CHRONICLES OF THE CHEYSULI: BOOK SEVEN

FLIGHT OF THE RAVEN

JENNIFER ROBERSON

D0032730

DAW BOOKS, INC.
DONALD A. WOLLHEIM, PUBLISHER

375 Hudson Street, New York, NY 10014

DAW Book Collectors No. 818.

First Printing, June 1990

1 2 3 4 5 6 7 8 9

PRINTED IN THE U.S.A.

GISELLA STARED UP AT HIM

She was mad, all too obviously mad, but there was more to her than that. Pale, feral eyes fixed on him—on the intruder—with a fierce intensity.

"Which one are you?"

"Aidan," he told her. "Aidan of Homana; Brennan's son."

"The throne will never be yours."

It stopped him in his tracks.

Gisella smiled, tilting her head to one side. "Never."

"Granddame—"

It denies you." She saw his shock, his recoil. "The Lion. I *know*, Aidan." Her voice was very soft; in its quietude, Aidan heard conviction, and the cant of prophecy. "Throneless Mujhar. Uncrowned king. A *child*, buffeted by fates he cannot understand . . ." She slumped back against the bolsters. "Touched by the gods, but ignorant . . . a man so touched, so claimed as one of their own can never know peace as a king." Gisella smiled warmly, yellow eyes alight. "You will never rule Homana."

Aidan blurted the first thing that came into his head. "Are you saying I will die? Granddame? Am I to *die*?"

This one is for S.J. Hardy, who, loving to read, married a woman exactly the same.

Eventually they begat four children who, in their turn, had the great good sense to pass along the reading gene to yet a third generation.

When my turn comes, I'll try my best to do the same.

Thanks, Granddaddy!

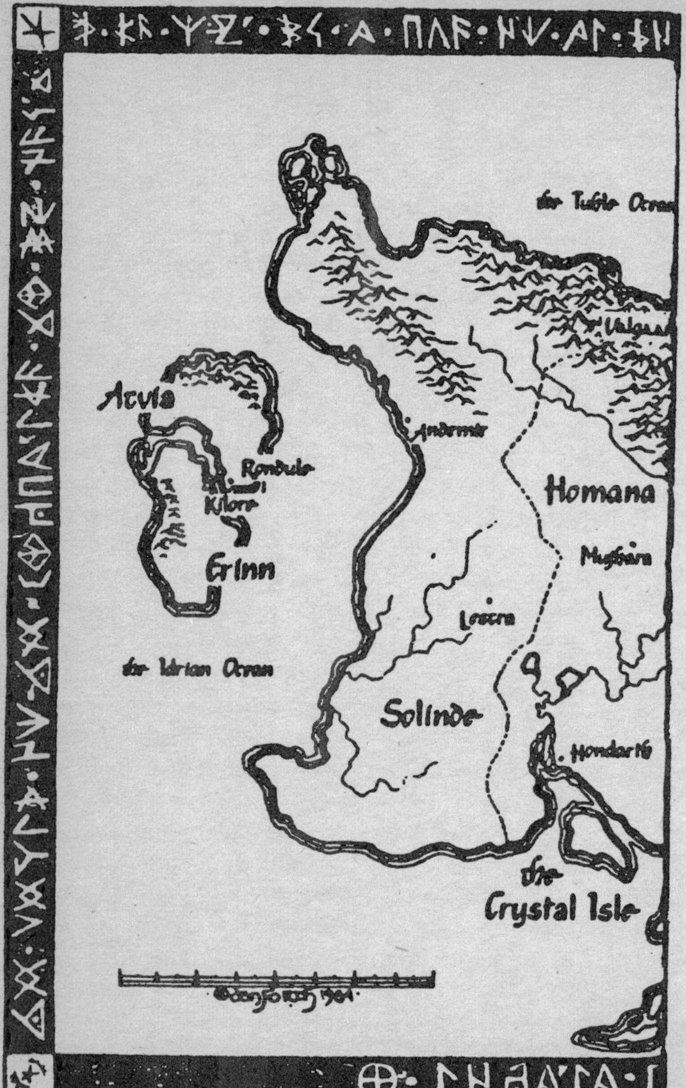
Atvia
Kilore
Erinn
Homana
Solinde
the
Crystal Isle

The Chronicles of the Cheysuli: An Overview

THE PROPHECY OF THE FIRSTBORN:

"One day a man of all blood shall unite, in peace, four warring realms and two magical races.

Originally a race of shapechangers known as the Cheysuli, descendants of the Firstborn, Homana's original race, held the Lion Throne, but increasing unrest on the part of the Homanans, who lacked magical powers and therefore feared the Cheysuli, threatened to tear the realm apart. The Cheysuli royal dynasty voluntarily gave up the Lion Throne so that Homanans could rule Homana, thereby avoiding fullblown internecine war.

The clans withdrew altogether from Homanan society save for one remaining and binding tradition: each Homanan king, called a Mujhar, must have a Cheysuli liege man as bodyguard, councillor, companion, dedicated to serving the throne and protecting the Mujhar, until such a time as the prophecy is fulfilled and the Firstborn rule again.

This tradition was adhered to without incident for nearly four centuries, until Lindir, the only daughter of Shaine the Mujhar, jilted her prospective bridegroom to elope with Hale, her father's Cheysuli liege man. Because the jilted bridegroom was the heir of a neighboring king, Bellam of Solinde, and because the marriage was meant to seal an alliance after years of bloody war, the elopement resulted in tragic consequences. Shaine concocted a web of lies to salve his obsessive pride, and in so doing laid the groundwork for the annihilation of a race.

Declared sorcerers and demons dedicated to the downfall of the Homanan throne, the Cheysuli were summarily outlawed and sentenced to immediate execution if found within Homanan borders.

Shapechangers begins the "Chronicles of the Cheysuli," telling the tale of Alix, daughter of Lindir, once Princess of

Homana, and Hale, once Cheysuli liege man to Shaine. Alix is an unknown catalyst bearing the Old Blood of the First-born, which gives her the ability to link with all *lir* and assume any animal shape at will. But Alix is raised by a Homanan and has no knowledge of her abilities, until she is kidnapped by Finn, a Cheysuli warrior who is Hale's son by his Cheysuli wife, and therefore Alix's half-brother. Kidnapped with her is Carillon, Prince of Homana. Alix learns the true power in her gifts, the nature of the prophecy which rules all Cheysuli, and eventually marries a warrior, Duncan, to whom she bears a son, Donal, and, much later, a daughter, Bronwyn. But Homana's internal strife weakens her defenses. Bellam of Solinde, with his sorcerous aide, Tynstar the Ihlini, conquers Homana and assumes the Lion Throne.

In *The Song of Homana*, Carillon returns from a five-year exile, faced with the difficult task of gathering an army capable of overcoming Bellam. He is accompanied by Finn, who has assumed the traditional role of liege man. Aided by Cheysuli magic and his own brand of personal power, Carillon is able to win back his realm and restore the Cheysuli to their homeland by ending the purge begun by his uncle, Shaine, Alix's grandfather. He marries Bellam's daughter to seal peace between the lands, but Electra has already cast her lot with Tynstar the Ihlini, and works against her Homanan husband. Carillon's failure to father a son forces him to betroth his only daughter, Aislinn, to Donal, Alix's son, whom he names Prince of Homana. This public approbation of a Cheysuli warrior is the first step in restoring the Lion Throne to the sovereignty of the Cheysuli, required by the prophecy, and sows the seeds of civil unrest.

Legacy of the Sword focuses on Donal's slow assumption of power within Homana, and his personal assumption of his role in the prophecy. Because by clan custom a warrior is free to take both wife and mistress, Donal has started a Cheysuli family even though he will one day have to marry Carillon's daughter to cement his right to the Lion Throne. By his Cheysuli mistress he has two children, Ian and Isolde; by Aislinn, Carillon's daughter, he eventually sires a son who will become his heir. But the marriage is rocky immediately; in addition to the problems caused by a second family, Donal's Homanan wife is also under the magical influence of her mother, Electra, who is mistress to Tynstar. Problems are compounded by the son of Tynstar and Electra, Strahan, who has his father's powers in full measure. On Carillon's death Donal inherits the Lion, naming his legitimate son, Niall, to succeed him. But to further the prophecy he marries his sister, Bronwyn, to Alaric of Atvia, lord of an island kingdom. Bronwyn is later killed by Alaric accidentally while in *lir*-shape, but lives long enough to give birth to a daughter, Gisella, who is mad.

In *Track of the White Wolf*, Donal's son Niall is a young man caught between two worlds. To the Homanans, fearful of Cheysuli power and intentions, he is worthy only of distrust, the focus of their discontent. To the Cheysuli he is an "unblessed" man, because even though far past the age for it, Niall has not linked with his animal. He is therefore a *lirless* man, a warrior with no power, and such a man has no place within the clans. His Cheysuli half-brother is his liege man, fully "blessed," and Ian's abilities serve to add to Niall's feelings of inferiority.

Niall is meant to marry his half-Atvian cousin, Gisella, but falls in love with the princess of a neighboring kingdom, Deirdre of Erinn. *Lirless*, and with Gisella under the influence of Tynstar's Ihlini daughter, Lillith, Niall falls prey to sorcery. Eventually he links with his *lir* and assumes the full range of Cheysuli powers, but he pays for it with an eye. His marriage to Gisella is disastrous, but two sets of twins are born—Brennan and Hart, Corin and Keely—which gives Niall the opportunity to extend his range of influence via betrothal alliances. He banishes Gisella to Atvia after he foils an Ihlini plot involving her, and then settles into life with his mistress, Deirdre of Erinn, who has already borne Maeve, his illegitimate daughter.

A Pride of Princes tells the story of each of Niall's three sons. Brennan, the eldest, will inherit Homana and has been betrothed to Aileen, Deirdre's niece, to add a heretofore unknown bloodline to the prophecy. Brennan's twin, Hart, is Prince of Solinde, a compulsive gambler whose addiction results in a tragic accident involving all three of Niall's sons. Hart is banished to Solinde for a year, and the rebellious youngest son, Corin, to Atvia. Brennan is tricked into siring a child on an Ihlini-Cheysuli woman; Hart loses a hand and nearly his life in a Solindish plot; in Erinn, Corin falls in love with Brennan's bride, Aileen, before going to Atvia. One by one each is captured by Strahan, Tynstar's son, who intends to turn Niall's sons into puppet-kings so he can rule through them. All three manage to escape, but not after each has been made to recognize particular strengths and weaknesses.

For Keely, sister to Niall's sons, things are different. In *Daughter of the Lion*, Keely herself is caught up in the machinations of politics, evil sorcery, and her own volatile emotions. Trained from childhood in masculine pursuits such as weaponry, Keely prefers the freedom of choice and life-style, and as both are threatened by the imminent arrival of her betrothed, Sean of Erinn, she fights to maintain her sense of self in a world ruled by men. She is therefore ripe for rebellion when a strong-minded, powerful Erinnish brigand—and possible murderer—enters her life.

But Keely's battles are increased tenfold when Strahan chooses her as his next target. Betrayed, trapped, and imprisoned on the Crystal Isle, Keely is forced through sorcery into a liaison with the Ihlini that results in pregnancy. But before the child can be born, Keely escapes with the aid of the Ihlini bard, Taliesin. On her way home she meets the man believed to be her betrothed, and realizes not only must she somehow rid herself of the unwanted child, but must also decide which man she will have—thief or prince—in order to be a true Cheysuli in service to the prophecy.

Prologue

He was small, so very small, but desperation lent him strength. The *need* lent him strength, even though fright and tension threatened to undermine it. He placed small hands on the hammered silver door and *pushed* as hard as he could, grunting with the effort; pushing with all his might.

The door opened slightly. Then fell back again, scraping, as his meager strength failed.

"No," he muttered aloud between clenched teeth. "No, I will not *let* you."

He shoved very hard again. This time he squeezed into the opening before the door could shut. When it shut, it shut on *him;* gasping shock and fright, Aidan thrust himself through. His sleeping robe tore, but he did not care. It did not matter. He was in at last.

Once in, he froze. The Great Hall was cavernous. Darker than night—a thick, heavy blackness trying to squash him flat. Darkness and *something* calling to him.

He would not be squashed. He would *not*—and yet his belly knotted. Who was he to do this? Who was he to come to his grandsire's Great Hall, to confront the Lion Throne?

Small hands tugged at hair, twisting a lock through fingers. Black hair by night; by day a dark russet, red in the light of the sun. He peered the length of the hall, feeling cold stone beneath his feet. His mother would have told him to put on his slippers. But the *need* had been so great that nothing else mattered but that he confront the Lion, and the thing in the Lion's lap.

He shivered. Not from cold: from *fear*.

Compulsion drove him. Aidan moaned a little. He wanted to leave the hall. He wanted to turn his back on the Lion, the big black beast who waited to devour him. But the need, so overwhelming, would not let him.

No candles had been left lighted. The firepit coals glowed only vaguely. What little moon there was shone fitfully

1

through the casements, its latticed light distorted by stained glass panes.

If only he could *see*.

No. He knew better. If he could see the Lion, he would fear it more.

Or would he? The light of day was no better. The Lion still glared, still bared wooden teeth. Now he could barely see it, acrouch on the marble dais. Could it see him?

Aidan bit a finger. Bowels turned to water; he wanted the chamber pot. But he was prince and also Cheysuli. If he retreated now, he would dishonor the blood in his veins.

But, oh, how he wanted to leave!

Aidan rocked a little. "*Jehana* . . ." he whispered, not knowing that he spoke.

In the darkness, the Lion waited.

So did something else.

Aidan drew in a strangled breath in three gulping inhalations very noisy in the silence. Pressure in his bladder increased. He bit into his finger, then slowly took a step.

One. Then two. Then three. He lost count of them all. But eventually all the steps merged and took him the length of the hall, where he stood before the Lion. He looked at eyes, teeth, nostrils. All of it wood, all of it. *He* was made of flesh. *He* would rule the Lion.

With effort, Aidan looked into the lap. In dim light, something glowed.

It was a chain, made of gold. Heavy, hammered gold, alive with promises. More than wealth, or power: the chain was heritage. His past, and his future: legacy of the gods. He reached for it, transfixed, wanting it, *needing* it, knowing it was for him; but when his trembling hand closed over a link the size of a large man's wrist, the chain shapechanged to dust.

He cried out. Urine stained his nightrobe. Shame flooded him, but so did desperation. It had been right *there*; now there was nothing. Nothing at all remained. The dust—and the chain—was gone.

He did not want to cry. He did not *intend* to cry, but the tears came anyway. Which made him cry all the harder, ashamed of his emotion. Ashamed of his loss of control. Of his too-Homanan reaction; Cheysuli warriors did not cry. Grief was not expressed.

But he was more than merely Cheysuli. And no one let him forget.

Only one more bloodline needed. One more outcross required, and the prophecy was complete. But even he, at six, knew how impossible it was. He had heard it often enough in the halls of Homana-Mujhar.

No Cheysuli warrior will ever lie down with an Ihlini and sire a child upon her.

But even he, a boy, knew better. A Cheysuli warrior *had;* in fact, *two* had: his grandsire's brother, Ian, and his own father, the Prince of Homana, who one day would be Mujhar.

Even at six, he knew. And knew what he was meant for; what blood ran in his veins. But it was all very confusing, and he chose to leave it so.

Grief renewed itself. *I want my chain.*

But the chain—*his* chain—had vanished.

A small ferocity was born: *I want my CHAIN—*

One of the doors scraped open. Aidan twitched and swung around unsteadily, clutching the sodden nightrobe in both hands. It was his mother, he knew. Who else would come looking for a boy not in his bed? And she would see, she would *know*—

"Aidan? Aidan—what are ye doing here? 'Tis far past your bedtime!"

Shame made him hot. He fought tears and trembling.

She was white-faced, distraught, though trying to hide it. He knew what she felt; could *feel* it, as if her skin was his. But she tried so hard to hide it.

The familiar lilt of Erinn echoed in the Great Hall. "What are ye doing, my lad? Paying homage to the Lion?" Aileen's laugh was forced. " 'Twill be *your* beastie, one day—there's no need for you to come in the night to see it!"

She meant well, he knew. She always meant well. But he sensed her fear, her anguish, beneath forced cheerfulness.

She hurried the length of the hall, gathering folds of a heavy robe. By the doors stood a servant holding a lamp. Light glowed in the hall. The Lion leaped out of the shadows.

Aidan fell back, thrusting up a warding arm, then realized it was no more than it ever was: a piece of wood shaped by man. And then his mother was beside him, asking him things fear distorted, until she gathered the reins of her worry and knotted them away.

She saw his hands doubled up in a soaked nightrobe. She

saw the urine stain. Anguish flared anew—he felt it most distinctly, like a burning band thrust into his spirit—but she said nothing of it. She merely knelt down at his side, putting a hand on his shoulder. "Aidan—why are you here? Your nurse came, speaking of a nightmare . . . but when I came, you were gone. What are you doing here?"

He looked up into her face as she knelt down next to him. Into eyes green as glass; green as Erinnish turf. " 'Tis gone," he told her plainly, unconsciously adopting her accent.

She wore blue velvet chamber robe over white linen nightshift. Her hair was braided for sleeping: a single thick red plait, hanging down her back. "*What's* gone, my lad?"

"The chain," he explained, though he knew she would not understand. No one understood; no one *could* understand.

Sudden anguish was overwhelming. He craved reassurance as much as understanding. The former he could get. As the hated tears renewed themselves, he went willingly into her arms.

She pressed her cheek against his head, twining arms around small shoulders to still the wracking sobs. "Oh, Aidan, Aidan . . . 'twas only a dream, my lad . . . a wee bit of a dream come to trouble your sleep. There's no harm in it, I promise, but you mustn't be thinking 'tis real."

" *'Twas* real," he insisted, crying hard into her shoulder. " 'Twas real—I *swear* . . . and the Lion—the Lion meant to *eat* me—"

"Aidan, no. Oh, my sweet bairn, no. There's naught to the Lion's teeth but bits of rotting wood."

" 'Twas real—'twas *there*—"

"Aidan, hush—"

"It woke me up, calling . . ." He drew his head away so he could see her face, to judge what she thought. "It wanted me to come—"

"The Lion?"

Fiercely, he shook his head. "Not the Lion—the *chain*—"

"Oh, Aidan—"

She did not believe him. He hurled himself against her, trembling from a complex welter of fear, anguish, insistence: he needed her to believe him. She was his rock, his anchor—if *she* did not believe him—

In Erinnish, she tried to soothe him. He needed her warmth, her compassion, her love, but he was aware, if distantly, he also required something more. Something very real, no matter what she said: the solidity of the chain in his small-fingered child's hands, because it was his *tahlmorra*. Because he knew, without knowing why, the golden links in his dreams bound him as fully as his blood.

A sound: the whisper of leather on stone, announcing someone's presence. Pressed against his mother, Aidan peered one-eyed over a velveted shoulder and saw his father in the hall. His tall, black-haired father with eyes undeniably yellow, feral as Aidan's own; a creature of the shadows as much as flesh and bone. Brennan's dress was haphazard and the black hair mussed. Alarm and concern stiffened the flesh of his face.

"The nursemaid came—what is wrong?"

Aidan felt his mother turn on her knees even as her arms tightened slightly. "Oh, naught but a bad dream. Something to do with the Lion." Forced lightness. Forced calm. But Aidan read the nuances. For him, a simple task.

The alarm faded as Brennan walked to the dais. The tension in his features relaxed. "Ah, well, there was a time it frightened *me*."

Aidan did not wait. "I wanted the chain, *jehan*. It called me. It *wanted* me . . . and I needed *it*."

Brennan frowned. "The chain?"

"In the Lion. The chain." Aidan twisted in Aileen's arms and pointed. " 'Twas *there*," he insisted. "I came to fetch it because it wanted me to. But the Lion swallowed it."

Brennan's smile was tired. Aidan knew his father sat up late often to discuss politics with the Mujhar. "No one ever said the Lion does not hunger. But it does not eat little boys. Not even little princes."

Vision blurred oddly. "It will eat *me* . . ."

"Aidan, hush. 'Tis fanciful foolishness," Aileen admonished, rising to stand. "We'll be having no more of it."

A dark-skinned, callused hand was extended for Aidan to grasp. Brennan smiled kindly. "Come, little prince. Time you were safe in bed."

It was shock, complete and absolute. *They do not believe me,* either *of them—*

His mother and his father, so wise and trustworthy, did not *believe* him. Did not believe their *son*.

He gazed blindly at the hand still extended from above. Then he looked into the face. A strong, angular face, full of planes and hollows; of heritage and power.

His father knew everything. But if his father did not *believe* him.

Aidan felt cold. And hollow. And old. Something inside flared painfully, then crumbled into ash.

They will think I am LYING.

It hurt very badly.

"Aidan." Brennan wiggled fingers. "Are you coming with me?"

A new resolve was born. *If I tell them nothing, they cannot think I am lying.*

"Aidan," Aileen said, "go with your father. 'Tis time you were back in bed."

Where I might dream again.

He shivered. He gazed up at the hand.

"Aidan," Aileen murmured. Then, in a flare of stifled impatience, "Take him to bed, Brennan. If he cannot be taking himself."

That hurt, too.

Neither of them believe me.

The emptiness increased.

Will anyone *believe me*?

"Aidan," Brennan said. "Would you have me carry you?"

For a moment, he wanted it. But the new knowledge was too painful. Betrayal was not a word he knew, but was beginning to comprehend.

Slowly he reached out and took the hand. It was callused, large, warm. For a moment he forgot about the betrayal: the hand of his father was a talisman of power; it would chase away the dreams.

Aidan went with his father, followed by his mother. Behind them, in the darkness, crouched the Lion Throne of Homana, showing impotent teeth.

He clutched his father's hand. Inside his head, rebelling, he said it silently: *I want my chain.*

Gentle fingers touched his hair, feathering it from his brow. " 'Twas only a dream," she promised.

Foreboding knotted his belly. But he did not tell her she lied. He wanted his mother to sleep, even if he could not.

PART I

One

Deirdre's solar had become a place of comfort to all of them. Of renewal. A place where rank did not matter, nor titles, nor the accent with which one spoke: Erinnish, Cheysuli, Homanan. It was, Aileen felt, a place where *all* of them could gather, regardless of differing bloodlines, to share the heavy, unspoken bonds of heritage. It had nothing to do with magic, breeding, or homeland. Only with the overriding knowledge of what it was to rule.

She knew what Keely would say; *had* said, often enough, phrased in many different—and explicit—ways. That women had no place in the male-dominated succession lining up for the Lion Throne. But Aileen knew better. Keely would not agree—she seldom agreed with anything concerning the disposition of women—but it was true. Women *did* have a place in the line of succession. As long as kings needed queens to bear sons for the Lion, women would have a place.

Not the place Keely—or others—might want, but it was something nonetheless. It made women important, if for womb instead of brain.

Aileen's womb had given Homana one son. Twin boys, enough to shore up Aidan's tenuous place in the succession, were miscarried; the ordeal had left her barren. She was, therefore, a princess of precarious reknown, and potentially threatened future. Brennan would not, she knew, set her aside willingly—he had made that clear—but there were others to be reckoned with besides the Prince of Homana. He *was* only a prince; kings bore precedence. And while the Mujhar showed no signs of concern regarding her son's odd habits, she knew very well even Niall was not the sole arbiter. There was also the Homanan Council. She was the daughter of a king, albeit the island was small; nonetheless, she understood the demands of a kingship. The demands of a council.

Only one son for Homana. One son who was—different.

She shivered. The solar was comfortable, but her peace of mind nonexistent. It was why she had gone to Deirdre.

Aileen stood rigidly before the casement in the solar with sunlight in her hair, setting it ablaze. A wisp drifted near her eyes; distracted, she stripped it back. The gesture was abrupt, impatient, lacking the grace she had mastered after twenty-four years as Princess of Homana; twenty-four years as her aunt's protégée, in blood as well as deportment.

She folded arms beneath her breasts and hugged herself, hard. "I've *tried*," she said in depair. "I've tried to understand, to believe 'twould all pass . . . but there's no hiding from it now. It started in childhood . . . he thinks we're not knowing . . . he believes he's fooled us all, but servants know the truth. They *always* know the truth—d'ye think they'd keep it secret?" Her tone now echoed the rumors. "The heir to Homana rarely spends a whole night in sleep—and he goes to talk to the Lion, to rail against a *chair* . . ." She let it trail off, then hugged herself harder. "What are we to do? I think he'll *never* be—right." Her voice broke on the last word. With it her hardwon composure; tears welled into green eyes. "What are we to do? How can he hold the throne if everyone thinks him mad?"

Deirdre of Erinn, seated near the window with lap full of yarn and linen, regarded Aileen with compassion and sympathy. At more than sixty years of age she was no longer young—brass-blonde hair was silver, green eyes couched in creases, the flesh less taut on her bones—but her empathy was undiminished even if beauty was. She knew what it was like to fear for a child; she had borne the Mujhar a daughter. But Maeve, for all her troubles, had never been like Aidan. Her niece's fears were legitimate. They all realized Aidan was—different.

Deirdre knew better than to attempt to placate Aileen with useless platitudes, no matter how well-meant. So she gave her niece the truth: " 'Twill be years before Aidan comes close to inheriting. There is Brennan to get through first, and Niall is nowhere near dying. Don't be borrowing trouble, or wishing it on others."

Aileen made a jerky gesture meant to dispel the bad-wishing, a thing Erinnish abhorred. "No, no . . . gods willing—" she grimaced "—*or* their eternal *tahlmorras*—Aidan *will* be old . . . but am I wrong to worry? 'Twas one thing to dream as a child—he's a grown man now, and the dreams are worse than ever!"

Deirdre's mouth tightened. "Has he said nothing of it? You used to be close, you and Aidan—and he as close to Brennan. What has he said to you?"

Aileen's expulsion of breath was underscored with bitterness. "Aidan? Aidan says nothing. Aye, once we were close—when he was so little . . . but now he says nothing. Not to either of us. 'Tis as if he cannot *trust* us—" She pressed the palms of her hands against temples, trying to massage away the ache. "If I say aught to him—if I ask him what troubles him, he tells me nothing. He *lies* to me, Deirdre! And he knows I know it. But does it change his answer? No, not his . . . he is, if nothing else, stubborn as a blind mule."

"Aye, well, he's getting that from both sides of his heritage." Deirdre's smile was kind. "He is but twenty-three. Young men are often secretive."

"No—not like Aidan." Aileen, pacing before the window, lifted a hand, then let it drop to slap against her skirts. "The whole palace knows it . . . the whole *city* knows it— likely all of Homana." She stopped, swung to face Deirdre, half-sitting against the casement sill. "Some of them go so far as to say he's mad, mad as Gisella."

"Enough!" Deirdre said sharply. "Do you want to give fuel to such talk? You're knowing as well as I there's nothing in that rumor. He could no more inherit insanity than *I* did, or you." She sat straighter in her chair, unconscious of creased linen. "He's Erinnish, too, as well as Cheysuli . . . how d'ye know he's not showing a bit of *our* magic? There's more than a little in the House of Eagles—"

Aileen cut her off. "Oh, aye, I know . . . but the Cheysuli is so dominant I doubt our magic can show itself."

Deirdre lifted an eyebrow. "That's not so certain, I'm thinking, with your hair on his head."

Aileen grimaced, one hand drifting to brilliant locks. Aidan's was darker, but still red; only the eyes were Cheysuli. "There's nothing about my son that bespeaks Erinnish roots— he's as bad as any of *them*."

Deirdre's smile was faint. "By 'them,' you're meaning Cheysuli?"

"Cheysuli," Aileen echoed, forehead creased in absent concern. "One moment they're all so human . . . the next, they're *alien*."

"Aye, well, they could say the same of us." Deirdre took up the forgotten embroidery in her lap, examining it critically. Her skills faded year by year, but not her desire. The worst thing about aging, she thought, was the inability physically to do what her mind wanted. "I think women have made that complaint many times before, whether the man in their bed is a shapechanger, or nothing more than a *man*."

For the first time Aileen smiled. She had never been beautiful, but beauty was not what made her Aileen. The beauty of Erinn's eagles lay in vividness of spirit, and a crude physical splendor. "You wouldn't be saying that of the Mujhar."

"I would," Deirdre retorted. "No doubt he's said it of me; no man understands a woman."

Aileen's brief smile faded. "Does a mother understand her son?"

Deirdre's hands slowed. "I'll not say you've naught to think about, with Aidan, but there's no madness in him. And there are worse things to a man than dreams; worse things to a throne than a dreamer."

"I wonder," Aileen murmured.

Deirdre schooled her tone into idle inquiry. "What does Brennan say?"

"Nothing." Aileen shifted on the sill, cocking one knee against the glazing so that her weight was on the stone. "He feels it as much as I, but d'ye think he'll admit it? Admit he doubts his son?" The line of her mouth flattened. "When Aidan was little, and so sick, Brennan and I shared everything. But Aidan withdrew, and then so did Brennan. There was nothing left between us. Now, when he speaks of it at all, he says merely 'tis Aidan's *tahlmorra* to hold the Lion Throne."

Deirdre sighed. "So says his birthright. But there are times, to my way of thinking, they put too much weight on what they believe instead of on what they feel."

"They believe in the prophecy, each and every one of them." Then Aileen laughed. Bitterness was manifest. "Except, of course, for Teirnan and his *a'saii*, lost in the woods of Homana."

Deirdre's mouth tightened. "Teirnan was a fool."

"You only say that because he seduced your daughter . . . you're not caring a whit what Teirnan thinks about anything else, after what he did to Maeve." Aileen shifted restlessly, adjusting heavy skirts. "Maeve is happy now, in Erinn, and perfectly safe—my son is neither, I'm thinking."

"Your son will do well enough." Deirdre bit through a thread. "As you said, Maeve is happy—and who would have thought *that* possible after what Teirnan did to her?" Deirdre sighed, untangling colors. "I thank the oldfolk of Erinn for hearing a mother's pleas . . . Rory Redbeard's a good man, and has made her a good husband."

"Since he couldn't be having Keely." Aileen smiled briefly. "He wanted her, you know. For all she was meant for Sean, and the Redbeard came here knowing . . ." She let it trail off. "Maeve is nothing like Keely. If that was what Rory wanted, he got something other than expected."

Deirdre raised a brow. "By the time Keely and Sean sailed for Erinn, only a fool would have thought he yet had a chance. After Teirnan's bastard was born, Rory took Maeve for Maeve's *own* sake, not as a replacement for Keely."

Aileen laughed aloud. "There *is* no replacement for Keely."

"And no replacement for Aidan . . . the boy will be whatever it is he's meant to be."

Brief amusement fled. Aileen stared at her aunt. Deirdre's composure occasionally irked, because she claimed so little herself. Just now, it made her want to shatter it, even as she longed for Deirdre's serenity. It was a thing unknown to her, with a son such as Aidan.

"There is something wrong with him. There is something not *right*." Aileen stared at her aunt, daring her to disagree. "Next time you see him," she said intensely, "look into his eyes. Then ask yourself these questions: "Is my grandson happy? Is my grandson *sane?*""

Deirdre stared, aghast. "I'd *never* do such a thing!"

"Ask," Aileen suggested. "Better yet, ask *him*. But don't listen to what he says—look in his eyes, instead. 'Tis where you'll find the truth. Cheysuli eyes or no, 'tis where you'll find the truth."

Two

He was up and out of his bed before he knew who or where he was; before he knew what he wanted. The need drove him to it. The compulsion preempted everything: thought, logic, comprehension, much as *lir*-sickness had. It overtook his body and carried him to the door, where he pressed himself against it in mute appeal for passage.

Inside his head tolled a certainty tainted with a plea: *This time I can touch it . . . this time it will be real—THIS time, I know—*

But the declaration faded, along with certainty, as he came sluggishly to himself from the depths of unsettling dreams. He realized, in despair, it had happened yet again.

Sweat filmed him. He slept nude, as always, disliking the bindings of sleepclothes, the excess warmth of covers. So now, damp with dreams and fear, he shivered in the chill of a cool summer night and cursed himself for a fool.

With great effort he stilled his breathing, pressing his brow against the heavy door as if the pressure of flesh on wood might drive out the dream he dreamed. But it never did, never, no matter how hard he tried, and at last he turned, giving up, scraping shoulder blades against wood, and stared blindly into darkness.

"Why?" he whispered raggedly, through the headache only beginning. "Why does this happen to *me?*"

In the darkness, something stirred. But no answer was offered him; after too many years of the asking, he no longer expected one.

The pounding of his heart slowed. He swallowed heavily twice, disliking the bitter aftertaste of the dream, and scratched irritably at a scalp itchy from dream-fear and reaction. He shivered once, controlled it, then stood up at last from the door.

He lingered only a moment, considering what might happen if he simply went back to bed; he knew better. He knew

14

very well, having tasted futility more often than dreamless slumber. So he gave up the sweet contemplation of what it might be like if he could simply *sleep*, as other people slept, and stumbled to the nearest clothing chest to pull out age-softened leather leggings.

No more: only leggings, enough for now, he thought; more would be too much. More would be too *hot;* the summer night was cool, but dreams banished comfort and basted him with warmth.

It would not be so bad, he thought wryly, *if at least I dreamed of women. They are worth the discomfort of a night become too hot.*

He had been a man, as manhood is reckoned, for nearly eight years. He had dreamed, and spilled his seed, into women and into his bed. But it was not of women he dreamed when the dreams were sent by gods.

A servant always left him a lighted candle; he always blew it out. Warrior training—and common sense—taught him safety lay in eyes well-accustomed to heavy darkness instead of blinded by too much light. But his room was an outer one, narrow casements slit the walls, and torchlight from the baileys crept through to bathe his chamber. Pale light burnished his arms: faceted *lir*-bands gleamed.

Bare of chest and feet, he swung back toward the door. He paused there, eyes shut, cursing himself for a fool.

"Leave it alone—*ignore* it—" Aidan bit into his lip. "Who is in control: a piece of wood, or you?"

Inside his head, the Lion roared. Aidan's belly knotted.

"Leave it alone," he repeated. "Gods—leave *me* alone—"

Time to go, someone said. *How can you turn back now? It has become ritual . . . and you are not the kind who changes anything regardless of the need.*

Stung, Aidan turned to glare through darkness at the rustling in the corner. "What am I to change? Would you have it be my *tahlmorra?*"

Now the tone was scornful. *You do not even have an inkling what your tahlmorra IS.*

Through the link, he lashed out. *I know very well what it is—Do you?*

I have known all along. What do you think I am? Are YOU not proof that my tahlmorra is undertaken?

Because I exist? No. The tone, now, was cool. *I exist because I am. Because the gods created me.*

To be my lir.

The tone spilled into smugness. *Or you to be mine.*

Aidan swore beneath his breath. Mockingly, he asked, "Has any warrior ever revoked the *lir*-link?"

No living *warrior.*

It reminded Aidan of something, as it was meant to do: the precariousness of his race. "Has any warrior petitioned the gods for a new *lir*?"

Undoubtedly others have asked. But it is not my duty to tell you how the gods deal with ungrateful children.

"Ungrateful," Aidan muttered. "How could any man be so foolish as to consider how peaceful life might be if his *lir* was other than you?"

How can any warrior contemplate peace when he stands ready to fight a chair made of wood?

"Agh, gods . . ." Aidan put his hand on the latch. "You do not need to come, Teel. Stay in the corner and sulk; I can find my own way."

He jerked open the heavy door and stepped through, leaving it ajar. He thought for the merest moment he *would* be unaccompanied, but the rustling grew louder. And then the raven left the darkness and flew to perch on his shoulder.

Aidan extended an arm. "Try my hand," he suggested. "Like this, you scratch my shoulder."

Too soft, his *lir* chided, but exchanged shoulder for hand.

Aidan briefly considered taking a lamp with him, but decided against it. No corridor in the massive palace was left completely without light so guards or servants, if needed, could see to serve or protect, but unnecessary torches and lamps were extinguished. And he was, after all, Cheysuli, with yellow Cheysuli eyes; he saw what there was to see whether light existed or not.

"A fool," Aidan muttered, but set off anyway. Ignoring the stubborn compulsion gained him nothing but sleepless nights.

He had known, for as long as he could remember, he was *different*. The dreams of childhood had faded during adolescence, dissipated by the intense need for and the bonding with his *lir*, but once adulthood was reached the dreams returned in force. Now, at twenty-three, he was accounted a warrior in the clans and a full-grown man by the Homanans who called him a prince, but he was still plagued by dreams. By the vision of the chain. By the *substance* of the chain—

unti he put out a hand to touch it, and the links dispersed into dust.

As a child, it had frightened him. Growing older, he believed it merely a manifestation of a want and desire he could not fully understand. But of late the dreams had worsened. The desire had become a *demand*. And Aidan fully believed, with a dreadful certainty, he was somehow, someway, tainted.

"Tainted," he murmured aloud, aware of familiar tension.

Perhaps, the raven agreed. *But why would gods choose a tool that is tainted?* Teel paused significantly. *Unless they merely* forgot—

It was not precisely the sort of reassurance he craved. It was true the *lir* were a gift of the gods, but he preferred to think of himself as a man, not a tool. Not even a divine one; he asked no favors of the gods, for fear they might give him one.

Enough, he said dismissively, sending it through the link. *Well? Well? Why* would *they?*

Firmly, Aidan said: *We are not discussing gods.*

Perhaps we should *discuss them. You discuss everything else, yet very little of substance.*

He gritted teeth, but did not answer. He merely walked, saying nothing, passing out of shadows into torchlight, into darkness again. Through countless corridors and passageways, knowing them all by heart, until he reached the Great Hall.

There are times, the raven commented, *even Cheysuli are fools.*

Aidan, searching for release from the tension, settled on irony. *It is because of the other blood.*

Teel considered it. *I think not,* he replied. *I think it is merely you.*

Muttering under his breath, Aidan shoved open the doors.

Go back to bed, Teel suggested. *You know how you feel in the morning when you spend the night chasing dreams. You know how you* look.

Irritated, Aidan shifted back into human speech as he shouldered into the hall. Against his flesh he felt the texture of the silver, the whorls and angles and patterns set by craftsmen into the metal. "You know very well when I try to ignore the dream, it only gets worse."

Because you allow it to.

He let the door fall closed behind him, hearing its distant grate. Irritation spilled away. Fear trickled back. He recalled all the nights very clearly. Especially the first, when he had come at the age of six to find the chain of gold in the lap of the Lion Throne. And how he had shamed himself, frightened by something of wood; and by things he could not fathom.

All came rushing back. Humiliation caused him to squirm; why could he not forget?

Tension made him curt. "Is it there?"

Probably, Teel observed dryly. *Is it not* always *there?*

Aidan sighed and moved away from the heavy silver doors. The flames of the firepit had died to coals, lending dim illumination to the cavernous hall. Shadows cloaked the walls: tapestries and banners; history set in cloth. Wheels of swords and daggers painstakingly bracketed in a perfect and deadly symmetry. Spears and pikes sprouted from display blocks set in corners; flagsticks dangled silk. In the folds crouched Homana. Beyond the pit, on the dais, crouched the Lion Throne.

Teel rode Aidan's hand easily, considerably lighter than the hawks, falcons and eagles other warriors claimed. It was, Aidan felt, a facet of his very *differentness* that his *lir* was a raven. The bird was hardly unknown in the history of the clans, but neither was it common. Aidan considered it a jest played on him by capricious gods. In addition to sending him dreams, they gave him an irascible *lir*.

Teel pecked his thumb. *I have ridden faster rocks.*

"Then get off my hand and go sit on one."

Obligingly, the raven lifted and flew the length of the hall. But he did not sit on a rock. He sat on the head of the Lion.

Aidan, ruddy brows lifted, stopped at the foot of the dais. "Surely sacrilegious—you profane the Mujhar's throne."

Teel fluffed a wing. *Considering the Mujhar is only the Mujhar because of lir like myself, I think it is allowed.*

Steadfastly, Aidan stared at the raven. Then, drawing a breath, he made himself look down at the cushion on which his grandsire sat when he inhabited the throne.

So, Teel observed, *the dream remains constant.*

Aidan shut his eyes. The painfully familiar sense of loss and oppression rushed in from out of the shadows.

Stiffly, he knelt. He waited. Felt the coldness of glossy

marble through the leather of his leggings. Smelled ash, old wood, oil; the scent of ancient history, intangible yet oddly vivid.

Let me touch it, he begged. *Let me know the chain is real.*

But when he put out a hesitant hand, the links dissolved to dust.

Breath spilled raggedly. "Oh, gods . . . oh, *gods*—why do this to me? What have I done to deserve it? What do you want from me?"

But even as he asked, futility overwhelmed him, much as it had the very first time. And, like that time, what he wanted was to cry. But he was twenty-three: a man fully grown. An acknowledged Cheysuli warrior with a *lir* to call his own . . . if Teel condescended to let him.

Aidan did not cry. He was no longer six years old.

Though there are times I wish I were, so I could begin again.

Teel's tone was cool. *What use in that?* he asked. *The gods made the child. Now the rest is up to the man.*

"Stop," Aidan declared.

When you do.

"I swear, you will drive me mad, hag-riding me to death."

Teel's irony slipped, replaced with an odd kindness. *I will keep you sane when you hag-ride* yourself *to death.*

Aidan let it go. He was too weary, too worn. There was something he had come for. The ritual to perform.

He sighed, cursing himself out of habit. He knew what he would find, but Aidan put hand to cushion. Touched the worn nap of the velvet. Felt nothing but the fabric. Not even the grit of dust.

Futility was overpowering. *"Why?"* The shout filled the hall. "Why do I always come back when I know what will happen?"

"Because the gods, when they are playful, are sometimes cruel instead of kind."

Aidan lurched to his feet and spun around, catching himself against the Lion. He had heard nothing, nothing at all; no scrape of silver on marble, no steps the length of the hall. He stared hard like a wolf at bay, thinking of how he looked; of what appearance he presented—hair in disarray, half dressed, haranguing a wooden beast. Heat flooded him. Humiliation stung his armpits. He wanted to shout aloud, to send the man from the hall, away from his royal—but embarrassed—presence; he did not. Because he looked at the man who faced him and recognition shamed him.

His grandfather smiled. "I know what you are thinking; it is written on your face. But it is unworthy of you, Aidan . . . you have as much right to be here, no matter what the hour, as I do myself."

On the headpiece of the Lion, the bright-eyed raven preened. *I have told you that, myself.*

Aidan ignored his *lir*. Embarrassment had not receded; if anything, he felt worse. What he wanted most was to apologize and flee—*this man is the Mujhar!*—but he managed to stand his ground.

After a moment's hesitation, he wet his lips and spoke quietly. "I may have the right to be here, but not to disturb your rest."

"The rest of an old man?" Niall's tone was amused. "Ah, well . . . when you are as old as I you will understand that sleep does not always come when you want it to."

He began to feel a little better; the Mujhar was now his grandsire. Wryly, Aidan smiled. "I know that already."

"So." Niall advanced, holding a fat candle in its cup of gleaming gold. "Why have you said nothing to me of these dreams? Do you think I have no time for my grandson?"

Aidan stared at the man who, by right of gods and men, held the Lion Throne of Homana. He, like Deirdre, was past sixty, yet as undiminished by age. Still tall, still fit, still unmistakably regal, though no longer youthful. Tawny hair had silvered, fading like tarnished gilt; Homanan-fair skin had creased, displaying a delicately drawn fretwork born of years of resonsibility; of the eyes, one was blue and bright as ever, the other, an empty socket couched in talon scars, was hidden behind a patch.

Aidan drew in a breath, answering his grandfather's question with one of his own. "How can you have the time? You are the Mujhar."

"I am also a man who sired five children, and who now reaps the benefits of my children's fertility." Briefly, Niall eyed the raven perched upon his throne. "You I know better than the others, since you live here in Homana, but there are times I fully believe I *know* you least of all."

Aidan smiled. "It is nothing, grandsire."

Niall arched a brow.

"Nothing," Aidan repeated.

"Ah." Niall smiled faintly. "Then it pains me to know my grandson feels he cannot confide in me."

Guilt flickered deep inside. "No grandsire—'tisn't that. 'Tis only . . ." Aidan shrugged. "There is nothing to speak about."

Niall's gaze was steady. "I am neither a fool, nor blind—though I have but one eye I still see."

Heat coursed through Aidan's flesh. The sweat of shame dotted a thin line above his lips. He made a futile gesture. "They are just—dreams. Nothing more."

"Then I must assume the servants are embroidering the truth." The tone was very quiet, but compelling nonetheless. "I think it is time you spoke. If not to Aileen or to Brennan, then to me. I have some stake in this."

Aidan clenched his teeth briefly. "*Dreams,* nothing more—as anyone dreams. Fragments of sleep. Thoughts all twisted up, born of many things."

The Mujhar of Homana forbore to sit in his throne, usurped by a black-eyed raven who, as a *lir*, had more claim than any human, Cheysuli-bred or not. Or so Teel told them. Instead, Niall sat down upon the dais, setting down the candle cup with its wax and smoking flame. "Tell me about them."

Aidan rubbed damp fingertips against soft leather. *Tell him. Tell him? Just like that?*

Niall's tone was kind. "Locking things away only adds to the problem. Believe me, I know; I spent far too many years denying myself peace because I believed myself unworthy of this creature looming behind me."

Aidan glanced only briefly at the Lion. Then sat down on the dais next to Niall, putting his back to the beast. He felt a vast impatience—how could he share what no one would believe?—but attempted to honor his grandsire by fulfilling part of the request. "This has nothing at all to do with unworthiness. I promise, grandsire, I know who I am and the task I am meant for: to rule as Mujhar of Homana." Easily, he made the palm-up Cheysuli gesture denoting *tahlmorra,* and his acceptance of it. "I think I will do as well as the next man when my time comes—you and my *jehan* have taught me very well; how could I *not* be worthy?" He flicked fingers dismissively, thinking it enough.

Niall waited in silence.

Discomfited, Aidan stirred. "No one can understand. Why

should I speak of it? When I was a child, I tried to tell them about it. But neither of them believed me."

"Who did not?"

"*Jehan* and *jehana*. They both said I was a child, and that what I dreamed was not real. That I would *outgrow* it . . ." Bitterness underscored the tone; Aidan pushed it away with effort. "Would you speak of a thing people would ridicule you for?"

"Aileen and Brennan would never ridicule you."

Aidan grimaced. "Not *them*, perhaps . . . not so obviously. But what is a child to feel when his parents call him a liar?"

Niall's brows knit. "I have never known you to be that. I doubt they have, either; nor would ever say such a thing."

"There is such a thing as *implying*—"

"They would not even do that."

It was definitive. Aidan shifted his buttocks and stared gloomily into the hall. "I wish there were a way I *could* explain what I feel. What I *fear*."

"Try," Niall suggested. "Tell me the truth, as you know it. Tell me what disturbs your sleep."

Aidan rubbed gritty eyes. What he needed most *was* sleep.

No. What he needed most was *the chain*.

He sighed and let it go. "What I fear is the meaning behind my dream. The same one over and over." Now it was begun. Tension began to ease. With it went strength. Slumping, he braced elbows on his knees and leaned his chin into cupped hands. "For as long as I can recall, the *same* dream over and over. I think it will drive me mad."

Niall said nothing. His patience was manifest.

Aidan sighed heavily and sat upright, scraping hair back from his face. In the poor light his thick auburn hair was an odd reddish black, falling across bare shoulders too fair for a Cheysuli. A man, looking at him, would name him all Homanan, or call him Erinnish-born. Until he saw the eyes.

"There is a chain," Aidan began. "A chain made of gold. It is in the lap of the Lion."

The Mujhar did not give in to the urge to turn and look. Mutely, Niall waited.

Aidan, abruptly restless, thrust himself upright and paced away from dais, Lion, Mujhar. Away from his *lir*, uncharacteristically silent. He stared in disgust at the firepit, letting the coals dazzle his eyes, then swung back to face his grandsire.

"I know—I *know* how it sounds . . . but it is what I feel, what I *dream*—"

"Aidan," Niall said quietly, "stop trying to look through my eyes."

Brought up short, Aidan shut his mouth and waited. He had been carefully tutored.

Niall's gaze was kind. "You are wasting too much time trying to imagine what I will think. Simply say it. *Tell* it; you may find me less ignorant than you believe."

Aidan clenched his teeth; how could anyone, kin or not, fully understand?

But in the end, it was very easy. "I have to have it," he said plainly. "If I do not, the world ends."

Niall's expression was startled. "The world—*ends?*"

Aidan gestured acknowledgment; it sounded as odd to him. "The entire world," he agreed dryly. "At least—for me." And then he gestured again. "I know, I *know*—now I am being selfish, to think of the entire world, and its fate, being determined by what I do . . . but that is what I dream. Over and over again."

He waited. Before him the old man sat hunched on the dais, silvered brows knit with thought. Niall frowned pensively, but his expression gave nothing away.

The thought was fleeting and unwelcome. *There is madness in my kinfolk—*

But Aidan knew better than to say it. Niall would only deny it; or, rather, deny its cause as anything other than accident. He had said, time and time again, the madness of Aidan's Atvian granddame, Gisella, was induced by an early, traumatic birth—but Aidan sometimes wondered. He was capable of intense thoughts and impulses, sometimes as disturbing as his dreams, though he always suppressed them. He had heard the same said of Gisella. And he knew from repeated stories his *su'fala*, Keely, had never been fully convinced the madness was not hereditary.

"Well," Niall said finally, "everyone dreams. *My* dreams are odd enough—"

For the first time in his life, Aidan cut him off. "I *have to have it*, grandsire. Do you understand? It is a need as strong as the need of a man for a woman . . . as the need of warrior for *lir*. There is no difference, grandsire . . . it *makes* me come here. Every time I dream it."

Niall stared at him, clearly startled by the passion. "If it disturbs you this much—"

Aidan laughed aloud. "Disturbs me? Aye, that is one way of saying it . . ." He banished the desperation with effort, striving for equanamity. "Grandsire, perhaps it is better put like so: what if, as you reached to take her into your arms, Deirdre was turned to dust? To *nothingness* in your hands, even as you touched her, wanting her so badly you think you might burst with it."

Niall's expression was arrested. Aidan knew, as he always knew, the emotions his grandsire felt. Shock. Disbelief. The merest trace of anger, that Aidan could compare a chain to the Mujhar's beloved *meijha* . . . and then the comprehension of what the failure meant.

After a moment, Niall got up with a muffled grunt of effort and mounted the dais steps. He paused before the Lion, placed a hand upon it, then turned awkwardly and sat down. It was not, Aidan knew, an attempt to use his rank, but the desire of an old man wishing for softness under his buttocks while he contemplated his grandson.

The Mujhar rubbed at deep scar-creases mostly hidden beneath the patch, as if the empty socket ached. "What happens, then, when you come looking for this chain?"

Aidan shrugged, trying to diminish the desperation he always felt. "I put out my hand to take it, and the chain is changed to dust."

"Dust," Niall echoed thoughtfully.

Aidan extended his right hand. It shook; he tried to suppress it. "I have to have it, grandsire . . . I *have to have the chain*—and yet when I touch it, only dust is left." He shut his hand tightly. "But even the dust goes before I can really touch it."

Niall's single eye was steady. "Have you seen the priests?"

Aidan grinned derisively, slapping his hand down. "They are Homanans."

A silver brow arched. Mildly, the Mujhar said, "They are also men of the gods."

Aidan made an impatient gesture. "They would laugh."

Niall rubbed meditatively at his bottom lip. "No priest of Homana-Mujhar would ever deign to laugh at the man who will one day rule."

Aidan sighed. "No, perhaps not . . . but they would tell those stories. *Already* people tell stories." He tapped his bare chest. "The servants are full of gossip about the Prince of Homana's fey son—the man who walks by night because he requires no sleep."

Niall's smile was faint. "Oh, you require it. And they should know it, too—they have only to look at your face."

"So it shows . . ." He had known it did, to him; he had hoped others were blind to it. "I have done so many things, trying to banish the dreams. Petitions to the gods. Even turning to women." His mouth twisted in self-contempt. "I have lost count of how many women . . . each one I hoped could do it, could banish all the feelings by substituting others. It is a sweet release, grandsire, but it gave me no freedom." He sighed heavily. "None of them was ungrateful —it was the heir to the Prince of Homana, grandson to the Mujhar!—and I like women too much to cast them off indiscreetly . . . but after a while, it palled. Physical satisfaction was no longer enough . . . all the dreams came back."

Niall said nothing.

"Gods—now I am started . . ." Aidan laughed a little. "*And* liquor! I have drunk myself into a stupor more times than I can count, hoping to banish the dream. And for a night, it may work—but in the morning, when all a man in his cups desires is for the sun to set again so it does not blind his eyes, the dream slips through the cracks." Aidan smiled wryly. "I'll be telling you plain, grandsire, the dream is bad enough when I've been having no liquor—'tis *worse* when I'm in my cups."

Niall's smile widened. "Did you know that when you are upset, you sound very like your *jehana*?"

Aidan's mouth twitched. "Or is it I sound like Deirdre?"

"No, no—Dierdre has been in Homana too long . . . most of Erinn is banished, in her . . ." Niall flicked dismissive fingers and straightened in the throne. "But we are not here to speak of accents. Aidan, if you will not go to Homanan priests, what of the *shar tahls*?"

Aidan stilled. "Clankeep?"

"There may be an answer for you."

"Or no answer at all."

"Aidan—"

"I thought of it," he admitted. "Many, many times, and each time I did I convinced myself not to go."

Niall frowned. "Why? Clankeep is your home as much as Homana-Mujhar."

"Is it?" Aidan shook his head. "Homana-Mujhar is my home—Clankeep is merely a *place*."

For a moment his grandsire's expression was frozen. And then the fretwork of Niall's face seemed to collapse inwardly. His eye, oddly, was empty of all expression, until realization crept into it. Followed by blatant grief and regret.

His tone was ragged. "So, it comes to pass . . . Teirnan was right after all." He slumped back in the throne, digging at the leather strap bisecting his brow. "All those times he said we would be swallowed up by Homanans; are you the first, I wonder? Is this the Homanan revenge; if Cheysuli must hold the Lion, we make the Cheysuli Homanan?"

Aidan stared in startled dismay. "Grandsire—"

Niall waved a hand. "No, no, I am not mad . . . nor am I grown suddenly too old for sense." He pulled himself upright in the massive throne. Now the tone was bitter. "I am speaking of Tiernan, your kinsman—cousin to your *jehan*, son to my dead *rujholla*. The one who renounced the prophecy and founded his own clan."

Aidan frowned faintly. "I know who he is. We all know who Teirnan is—or *was*." He shrugged. "How many years has it been since anyone has seen him? Fifteen? Twenty? He may well be dead."

Niall's expression was pensive. "He took his clan into the deepwood somewhere in Homana . . . he is still out there, Aidan—he still plots to take the Lion."

Aidan did not really believe his grandsire was too old to rule, or growing feeble in his wits, but he did think perhaps too much weight was given to a man no one had seen for too many years. The Ihlini were past masters at waiting year after year to strike at their enemies, but from what he knew of his kinsman, Teirnan was not that kind.

"Grandsire—"

Niall did not listen. He heaved himself out of the Lion and bent to retrieve the candle in its cup. He straightened and looked his grandson dead in the eyes. "Go to Clankeep, Aidan. Discover your true heritage before it is too late."

Dumbfounded, Aidan automatically gave way to his grandfather's passage and watched him go, saying nothing. Then turned to look at his *lir* once the silver doors had closed. "What does that mean?"

Teel observed him thoughtfully. *I did not know you were deaf.*

Aidan scowled. "No, I am not deaf . . . but what good will Clankeep do?"

Give you ears to hear with. Give you eyes with which to see. Teel rustled feathers. *Go back to bed, deaf lir. No more dreams tonight.*

Aidan thought about retorting. Then thought instead about his bed and the sweetness of dreamless sleep. "Coming?" he asked acerbically, turning away from the dais.

Teel flew ahead. *I could ask the same of you.*

Three

The stallion was old, growing older, but retained enough of his spirit to make handling him occasionally difficult. The horseboys and grooms of Homana-Mujhar had long ago learned the tending of the black—appropriately named Bane—was best left to his owner, who had a true gift. They dealt with him as they could, then gave him gladly into Brennan's keeping whenever the prince came down to the stableyard.

He came now, dismissing the horseboys flocking to offer attendance, and went into the wood-and-brick stable to see the stallion. But a true horseman never merely *looks;* he can but tie his hands to keep from touching the flesh, from the strong-lipped, velveted muzzle, blowing warmly against his palms.

Bane, by right of rank, had the largest stall in the stable block; a second block housed the Mujhar's favorite mounts. Brennan slipped the latch and entered the straw-bedded stall. The stallion laid back ears, cocked a hoof, then shifted stance to adjust his weight. One black hip briefly pressed Brennan into the stall; automatically slapped, the hip duly shifted itself, ritual completed. Raven ears came up. One dark eye slewed around to look as Brennan moved in close. Bane blew noisily, then bestowed his chin upon Brennan's shoulder, waiting for the fingers that knew *just* where to scratch.

The murmured words were familiar. Bane spoke neither Homanan nor the Old Tongue of the Cheysuli; Bane spoke motion and voice and touch and smell, the language of horse and rider. He listened but vaguely to the words Brennan crooned, hearing instead the tones and nuances, knowing nothing of meaning. Only the promise of affection. The attendance upon a king by a royal-born man himself.

Bane did not mark the underlying anguish in Brennan's tone, the soft subtleties of despair. He was horse, not human; he did not answer to anything unless it concerned his few wants and needs. But even if he *were* human, even a Homanan, the emotions would escape him. Cheysuli-born were different. The unblessed, regardless of bloodlines, of humanness, were deaf to things unsaid. Blind to things suppressed.

But Ian was not unblessed. Ian was Cheysuli. His own share of anguish and despair, though mostly vanquished by time, made him party to them in his nephew.

He moved close to the stall, pausing at the door. Briefly he watched Brennan with his stallion, noting tension in the movements, marking worry in the expression. Seeing such indications was what he had learned to do as liege man to the Mujhar, and as kin to volatile fledglings not always cognizant of caution.

"I have," Ian began quietly, "spent much of my life offering succor—or merely an attentive ear—to those of my kin in need. You have always held yourself apart, depending in great measure on a natural reserve and full understanding of your place. But I have never known a Lion's cub to be beyond the need of comfort."

Brennan, startled, stiffened into unaccustomed awkwardness, then turned. One arm rested on Bane's spine, as if maintaining contact might lend him strength. The other fell to his side. The gold on his arms gleamed in a latticework of sunlight, vented through laddered slats in the outside stable walls. "Did *jehan* send you?"

Ian, hooking elbows on the top of the stall door, smiled with serene good humor. His arms, like Brennan's, were bare of sleeves, displaying Cheysuli gold. "I am not always in his keeping, any more than you. Give me credit for seeing your pain independent of the Mujhar."

Brennan grimaced, looking away from his uncle's discerning eyes to the black silk of Bane's heavy rump. Idly he smoothed it, slicking fingers against the thin cloak of summer coat. Thinking private things. "It was always *jehan* you went to, or Hart—then Keely, when Hart was gone. There were times I wanted to come, but with so many others to tend, I thought your compassion might be all used up."

Ian's eyes were on Bane. He was, like the stallion, past his prime, with hair more gray than black, and white creeping in. By casual reckoning, he was perhaps fifty; in truth, nearly seventy. It was the good fortune of the Cheysuli that age came on them slowly, except for prematurely graying hair. The bones and muscles stiffened, the skin loosened, the hair bleached to white. But nothing about Ian's manner divulged a weakening of spirit any more than in the stallion.

He shifted slightly, rustling boots in straw and hay and bits of grain dropped by Bane over the door. "Niall's children cannot escape the often too-heavy weight of *tahlmorra*, except perhaps for Maeve." Still-black brows rose in brief consideration. "But even then, I wonder—who are we to say there is no magic in her? Niall's blood runs true . . . even in Aidan."

Brennan winced. And Ian, who had baited the hook with quiet deliberation, saw it swallowed whole.

"Oh, aye," Brennan sighed wearily. "The blood runs true in Aidan . . . including Gisella's, I wonder? It is what everyone *else* wonders, regardless of the truth." Brennan turned again to the stallion. A lock of raven hair, showing the first threading of early silver, fell across a dark brow deeply furrowed with concern. "You know and I know my *jehana's* madness is not hereditary, but the Homanans overlook it. All they see is his *difference*, then they mutter about Gisella."

"You cannot ask a man to hide his true self," Ian said gently, "and yet Aidan does so."

Brennan's mouth tightened. "You refer to what *jehan* told me. About Aidan's dreams."

"There was a time he would have told you himself."

Brennan's expression was bleak. "Not for many years. He changed, *su'fali* . . . somehow, some*when,* he changed."

"Perhaps he believed he had to."

The tone now was anguished. "I did not *want* him to! Why would I? After so many years of sickness . . . after so much worry and fear . . ." Brennan sighed, shutting his eyes. "We thought he would die, *su'fali*. In fever, he often babbled. We learned not to listen."

"Because what you heard made no sense."

Mutely, Brennan nodded.

"And so now he does not speak." Ian shook his head. "Aidan is perhaps not what you expected . . . but trying to reforge a sword will only make the steel brittle."

Brennan swung abruptly from the horse. "Have I tried?" he cried. "He is as much a man and warrior as you or I. There is nothing in him I would curse, wishing for alteration . . . he came through a sickly childhood in better fashion than we hoped for, and now there are no doubts he will live to inherit the Lion. But I cannot say what he *thinks*—" Brennan broke it off. The stallion shifted restlessly, disturbed by the raw tone. "*Su'fali*, have you never seen him look through you? Not *at* you, but through. As if you were not present. As if *he* were not, but in another place."

Ian felt serenity slipping. He was one of those men others spoke to freely, finding him easy to confide in. It was a trait not well known among the Cheysuli, who had, in the old days, forbidden the showing of private emotions before others for fear of divulging a weakness to enemies. But those days were past. Things changed within the clans— some said too many things—and he saw no oddity in listening to the sometimes illogical initial commentary of a man—or a woman—trying to find the proper way. It had been so with Niall, and with Hart, and Keely. Brennan had needed no one; Corin had *wanted* no one, unless she be twin-born Keely. But even that had changed.

As everything changed. Now Brennan needed someone to explain a son to his father. And Ian could not do it.

"So you have," Brennan said dully. "You have seen it as well."

Ian sighed. "How can I give you an answer? How can anyone? Aidan is like none of us in many ways, while very like us in others. I see Aileen in him. I see you in him. But perhaps all of us look too hard for unimportant things, such as who he resembles or sounds like. Perhaps Aidan is merely *Aidan*—"

"That bird." Brennan's tone was intent. "That raven—"

Ian smiled. "Teel is a *lir*."

Brennan shook his head. "More. I swear, he is more. Have you seen the look in Aidan's eyes when he goes into the link?"

Ian's smile broadened. "If Keely were here, no doubt she could tell us what it is they converse about, but I would imagine what they say to one another—or what Teel says to him—is little different from what we say to our own *lir.* You should see *your* expression when Sleeta links with you."

"Aye, well, she is sometimes difficult to deal with." Brennan's brow smoothed as a faint smile pulled his mouth crooked. "Aidan himself has said Teel hag-rides him unmercifully."

Ian stepped aside as Brennan left Bane and unlatched the door to exit the stall. "For too many years he was sick, too many times close to death. It marks a man, Brennan. It marked your *jehan.* It marked you. It marked Hart and Corin and Keely. Did you think your son would escape it?"

Brennan swung shut the door and slammed the latch into place. "The Lion requires a man who can rule with intellect, not with dreams and fancies."

"Ah," Ian murmured. "Is that why you allowed yourself none?"

Brennan's face hardened. "You understand what responsibility is, *su'fali.* Do you blame me? When it comes to levying war, dare a king think of dreams?"

"There is no war in Homana. Nor in Solinde. Nor in Erinn or Atvia. What war are you fighting, *harani*?"

Brennan shook his head. "No one understands what it is to look at Aidan and wonder what he will be. To wonder what he *is*."

Ian refrained from answering at once. There was wildness in the Cheysuli, for all they practiced control; he knew from personal experience how difficult it was to maintain balance under trying circumstances. Some said it was the beast in the blood. Ian knew better. There was a price to pay for control: the occasional loss of it.

His royal nephew, for all Brennan's reknowned maturity, was as capable of anger as his volatile brother, Corin, or Keely, his prickly sister. He simply did not show it as much, yet Ian thought it best now to avoid provocation. It was next to impossible to make a man see reason if his mouth was busy shouting.

He watched Brennan a moment, marking redoubled tension. "Do you wonder, then, why he says nothing to you? Why he goes so often to the Lion? If you have, in any fashion, caused him to wonder if he is—*askew*—in any way, should he trust himself with a throne shaped like a mythical beast? Or believe it an enemy?"

"By the gods, Ian, he is a grown man, a *warrior*."

"This began when he was a child. Children view things differently."

"Children are often too fanciful. They frighten themselves." Brennan's eyes, oddly, were black. "Do you think I know nothing of that? Even within Bane's stall, knowing the door is *there*, I still feel the fear of being closed in."

"Do you blame yourself for that?"

Brennan's expression was ravaged. "I was locked in the Womb for a very short time . . . and yet I believed it days." He raked a hand through his hair. "Gods—how I frightened myself. I made all those *lir* into beasts . . . *carved marble shapes,* I remade into living beasts. And now I reap the reward . . . shut me up in darkness, and I lose myself utterly."

Ian nodded slightly. "And so the *jehan*, seeing a child's fear fed by fancies, told him it was not real. Over and over again, until the child thought it best to keep everything to himself."

Desperation threaded Brennan's tone. "They are *dreams,* Ian. What else was I to do? Allow him to frighten himself?"

Ian shrugged a single shoulder. "I have no answer for you. But Aidan still dreams . . . fear or no fear, *something* is real to him."

"And I gave it no credence, ever." Brennan collapsed against the wall, mouth pulled awry. "I am not and have never been the most discerning of men."

Ian watched him closely. Quietly, he suggested, "I think Aileen might understand what you feel. She has as much stake in Aidan's future as you."

Brennan's expression was bleak. "She says nothing of it to me."

Ian did not smile. "Have you ever thought to ask her?"

Brennan shrugged. "She is too quick to defend him. She hears nothing of my concern, gives no weight to what I say." He grimaced. "He is her only child; she will hear no wrong of him."

Ian shook his head. "Aileen is neither blind nor deaf. She defends him to *others;* is there need to do that with you?"

The stallion, now turned, thrust his head over the door, blocking their view of one another. Brennan cupped a hand

over the bone of the nose and pulled the black head down
so he could see his uncle. "I have the right to worry."

Ian stroked the silken neck. "No one will take that from
you. But Aileen might help you bear it."

Brennan's expression was odd. "He needs to sire a son."

Ian's motion was arrested. "Why? Do you think it might
be best if you replaced your son with a grandson? Just *in
case*—"

"No!" The response came too quickly. "But he is twenty-
three, *su'fali* . . . I had a son by then. My *jehan* had three of
his own, as well as two daughters."

Ian said nothing a moment. Then, in precise, staccato,
tones, "Have you never thought that, given more time, you
and Aileen might have made a true match? One much like
Niall's and Deirdre's?"

"There was Corin—"

"That was very nearly twenty-five years ago!"

Muscles clenched in Brennan's jaw. "You are saying I
should give Aidan time."

"There is enough of it yet; aye. You know the price you
and Aileen have paid . . . why ask *him* to pay it?"

Brennan's tone was as clipped. "Kings must beget sons."

Ian lost his patience. "The present king is living. His own
heir is perfectly healthy, and *he* has an heir. I think the
Lion, just this moment, requires no more than that."

Brennan shut his eyes. When he opened them, Ian saw
bleak despair. "And if my son is mad? How do I get
another? Aileen can give me no more . . . and I will not set
her aside. I *need* a son from Aidan."

Ian shook his head. "Aidan is not mad. Aidan is only—
different."

Brennan cupped Bane's black muzzle. "Kings cannot be
different. It makes the Homanans afraid."

His uncle's expression was compassionate. "No more afraid
than you."

The day was gray, growing grayer. Aidan, who had ridden out of Mujhara not long after a mid-morning meal,
scowled irritably at the pewter-hued sky. Teel was in it
somewhere, riding out the wind; Aidan looked, found him,
sent his feelings through the link.

As if to spite the wind, Teel's tone was undiminished.
Some things are worth discomfort.

"But it is *summer*," Aiden protested. "Summer rain I understand—*this* feels more like winter!"

Only yesterday you complained of the heat . . . I think you are merely perverse.

He could be, Aidan admitted. But now was not one of those times. Yesterday, it *had* been hot; now it was much too cold. Not so cold as to make him shiver, but enough to make him wish he had brought at least a fall cloak. Arms left bare by Cheysuli jerkin protested the chill. *Lir*-bands felt icy.

Wind changed direction and blew ruddy hair into pale eyes. Aidan stripped it back, peeling strands free of lashes, then forgot about hair altogether as his horse shied violently sideways to make his own discomfort known. The dun gelding did not bolt, but only because Aidan was ready for him.

"No," he said calmly, speaking also through the reins. "I think it would be best for both of us if you let me do the choosing of whether we walk or run."

Lir. Teel's voice. *The storm is growing worse.*

Aidan, who could feel the blast of the wind as well as the raven, offered no comment. He was too busy with the horse, who threatened to run again. Aidan did not really blame him. If he himself were a horse, he might run as well. The wind was full of urging, wailing down hilly croftlands. Its song was one of winter; of hearthfires and steaming wine. Or, if he were a horse, of windtight stable and warm bedding straw, with grain for the asking.

"Summer," Aidan muttered. "What will winter be like, I wonder?"

There was nothing for it but to ride on, to reach the fringes of the wood that would provide some protection. The track, warded by trees and foliage, would be free of much of the wind, and he could go on to Clankeep screened from the worst of the weather.

Debris littered the air: leaves, dirt, torn petals of wind-tattered flowers. Aidan ducked his head, squinted, spat, urged the gelding a little faster. And then faster still.

"Go ahead," he agreed, giving the dun his head. "A bit of a run will do no harm, and will get us there the faster."

The gelding required no urging. By the time they reached the trees, Aidan was almost sorry. A gallop through the wind blew away the dull dregs of a troubled night's sleep, leaving him refreshed and in good spirits. He gloried in the sensation of horse against the storm, himself bent over the neck so as to give the wind no purchase. But he did not give into the impulse that told him to run again; the gelding deserved a rest, and the track was littered with stormwrack, providing treacherous footing for a horse already spooked.

"*Shansu*," he said, patting the gelding's neck. "Another time, I promise—for now we will walk."

The dun was ordinarily a well-mannered, settled horse, neither young nor old, and not given to coltish antics. But clearly the storm had set him on edge; now, as Aidan attempted to calm him, he pawed and swished his tail, indicating displeasure.

Aidan lifted an arm and pointed. "That way," he suggested.

The dun backed in a circle, eyeing the way they had come.

"No, I said *that* way—" Aidan turned him forcibly. "We have been to Clankeep uncountable times before . . . there is no reason for this. If there were danger, Teel would say so; I trust him more than you."

The gelding protested, snorting nosily. Dark eyes rolled.

Frowning, Aidan went into the link. *Lir—is there danger?*

So much for trust, Teel answered. *No, there is no danger . . . nothing but the storm.*

Relieved, Aidan aimed the dun yet again toward the east. "If this is a show of will, I could choose a better time . . . shall we discuss this a bit later?"

The gelding stood still and quivered.

Aidan stroked the ocher-brown neck again. "*Shansu*, my lad, my boy—'tis naught but a bit of a blow . . . d'ye think I'd be wanting you harmed?"

Erinnish, many held, was a tongue made for horses, but the gelding was Homanan. He chose to misunderstand.

Wind roared through the trees. The dun bolted and ran.

It was, Aidan thought grimly, an entirely horselike flight. After refusing to go east, fright had forced the gelding. If the storm had not worsened matters, Aidan might have let him run on since he was heading toward their destination. But he dared not in the wind. The track was fouled with debris. If the gelding tripped and went down—

"Never *mind*," Aidan muttered, cursing imagination.

He drew the reins in tautly and attempted to apply force of will to the restraint. He had gentled many a colt and won many a horse's trust, sharing much of his father's skill. But the gelding was having none of it.

Concern instantly deepened. Aidan knew the feel of it: the bit had been rolled forward, free of tender bars, and now was lodged in teeth. The horse was in control. The man on his back was nothing more than a minor inconvenience not worth the trouble of throwing off.

Aidan, amused by the all-too-accurate vision, grinned, then wished he had not as dirt fouled his teeth. He spat. *I could simply take lir-shape and let this fool of a boy run on without me*—

But the thought of risking the gelding made him reconsider. His father had trained him too well; when it came to welfare, he thought of the horse's in place of his own.

Or, I could—

But what else he could—or could not—do, went unthought. Without altering his pace, the gelding dodged off the track and crashed into deadfall and foliage, neatly avoiding a tree trunk. Aidan also avoided the trunk, but did not miss the limp sweeping down from the rack of low boughs.

In reflex, he thrust out a warding forearm, knowing it much too late. *Lir*—

It was all Aidan managed as the tree limb embraced his ribs and swept him out of the saddle.

Four

He dreamed. He dreamed he was made of smoke and fire in place of flesh and blood. His heart was a white flame and his soul whiter still, so brilliant it was blinding. Out of the white flame of his heart and the whiter brilliance of his soul came the music that poured through his veins like quicksilver, burning what it touched with a pain exquisitely sweet. He wanted to cry with its beauty, but knew he dared not.

Water extinguishes flame. Extinguished, I will die.

He saw himself, but it was not himself. The Aidan he saw was another man, insubstantial, incorporeal, substantive as smoke. He drifted this way, that way, shredding himself as he moved, then forming himself again. And then the man of smoke congealed into anther shape, taking the form of a raven, also made of smoke, and the raven flew swiftly skyward in a bid for needed freedom.

South: to an island: away from Homana-Mujhar and all the Cheysuli Keeps; away from the world everyone else called home, until the raven found a new home among the standing stones now fallen, cold and green and gray, where he perched upon a shattered, rune-scribed altar as if he wished to speak of gods.

The altar was overturned. From beneath it, something glinted with the dull brilliance of muddied gold. The raven, knowing need, left his perch and descended.

A chain. Coiled beneath the altar, perfect and unblemished. Its beauty was so compelling that even the raven was moved to desire it. But a raven has no hands; he shapechanged himself to a man and knelt down to pick up the chain.

He touched it. It was whole. He lifted it. It was whole. He took it from the shadows, unable to breathe, and held it in the light.

The links were the size of a man's forearm. Seamless, flawless gold, filled with twisted runes too intertwined to decipher.

He dared to breathe on it. One of the links broke.

Grief swallowed him. *Why do I destroy when all I want is to make things whole?*

He still held half of the chain. The other half had fallen, spilled on leaf-molded floor.

A sound. He turned, still kneeling, still grasping his half of the chain, and saw the shadowed figure in the tumbled doorway of lichen-clad stones.

The voice was firm and commanding. "You hold me in your hand. What do you want from me?"

Aidan tried not to gape. Where had the stranger come from?

For that matter, where was *he*?

"Who are you?" he blurted.

Disbelief was manifest: black brows arched up, then snapped together over a blade-straight nose. "The Mujhar," he said. Clearly the stranger believed Aidan could surely name him; only a fool could not, or a man with no eyes to see.

Aidan heard the undertone of expectation couched in blatant arrogance. But he *heard* it, he did not feel it; something was not right. Something was not *real*.

The Mujhar—? he echoed blankly.

Certainly the man looked it. He wore black velvet and leather of exquisite quality and cut; a scarlet rampant lion clawed its way across the black silken overtunic belted with heavy gold. Hands, hooked into the belt, were strong, long-fingered, callused, the hands of a soldier; no Cheysuli, he. The eyes were a clear, piercing gray. Black hair was frosted silver.

Neither young nor old. Aidan thought him fifty. But something he could not name whispered of agelessness.

It would do no good to wonder when he knew the man lied. "Who are you?" he repeated.

Gray eyes narrowed. "I have said: the Mujhar."

It was too much. Aidan, frowning, glanced around the ruins, trying briefly to place himself. And then the arrogance of the tone—and the claim—restored his attention to the stranger.

Who is he *to say such a thing?* And then he nearly laughed. *And to* me, *when it comes to that; I know the truth.*

"Mujhar, you say?" Aidan sat back on his heels. "And *I* say you are lying."

Well-cut lips tightened. "That is punishable by death."

"Oh?" Aidan smiled. "Then kill me, Mujhar . . . kill the man who *will* hold the Lion when the proper time is come."

"You?" Black brows swept up again. "*You* will hold the Lion?"

Aidan spoke lightly. "So I have been told. It has to do with my birth—I am Brennan's son, and grandson to Niall."

"Ah." It was succinct, yet brimming with comprehension. "Where I am, there is no time . . . and I did not realize so much had already passed." He smiled consideringly. "Are we to Niall already?"

This man is mad. And I am mad for listening.

He adopted a coolly condescending tone. "You will forgive me, I hope, if I fail to display the deference due a Mujhar—I show it to my grandsire, who is deserving of it. You I do not know."

"Oh, I think you do." The gray eyes were oddly lambent. "The history of the Cheysuli is full of my name and title."

Aidan held on to his patience. "Then why not give me both."

"You have the title: Mujhar. The name I am called is Shaine."

Shaine. Shaine? *Shaine?*

He wanted to laugh, but could not. This man touched his pride, as well as heritage. "I will thank you to keep your mouth from the name of my ancestor."

Gray eyes glinted. "But it is *my* name."

"Shaine is dead," he said flatly.

The stranger merely nodded. "A long time ago. Would you like to hear how?"

"I know how. I was taught. All of us were taught." Aidan did not smile. "Shaine killed himself when he voided Ihlini wards set to keep Cheysuli from Homana-Mujhar."

"A painful death, and somewhat unexpected," agreed the other. "But by then it no longer mattered . . . Finn would have killed me once he walked the hall. It was what he came to do." Briefly the eyes smoldered. "Hale's shapechanger son . . . gods, but I hated them. And Alix was the worst, coming before me like Lindir, but dark instead of fair." Lips writhed briefly. "Carillon would have wed her, and made her Queen of Homana. I could see it in his eyes."

Dumbstruck, Aidan stared. The words came very slowly. "She married Duncan instead."

"Duncan. Your great-great-*great*-grandsire." Gray eyes narrowed. "A long history. I weary of it all."

This cannot be happening. None of this is real. Aidan stared at the man. He filled his eyes with the man, stretching lids wide, then swallowed back the sour taste filling his mouth. *Am I dead?* he wondered. *Could this all be real?*

The knots in his belly tightened. Aidan felt numb. "If you are Shaine . . ." he mumbled. "If you *are* Shaine . . ." He twitched the thought away. "Am I dead?" he asked flatly. "Oh, gods, am I dead? Is this what it is to die?

"Dead? You?" White teeth parted the beard. "No, not yet. There is time still left to you."

Fleetingly, Aidan wondered how much; he forbore to ask. Relief was too overwhelming, until he considered again the circumstances.

He wiped one sweaty hand on a legging-clad thigh. His only chance was to focus on something, anything, to keep himself from losing control. "If you are Shaine the Mujhar, you *are* dead."

The man did not reply.

Aidan felt sick. He wanted to spew out the contents of his belly across the fallen altar, or onto leaf-thickened floor. Sweat bathed his flesh. His head began to ache. Worst of all was the fear.

I HAVE gone mad.

And then, *Gods, where is Teel? What has become of my lir?*

Still kneeling, he shuddered. Hands clenched on the links. *This is a new dream . . . gods, let it BE a dream—*

Shaine the Mujhar stared back. "We are not discussing me. We have come to speak of you."

"Me?" Aidan blurted. "What have you to do with me?"

"Stand up," he was told.

Aidan slowly rose. Links in his hand chimed.

The man examined him. "Cheysuli," he said in disgust. "I should have known Carillon would lift my curse as soon as he claimed the Lion . . . well, it took him five years to win it back from Bellam, and longer still to end the extermination." The line of the mouth was bitter. *"Qu'mahlin,* you shapechangers call it? Aye, well, nothing lasts, not even the

Cheysuli . . ." Gray eyes narrowed. "Red hair, fair skin . . . is it merely you mimic the fashion?"

Sickness was unabated. His belly writhed within. But he focused on something else so as to ignore his discomfort.

"Mimic the fashion—?" Abruptly, Aidan understood. It made him angry, very angry; it gave him courage again. "These *lir*-bands and the earring are mine, gained in the usual way, and properly bestowed during my Ceremony of Honors. There is no *fashion* to them; nor to me, my lord apparition: I am Cheysuli and heir to Homana."

Shaine the Mujhar smiled. "Are you so certain of that?"

Aidan struggled with himself. *I am mad—I must be mad— why else am I standing here arguing with a fetch?* He glanced around for Teel. *Where is my lir?*

Shaine the Mujhar still smiled. "Are you so certain?"

The derision snared Aidan's attention. "Of course I am certain," he snapped. "I have told you who I am, and you say I am not dead; how would I *not* be heir?"

"By never accepting the throne."

Aidan swallowed a shout. Quietly, he said, "I was born to accept the throne. The Lion will be mine."

Shaine lifted a hand and pointed to the chain dangling from Aidan's hand. "Men are but links," he said. "Links in a chain of the gods, who play at the forge as a child plays at his toys. Make a link, and solder it here—solder another there . . . rearrange the order to better please the eye." The arrogance had faded, replaced by intensity. "Some links are strong and never yield, bound to one another . . . others are flawed, and break, replaced by those who are stronger so the chain is never destroyed. It is a game of the gods, Aidan, to forge a flawless link, then join it to the other. One by one by one, making the chain strong. Making the chain perfect. Disposing of weakened links so as not to harm the whole."

Holding the broken chain, Aidan said nothing.

Shaine did not smile. "The weak link has a name: Aidan of Homana."

Anger rose, was suppressed. It would do no good to argue with a man who did not exist. "You are in my dream," Aidan rasped. "Dreams have no substance. This *chain* has no substance. Nothing you say is real."

"Then why did you summon me?"

Aidan shook his head. "I did not summon you. A man cannot summon a dream . . . nor can he raise the dead."

"But I am there, in your hand." Shaine pointed precisely. "The chain, Aidan; that link. I explained it all to you once, must I explain it all again?"

Aidan looked at the link clutched in his hand. His fingers tightened on it. If, in his twisted dream, this link was Shaine, who were the others?

But he banished the question at once; Shaine was his concern. "Begone," he said tautly. "I want none of you."

Gray eyes glittered. "But I am *in* you, Aidan. All of us are."

Aidan threw down the chain. Shaine disappeared.

The tremor ran through his body. It convulsed legs, arms, neck, then snatched at lax control. He felt the spasm, the jerk, then the sudden cessation of movement. He lay limply on the ground, sprawled in broken foliage now compressed beneath his body.

What—? he asked vaguely, numb with disorientation.

"*Shansu,*" a voice said quietly. "Let the world settle."

Aidan had little choice. For the moment he knew nothing of who he was or where he was, or what had happened to him. Only that somehow—*how?*—he had come to be lying on his back on the ground.

"*Shansu,*" the voice repeated. "I would be the last to harm you."

Who—? Aidan forced open eyes. Dazzled, he stared blindly up at the pewter-gray sky screened by a lattice of limbs, and recalled he was in the wood.

Not inside a ruined chapel with a dead Mujhar standing before him.

Consciousness solidified. "Teel," he managed aloud, groping through the link for familiar reassurance.

There was nothing. Nothing. No Teel. No link. Only the absence of everything, as if he had been emptied.

"*Teel!*"

The spasm returned in full force, this time prompted by the frantic flailing of his limbs. He still had no control, but this time he was the cause.

A hand touched his brow and pressed him gently against the ground. "*Shansu.*" A third time. "Your *lir* is safe, I promise. I only sent him ahead. Clankeep is not so far . . .

unless, of course, I have misreckoned the distance." The tone was wry. "That is possible, I suppose; I am not accustomed to human time divisions, or distances reckoned as leagues. Still, as the raven flies . . ." Now the tone was amused.

"Who—?" Aidan squinted.

The hand was cool on his brow. "For now, it makes no difference. I have a name, aye, but we do not bestow them on men, who cannot deal with the power held in a true name. If you like, you may call me the Hunter; it will do as well as my real one, which means very much the same."

Another one, Aidan thought dimly. *First the one calls himself Shaine, and now* this *one* . . . It drifted away on a wisp of disbelief. He would not allow himself. Self-possession was the key, if he was to survive.

Aidan licked dry lips. "I came off my horse."

"Most dramatically. Unlike you, the horse is unhurt." The voice was amused.

Aidan focused with effort. Now he could see someone. A man, kneeling by his side. A *brown* man: hair, skin, eyes, leathers, all degrees of peat-brown, as if he hid himself in the wood—or, Aidan thought dimly, as if he was *of* the wood. Not old, not young, but in between; a score of years older than Aidan, a score younger than Niall. Dark eyes were kind, but compelling.

Something in Aidan answered. "You are Cheysuli—?" But he broke it off almost at once. "No—no, of course not . . . how could I think such a thing?"

The Hunter smiled. "There is Cheysuli in me. Or, to be precise: there is *me* in Cheysuli."

For a man only recently revived from unconsciousness—and with an aching head—it was much too confusing. Very like his meeting with Shaine, which, Aidan was certain, came as reaction to the fall. "Let me sit—*aghh*—"

"Perhaps not," the Hunter said mildly.

Aidan was appalled by the pain. His head hurt, aye, but not so much as his chest. A demon was kicking his ribs. "Am I broken?" he asked faintly.

"Bruised, a little. Repairable, certainly. I could do it for you, but that is not my gift. I Hunt; I do not Heal."

That won Aidan's attention. "Hunt—" he muttered blankly. "What is it you hunt?"

"Men."

Something jumped inside painful ribs. "But—" He stopped. "No—I think not . . . you could not be—"

"—hunting you?" the brown man finished. "Oh, indeed I could be . . . in fact, I am certain I *am*."

Sweat sheened Aidan's face. He felt it under his arms; in the hollow of his belly, beneath aching ribs. "What have you done with my *lir*?"

"Sent him ahead, as I said. Do you think I could hurt a *lir*?" The tone changed to shock. "No more than harm *you*, who are true-born of the Cheysuli . . ." The Hunter's voice faded. His face registered concern. "I have little experience with humans, even with those of my blood . . . perhaps I would have done better to come in another guise." He frowned thoughtfully. "But this one has always served me . . . it has always been so *benign* . . ."

Aidan lost fear and patience. "Who exactly *are* you? And why are you hunting me?"

The dark face creased in a smile. "To discover what you have learned."

"Have—learned—?" It was incongruous to Aidan that any of what he saw was real. That what he *heard* was real; the fall had addled his wits. First Shaine, and now the Hunter. "Am I supposed to have learned anything in particular? Or anything at all?"

"Oh, I think something. You have been alive for twenty-three years . . . I think you *must* have learned something." The smile was undiminished, though irony laced the tone.

And yet another time, as if repeated asking would eventually win him an answer: "What have you done with my *lir*?"

The brown man's smile vanished. "Ruefully, he rubbed his jaw. "I see the link is even stronger than we expected . . . we might have done better to lessen it, to make *lir* and warrior less dependent upon one another, but without the strength of that bond, there could be repercussions. And we could not afford those." He shook his head. "No, I think it is as well."

Patience frayed. "*What* is as well?"

"The bond," the Hunter answered equably. "The thing you call the *lir*-link. The thing that sets you apart from all the others we made . . . except, of course, the Ihlini." He sighed. "We do not succeed in everything. Imparting free will was a risk we decided to take . . . the Ihlini were the result." He paused. A trace of grimness entered his tone. "And, now, the *a'saii*."

Aidan gritted his teeth. "You have not answered my question."

"About your *lir*? But I have. I sent him ahead, to Clankeep."

Response was immediate. "Teel does no man's bidding! Teel can be *sent* nowhere, unless I do the sending!"

"Ah, but the *lir* answer to a higher power than that of the Cheysuli. They can be sent wherever we say."

"There is only one other power—" Aidan broke it off. He stared hard at the man, daring him to repeat the oblique claim, but nothing was forthcoming.

The wind, for a moment, rose, then died away to nothing. Storm clouds peeled away, leaving behind a clear sky. It was, abruptly, *spring*, not summer; grass grew, trees budded, the air was warm and light. Even as Aidan sat there, braced against the ground, a flower grew up between the fingers of one hand. And blossomed.

The Hunter's smile was mild. "Perhaps you begin to see."

Aidan snatched his hand away. The denial was absolute. "No."

The Hunter nodded in silence.

I am mad. I am. I must be. Or sick in the head; the fall—it was the fall . . . I landed on my head, and everything is a dream—yet another dream . . . first Shaine, now this Hunter— Aidan squinted fiercely. *If I look at things more closely—*

What he looked at was a man who claimed he was a god.

Spring dissolved itself. It grew cooler as Aidan stared, until he began to shiver. It was cold, too cold; in winter he wore fur-lined leathers, forsaking the linens of summer. But now he was caught, bathed by winter's breath. The ground around him hardened. The trees sloughed leaves. The grass beneath was dead, and all the flowers gone.

But a moment ago it was spring . . . Aidan shivered. And then it was warm again.

When he could, he cleared his throat. Perhaps if he proceeded with extreme caution . . . "*Why* did you send Teel away? If he is of your making—"

"Oh, not of *mine*—I do not do the making. That is a task for others, though all of us, of course, have some say in the matter." The Hunter's expression was kind, as if he understood all too well what Aidan was thinking. Which perhaps he did, if he was what he claimed. "As to why I sent him away, the answer is simple enough. This is a thing between you and I, Aidan, not among you and I and the raven. Even the *lir* are not privy to all we do."

The seasons, without fanfare, continued changing. Grass grew, then died; flowers bloomed, then died; trees changed their shapes; the sky was day, then night; then night and day again. And all without a single word from the brown man watching Aidan. Without a single *gesture* to say he realized what he did was not done—could *not* be done—by anyone but a god.

Think about something else . . .

Aidan stirred, then ventured another question. "Why are the *lir* not privy to all you do?"

"Oh, they are quite arrogant enough without requiring another reason. They are familiars, not gods—they cannot know everything, or they become quite insufferable."

"No," Aidan said faintly, letting it sink in. "Teel needs no more cause for any additional arrogance. He has quite enough as it is."

White teeth gleamed. "I thought you might agree. I think any warrior would, faced with such a course." The Hunter rose, stretched legs, moved to a shattered tree stump. As he sat down, a tiny sapling sprouted at the base of the broken stump. "Teel is—different. I thought him well suited to you."

Aidan sat upright carefully, holding himself very straight. *I will say nothing of this to him—all these* wonders *he performs. Perhaps I am not meant to notice.*

But that seemed incongruous. How could he not notice?

Once more, Aidan focused. "Why? Why is Teel suited to *me?* Why not another warrior?"

"Because you also are different." There was no sting in the quiet words; from a god, they were revelation. "You will spend much of your time questioning things; that is the way of you. Many men act first with little thought for result— rashness is sometimes a curse, sometimes a virtue— but your gift is to think things through before acting." The Hunter smiled. "You will make mistakes, of course—you are man, Aidan, not god—but you are also exceedingly cautious. Some might call you reluctant, others will name you afraid, but cowardice is not your curse."

Aidan wet drying lips. "What *is* my curse?"

The god looked down at the sapling trying mightily to be a tree. He bent, cupped its crown in his fingers, murmured something quietly in a tongue foreign to Aidan. Then, in clear Homanan, "Not so quickly, small one . . . there is time for you to grow. For now you must wait on men." He took his fingers away and looked again at Aidan. "You are simply you. Try to be no one else. Let no one force you to be."

"But—" Aidan, staring at the tiny tree, did not finish, forgoing the question he meant to ask in a flood of others like it. "Is that all?"

"All?" Brown eyebrows arched. "Trying to be himself—or *her*self, as Keely learned—is one of the most difficult tasks a human can face."

Aidan waited a moment. "But I have to be Mujhar."

The Hunter was very solemn. "That, too, is a task. Not every man succeeds." He shifted on the stump. "I am here to tell you nothing more than I have. It is not the nature of gods to tell their children everything—man does not learn by being told; he must *do*. So, you will do." One leather-clad shoulder lifted and fell in a casual shrug.

Aidan, who felt in no way enlightened *or* casual, scowled at the Hunter. "Are you really here?"

"Are *you?*"

In spite of himself, he smiled. "With this pounding in my head, I could not begin to say."

Brown eyes glinted. "Horses are made for riding, not for falling off of. Now you must pay the price." He paused. "You might have flown, you know."

"I might have," Aidan agreed. "There is nothing so free as flying . . . but riding a good horse has its own brand of magic."

The Hunter laughed. "Aye, well, we gave you free will . . . choosing to ride instead of fly is one of the smaller freedoms."

Aidan shifted restlessly, then surpressed a wince. "That is all—? You came merely to say I must be myself?"

"Enough of a task, for now. But since I am here, you may as well tell me about your dream."

Ice encased his flesh. "You know about my dream? You know about the chain?"

The answer was oblique. "I mean the dream you dreamed just now, before coming to yourself. Your eyes were wide open, but you saw nothing of the day. Only inside yourself."

Aidan felt moved to protest. "But you are a *god*."

The Hunter looked annoyed. "You are a man," he said plainly. "We made you deliberately impulsive and idiosyncratic, and gave you minds with which to dream . . . do you think we also put thoughts in your heads? Why would we want to do *that* when it defeats the purpose of living?"

"My heads hurts," Aidan replied. "That is my only thought."

The Hunter displayed white teeth. "We gave you the freedom to rule yourselves, Aidan, because we wanted children, not minions. Devotion is appreciated; respect we honor highly. But we do not want fanatics and zealots. That is not why we made men." He paused, then softened his tone. "Now, tell me of the dream."

He did not want to, any more than tell Niall. But he had spoken to the Mujhar. Surely he could find it within himself to divulge the dream to a *god*.

He drew in a trembling breath. "Shaine," Aidan said, and told him the whole of it.

He thought, at the end, the Hunter would disparage him for it, saying he was too fanciful, or blame it on the fall. But the Hunter did no such thing.

"It was not false," he said quietly. "Who calls it so is a blind man, with no soul to use as eyes. Those in your head can play you false; those of your soul cannot."

"But Shaine has been *dead* for nearly one hundred years!"

Frowning, the Hunter nodded.

It frightened Aidan badly. "Have *you* no explanation?"

"There are tests," the Hunter replied absently. "I am only one among many; I cannot tell you what others plan for you. There are tests, and tasks . . . no *tahlmorra* is fulfilled without pain, or there can be no growth. Without growth or evolution, there can be no change. Without change, the world dies."

"Evolution?" Aidan echoed.

The Hunter's smile was sanguine. "A mechanism for change. For the *betterment* of a world."

Aidan, lacking reply, merely stared at the god.

"So." The Hunter rose. "I have said what I came to say. There remains only this." He reached into his belt-pouch. "This is for you, and only you. When you have learned both use and meaning, you will be closer to finding the answers to all those questions you ask aloud in the darkness of the night."

Something arced through the air. Aidan, scrambling forward painfully, caught it. And knew it instantly by touch. By the texture of the gold, formed into a seamless, flawless link big enough for a man's wrist.

"You *do* know—" he began, but found the Hunter gone. In his place reared a tree, in full-blown majesty.

Five

Aidan made his way through Clankeep and rode straight to the blue pavilion bedecked with a painted black mountain cat. It was not his own; he had none. It was his father's pavilion, though Brennan rarely came. Its use had fallen to Aidan, though he also spent most of his time in Homana-Mujhar.

He reined in the dun before the laced doorflap. And scowled up at his *lir*, perched in perfect indolence atop the pavilion ridgepole.

You knew, he charged, sending annoyance through the link.

Teel fluffed feathers.

"You *knew*," he said aloud, as if the dual challenge carried more weight than one or the other.

I knew nothing, the raven retorted.

Aidan's brows shot upward. His tone dripped sarcasm. "Oh? Is this the first crack in your vaunted self-assurance? You admit to ignorance?"

Teel thought it over. *I knew what he was,* he conceded at last. *But not what he wanted.*

It was, Aidan thought, a compromise. Something Teel rarely did. "Why?" he asked aloud. "Why did he come to me?"

Teel turned around twice on the ridgepole, then stared down at his irritated *lir*. *You are angry.*

"Aye," Aidan snapped. "Should I not be? I have just

spent a portion of my life—I'm not even knowing how much!—talking with dead men and gods."

Ah. Black eyes were bright. *Anger is good.*

Aidan glared. "Why?"

Because it is better than fear. If you give in to the fear, it can overwhelm you.

"For now the only thing overwhelming me is frustration," Aidan retorted. He scowled blackly at the raven. "You did not answer my question. Why did he come to me? This *god.*"

Teel fluffed feathers. *I am quite certain he told you.*

"Something of something," Aidan agreed. "Not enough to make sense, merely to confuse."

Teel cocked his head. *Gods are often like that.*

Aidan drew breath for waning patience, caught it on a hiss as the pain of bruised ribs renewed itself. "Then I am to assume you will give me no answers to the questions I still have."

We are not put here to answer all *your questions*, Teel said brusquely. *Only some of them.*

"With you choosing which ones."

We answer what we can, if the questions are in your best interests. Teel dug briefly under a wing, then looked down at Aidan once more. *You will know what you must know when the time to know is come.*

Aidan gritted teeth. "Obscurity," he said grimly, "is a game I do not care for."

The raven's tone was amused. *But it is the one I am best at.*

Giving up, Aidan kicked free of stirrups and carefully let himself down from the saddle. It was a painful exercise and one he regretted immensely, clutching impotently at ribs. Likely he needed them strapped, which meant admitting to the accident. His father would be amused; Brennan *never* came off a horse.

Or, if he had, his son had never known of it.

"Hungry," he muttered aloud. "But chewing will hurt my head."

Out of sorts, are we?

Aidan went into the link. *Out of sorts and out of patience; I am here for the shar tahl. Perhaps* he *will have my answers, even if you do not.*

Teel eyed him archly. *Oh, he may have them . . . but are you worthy of them?*

Aidan looped the reins over a post set into dirt before the pavilion. *Surely a warrior with you for a lir is worthy of anything.*

It was sufficiently double-edged that Teel did not respond.

The *shar tahl's* pavilion was larger than most, since he required additional room for storage of clan birthlines and assorted ritualistic items. It was customary to wait no farther inside a *shar tahl's* or clan-leader's pavilion than a single pace; Aidan therefore sat very precisely near the open doorflap on a gray-blue ice bear pelt brought from the Northern Wastes. The *shar tahl* was not yet present, although word had been carried throughout Clankeep the Mujhar's grandson had arrived.

Even though Aidan was well-accustomed to the immense size and overwhelming presence of Homana-Mujhar, he felt daunted by the pavilion. It was here the history of the clan was kept, rolled tightly in soft leathers and tucked away inside strong chests. His own history resided somewhere in the pavilion, reduced to a single rune-sign on pale, bleached doeskin. A rune, no more than that, yet he felt small because of it. Small because of doubts; was he doing the right thing? The Hunter had not admonished him against displaying the golden link, merely said it was *for* him. He could not imagine anything to do with gods could be denied a *shar tahl*. Such men served those gods with steadfast loyalty.

He waited, legs folded beneath him, with the link clutched in two hands. Teel was not with him, leaving his *lir*, with some trepidation, to find his own way. Aidan was alone, and feeling immensely lonely.

He will say I am mad. Or, if he does not say it, he will think it . . . and soon even the clans will say I mimic Gisella—

Aidan cut it off.

I should look at another side . . . perhaps he will have my answers and share them willingly. Perhaps he will know what this is and what I should do with it—

Aidan gritted teeth. "Why does this happen to me? First all those dreams, now this nonsense of dead Mujhars and gods—" He clenched fingers around the link. Fear was unavoidable, no matter what Teel said. "What if I *am* mad?"

"Aidan."

He stiffened, then bowed, showing homage, and was startled when a hand touched the crown of his head.

"No, Aidan—not from you." The hand was removed. The *shar tahl* came more fully into the pavilion and moved around to face his guest. He was surprisingly young for his place, still black-haired and firm of flesh. He was, Aidan thought, perhaps thirty-five or thirty-six.

But the *shar tahl's* physical appearance was not the matter at hand. "Why not?" Aidan asked, glad to think of something else. "Honor is your due."

"And I do not disparage it. I only resent the time it wastes when there is distress to be addressed." The *shar tahl* sat down in front of Aidan. It seemed somehow incongruous to see a *shar tahl* in leathers; Aidan was accustomed to linen or woolen robes, though neither was required. But this particular man, displaying armbands and earring—his absent *lir* was a fox—was different from the others. Aidan knew it at once.

It is not merely age . . . the fire in him is different. It burns a little brighter— Inwardly, he frowned. *I have only known old shar tahls . . . this one is not old. This one is more like a warrior. Perhaps that is the difference.*

The *shar tahl's* tone was mild. "You come so rarely, or so I have heard, that the reason must be quite important."

Guilt pinched Aidan's belly. He answered more brusquely than intended. "Aye, it is. This." He set down the link on the fur between them, then took his hands away.

The *shar tahl* did not at once look at the object. He looked only at Aidan, who felt years stripped away until he was a boy, staring guiltily but defiantly into the face of authority. Yellow eyes were kind, but also very attentive. "You do not know who I am."

Aidan maintained a blank expression. "The *shar tahl*, of course."

"I mean, which one."

He debated answers. This *shar tahl*, a stranger to Aidan, was as odd as the brown man who called himself the Hunter, who called himself a god. Aidan decided to avoid possible problems by stating the obvious. "The *shar tahl* of Clankeep."

The other smiled. "You take the easy road. That is not your reputation."

Aidan's answering smile was twisted. "My reputation is

founded on many things, and so there are many reputations. Which one do *you* know?"

"The one I heard up north across the Bluetooth, in my home Keep." The *shar tahl* crossed his legs and linked dark fingers. "My name is Burr. I am but newly come to Clankeep—I thought it might be worthwhile for me to live nearer the Lion."

Something pricked at Aidan's awareness. Something sounded a faint alarm. "*How* nearer?" he asked. Then, very quietly, "As near as Teirnan might like?"

Burr's eyes narrowed, if only minutely. And then he smiled. "Teirnan, as you know, has been proscribed by all clan councils. He forgoes the teachings of the *shar tahls*; therefore he forgoes my own. And, undoubtedly, anything else I might say to him."

Certainty firmed Aidan's tone. "But you know him, my proscribed kinsman."

"Everyone knows of him."

Aidan spoke very precisely, so no mistake could be made. "I did not say *of* him. I said you knew *him*."

Quiet reassessment. Burr altered manner and tone, as if casting off prevarication and the habitual obliqueness of *shar tahl*. "I know him. I knew him. I *met* him, once." The tone was uninflected, shielded behind self-assurance.

Oddly, it rankled. "But you did not see fit to send word to the Mujhar."

"Teirnan has more to concern himself with than what the Mujhar might say, or do."

Aidan felt a flicker of irritation. For a fleeting instant it shocked him—this man was a *shar tahl*, due honor and respect—but it passed. What they spoke of—prince and priest-historian—could affect Homana's future, as well as the prophecy.

"What 'more' is there?" Aidan demanded. "You know what he has done."

"And paid the price for it." Burr's eyes did not waver. "Teirnan has lost his *lir*."

"Lost his—" It brought him up short. Aidan spread a hand, made the gesture denoting *tahlmorra*. "Then Teirnan is dead. We need not concern ourselves with him further."

"I did not say he was dead."

"But he *must* be—he lost his *lir*."

Burr's smile was very faint. "The death-ritual is voluntary. It is, to my knowledge, undertaken when a warrior truly believes in such binding clan custom."

Aidan nodded impatiently. "Of course. It is always done—" And then he understood. "You are saying Teirnan rejected *that*, too?" It was impossible to believe. "But that means he is mad. *No* Cheysuli warrior will countenance that. He has to die. The loss of control, the awareness of loss of balance, drives him to it. There is no other choice."

Burr did not answer. Aidan, staring, heard the echo of his own words inside his skull.

Am I mad, too? he wondered with a new insight. *Am I bound for Teirnan's course, to throw myself away? Is that why Shaine—or whatever he was—tells me I will not rule?*

It nearly overwhelmed him. *Lir*-bonded or not, was he meant to give up his life to keep the blood free of taint?

Numbly, he echoed, "There is no other choice."

The *shar tahl* spoke quietly. "He does choose, Aidan. Every warrior *chooses*. He dies if he wants to die. But that is not Teirnan's way."

Teirnan, not Aidan. He pushed away thoughts of himself and focused on his kinsman.

More than bruised ribs ached. Also family pride; the awareness of a betrayal he had never experienced. He had been told all about Teirnan's defection from the clan, his rejection of the prophecy and betrayal of heritage, but Aidan had been conscious of it with a pronounced sense of detachment. He had been too young to know Teirnan, to comprehend the issues.

But he was no longer too young. Now he began to understand why all his kin hated Teirnan.

Speculation took precedence over fear of his own ends. "He wants the Lion," Aidan said flatly. "He has always wanted the Lion."

"Aye, well, men want many things . . ." Burr neatly turned the subject. "What is it *you* want?"

Aidan was no longer certain he cared to continue the discussion with Burr. The man was different. He was unlike any *shar tahl* Aidan had ever known. That he thought differently was obvious. And what he might do with such thoughts—

Abruptly, Aidan laughed. *Is this what they say of me?*

Burr's smile lapsed. The eyes, so like Aidan's own, were fixed and uncannily feral. The voice was very quiet; the tone a whiplash of sound. "If you question my own commitment to my race, let me reassure you. My belief in the gods is unshakable. It has been since I was quite young—I knew as clearly as I knew my *lir* what I was meant to be. It was my *tahlmorra:* I could be nothing else. No man, no woman, no warrior—proscribed or otherwise—could ever turn me from that, any more than Teirnan or anyone else could turn you from the Lion. I am a Cheysuli *shar tahl*, fully cognizant of my service." Intensity dispersed abruptly, as if no longer needed. The calm smile returned. "What service may I do you?"

Something in Aidan answered. His distrust of Burr faded, replaced with an odd recognition. *This man is very like me—* He smiled back slowly, though its twist was decidedly wry. "I have many questions." He pointed at the link. "What do I do with that?"

Burr, for the first time, looked at the link. Aidan knew what it looked like, what it *felt* like; he had carried it by hand all the way to Clankeep, unable to hide it away. It was nothing and everything, all bound into the gold and runes, and he dared not let it go.

For Burr, he had let it go. It waited on the pelt, glinting dully in wan light.

Abruptly, the man was *shar tahl*. Aidan was startled by the sudden transformation. It was, he thought, merely his own perspective, somehow altered; this Burr was no different from the Burr of a moment before, in appearance or manner. And yet Aidan felt the change, the slow comprehension, that flooded the man with an eerie exaltation.

Burr unlaced his hands and reached out, as if to pick up the link. But he refrained. Fingertips trembled a moment. Then quieted into stillness. He did not touch the link. He looked searchingly at Aidan. Then abruptly looked away.

Aidan frowned. "What is it?"

Burr quickly rose to his feet and went directly to the open doorflap. The gesture was blatant: Aidan was to leave. "I cannot help you," he said. "You must find your own way."

Unquestionably dismissal, in tone and posture. Part of Aidan responded instinctively—a Cheysuli warrior was carefully tutored to honor a *shar tahl*—until he recalled his other self. The self meant for the Lion.

"No," he said quietly, still kneeling on the pelt. "I came to you with questions. You promised answers." Slowly he twisted his head and glanced over a shoulder at the *shar tahl*. "Are you the kind of man who can refuse to give them?"

Burr did not hesitate. "You ask too much."

Aidan was deliberate. "As warrior? Or as a prince?"

Burr drew in a breath, then released it audibly. His expression was peculiar. "We spoke of choices, my lord. We spoke of a warrior's *tahlmorra*. No Cheysuli is truly *forced* to accept his *tahlmorra*—he does have free will—but if he is truly commited to his people, to the prophecy, to his belief in the afterworld, he never refuses it. So we are taught: so I believe." The phrasing was deliberate; Aidan understood. "I came to my own arrangement with the gods when I was very young. Now you must come to yours."

"I know my *tahlmorra*," Aidan declared. "I came to you for this."

Burr did not look at the link. "I have no answer for you."

Anger flickered dully. He had come for help, as advised by his grandsire, and this was what he got. More obscurity. His belly was full of it.

"Tell me," he said quietly. "You see something in this. You know what this is. Why will you not tell me?"

"I am not meant to tell you."

Control slipped askew. *"Gods,"* Aidan rasped, "will anyone speak plainly? My *lir* practices obscurity; now so do you. Tell me, *shar tahl*: am I to live, or die?"

"The gods will decide that."

Aidan's laughter was a sharp bark of blurted sound. "The Hunter tells me differently. *He* speaks of choices, even as you do."

Burr's eyes glittered. "I do not know everything."

"Neither do I," Aidan gritted. "I'm knowing nothing at *all*—d'ye think this is pleasant?" He sat rigidly on the pelt. "I came to you for help, because grandsire suggested it. Because I think I am going mad."

There, it was said. The silence was very loud.

Burr swallowed tightly. For a brief moment there was war in his face, a battle that underscored, to Aidan, the great need for him to know. Then the *shar tahl* muttered a brief, sibilant petition and pulled aside the doorflap.

Aidan was filled with emptiness. He was six years old once more, faced with adult betrayal; the inability of anyone—even those who should—to understand the pain that drove him so desperately. "Nothing," he murmured numbly. "You give me nothing at all."

Burr's jaw was clenched. "If I could, I would. But if your *lir* will not, who am I to do it?" He gazed at the link, glowing wanly in the light. "I only know part of it."

Aidan scooped up the link and rose, turning to face the *shar tahl*. Contempt shaded his tone. "What *do* you have for me?"

The yellow eyes were kind. "My lord, my sympathy."

Six

It was dark when Aidan rode into Mujhara, well after sunset. He had come close to staying one more night at Clankeep, but judged three enough; it was time he tested his newfound "knowledge" regarding links, Mujhars, and himself.

He rode in through the massive gates of Homana-Mujhar, only vaguely acknowledging salutes and greetings—he was too weary to offer more—and gave the dun into the keeping of the horseboy who came running. Brief instructions passed on, Aidan then went into the palace by way of the kitchens, studiously avoiding his kinfolk, who would no doubt ask him questions he did not wish to address. He was not yet in the mood. First things first.

Word of his return would not be carried to the Mujhar or his parents once they had retired for the night. Aidan kept himself to the kitchens, cadging meat, ale, and bread from servants startled by his presence, until well after bedtime. Then he sent Teel to his perch in private chambers, and went by himself to the Great Hall.

Bootsteps echoed as he walked the length of the firepit, dividing the hall in half from dais steps nearly to the doors. As always, he took no lamp or candle; this was better done in dimness, with only the summer-banked coals for light.

He silenced his steps, and stopped. In the darkness, Aidan laughed: bitter irony. Speaking with the Hunter had changed nothing for the better. Now the dream was real even when he did not sleep.

He stood, as he had stood so often, before the Lion Throne. In its seat was the chain.

Aidan linked hands behind his waist. "No *lir*," he declared. "Is that what makes the difference? You want me to come alone?"

Nothing answered him.

The challenge faded away. Aidan sighed, smearing one palm against his brow hard enough to stretch flesh. He was twitching from exhaustion, both mental and physical; he had not slept very well in the three nights at Clankeep. "—tired," he said aloud. "Will you never let me rest?"

In dim light, gold gleamed.

Go, he told himself. *Just go, go to bed—turn your back on this idiocy. Think of something else. Dream of something else. Imagine yourself with a woman—*

But the chain transfixed his eyes, washing him free of all thought except the need to touch it. To hold it in his hands.

I think I begin to hate you—

But nothing could make him ignore it.

Wearily Aidan mounted the dais steps. He halted briefly before the Lion, rubbing absently at gritty eyes, then slowly knelt. The motion was awkward and painful; his ribs still ached. He placed both hands upon the curving, carved armrests and gripped the Lion's paws. The throne was dead to him. A thing of wood; no more. He sensed none of its power or the ambience of its age.

Burning eyes locked on the chain coiled against dark velvet. "So," he said unevenly, "I shall put out my hand to touch it, and the gold will crumble to dust."

Aidan put out his hand. Fingertips touched gold. He waited for it to crumble, but the chain remained whole.

"Something," he breathed, "is different."

Nothing answered him. Silence was very loud.

He waited. He knew what had to happen. It happened without fail. It had *always* happened.

He clung one-handed to the Lion. "This time, something is *different.*"

The hissed declaration filled the hall. He heard himself breathing; the uneven rasping of air sucked through a throat nearly closed off by emotions. He could not name them all, only two: a slowly rising despair and a burgeoning exhilaration.

They were, he thought, contradictory emotions, even as

he felt them. How could a man experience exhilaration and despair, both at the same time? From the same cause?

He allowed his fingers to move. Now the palm touched the chain.

Cool, rune-scribed metal. No different from that on his arms. Solid, substantial gold.

"I know you," Aidan challenged. "You entice me, you seduce me, promising fidelity—the moment I pick you up, there will be nothing left but dust."

Nothing answered him.

Sweat prickled flesh. He ached, yet felt no pain, only a brittle intensity. A growing, obsessive hunger.

Aidan dared to close his fingers. The chain remained solid.

He laughed softly into the darkness. "Such a sweet, subtle seduction . . . if I but pick you up—" He suited action to words.

Links rang softly, chiming one against another.

Aidan knelt before the Lion. One hand steadied himself. The other held up the chain. It dangled in the dimness, one perfect link clutched in rigid, trembling fingers.

Jubilation crept closer, hand in hand with apprehension. Aidan stared, waiting. The hair stood up on his arms, tickled the back of his neck. He drew in a tenuous breath, taking care to make no sound. "What now?" he whispered.

In answer, the link parted. Half of the chain fell, spilling across crimson velvet.

Oh, gods—oh, no—not AGAIN—

A blurt of sound escaped him: forlorn, futile protest. Sweat ran down his temples, tracing the line of his jaw. "So," he rasped hoarsely, "you tease me a little *more*—"

Intrusion. He heard the scrape of silver on marble; the step of booted feet. Humiliation bathed him. If his father found him like this, or even the Mujhar—

Aidan set his teeth and turned, still kneeling, still clutching the remaining links against his bare chest. That much he had gotten, he had *won* . . . if he showed his father—if he displayed it to the Mujhar, or to anyone who asked—

Halfway breathed, breath stopped. The man was no one he knew.

And yet, somehow, he did. He knew that face; had *seen* that face. The same tawny hair, now silvered. The same blue eyes, but no patch; both eyes were whole. Even the same remarkable physical presence, though this man, Aidan thought, was a trifle taller than the Mujhar. The breadth of shoulder was startling; that, and his expression.

No, Aidan mouthed. And then, almost laughing: *Aye. First Shaine, now—this. Now HIM—*

Transfixed, he stared at the man. At the slow transformation in the features. First a quiet acceptance of his presence in a place not quite expected. Then the realization of what that place, and his presence, meant. Lastly the quiet joy, the subtle recognition of a man returned to his home after too many years—and deaths—away.

It was not an old face, not as old as the Mujhar's, though the lines were similar. But there was an odd awareness of age, an eerie aura of knowledge far greater than Aidan's own, so well-tutored in heritage. This man was not Cheysuli, but clearly he knew the Great Hall. Clearly he knew the Lion.

Unlike Shaine in his velvets, he wore plain soldiers' garb: ringmail over leather. Ringmail stained with blood; leather scuffed from usage. On his hand glinted the ring Aidan's grandsire wore.

Ringmail in place of velvets.

Aidan stared blankly, recalling Shaine, whose arrogance dominated. This man was as proud, but less of himself than of things that had occurred in a realm once his own.

Aidan's lips were dry. *A different kind of Mujhar—*

The length of the hall, he came. Then stopped before the dais, before the throne, before the prince still kneeling in rigid silence, pale Erinnish flesh stretched nearly to cracking over unmistakable Cheysuli bones.

"So *long*," the man whispered. "I thought never to see it again."

Numbly, Aidan murmured, "This is Homana-Mujhar."

The other man's jubilant smile was brilliant. "I know where I am. I know who you are. Do you know who *I* am?"

Aidan wet dry lips. "I can make a guess."

The stranger laughed aloud, in eerie exultation. "Then let me save you the trouble: my name is Carillon. That throne once belonged to me." He paused delicately. "And are you kneeling to me, or to your own *tahlmorra?*"

Aidan did not move. "Carillon was Homanan. He knew nothing of *Tahlmorras*."

Tawny eyebrows rose. "Nothing? Nothing at all? When it

was *my* doing that the Lion Throne of Homana was given back into Cheysuli hands?" Blue eyes were assessive. "Ah, Aidan, have they neglected your history? Or are you merely being perverse?"

"Homanans have no *tahlmorras*."

"Oh, I think they do. I think they simply lack the imagination to accept them." Carillon's voice was kind, pitched to a tone of quiet compassion. "It hurts to kneel on marble. If I were you, I would not."

Aidan put out a groping hand and caught at the Lion, dragging himself from the dais. He stared at his kinsman. His great-great-grandsire, with no Cheysuli in him.

I am so tired—so confused—

He sighed gustily, trying to summon respect for a man dead so many years even though the pragmatic part of him suggested he might be so tired and sore he was merely dreaming the whole thing. "I suppose you have come with a message, much like Shaine. I suppose you are here to talk about this chain, much like Shaine." He held it up; it dangled. "The rest of it is in the throne . . . I am only worth half of it." He grimaced, shoving away the acknowledgment of pain. "But more than I was before."

Carillon said nothing.

Aidan looked down at his kinsman, taller than Carillon only because of the dais. He lacked the height of his father or the Mujhar; certainly that of the man—or fetch—he faced now. "Shaine mouthed nonsense. Have you come to do the same?"

Now Carillon smiled. "I did not come: I was *brought*. By you, whether or not you know it. There is a certain need . . ." But he did not finish. "As for Shaine, he often mouthed nonsense. My uncle—my *su'fali*, as you might say—was a hard man to know, and a harder man to like. Respect, honor, even admire, aye—"

"Admire!" Aidan's astonishment echoed. "The *ku'reshtin* began the *qu'mahlin*! He nearly extinguished my race!"

Some of the fire dimmed in old/ageless blue eyes. "Aye, he did that. But I was speaking of the man before the madness. The man who was Mujhar, was *Homana*, before the fool who began a purge." Carillon sighed. Wan light glinted on ringmail. "He was a man of great loves and stronger hatreds. I will excuse him for neither; I did not understand him, save to serve him as an heir. And, as you know, even that was never intended; I was not raised to be Mujhar."

"No," Aidan agreed, giving up the last vestige of disbelief. It seemed he was meant to have discourse with all manner of men and gods.

"I was raised to be a soldier, and to inherit my father's title. Never my uncle's—that only became *my* place when Lindir ran away with Hale, and Shaine got no other heirs." Carillon glanced down at a lifted hand: blood-red ruby glowed. "So, I was made heir to Homana . . . and heir to travesty—" Abruptly he broke it off, smiling ruefully. "But you know all of this . . . I will bore you with old stories." Now the smile was twisted. "Finn would say it is my habit, to prate about history."

"Finn," Aidan echoed. "Could he come here? Could I summon him, if what you say is true?" He paused. "Finn—and *Hale?*"

After a momentary stillness, Carillon shook his head. "They were never Mujhars."

"Mujhars," Aidan murmured. He looked at the chain in his hand. Realization was swift. "Mujhars—and links. Is that what this is about? Is that what the dreams are for?" He held out the portion to Carillon. His voice shook, even as his hand. "Is that *it*, my lord? Each of those links—"

"—is a man." Carillon's voice was steady. "A man caught up in the game of the gods. But you should know that, Aidan. You should know very well."

I know nothing at all . . . Aidan strung out the chain, touching individual links. "You. Donal. Niall. Here: my *jehan.*" The chain ended abruptly.

Suspicion blossomed painfully. So did fear.

White-faced, Aidan swallowed. Looked at the Lion. Reached down and picked up the two halves of the broken link. They chimed in his hand. "And Aidan?" he asked softly, looking back at Carillon.

His kinsman's gaze did not waver. "You know what you know. Now you must deal with other things: acknowledgment and acceptance. Knowing is not enough."

Bitterness rose; engulfed. "I have been very well-tutored. Do you truly think I would not acknowledge nor accept? Do you think I *could* not?"

Now Carillon's eyes were bleak. "We have each of us, in

your birthline, done things we did not desire. Become what we did not want. We each of us chose our road, always cognizant of the choice . . . but none of it was easy. The gods gave us free will. Regardless of tutoring, refusal is always an alternative. The gods do not strike us dead, unless our time is done."

The response was automatic: "If we say no to our *tahlmorras*, the afterworld is denied us."

Carillion's tone was steady. "That is a choice, too. Teirnan made it; will you?"

Aidan met the eyes of a dead Mujhar, only dimly surprised he could. Such miracles, now, were expected; they had, each of them, beaten belief into him. "I have to be what I am."

Slowly, Carillon smiled. "Then the gods will be satisfied."

In Aidan's hand, gold melted. At last he opened fingers. The chain flowed out of his hands and into nothingness.

He looked up to ask Carillon why. He found himself alone.

Seven

Aileen slammed down her goblet. Cider splashed over the rim. "Not so soon!" she cried, astonishing them all. "I'll not be letting you do it!"

It stilled the room instantly. Servants with trays of food and pitchers of cider stopped dead in their tracks, staring at their angry princess, then cast furtive glances at one another to see what should or should not be done.

The outburst came in the midst of the midday meal. It had, heretofore, been an entirely normal gathering uneventful in the extreme. The Mujhar and all his family—excepting the absent Aidan—were halfway through the meal.

Now it appeared one of them would not finish. Or possibly *two* of them; it was at Brennan she had shouted.

The Prince of Homana, frozen in the act of lifting his own goblet to his mouth, also stared at Aileen. His astonishment rivaled that of the servants who, upon a subtle signal from

Deirdre, melted out of the room. Food and drink could wait until the storm had blown over.

Brennan, thawing at last, quietly put down his goblet. He did not spill his cider. "I only meant—"

"I *know* what you meant!" Aileen's green eyes blazed. "D'ye think I'll sit here all mealy-mouthed and listen to such drivel?"

Brennan's face tightened. "What 'drivel' do you mean? I was discussing our son's future."

"Discussing his *marriage*, ye *skilfin*!" Aileen flattened her hands on the table and leaned down on braced arms. "I'll not allow it so soon. The boy deserves some time."

"The 'boy,' as you call him, is twenty-three years old." Brennan very carefully did not look in Ian's direction.

"Twenty-three years *young*," Aileen snapped. "The House of Homana is long-lived—he'll be having time for marriage. Let him have time for himself."

Now Brennan did cast a sharp glance around the table. He saw three carefully neutral expressions, which did not particularly please him. He had expected support—except from Ian; clearly, they offered none. *"Jehan,"* he appealed.

Niall lifted both hands in a gesture of abdication. "I married off four of my five children. This is for you to do."

Inwardly Brennan sighed. He looked again at Aileen. "This can be discussed another time—"

"You brought it up," she charged. "Oh, Brennan, d'ye not know what you're doing? Can ye not see what might happen? D'ye want him to be like us?"

Brennan lost his temper. "By all the gods, I love you! I have never kept it a secret!"

The admission was not precisely what any of them had anticipated, least of all Aileen. She had expected a different issue.

White-faced, she glanced at the tactfully averted faces of the Mujhar, his *meijha*, his *rujholli*. Only Brennan looked at her; no, he *glared* at her, with an angry, defiant expression. It belied the words he had shouted.

"Not now," she said weakly, turning toward the door. "Not now; not *here*—"

Brennan rounded the table and met her at the door, jerking it open. "Now," he said grimly. "But I will agree with the 'not here.' Shall we retire to our apartments and discuss this issue in private?"

Color set her afire. What she thought was obvious.

Brennan grasped her arm and steered her out of the room, lowering his tone. "That is not what I meant. I *meant* to discuss it; nothing less, nothing more. You know very well I would never shame you that way in front of kin and servants—that is not my way. . . ."

Aileen was not placated. "You are a fool!" she snapped, gathering heavy skirts as he pushed her up the stairs. "You see only whatever it is you *want* to see, being blind to people's feelings."

"I am not being blind to anyone or anything," he retorted, ascending rapidly to keep up with his angry wife. "What I am is being careful."

"What you *are* is being a *skilfin*, as always. You've lost whatever sense—*and* diplomacy—you might once have had."

"Oh? I have never believed thinking about the future of one's realm—"

" 'Tisn't your realm *yet*—here, will this do?" Aileen shoved open a door and watched it slam against the wall. "Is this sufficiently private?"

Brennan advanced through the doorway. "It was a topic of discussion. It was not a royal decree. I was merely suggesting it might be time we thought of Aidan's future."

"Aidan's future is Aidan's *future*. Let it remain so, Brennan." Aileen swung to face the doorway. "Give the boy—" She stopped. "Oh," she said weakly. "Have you heard everything?"

Brennan turned abruptly. Their son stood in the corridor.

"Enough," Aidan said calmly, folding hands behind his back.

Brennan frowned. "When did you come home?"

"Last night. Late." Aidan's crooked smile was private. "There was something I had to do . . . something to be resolved."

"And was it?" Aileen asked.

The smile became a scowl. "Not entirely," he muttered, then flicked dismissive fingers as he altered tone and topic. "Am I to be married, then?"

Brennan swung back jerkily and walked directly across the chamber. It was a small room, no more; a nook for private withdrawal. Not unlike Deirdre's solar, though lacking amenities. It was little more than a cell, or an awkward, forgotten corner.

A bench was against the wall. Brennan sat down on it. "Your *jehana* and I were discussing it."

Aidan arched one eyebrow. "It was a loud—discussion. The servants were talking about it."

Aileen's face flamed. "Your father is being a fool."

Brennan sounded tired. "At least I know that word. You have never translated *skilfin*."

She had the grace to look abashed. " 'Tisn't a polite term."

"I had gathered that." Brennan looked at his son. Aidan did not, he thought, appear particularly disturbed by the topic. He was, as usual, keeping himself detached from the emotions he and Aileen battled, as if he feared to share them. "Well? Will you come in and give us your opinion? It *is* your future, as the Princess of Homana has taken great—*and* loud—pains to point out."

Aidan smiled lopsidedly. He came through the doorway, lingered idly a moment near his mother, then drifted farther into the chamber. Brennan thought his expression odd. There was distance in his eyes; and an eerie *otherwhereness* that Brennan found unsettling.

"Come back," Brennan snapped impatiently. "You had best attend this."

Aidan glanced sidelong at his father. "I fell off my horse," he said inconsequentially. Then, smiling wryly, "No—I was *swept* off. It does somewhat make a difference."

Aileen made a sound and moved as if to go to him, but a lifted hand kept her back. She contented herself with a question. "Are ye hurt, then? I thought it was dirt; 'tis a *bruise*, then, there on the side of your face."

Aidan briefly touched a cheekbone. "A bruise, aye—so it should be." Then, as if shaking himself, he looked more clearly at his father. "Do you want me married, then?"

There was only the slightest hint of Erinn in the inflection. It made Brennan smile; his son sounded, on occasion, very like his mother. "I want you content, though undoubtedly your *jehana* will not agree that I would consider your feelings."

" 'Tisn't sounding like it," she muttered.

Brennan cleared his throat. "I want you content, Aidan. I want you settled. I want you less disturbed by whatever it is that disturbs you."

Aidan laughed. "And marriage is the answer? With yours as the example?"

Brennan nearly gaped. The question had been so *blatant*—and so keenly on the mark. *As if he reads my thoughts . . .*

Aileen's face flamed red. "D'ye not care?" she demanded. "He'd have you wedded and bedded before nightfall, if he could—and all for the Lion, he says."

"Well, perhaps it is." Aidan went over to the bench occupied by his father and sat down at the other end. He looked tired, worn through, clearly thinking of something else. "I have no objection."

The negligent tone and manner set Aileen's eyes to blazing again. "No objection, have you? To being pushed this way and that? For being made to take a wife?"

Aidan scowled briefly, then wiped it away instantly. His tone, usually circumspect and polite, was pitched to cut through them both, as if he knew just where to aim. "I am not you, *jehana*. I am not and never have been in love with the wrong person. Nor am I my *jehan*, so badly hurt by an Ihlini witch's meddling." He cast a glance at Brennan, mouth twisted, as if to ask his pardon for speaking of private things. "I am not in love at all, so it really makes no difference."

His parents, stunned, stared. Aileen roused first. "It *should!*" she snapped. "The woman you'll be taking will share your bed for the rest of your life. D'ye think *that* makes no difference?"

Aidan sighed wearily, murmuring beneath his breath. Then, more clearly, "After the events of four days ago—when I got this bruise—I think debating the merits of marriage is the least of my concerns." He slumped against the wall and yawned, then straightened as if the position hurt. Indifferently, he asked, "Have you a woman in mind?"

Aileen stared at her son. Dark red hair tumbled into his face, until he flung it out of his eyes like a horse tossing his mane. It was, as usual, badly in need of cutting; he was lazy about such things. Thick lashes screened his eyes, but that did not disturb her. His eyes were like his father's; she could not read *his*, either. Aidan was a trifle paler than usual, and the bluish bruise was temporarily disfiguring, and he acted as if his ribs hurt; all that aside, he seemed perfectly normal, she thought—except for a sharper, more pronounced detachment that was, even when weighed against Aidan's customary feyness, something out of the ordinary.

"What events?" she asked suspiciously.

Aidan shrugged slightly. "Nothing worth the telling." He scratched gingerly at the bruise. "*Have* you a woman in mind—or are you simply wanting to argue?"

It was Brennan's turn to stare, albeit from a more awkward position. He frowned, marking the bruise, the pallor, the unfeigned detachment that spoke, to him, of boredom. Aidan was often detached, but rarely ever bored.

Brennan glanced at Aileen, seeking an explanation. Clearly she was as baffled by Aidan's demeanor. In that they always agreed. "No," he answered finally. "It had only just come up."

"*Brought* up by your father." But Aileen's tone was less than hostile. "D'ye really not care?"

Aidan smiled at her. "You cared because you loved Corin. *Jehan* cared because he knew it, and because he thought you might be worth the loving." He glanced briefly at his father, then back at his mother. "It makes no difference to me. There have been women in my bed, but none I want to keep there. If you have a candidate for eternity, I am willing to listen."

Aileen glanced at Brennan. "Hart has four daughters."

"And Keely, one." Brennan pulled at a lobeless ear, reaching for a long-absent earring. "Maeve has a daughter. Maeve has *two*."

Aileen's tone was odd. "Legitimate, if you please."

Brennan scowled; Maeve was his favorite. "Maeve's daughters *are* legitimate. She and Rory are married."

Aidan's tone was amused. "She wants a princess for me."

Aileen folded her arms. " 'Tis better for a prince."

He grinned, laughing in silence. "Very well, five princesses to pick from. Unless you take bids from other kingdoms, such as Ellas and Caledon."

"No," Brennan said thoughtfully. "There is the prophecy to think of. We now know the four realms mentioned . . . we need add no other blood."

"No," Aidan agreed. "Only the Ihlini."

Brennan looked at him sharply. "No son of mine—"

"Of course not, *jehan*." Aidan's tone was dryly deferential as he stretched out booted feet and planted both heels. "So, am I to choose sight unseen?"

Aileen frowned. " 'Twas what was done for us, your father and I. We saw naught of each other."

"And look at the result." Aidan's smile was so charmingly disarming, neither of them could respond immediately. "You are both of you fools—or *skilfins*," he continued, ignoring their stricken stares. "The Prince of Homana at least has the courage to admit he loves the Princess . . . she might do as well. Old wounds do heal—if you give them the time." He looked straight at his mother. "Twenty-four years is a long time. I'm thinking the two of you might be happier if you started all over again."

"How can you—" Aileen cut it off. Color waned in her face. "Oh, no," she whispered dazedly. "Deirdre said it might be true—she did say it might show itself . . ." Even her lips were white. "How long have you known how I feel? How your father feels?"

Aidan frowned. "I have always known how you feel. How either of you feel. How *everybody* feels."

"Always?" she echoed blankly.

Brennan sat erect. "What are you talking about?"

Aileen's hand was on her throat. *"Kivarna,"* she murmured. "Oh, Aidan, after all this time . . . and none of us knowing—none of us *thinking*—"

"Knowing *what?*" Brennan asked testily. "What are you talking about?"

"Kivarna," she repeated. "Oh, gods, Aidan—is that what it is? All this time—is *that* what this is?"

Her son and husband stared.

Aileen pressed rigid fingers against her face. "All those things we've felt, the both of us, and you knowing them all—" She squeezed shut her eyes. "And you not knowing *why*—"

"Aileen!" Brennan said sharply. "What are you talking about?"

"Aye" Aidan agreed, detachment shredding abruptly. *"Jehana—"*

Aileen's face was white. Hands shook as she clasped them tightly in her lap. She tried to smile at Brennan, but it faltered. *"Kivarna,"* she said only. "Your son is *Erinnish*, too." And with that she went out of the room.

Brennan stared after her. He had not seen her so distraught in years. Not since Aidan was young, and troubled by the dreams.

Frowning, he turned to his son. Aidan put up his hands. "A word, nothing more. But I am Erinnish, aye; I have been all my life." He grinned. " 'Twas her doing, I'm thinking."

"But what is it—?" And then he gave it up. "Agh, gods—" Brennan collapsed once more against the wall. "Perhaps I *should* give you more time—sharing your life with a woman is never an easy thing."

Aidan, like his father, leaned against the wall, but took more care to settle still-sore ribs. "She really does love you.

She always has, in her way. But she has never admitted it to herself; certainly not to you. She thinks of Corin, and feels guilty. She believes you deserve better, and so she blames herself."

Brennan sat in silence. Something pinched deep in his belly. Something that whispered of dread; of a thing left unattended to fester in someone's spirit, shaping a life for too many years.

He swallowed tightly and rolled his head against the wall to look at his son. "This is what she meant? This—*kivarna*?"

Aidan shrugged. "The word is as foreign to me. I have never heard it before."

Brennan, tensing, sat up a little. Very carefully. "But—you can do this? Always? This reading of people's thoughts?"

"Not thoughts. Feelings. And only bits of them. I thought everyone did." Aidan carefully felt his discolored cheekbone. His tone, now, was deliberate: he wanted to change the subject. "Have you ever come off your horse?"

"Many times." Brennan's thoughts were not on enforced dismountings. "Aidan—" He frowned. "You have been able to do this since childhood?"

Aidan lifted a single shoulder. "It began very young. I cannot say precisely when."

Gods, he can be cold— "—young," Brennan echoed. "Such as a night in the Great Hall, with the Lion . . . and a chain."

Aidan turned his head deliberately and looked into his father's eyes. What Brennan saw made him cringe. "I thought everyone felt it. That it required no explanation."

"I should have listened," Brennan rasped. "I should have listened then. Even Ian sees it."

"Jehan—"

"How is a child to trust when his parents give him no chance to say what troubles him most?" Brennan shut his eyes. "Gods, I have been a fool . . . and I have made you this way."

Aidan's tone was tight. "What way, *jehan*? What 'way' *am* I?"

"Different." The answer was prompt. "Private. Withdrawn. Guarded. As if you trust none of us." The pain tore at his vitals. "I did that to you."

"If you are concerned that I know everything you think, everything you *feel*—"

"No." Brennan cut him off. "What you know, you know; how much does not matter. What matters now is that you have this ability . . . and that you dream dreams."

Aidan's smile was wintry. "Everyone dreams."

"*Gods—*" But he let it get no farther. His mind was racing, running back over the years, over the memories, drawing from the deepest part of the well the things that glittered most brightly, like the keen edge of a new blade. "You were ill so often, and for so long . . ." It was not an explanation. It was not a just excuse. It was nothing more than a father's plea for understanding from a child he has turned away through misinterpretation. "You spoke to the Mujhar."

Aidan's tone was closed. "I spoke to my grandsire."

"But not to me, nor your *jehana*." Brennan's jaws clenched. "I suppose we deserved it, your meticulous privacy. But it was so long ago—did you never think to try again?"

Aidan's gaze was unflinching. "I sense *feelings*. At first, I knew you were only frightened, worried for my welfare. But you changed, even as I did. You began to realize a child's fancies were being carried over into adulthood." Aidan's expression was taut. "Your feelings were all too blatant: you questioned my sanity. My worthiness for the Lion." His mouth warped a little. "How many children, even those in a man's body, care to discuss it with a *jehan* who wonders such things?"

Brennan's face was ravaged. "If you had told us of this ability—"

Aidan's tone sharpened. "I did not know what it was."

"If you had said *anything*—"

"You gave me no leave to try." Unsteadily, Aidan straightened. "But now you have, and I have said something of it. Enough. It has a name, now . . . better we leave it at that."

"How? There are things to be settled . . ."

"Such as marriage?" Aidan smiled. "Perhaps it is not such a bad idea."

Again, he changes the subject. And perhaps I should let him. Brennan made a dismissive gesture. His tone was conciliatory. "Perhaps your *jehana* has the right of it. Perhaps I *do* move too soon, pushing you this way and that—" He broke off, sighing, to look at his son. "There are times I think too much about what will become of the Lion, when the throne is not even mine. I look back at our history and see how tenuous is our claim—how vulnerable our race. We are still badly outnumbered . . . if the Homanans ever turned against us again . . ." But he let it trail off. Aidan was not listening. "Aidan . . ." He waited. "Aidan, I want to do right by you. If now is not the time—"

Aidan's response was detached. "It makes no difference."

Brennan held onto his equable tone with effort, knowing instinctively that to press his son now was to lose him. "Marriage is a large step for any man. For a prince—"

"It makes no difference." Aidan insinuated careful fingers into the folds of his jerkin, as if testing for soreness. "Perhaps a change such as this is precisely what I need, after everything else."

Concerned, Brennan frowned. "Aidan—"

His son smiled lopsidedly and raised a preemptive finger. "First you suggest I marry, now you attempt to talk me out of it. Which do you want?"

Brennan stirred restlessly; Aidan was, as usual, cutting too close to the bone. "I want you content."

Aidan's smile faded. He stared blankly at the door, distance in his gaze. "Perhaps that is not my *tahlmorra*. Perhaps, instead—" But he waved it off without finishing. Detachment faded, replaced by dry irony. "A wedding will change many things."

If he wants to let it go . . . Brennan forced a smile. "A wedding usually does."

The tone altered oddly. "And if it changes *everything*—" Yet again Aidan did not finish, but his expression was intense.

Brennan's smile faded. Something cold touched the base of his spine. "Are you all right? Is there something troubling you?"

Aidan did not answer, staring fixedly into the distance.

He is not here, Brennan thought. *In the flesh, perhaps, but not in the mind. He goes somewhere—else.* "Aidan," he said aloud. Then, more urgently, "*Ai*dan!"

His son stirred, clearly startled. And then he sighed, scrubbing at a wan, discolored face. "I am—confused. Forgive me . . . I have not been paying attention."

Brennan leaned forward. "Then tell me. Share it with me. Let me be the *jehan* I should have been years ago."

Aidan weighed his words, then sighed in resignation. His crooked smile was, Brennan thought, oddly vulnerable. "More than confused—*irritated*. There are things in my life I can-not understand, and no answers are forthcoming. No matter *who* I ask—" He sighed heavily, fingering the bruise. "Have you ever spoken with a god?"

It was an odd tack. "*To* them; many times."

"One particular god?"

He strived for lightness; to keep his head above water. "No. I generally address my comments—or petitions—to as many as possible, just to improve my chances." Brennan waited for laughter. When he heard no response at all, he dismissed forced levity. His son was revealing more of him-self than ever before. This time the *jehan* would listen. "Why? Do you speak only to one?"

Aidan sighed. "I had never thought it necessary—like you, I spoke to them all. But now—" Abruptly he broke it off and rose, heading toward the door. "If there are five princesses to be considered, perhaps I should go to see them."

He is gone—I have lost him—

Nonplussed by the abrupt change in subject and his son's implicit dismissal, Brennan rose hastily. "But none of them are here."

Aidan paused in the doorway, arching ruddy brows. "Then perhaps I should go where they *are*."

Eight

The fire had died to coals. The horses, a few long paces away, were hobbled for the night, tearing contentedly at the now-sparse grass surrounding their plots. Food was packed away, bedrolls unfurled, skins of wine unplugged. Sprawled loose-limbed against saddles, two Cheysuli warriors stared up into star-peppered darkness and shared the companion-able silence.

Eventually, Aidan broke it. "Tomorrow," he mused idly, scratching an itching eyelid. "Solinde in place of Homana."

His companion grunted absently, fingers stroking the hud-dle of chestnut fur slumped across most of one leg.

"It will feel good to leave Homana behind awhile. It will give me a chance to start over again," Aidan mused. Then, thinking he had given too much away, he sighed and rolled his head to grin at his great-uncle. "Escort enough, I'm thinking . . . Teel, you, and Tasha."

"Certainly more comfortable; I prefer it this way, myself." Ian's answering smile was wry. "But Aileen nearly won the battle."

Aidan swallowed wine, mopped up a few spilled drops dampening his chin, then shook his head in detached irritation. "Why do women insist on so much ceremony? There is no need to send me into Solinde trailing a hundred men in my wake . . . and as for that chatter about protection, I say it is nonsense. We are at peace with Solinde—we *have* been for tens of years—Teirnan's *a'saii* have disappeared, and even the Ihlini are silent. What is there to protect me *from?*"

Ian's smile faded. The tone was carefully neutral as he stroked the huge cat at his side, chin resting on his thigh. "From yourself, perhaps?"

Aidan's contentment spilled away. The aftertaste in his mouth turned sour. "She wasted no time, did she? Or was it *jehan*, instead?" He shifted irritably against the saddle. "I should have said nothing of it. It is private, personal . . . it should make no difference—"

"That you know what others feel?" Ian tipped his head. "You must admit, *harani*, it is a powerful gift—"

"Is it?" Scowling, Aidan cut him off. "I did not choose to have it. I do not choose to use it. I only know what I know, what I *feel*—"

"—and what others feel." Ian's tone remained affable. "I only remark on it because it may be an explanation—"

"—for why I am so different?" Aidan twisted his mouth. "No man is like another."

"No." Ian drank from his wineskin with less spillage than Aidan; he had had much more practice. "And that very differentness is something all Cheysuli must deal with, when faced with an unblessed Homanan trying to comprehend how we can shapechange. We are *alien* to them, trading flesh and bone for fur . . . but this Erinnish gift you apparently have augments even that. And so I begin to see why we confuse the unblessed; you confuse *me*. You confuse us all."

Aidan's hand stole to his belt. Fingers touched the heavy link looped over leather next to his buckle. He stroked the gold absently. *I confuse myself.*

"But it does not matter." Ian settled more deeply into his blanket pallet, adjusting to Tasha's weight. "You are you, and I am I; we are what the gods decree."

Something thrummed across the *lir*-link: a feather-touch of amusement. Aidan glared hard through the darkness at Teel, perched upon a pack slumped on the other side of the fire. The raven said nothing, but Aidan translated the silence. He had had years of practice.

Gods, indeed— Abruptly, he was restless. He sat upright, slinging aside the stoppered skin, and swung on his knees to face his kinsman. "I *am* different," he said intently. "But no one knows how much. No one knows who I am. No one knows *what* I am . . ."

The light from the coals was dim. But Ian's expression was visible: Aidan's vehement outburst had clearly startled him. "Aidan—"

Everyone says I should speak, to divulge what I think; that it will do me good . . .

He did not necessarily think so, but was willing to try. There was too much pressure inside, too much apprehension. He needed to share it with someone other than a *lir* who couched so much truth in obscurity.

If only they could *listen*—

"I talk to gods, *su'fali*. To gods—and to the dead."

Ian's hand stilled on Tasha's head.

Aidan smiled a little. There was no amusement in it. "Ten nights ago, I met with Carillon. Before that, it was Shaine."

"Shaine," Ian echoed.

"The father of the *qu'mahlin*." Aidan shifted slightly, relaxing the tautness of bunched thighs. "Then, of course, there was the Hunter, the god himself . . ." He let it go unfinished. "But you could argue that it was the fall I took—that it addled my wits, and I merely *dreamed* all of it." Aidan's tone was elaborately dry. "But how would that explain seeing Carillon? I did not dream that. He was as real as you, standing before the Lion. He made the Great Hall his own, even with me in it. Even dead so many years . . . however many it is."

"Sixty-six," Ian murmured. "Have you learned nothing at all?"

Aidan looked at him sharply. Ian still lay stretched out
against his saddle, one side engulfed by Tasha. His expression now was calm, but the mouth smiled a little. The eyes,
so eerie a yellow, gazed serenely into the heavens.

"You *believe* me?"

"I have never known you to lie."

Now he distrusted the truth, certain no one could understand so easily, or in such a calm frame of mind. "But it was
Carillon I saw! Carillon I *spoke* with!"

"And what did he have to say?"

Aidan frowned. He had expected startled reassessment,
the mention of possible madness. Even though Ian had
always given him the latitude to be himself, Aidan had not
believed it could remain so. Not in light of his revelation.

But now something else caught his attention. "You knew
him," Aidan said. "You knew him personally."

"Carillon?" Ian grunted amusement. "In a manner of
speaking. I was four years old when he died."

"He was killed."

"In battle, aye. Actually, *after* a battle; the Atvian king
killed him. Osric himself." Ian drank again. His tone was
meditative. "A long time ago."

Aidan reached out and recaptured the skin he had tossed
aside, dragging it across grassy ground. "What was he like?"

Ian quirked an eyebrow. "I thought you said you met him
yourself ten nights ago."

Aidan waved a hand. "Aye, aye—I did . . . but how am I
to know if he was real or not? *You* met the real man. The
warrior Mujhar who won Homana back from Solinde and
the Ihlini."

"Your great-great-grandsire." Ian smiled, tugging Tasha's
tufted ears in absentminded affection. "I remember little
enough. I was three the last time I saw him . . . to me he
was little more than a huge man dressed in leather and
ringmail, glinting and creaking when he moved. He was
entirely Homanan, in appearance as well as habits . . . to
me, that was what counted. Carillon the Homanan: my
jehana made it so. He was Mujhar, aye—but I was taught to
be aware his blood was different from mine."

"But you were kin to him."

Ian shrugged. "My granddam was his cousin . . . aye, we
were kin, but the link was never explored. There was something else that took precedence—" He shifted against his

saddle, resettling Tasha's weight. "I was the bastard son of Donal's Cheysuli light woman. I was not entirely *approved* of by the Homanans, who knew Donal was pledged to marry Carillon's daughter."

"Aislinn," Aidan murmured.

"Aislinn of Homana." Ian sighed and thrust one arm beneath his head. Gray-white hair, in the darkness, was silvered by the moon. "My *jehana* was half Homanan herself, but she hated it. I remember her petitioning the gods to let her spill out the Homanan in her blood many times—whenever my *jehan* left the Keep for Homana-Mujhar." Ian was silent a moment. "Eventually, she did . . . in the Keep across the Bluetooth, she spilled *all* of her blood. Homanan as well as Cheysuli."

Aidan made no comment. The history was his own, and well-learned in now-distant boyhood, but hearing it from Ian made it come alive. His great-uncle had known those people. Carillon, Finn, Donal—even Alix herself, who had proven to be the catalyst for the resurgence of the Old Blood. Others carried it, aye, but it was Alix who, by bearing a son to Duncan, breathed new life into the prophecy.

Who put new blood into the stable— Grimly, Aidan smiled. *When the old blood grows too weak, the new blood makes it strong.*

But his thoughts did not linger there. From his great-uncle, as with others, the emotions were tangible things. Aidan sensed shame, regret, grief; a tinge of bitterness. He put aside his own.

"*Su'fali,*" he said softly, "has it followed you so long?"

Startled, Ian glanced over. His eyes asked the question.

Aidan answered it. "She killed herself, your *jehana*. She brought dishonor to her name, expunged her rune-sign from the birthlines . . . but that does not destroy the memory of the mother in the mind of her son."

"No." Ian's tone was rough.

With care, Aidan proceeded. "Once a year you carry out *i'toshaa-ni*—"

Ian cut him off. "That is my concern."

Aidan drew breath and tried again. "I think it is wrong for one man—one warrior—to assume responsibility for things he had nothing to do with."

"And you think that is why I carry out *i'toshaa-ni*?" Ian's eyes in the darkness were black, save for the rim of feral yellow. "You do not know everything, regardless of your 'gift.' "

Aidan gestured placation. "No, perhaps not—but I think that is a part of it. As for the rest, there is also the knowledge of what Lillith did to you, and what your child on her became."

Ian plugged the wineskin abruptly, squeaking the stopper home. "These are personal, private things."

"So is what *I* feel. Yet everyone wants to know."

Ian's motion to toss down the wineskin was arrested. Then, in silence, he set it carefully by his saddle. "Aye," he said finally, "everyone wants to know."

Aidan wet dry lips. "And yet when the taboo topic is raised, everyone turns away."

Ian's silence was loud.

"Taboo," Aidan repeated. "Even mere *contemplation* that a Cheysuli warrior might lie with an Ihlini woman."

Ian was, if nothing else, a man of much compassion. Yet now the emotions Aidan sensed were anger and bitterness. "We have little reason to consider such a bedding a benevolent thing," Ian declared. "Look at Lillith—daughter to Tynstar himself, half-sister to Strahan . . . servant of the Seker." He sighed, rubbing at tired eyes; age, all of a sudden, sat heavily on him. "Lovely, lethal Lillith—who, holding my *lir*, ensorcelled me so well I had little choice in the matter . . . and then bore me abomination."

"Who then bore *my* father a daughter." Aidan stroked back hair. "You see, *su'fali*, it has been done before. And children have been born."

"But children who are not Firstborn." Ian's voice was emphatic. "Now, more than ever, we must be vigilant. The Ihlini have proved we can be tricked, even into bed . . . they have proved they have the power to alter the prophecy. It is only our good fortune the bloodlines were not whole . . ." Abruptly, his tone altered. "Aidan, if ever a child of the Lion sires a child for the Seker, everything is undone. *Everything* is undone."

Tension was palpable. Aidan sought to break it. "Do not fret about me, *su'fali*. I may be bound for my wedding, but she will not be an Ihlini."

Ian's face was taut. "There is danger in complacency."

"Aye," Aidan agreed. "But even if I should fail, the gods will tend to the outcome."

"Do not—" But Ian broke it off.

Aidan nearly laughed. "You were intending to suggest I not trust so much to the gods? But that is heresy, *su'fali*. And you a devout believer."

Ian fought to retain his composure. "This is not a topic for jest and mummery. We have dedicated our lives to the prophecy, devoted all honor and commitment to the gods—"

"—with whom I speak." Aidan shrugged correction. "Or, at least, with one."

"*Aidan—*"

"Fate," Aidan declared. "The Homanan word for *tahlmorra*. If it is meant to be, surely it will be. And nothing I do can change it."

Desperation underscored Ian's tone. "But it *can* be changed. By me, by you, by—"

"—Ihlini?" Aidan nodded. "Certainly they may try. And perhaps they can *win*—the gods gave us all free choice."

Staring in dismay, Ian slowly shook his head. "Does it make no difference to you? Does any of it matter?"

Aidan sighed. Weariness swept up out of the darkness and threatened to swallow him whole. "*Su'fali*, I do not mean to be contentious or perverse. But I have these thoughts, these *feelings*—" He shook his head, dismissing it. "I promise—all of it matters to me. But as for making a difference . . ." He collapsed against his saddle, too tired to stay upright. Through a yawn, he said, "—we shall have to wait and see."

The day dawned bright and warm, with no hint of rain in the air. They rode in companionable silence, taking comfort in mere presence, and lost themselves in the season. It was very nearly midday when Ian pulled his gray to a halt atop a hillock. "There," he said. "Solinde."

Aidan, reining in his dun, squinted across the distance. "How can you tell?" he asked. "It looks the same as Homana."

"There speaks ignorance." Ian grinned. "Is this land the same as the land around Mujhara?"

"No, of course not—"

"Is this land the same as that we left yesterday?"

"No, no—of course not—"

"And while there *are* similarities between this patch of ground and that, there are also differences." Ian resettled reins, unthreading tangled gray horsehair from red-dyed braided leather. "Just as there are in people."

Aidan forbore to answer. His great-uncle was being obscure.

No more than you, reminded Teel. The raven was a black blot against blue sky, swinging back from the border to return to his *lir*.

Aidan scowled into air. "How much longer to Lestra?"

Ian shrugged. "A six-day or so . . . I am not certain. The only time I went there was in *lir*-shape. It changes the measure of distance."

Aidan nodded vaguely. He sat quietly a long moment, soaking up the sun, then relaxed into the saddle. The depth of his relief was unexpected as well as welcome. Then he sat rigidly upright, thrusting arms into the air to cloak himself in the day. "Gods—I can *breathe* again!"

Ian's question was quiet. "Has it been so very bad?"

Aidan shrugged, lowering his arms. He was unwilling to discuss it. Not now. Not *here;* he did not want to destroy the new freedom he was feeling. "Not all of the time. But now it does not matter. I am no longer in Homana, hounded by gods and fetches, but in a new realm. And beginning a new life—complete with a *cheysula*." He grinned at his kinsman. "Four daughters," he laughed. "Hart must be hungry for sons."

"Hart is hungry for nothing except the means to wager." Ian's tone was dryly affectionate.

Aidan laughed. "*Jehan* said I will like him."

Ian nodded agreement. "Everyone likes Hart . . . until he wins their coin."

Lir. It was Teel. *Lir, there comes a storm.*

"Storm?" Aidan spoke aloud. "The sky is blue as can be—"

Look behind you, lir. There the sky is black.

Aidan, sighing, twisted in his saddle to glance back the way they had come. "Teel says there is a storm . . ." He stopped speaking to gape inelegantly. "Where did *that* come from?"

"Tasha, too—" Ian also broke off. Then, with exceeding mildness, "I think we had better run."

Behind them the world was dark. Aidan glanced back toward Solinde—summer-clad Solinde—then back again to Homana, wearing wind-torn robes of black and gray, edged with a hem of lightning. "How do we outrun *that?*"

"By trying," Ian suggested, setting heels to his horse.

Aidan wasted a moment staring at the storm sweeping inexorably toward them both, rolling out of Homana like a wave of brackish ocean. It was impossible to believe; where they were it was warm, bright, still.

Then stillness began to move. Brightness began to fade.

By trying, Aidan agreed, then followed Ian's lead, sending his dun after the gray. Above him the rising wind buffeted Teel, who cried his displeasure.

"There is no cover!" Aidan shouted ahead to his kinsman. "The border is too barren . . . there is no place we can go!"

"Just run!" came Ian's reply, tossed back over a shoulder.

Aidan hunched down over the dun's neck, recalling the last storm-flight he and the gelding had shared. Then it had proved disastrous; he feared now might be the same. There were no trees with which to collide, but the scrubby grass of the borderlands could hide all manner of holes. A horse, falling in flight, could easily break his neck.

Or the head of the man who rides it—

He chanced a glance over a shoulder, squinting back stinging hair. The sky was indigo-black. He could not see the horizon. "Teel!" he shouted. *Lir—*

Here, the raven answered. *This wind disturbs my feathers.*

Aidan peered upward, reassured to see the raven. Teel was battling wind and winning, though his pattern was erratic.

We need trees, Aidan sent. *Trees—or better, a croft—*

Too late— Teel cried.

The curtain of darkness caught up, then settled its folds about them. It turned the day to night.

The dun was laboring. Fear dotted a line of sweat across summer-slick shoulders, brown in place of dun. Cold, clammy wind bathed exposed flesh. *"Su'fali—"* Aidan shouted. "We cannot run them forever!"

The first bolt of lightning broke free from the sky and struck the ground in front of them, blasting apart the earth in a rain of dirt and grass. The brilliance blinded Aidan. The explosion of thunder was deafening, buffeting his skull.

The dun gelding screamed, then tried to bolt. That he did not was only because Aidan used all the strength and skill he had to hold the horse in place; a blind man tipped off a frightened horse was surely bound for death. He fought even as the horse fought, spitting dirt from a gritty mouth, and blinked burning eyes repeatedly, trying to banish blackness.

—not blind—I am not—

"Teel!" he shouted. *"Su'fali—"* In thunder-bruised ears it was merely noise.

No rain, only wind. The darkness was absolute. It muffled the world around him like swaddling cloths on a corpse.

Teel— Through the link.

Lightning plunged into earth before him. The air stank and sizzled, raising the hair on his arms. Silhouetted against the brilliance was the shape of a man on horseback.

"*Ian—*" Aidan screamed. "Oh, gods—no—not *him* . . ."

The gelding thrashed and reared, as blinded and deafened as Aidan.

"Wait—*wait,* you thrice-cursed nag from the netherworld—"

But the dun chose not to wait. He shed Aidan easily and galloped off into keening darkness.

Aidan landed hard, one arm crooked awkwardly, but scrambled up without thinking about his own discomfort. Somewhere before him was his great-uncle and the gray horse who had fallen.

Teel, he sent frenziedly. *Lir—where is he . . . ask Tasha—*

Through the link came the familiar tone, naked of customary bite. *Six paces ahead, no more.*

Six paces . . . Aidan counted. And nearly tripped over Tasha, huddled by Ian's side.

"*Su'fali—? Su'fali—*"

Ian offered no answer.

"Oh, gods, not like this . . . please, do not be dead—"

Eyelids twitched. "No," Ian blurted. "No—not like this . . . agh, gods, *harani* . . ." The voice was tight with pain. "How—is the horse?"

Aidan looked, scraping hair out of his face. The wind was merciless. "Where—oh." The gray stood exhausted on three legs; a shattered foreleg dangled. Aidan looked back to his kinsman. "Broken leg," he answered tersely. "*Su'fali*—what of you?"

Ian's smile was faint, then spilled away. "Broken, too . . ." he gasped. "But I think hip in place of leg . . ." One hand hovered over a hip. "The horse fell, and rolled . . . gods, I will shame myself—"

"Because it hurts?" Aidan loosened Ian's belt gently. "You can *cry,* if you like—do you think I will complain?"

Ian's face was gray. His bottom lip bled from where teeth had broken through. "First, tend the horse. He has been a good mount."

Aidan did not answer, squinting against the wind and grit and hair as he peeled the waistband from Ian's abdomen.

The weak voice gained authority. "*Harani,* I will wait. The horse deserves a good death."

"And you, none at all." But Aidan knew his kinsman; he went to tend the horse.

It was not an easy task. He cared for horses as his father cared: with every bit of brain and body. But a broken leg was a death sentence, requiring immediate action. Aidan, with his Erinnish gift, sensed bewilderment and pain as the gray attempted to walk.

In Erinnish, he tried to soothe; the language was made for horses. He eased saddle and packs from the mount, then stroked the sweating neck. "*Shansu,*" he whispered gently, sliding long-bladed knife from sheath. "The gods will look after their own."

He went back to his kinsman wet with blood, then knelt at Ian's side. Tasha growled a warning. "*Shansu,*" Aidan repeated, one hand brushing her shoulders. Tasha growled again, ears flattening.

Ian's eyes were closed. In lightning, his years showed clearly, sharp bones protruding beneath aging flesh changed from bronze to linen white. Blood smeared his chin. Thunder boomed distantly.

"How can I move you?" Aidan pleaded, mostly of himself. "The pain alone could kill you. And if not that, what is to say the movement itself will not?" Wind whipped gray-white hair across Ian's face. Aidan peeled it back. "*Su'fali,* what do I do?"

Ian's eyes opened. From pain, they were nearly black. "Bones grow brittle with age," he remarked. "Take ten years away, and I would only have bruised."

Aidan tried to smile, because Ian wanted him to. "*Su'faili,* what can I do?"

"Be true to yourself," Ian murmured. "Be true to the blood in your veins."

"Earth magic," Aidan said numbly. "But—I have never required it. I have never even *attempted*—" Futility was painful. "I'm not knowing how to do it!"

"Ask," Ian said raggedly. "You are Cheysuli—*ask*—"

Aidan flung back his head, searching black sky for a smaller blackness. *Lir*— he appealed. *Teel*—

Would I tell you any different? Use what you have been given!

Beside her *lir*, Tasha wailed.

"—time—" Aidan muttered. "Gods—give me the *time*—"

You waste it! Teel told him. *What are you waiting for?*

Aidan did not know. Courage, he thought dimly; assurances of success.

Tasha's wail increased.

The raven's voice intruded. *Old men die of this!*

Old men, Aidan echoed. And looked again at his kinsman, who once had known Carillon.

Tasha's tail beat the ground. Angry eyes glowed dimly. The storm raged unabated, buffeting them with wind. It keened across the land, spitting dirt and grass and dampness.

"Now—" Aidan murmured, digging fingers into soil. "Let us see who is Cheysuli—let us *see* what gods can do—"

The lightning came down a third time and blasted him apart.

Nine

He stood before a door. The door swung silently open.

"Come in," the woman invited, and put her hand on his arm.

She drew him into the croft, where no croft had existed before. It was small, thatched, lime-washed white, smelling of warmth and wool. He saw three cats: the black on the hearth, the brown on a stool, the white-booted silver tabby curled in the tangle of colorless yarns piled in haphazard fashion on the floor. In the center of the room stood a loom.

She shut the door behind him. And, when he tried to speak, closed his mouth with her hand. "No," she said quietly. "Ian will be well. There is no need to fear." She gestured toward a chair.

He did not intend to sit, but found himself obeying. And staring at her in wonder.

She was unremarkable. A small, fragile woman with callused hands, graying hair snugged back in a knot pinned against her head. She wore a woolen skirt of many patches, as if she added a swatch of weaving each time the skirt wore thin. Over it was a tunic the color of winter grass: dull and lacking luster. A single colorless stone shone on her buckle: lone, unwinking eye. Her own eyes were blue, faded with time, and the flesh of her face was worn.

Aidan stirred sluggishly, coming out of disorientation. Urgency made him curt. "Lady, I have no time—"

"You have as much time as I give you."

Her serene certainty filled him with trepidation. Aidan tried again, exerting more authority. "There is the storm, and my kinsman—"

Her composure remained unruffled. "Ian will be well. The storm is of my sending."

"*Your* sending—" He stopped, banished shock, summoned anger on Ian's behalf. "Lady, he is *harmed*—"

"He can be healed." Quietly she lifted the cat from her stool and sat down before the loom. The cat found a home in her lap, collapsing once more into sleep. She reached out and took up the shuttle.

Aidan, staring at her, knew it was the only answer he would get until she chose to give another. Nothing he said would shake her. She was not the kind touched by emotions; her concerns lay in other directions.

Impatience will not serve . . . With effort, Aidan banished it. He turned instead to the quiet courtesy Homana-Mujhar had taught him. "What do I call you, Lady? The first one was the Hunter."

"You may call me the Weaver." Her smile was luminous. "Come to my work, Aidan. Come and look upon the colors."

He did as he was bidden, dragging himself from the chair. A part of him denied what was happening, recalling the blast of lightning; a part of him counseled patience. He had met Shaine, Carillon, a god; now he met a goddess.

"Teel," he murmured dully. The link was empty of *lir*.

"Teel is very patient . . . come look upon the colors."

Aidan moved to stand before the loom. He was aware only dimly of the warmth of the croft, the purring of the cats, the scent of fresh-spun wool. She was gray, gray and dun, weaving gray and dun homespun—and then he looked at the loom. He looked upon her colors.

He could not name them all. He had never seen such brilliance.

The Weaver worked the shuttle. Back and forth, to and fro, feeding dullness into the pattern. Aidan thought it sacrilege—until he saw the truth.

The colors came from her. As 'she carried the shuttle through, each strand took on a hue.

"There is a thing you must do," she said quietly. "A task to be undertaken, but one you will deny. It is a task of great importance, of great *necessity,* but we cannot be certain you will do it. We gave humankind the gift of self-rule, and even gods cannot sway those who choose not to hear." In renewed silence, she worked the shuttle. "We make things easy; we make things hard. Humankind makes the choices." She stilled the shuttle, and held it. "Look into the colors. Tell me what you see."

He swallowed to wet his throat. "A man," he said huskily, "and a chain. The chain binds him, binds his soul . . . but it is not made of iron—" Aidan shut his eyes. When he looked again, afraid, the colors were brighter yet. "Gold," he said hoarsely. "Gold of the gods, and blessed . . . but there is a weakness in it. One of the links will break."

The Weaver's smile was sweet. "There is sometimes strength in weakness."

He fought down the urge to run. "Am I to fail, then? Am I the weak link?"

"Not all men succeed in what they desire most. As for you, I cannot say; your road still lies before you."

"And my—task?"

"The time has not come for you to make your decision."

"But—this—?"

"This is only a prelude to it."

Aidan shivered. "Why did you send the storm? Why did you send him pain?"

The Weaver looked at him. Her eyes were no longer kind. "If a man will not listen, we must make ourselves be heard."

"It was not necessary to harm *him*—"

Her voice was a whiplash of sound. "You are meant to go alone."

"By the gods—" he began, then stopped. Incongruously,

he laughed. "Aye, well, so it is . . ." Aidan rubbed a stiff face. "You will forgive me, I hope, if I consider your actions unnecessary. He is a devout, committed Cheysuli—"

"One who will be rewarded." The Weaver's tone was gentle. "This is your journey, Aidan. Your task. You are meant to go alone."

"You might have *asked*—"

"Gods often ask. Too often, we are ignored." She gestured again to the loom. "Tell me what you see."

Wearily, Aidan looked. The colors, oddly, had faded, except for the chain of wool. Its hue was still brilliant gold, the gold of purest refining, glinting in firelight.

As he always did, Aidan put out his hand. He knew he would touch wool; when he touched metal, he promptly dropped it.

The link fell. It rang dully against beaten earth, then lost part of itself in wool. Dull, colorless wool.

Slowly Aidan bent down and peeled back the strands. The link was real, and whole.

He rose, clutching the link. Then fumbled at his belt, undoing leather and buckle, threaded the belt through. He slid the new link to the old. They clinked in harmony, riding his right hip. Aidan rebuckled his belt.

He looked at the tapestry. The colors, for him, were faded. "What *tahlmorra* do you weave me?"

The Weaver smiled: small, gray-haired woman with magic in her eyes. "You will weave your own, Aidan. That I promise you."

He opened his mouth, closed it. Then opened it again. "Am I worthy of this?"

"Perhaps. Perhaps not."

Aidan closed one hand around the links. Edges bit into his palm. It was all he could do to keep the frustration from his tone. "Is this how I am to spend my life?" Control frayed raggedly: now the frustration was plain. "Jerked out of the day or night to trade obscurity with gods—*and* goddesses—who play a private game? Am I to do your bidding like a tame little Cheysuli, never questioning this unknown task?" Anger replaced frustration. He shouted aloud in the croft. "Do you know what it is like having everyone think you are mad?"

Silence as the shout died. For a moment, he was ashamed. Then knew it had been required. Too much more locked away would make him lose the balance, and what would he be then?

The gods made us this way. They gave us the gift of the shapechange as much as the curse of knowing the loss of balance is loss of self.

"Do you know?" he repeated, because he needed an answer.

Tears glistened in the Weaver's eyes. "Do you know what it is like having to ignore petitions and prayers? To let a child die even though others beg for its life?"

Aidan was dumbfounded. "Why *do* you ignore such things?"

"Because sometimes the greatest strength comes out of the greatest pain."

"But a *child*—"

"There is reason for everything."

Aidan's tone slashed through her words. "What reason in the death of a child? What reason in the destruction of a race?"

The Weaver set down her shuttle, the cat, and slowly rose to face him. Aidan was much taller; it did not diminish her. "The world is complex," she told him. "The bits and pieces of it are very hard to see, even if you have eyes. The eyes of humans are blind."

It was not enough for Aidan, full to choking on obscurity. "I think—"

She did not allow him to finish, silencing him with calm. "Some see more than most. *You* see more than most; it is why we gave you the task. But if you saw it all, if you saw *every piece,* surely you would be mad."

He felt helplessness gathering. "Then a *tahlmorra* has no bearing on how we live our lives."

"There is a fate in everything. People choose not to see it. They see only the immediacy; they demand gratification even in their grief." The Weaver drew a breath. "If no one ever died, the Wheel of Life would stop. It would catch on the hordes of people, and eventually it would fail."

Aidan's tone was bitter. "Blood greases it."

"The Wheel of Life must turn."

"If it stopped, would *you* die? Would the gods disappear?"

The Weaver's eyes were bleak. "We disappear every day."

Helplessness crashed down. Aidan stretched out his hands, angered by impotence. "What am I to do? How am I to serve? You tell me you kill children, yet you expect me to do this task, which you then refuse to divulge. Is this how the Wheel turns? Is this how our worth is judged?''

Her expression altered. The eyes now were masked. "Is it cruel to keep the child from jumping off the wall because she believes she can fly?"

Irreverence bubbled forth. "If the child is Cheysuli, perhaps she *can* fly . . ." But the irony spilled away. "You make it black and white."

"Choices often are."

"But what of the *gray* choices? What of the subtleties?"

Her voice was implacable. "To a man who does not care, there are no subtleties. But there is no compassion, either. There is no empathy."

He let his hands fall slack. "I cannot deal with this."

"Every man deals with this. The result is not always pretty; the result is often bloody. But every man deals with this. Every man makes his choice."

It was too much, too *much;* he was incapable of comprehension. He smelled wool, cats, himself; he tasted futility.

Aidan scrubbed his face, warping syllables. "I have to go—there is Ian . . . I have to go from here—"

The door swung open in silence. "Then go," the Weaver said.

Aidan lay sprawled on the ground, stunned by the force of the lightning. His head rang with noise, filled up with tight-packed wool. Vision was nonexistent. Flesh writhed on his bones; all the hairs on his body rose.

He blurted something and thrust himself up, clawing into the daylight. Blood and dirt was spat out; he sucked in lungfuls of air. Links chimed at his belt.

Links—? Aidan caught them. And then he looked at Ian.

The aging face was wasted. "I saw it," Ian gasped. "I saw the lightning *strike*—"

"No. No—*su'fali*—"

"I *saw it*—" Ian repeated. "You lit up like a pyre, and when it died you were gone. When it died, you were *gone*—"

Aidan began to tremble. Shock and fatigue were overwhelming. "You would not—you would not believe—" Dazedly, he laughed. "You would never believe what happened—"

"Aidan, you were *struck*—"

"You would never believe what I saw—"

Ian's hand clutched Tasha's neck. "You would never believe what *I* saw!"

Aidan tried to stifle the laughter. He knew very well he walked much too close to the edge. "What I saw—what *I* saw—" He smothered his face with both hands, stretching the skin out of shape. "Oh, gods—" More laughter. "Oh, *su'fali*, if only I could tell you—" Abruptly he cut it off. "She said you would be well. She *promised* you would be well."

"Who—?" Ian's eyes widened. His silence was absolute.

Aidan, on hands and knees, moved to crouch by his kinsman. He ignored the cat's snarl. "Then *I* am meant to do it—she left this task for me . . ."

Ian still said nothing.

"She said you would be well, so I will have to do it." Grimly, Aidan smiled. "But I'm *still* not knowing how."

"Oh, gods," Ian murmured. "No wonder they whisper about you— "

"You will have to go back, *su'fali*. I am to go alone."

Ian shut his eyes. The *lir* by his side growled.

Teel? Aidan appealed.

The raven's tone was amused. *All one must do is ask.*

Aidan asked, and was given.

PART II

One

The city of Lestra, unlike Mujhara, was situated on a series of hills. None rose much higher than its brother or sister, but there were distinct prominences scattered throughout the city, each capped with clusters of buildings like curds of souring milk.

It gave Lestra a scalloped look, Aidan decided, as he wound his way through the warren of cobbled streets, each turn more confusing than the last. He asked directions to the palace several times, each time receiving an answer distinctly different from the last, and despaired of ever finding his way to his *su'fali's* home.

Teel's contempt was dry. *Shall I find you the way?*

It was, of course, the simplest method of all, except Aidan preferred, at this point, to find the palace himself. He disliked giving Teel any more reason to feel superior than was absolutely necessary, as the raven took especial care to point out Aidan's human shortcomings all too often as it was.

Except they seemed to be lost—or *he* seemed to be lost—and he saw no help for it.

Aidan sighed and shifted in the saddle. *All right. I give in. Go find us the palace.*

Teel, perched on the saddlebow, did not leave at once. *You might find it yourself, if you gave up this useless horse. Why you persist in riding when you have the means to fly . . .* In the link, Teel sighed.

I persist in riding because, as I explained to the Hunter, there is a marvelous freedom in such things. I persist in riding this *particular horse because, if you will recall, Ian refused to accept him in place of his own.*

Teel ruffled one wing. *Because he went home in lir-shape, instead. Like any sensible Cheysuli.*

Aidan smiled grimly. *I am what you have made me.*

The raven demurred. *I made nothing. I bonded, no more,*

93

*in order to give you the aid all warriors require—though you
do, I will admit, require more than most.* Teel's eye was
bright. *Moreover, you are much too stubborn to accept anyone's guidance, god's or otherwise. You have made yourself.*

Aloud, Aidan suggested: "Then render me aid, *lir:* go
find the palace."

The raven did, taking much less time than Aidan had
hoped, and reported explicit directions that led Aidan—and
his horse—directly to the front gate. Aidan tried to give his
name and title to the guards, but they merely waved him
through. He then tried to find the duty captain—who would,
of course, carry word into the palace, then return with the
proper summons—but was yet again waved along. Bemused,
he rode through the outer bailey into the inner one without
being challenged at all. And when, in growing frustration,
he tried to pay a horseboy to carry word into the palace, the
boy merely grinned and bowed his head, then took his horse
away after nodding at the front door.

Teel, on the nearest wall, suggested Aidan go in. *They
seem a welcoming sort, these Solindish.*

After an aimless hesitation, Aidan approached the massive front door. *My su'fali is not Solindish, as you well
know.* He climbed the first flight of steps. *Could you at least
send word through the link to Rael? I think it would be best if
someone knew we were coming.*

Why?

Common courtesy. Aidan climbed the second flight. *As
well as a proper defense . . . if I were an enemy, I need only
walk through the door.*

You are not, and there is the door.

Aidan paused, glancing back. *Are you not coming in?*

Later. For now, I prefer the sun.

So Aidan left Teel upon the wall, in the warmth of a
summer day, and entered, unannounced, his *su'fali's* un-
guarded front door.

It was not, Aidan soon discovered, guarded any better
inside than out. He stopped inside the front door, lingered
politely a moment as he waited for servants to come running; when no one at all came, even walking, Aidan at last
gave up. He headed down the first hall he could find.

No one appeared to ask him who he was or what he
wanted. Disgruntled, he began opening heavy carved doors.
All the rooms were empty. *If I were bent on assassination,*

surely I would succeed. He boomed shut yet another door and turned again into the hall. *Then again, perhaps not—I cannot find anyone to kill!*

Sound interrupted disgust. Aidan stopped walking at once, listening expectantly, hoping for someone at last who might be able to guide him to living bodies, or at least tell him the way.

Echoes threaded corridors. Over Aidan's head arched wooden spans in scalloped, elaborate beamwork, drooping from ancient stone. The immensity of the palace dwarfed and warped the sound, distorting clarity.

I could die in here, Aidan thought in wry disgust. *I could starve to death on this very spot, and all anyone would find would be my dessicated corpse—*

A voice. A young, childish voice, raised to a note of possessive authority. He could not make out the words, but recognized the tone. Someone was put out.

And then the words came clear. "It was *me* he made eyes at, Cluna! Not you! He did not even *look* at you!"

"You!" scoffed a second voice, very like the first. "Why would he look at you when *I* am there? You only *wish* he would look at you!"

Aidan, smiling, folded arms across his chest, found the nearest pillar to lean against, and waited.

"It is *me* he likes, not you! He gives me sweets whenever he can."

"Sweets are no way to judge a man. *Words* are how you judge—"

"But *you* never give him a chance to speak, Cluna! How would you know what he says?"

"Oh, Jennet, just because he was polite to you does not mean he really cares. He was only being kind—"

"Kind to *you*," Jennet rejoined. "While, as for me—"

But they came around the corner and into Aidan's hall. Seeing him, they stopped.

"Oh," said one.

"Ummm," said the other.

Aidan merely smiled.

They scutinized him closely, marking clothing and ornamentation, especially the *lir*-gold on his arms. Clearly he was more than a servant, while something less than what he was, if using Homanan rank. They had learned, even as he had, how to judge others by subtleties, trained not to jump to conclusions when the conclusion might offend.

Which told him who they were, even though he already knew.

"Cluna and Jennet," he said. "Which of you is which?"

Two sets of blue eyes glinted. "Whichever we choose to be."

"Ah." Aidan nodded. "A riddle, then, is it? I am to guess?"

Two heads nodded. Expectantly, they waited.

They were identical. Both fair-haired, blue-eyed, a little plump, with a sturdy femininity. One wore violet-dyed skirts and tunic, pale hair tied back in a matching ribbon with gem-weighted ends now straggling down her back much as loosened hair did; the other similar garments—and tattered ribbon—in pale blue, but the colors told him nothing. He did not know the girls and therefore could not judge the small things, such as a lift of the chin, a tilt of the head, the level set of small shoulders, but there was no need to judge. For the first time in his life, Aidan used his Erinnish *kivarna* to answer specific needs.

"You," he said to the one in violet, "are Jennet. And you, of course, are Cluna."

Identical mouths dropped open. It was Cluna, in blue, who spoke. "*No one* has gotten us right. Not on first meeting!"

Jennet assessed him closely. "How did you do it?"

"Easily," he answered. "To the stranger, you look very much the same. But two people are never truly one. You think differently, feel differently . . . you want different things."

They stared. First at him, then at one another. Then once more at him. Cluna shook her head. "No one else thinks so."

Aidan shrugged. "Because no one else is truly twin-born, not as you are. Even your *jehan* is different—twin-born, aye, but he and my *jehan* are quite dissimiliar in appearance and temperament. No one *expects* them to be the same. But they do expect it of you, and so neither of you is given the leave to be individual."

"He *knows!*" Cluna gasped.

Jennet reassessed him. "Your *lir* is telling you that."

Aidan laughed. "No, my *lir* is at this moment perched outside in the sun."

Blue eyes narrowed as she absently tugged her tangled ribbon. "Then how *can* you know?"

He forbore to explain the gift. "I understand feelings," he said, thinking it enough. "Now, as for you—"

"Are you *Aidan?*" Cluna asked.

Jennet cut off his answer. "He *cannot* be Aidan," she declared, flipping violet ribbon behind a shoulder. "Aidan is very sickly. Everyone says. He is not expected to live."

It was a sobering summation. Aidan eyed both girls a moment, then sighed faintly. "There was a time I was sickly," he agreed. "There was even a time they feared I might die. But not anymore."

Jennet lifted pale, inquisitive brows. "Well, then," she began, "who are you going to marry?"

Cluna was horrified. "Jennet, you cannot ask him that!"

"Why not? It is a fair question, I think." Jennet twined a lock of fallen hair around one finger. "We are thirteen now, and there has been talk of betrothing us into this kingdom or that. Even Homana has been mentioned."

"Oh, has it?" Aidan's tone was bland. "I'm thinking I might yet have something to say on that order."

Jennet was speculative. "I doubt they will let you. It makes them feel important to decide how we should live."

"*Jen*net!" Cluna wailed.

Her sister did not respond. "*Have* you come for a wife?"

Aidan smiled. "Perhaps."

Cluna's face was burning. "He will never have *you*," she asserted. "A queen must know her place—"

"I *do* know my place!" Jennet snapped. "As any fool can see, we are of marriageable age and excellent family."

A new voice intruded. "But *not* of excellent manners." A young woman advanced on them quickly, yellow skirts gathered in both hands. "I could hear you screeching all the way to my chambers. That is *not* how our lady mother desires you to behave . . . you are princesses, not street urchins— though you look more like the latter with your hair all pulled awry." She glanced briefly at Aidan, then back to the girls. "Jennet, have you no sense at all? You tax a stranger with inappropriate talk . . ." She cast a polite smile at Aidan, smoothing yellow skirts and the amber-studded girdle binding a narrow waist. "You will forgive them, I hope, if they spoke too plainly. Jennet has cost herself more than one friend by such bold talk."

"Not Tevis," Jennet declared. "He *likes* such talk."

Cluna disagreed. "Tevis is merely polite. He has no wish to offend our father."

"Enough," the woman chided. "Have you no sense of decorum? This man is a stranger!"

"Cousin," Janet supplied.

It stopped the other at once. For the first time she gave Aidan all her attention. She was as unlike her sisters as could be, but by color and age he knew her. The oldest of all Hart's brood: Blythe, only months younger than he himself.

She was, he thought, magnificent. The heavy velvet gown, dyed a rich, warm yellow, set off her dusky Cheysuli coloring, though the eyes were blue instead of yellow. Her face was much like the faces of the Cheysuli women in Clankeep, formed of arresting planes and angles. There was little Solindish in her; that was Cluna's and Jennet's province. Blythe's black hair had been twisted and looped against the back of her head, showing off an elegant neck.

She was worth coming for— Aidan cut it off. He had spent too much time with women of lower rank, who encouraged his attention. He had become adept at dealing with them, and at judging their worth very quickly. *But this woman is not like them . . .*

Blythe's gaze was level. "Are you truly Aidan?"

He gazed back at her. *SHE could make me forget. All the dreams, the chain—* Again he cut himself off. "Aye," he offered calmly. "I was not expected, so I hope you will forgive me for arriving without a warning. My *jehan* did not think Hart would turn me away."

"Of course not. You are well come to Lestra." Blythe's Homanan was accented with the nuances of Solinde. Aidan found it attractive. "But you must promise me you forgive these little magpies, croaking about private things."

Both magpies glared at their sister, then turned their attention to Aidan. Summoning gallantry, he assured them he would.

Jennet banished contrition. "*Have* you come for a wife?"

Blythe's eyebrows rose. "What has possessed your tongue to be so heedless? Do you think Aidan came all the way from Homana simply to look for a wife?"

Aidan opened his mouth, shut it, scratched eloquently at his scalp.

"See?" Jennet challenged.

Blythe's eyes widened. "*Have* you, then?"

"See?" Jennet repeated. "You want to know as much as we do."

Aidan maintained a neutral tone. "There is some possibility—"

"Queen of Homana," Jennet considered.

Cluna glared at her. "Not for years and years. First there is *Princess* of Homana—"

Blythe's turn. "And *that* not for years," she declared. "There is one of those already: Aidan's mother, Aileen."

Cluna smiled shyly. "Jennet may be older, but I am nicer."

Jennet eyed her askance. "And Blythe the oldest of all. *She* comes first in everything."

"Enough!" Blythe cried, before full-scale war was begun. "All of you, come with me. Aidan must meet *jehan*."

Jennet twitched at skirts. "He is playing Bezat with Tevis. He sent us out when Cluna knocked over the bowl and scattered all the pieces."

"It was an accident!" Cluna cried. "And it was *really* your fault—if you had not left the bowl so close to the edge of the table—"

"And if *you* had kept your sticky fingers out of it—"

"Never mind," Blythe said ominously. "I know where Tevis is. I know where *both* of them are. And I know where you are going." Blythe locked a hand over Jennet's shoulder and steered her down the hall. "Cluna, you also. And Aidan—" Blythe's smile was both beautiful and beseeching. "Will you come with us?"

Aidan was a man who had grown up with no sisters. He liked women very much, but the ones he had spent most of his time with had been quite different. Looking at his kin, allied against refusal, he doubted he could do otherwise. Not in the face of so many females bent on a single thing that had nothing to do with bed.

Two

The round room was tiny but comfortable, lime-washed white for brightness, and tucked into a corner tower of the castle. A handful of casement slits let in the light of a fading day, painting the room in muted stripes. There were stools, chairs, tripod candle stands; one low table. At the table were two men: a Cheysuli in indigo leathers, gold gleaming on dark arms, and a younger, more elegant man dressed in russet velvet doublet over brown hunting leggings.

Aidan knew the elder, though they had never met. He was very like his own father.

Lost within their game, neither man looked up. Blythe sighed, exchanging an amused glance with her newly-arrived cousin, then silenced Cluna and Jennet with a raised finger. With eloquent, purposeful gravity, Blythe made the introduction.

A pair of heads lifted and turned, displaying startled expressions. Hart stared, then abruptly suspended movement in the midst of drawing a bone-colored stone from a rune-wrought silver bowl. Blue eyes at first were stunned; then disbelief entered. "No," he said only.

Aidan, amused, grinned. "Aye."

Hart frowned. His eyes were shrewdly attentive as he made a brief, alert assessment, marking hair, eyes, gold; the shape of facial bones. Then the frown faded. Doubt shaded his tone. "Aidan of *Homana?*"

"Not Aidan of Falia." Aidan's tone was dry. "Am I to spend the rest of my life reassuring my kinfolk I am well and truly alive?"

"Brennan's son," Hart murmured, the slow smile stretching his mouth. And then he was on his feet, dropping the forgotten Bezat stone. "By all the gods, *Aidan!*"

The fleeting thought was ironic. *By all the gods indeed—* But then Hart was hugging him, pulling him into a kinman's proud embrace, and Aidan had no more time for thought.

Hart said something in the Old Tongue, something to do with prayers answered for his *rujholli*, then released Aidan. Blue eyes were very bright. "You must forgive my doubt . . . all those years everyone feared for your welfare, and now you stride into my castle every inch the warrior!"

Aidan indicated his hair. "Except, I think, for this."

Hart waved a dismissive hand. "Aye, well . . . you have noted, I am sure, two of my *own* children lack the Cheysuli color." He grinned at his fair-haired daughters. "It comes from outmarriage. First Aileen, then Ilsa. If we are not careful, we will lose the coloring."

But he did not sound particularly concerned by the dilution of true Cheysuli characteristics. Aidan, looking at Hart's face, saw the same bones his father had, and hair equally black—or once equally black; now equally threaded with silver—but Hart's eyes were blue. Blythe looked very like him.

Blythe. Aidan glanced at her. Upon making the introduction, she had crossed the room to stand beside the young man in russet velvet. He waited in polite silence, displaying only a profile, and idly stirred the stones. Blythe reached down and took the wine cup by his elbow, murmuring in a low tone.

Aidan felt a flicker of unexpected apprehension. He was very accustomed to seeing approval or invitation in the eyes of attractive women. Blythe was different, but he found he wanted the same reaction. Yet her thoughts, clearly, were with another man. And Aidan, for all his experience, knew the rules were different. He had come looking for a wife, not a bedpartner of brief duration.

Apprehension mounted. *Am I too late for Blythe?*

Hart's ebullient voice overruled thinking. "How is my royal *rujho*? And *jehan*? Is Mujhara the same, or has it grown? Has Deirdre—"

But Jennet and Cluna, freed now of requested silence, began chattering at their father.

"Not now," he said above the high-pitched din that was, to Aidan, indecipherable. "There are too many things I have to ask of Aidan—" Then, in affectionate exasperation, "Not *now;* I have said. You will have Aidan thinking I spoil you."

Aidan, who had already seen he did, smiled privately. Across the room Blythe glanced up, caught his expression and smiled back. They shared the tiny moment of acknowledgment, then Blythe set down the cup and came away from the table.

"Jennet," she said, "enough. *And* you, Cluna. There will be time for your chatter later . . . for now we must host our kinsman and treat him with Solindish honor." She flicked eloquent fingers. "You know where the kitchens are. Send for food and wine."

Jennet's mouth pursed mutinously. "If he has come to find a wife, it concerns me. I should be allowed to stay."

At the low table, the young man stopped stirring stones. "A wife?" Hart echoed.

"Not *now*," Blythe told Jennet. "Settling a marriage is something done by adults, and *you* have yet to prove you are anything more than a child. Go, and take your sister."

Brief rebellion from quieter Cluna. "But he might choose *me*."

Blythe pointedly opened the door. "He might even choose Dulcie."

Two mouths dropped open. Two voices chorused, "But Dulcie is only a *baby*."

"All the better," Blythe told them briskly. "Babies are easier to train." She smiled at Aidan, then motioned her sisters out. Eventually, they went.

"A wife?" Hart repeated. "But Brennan has said nothing of that in any of his letters."

His father and Hart corresponded often, Aidan knew, trying to compensate for the separation. Too distant even for the *lir*-link, the twin-born princes took what solace they could from parchment.

Aidan shook his head. "It came up of a sudden. They discovered, *jehan* and *jehana*, that I was twenty-three . . . apparently there is some significance attached to the age." He smiled at Blythe, not so much younger than he. "It must be a family custom than no man or woman be allowed to reach twenty-four without having married."

Blythe's color darkened. She turned jerkily to her father. "Perhaps I should go . . . perhaps I should accompany Cluna and Jennet—"

"Cluna and Jennet will do very well without you." Hart waved her back, then glanced across at the table. "No, Tevis—sit down. There is no need for you to go."

"But—my lord—" The young man was standing. He was

tall, dark-haired, handsome, filling out leather and velvet with an elegance edged with power. Aidan recalled Cluna and Jennet were quite enamored of him. "If you truly intend to discuss a royal marriage—"

"Not now," Hart declared. "By the gods, not now. I am a man with four daughters . . . there will be time aplenty for that. And time aplenty to speak of family matters." He kicked another stool over toward the table, looking expectantly at Aidan. "Do you play?"

"Not that. I have heard of Bezat; I thought it best to avoid it. It carries—consequences."

"*All* games carry consequences." Hart reseated himself. "If you mean my missing hand, that had little to do with Bezat. It had to do with being a great fool . . . since then, I have learned better." He motioned impatiently. "Sit down, Aidan. Talk of marriages can wait . . . there is a game to learn!"

Aidan hesitated. "I was warned about you."

"All true," Hart agreed cheerfully. "Shall we add to the stories?"

"*Jehan,*" Blythe said warningly. "You know what *jehana* will say if you stay up all night again."

"Your *jehana*, at the moment, has more to concern herself with than what time I come to bed. She would more likely prefer me *out* of it . . ." Hart's eyes were bright as he grinned at Aidan. "Sit you down, *harani*. How best do we meet one another save over wine and a game?"

The gaming continued until dawn. Tevis, yawning, gave up at last and excused himself, pushing all of his coin across the table to Hart. His bloodshot eyes were red-rimmed.

"No more," he murmured sleepily. "You have all my wits and now my coin . . . I am for bed, my lord. You promised me one last night."

Hart leaned back on his stool, rolling a stiffened neck. Black hair touched his shoulders; the silver was in his forelock. "There is always a bed for you . . . if I refused, all four of my daughters would ply my name with curses." He grinned, working shoulders. "Even Dulcie adores you."

"She has excellent taste." Tevis rose, rubbing absently at thick hair. It was so brown as to verge on black, cut closely to his head. Equally dark brows arched smoothly over ale-brown eyes, defining the bone of the forehead. "Of course, at all of two, her allegiance is easily won." He yawned, stretched briefly, looked down at Aidan. "My lord. If you yet have the wits to think, you might consider ending this travesty. He will have all of *your* coin, too."

Aidan grunted and reached for wine, then thought better of it. "I am a careful man."

"So was I, once." Tevis bowed briefly in Hart's direction, then headed for the door.

Hart waited until it was closed. "He is here to marry Blythe."

Wandering wits snapped back at once. Aidan blinked. "Ah."

"Of course, nothing has yet been settled—nothing has been *said* . . . but it is why he came." Hart rose and walked stiffly to the nearest casement and shoved the shutter open to let in pale pink dawn. "He is of one of the oldest and finest families of Solinde . . . a *jehan*, prince or no, could ask for no better match."

Aidan recalled Blythe's subtle intimacies, the expression in Tevis' eyes when the subject of marriage had come up. He had suspected as much, though he wished it were otherwise. "You must do what is best, *su'fali*."

"No." Hart strode to another casement, pushed open another shutter. "No, I must do as my daughter desires." Aidan watched in startled silence as Hart opened shutters at two more casements, then swung to face his audience of one. "*You* should understand the need."

"I?"

"Of course." Hart's nostalgic smile was lopsided. "Aileen and Brennan married out of duty, and out of honor for a betrothal made without their consent. Before they were born."

"Ah," Aidan said.

"I was the middle son, the son whose disposition was not so important as Brennan's . . . no one linked me to anyone. Ilsa and I married for the sake of Solinde, but by then the point was moot. We were already bound." Hart leaned against the sill, folding arms across his chest. *Lir*-bands gleamed. "Given the choice, Aileen never would have married Brennan. She wanted Corin. But he left for Atvia, so Brennan got his *cheysula*." Hart's expression was blank, his tone carefully bland. "I will give my daughter the choice."

Aidan sighed, staring blankly at the bowl of bone-colored

stones. "A man come to sell his horse would list its obvious assets. I am to be Mujhar, one day . . ." Aidan lifted his head. "But that makes no difference, does it? Not to you. The stories I have heard say you were always the least impressed by titles and rank."

Hart shrugged. "The only thing that impressed me was a man's willingness to wager." But he said it without smiling. Wearily, he threaded the fingers of his remaining hand through fallen hair and scooped it back from his brow. The gesture displayed a dual circlet of lines graven deeply into the flesh. Age sat lightly on him, as lightly as on Aidan's father, but nonetheless it encroached. "You have my permission to ask her, if you choose—that much I can give you . . . but it will be Blythe's decision."

Aidan lifted one shoulder in self-conscious concession; they both knew what she would say.

Hart's voice was neutral. "If it is kin you want, to keep the bloodlines whole—I have three other daughters."

Aidan shrugged again. "By now, the blood is everything we need to fulfill the prophecy, except . . ." He let it trail off; the ending was implicit.

Hart said it anyway. "Except Ihlini." He sighed and rubbed absently at the flesh of his left forearm where the leather cuff bound the stump. "Aye, there is that . . . but who of us will take on the distasteful task?" Black brows arched curiously. "You are the likeliest one."

Aidan shook his head. "Not I, *su'fali*. I am not my *jehan*."

Hart's expression stilled. "Brennan was tricked."

He did not like being reminded. He protects my jehan as much as jehan protects him. Even now. Aidan made his tone light. "Aye, so he was; I do not hate him for it, or think him due less respect. He was not the first . . . it happened even to Ian."

"And Ian still pays the price . . . I think my *rujho* does, too." Hart stopped kneading his arm, changing the topic abruptly. "There are the other girls. Young, I know . . . but such things are not uncommon when House marries House."

Aidan thought of Cluna and Jennet. Thirteen-year-old hellions. The other was Dulcie, age two. He was a man who wanted a woman, not a child to raise. Not girls who thought they were grown, not knowing what else was expected. While it was true he would not inherit the Lion for many years yet, he wanted those years spent properly, not waiting for a girl-wife to discover she was a woman.

There is one last thing . . . He rubbed gritty eyes. "You have no son," he said softly. "What will you do for an heir?"

Hart did not smile. "Are you promising me one in exchange for persuading Blythe?"

Aidan sighed. "No."

Hart pressed himself off the sill and came to the table. He poured himself fresh wine, lifted his cup and sipped. Then set down the cup again. "Ilsa is in bed because she is very near to term. In a week, possibly two, I may yet have an heir."

The words rose unbidden: *"Ru'shalla-tu, su'fali. Tahlmorra lujhalla mei wiccan, cheysu."*

"You sound like a *shar tahl.*" Hart smiled. *"Leijhana tu'sai, harani.* I, too, hope it is so."

"So." Aidan rose, kicking back his stool. "There is yet a princess left—an *older* princess—Keely's daughter, Shona. She is—nineteen? Twenty? Perhaps I should go at once, to set Blythe's mind at ease. She knows why I am here, as does Tevis. It would discomfit them to think I mean to come between them."

"Stay," Hart said. "There is no need to go in such haste. If Blythe and Tevis cannot survive your presence, they cannot survive a marriage. Stay at least until the birth. You can give the kinsman's blessing."

Aidan grinned. "And keep the hellions busy?"

"They will keep *you* busy." Hart eyed him consideringly. "Are you awake enough to ride?"

Aidan blinked. "Now?"

"Dawn is my favorite time, and Rael will be glad of flight. Will you come with me?"

He had been thinking of bed. But the morning air would refresh him after a night spent in a game, so he agreed readily. Teel would approve, also.

"Good. Mounts are always waiting; the privilege of rank." Hart swung open the door. "I will show you Lestra as Lestra should be seen."

Three

Hart led Aidan back through empty halls and corridors, striding purposefully without pause, and out into the bailey. He waited, smiling faintly, and after only a moment horseboys came running from the stable block. A tall black stallion was brought to Hart, saddled and waiting; a bay was given to Aidan.

"I have a horse," he said.

Hart's voice was bland. "Undoubtedly weary from the journey. Try this one instead." He swung up and gathered reins into the only hand he had, looking down patiently at Aidan. "What is it?"

Aidan sighed and gave in. "The way you keep your castle . . . *su'fali*, you know I mean no disrespect, but when I came here no one seemed perturbed by a stranger's presence. No one even asked if I was here to see *you*, or merely a tradesman come for business." He stroked the bay's nose. "And when I went into the castle—"

"—no one even bothered to ask who you were," Hart finished. "Aye, is it not soothing? No servants underfoot, no 'my lord' this, 'my lord' that before you can even think." He smiled down on Aidan. "I am not much like the Mujhar, drowning in too-helpful servants, and little like my *rujho*, so weighed down by responsibility that he can barely breathe. Protocol I find tedious . . . oh, I do what I must when I must—Ilsa sees to that—but I am happiest with my children and the freedom to be what I am." He swung the stallion gateward. "Do you plan to wait all day? Dawn only lasts so long."

Hastily Aidan mounted, settling into the bay. The stallion had a fiery eye, but his manners were excellent. Aidan smiled with pleasure and turned him after the black.

Hart led him through the winding streets without apparent confusion—Aidan expected none—and up toward the line of hills on the western outskirts of the city. When at last they climbed to the summit, Aidan was suitably impressed. Whitewashed buildings damp with dew glittered in the sunrise, pale pink and silver-gilt. Skeins of woodsmoke drifted from gray stone chimneys, knotting and tearing apart; Aidan was abruptly reminded of the Weaver's colorless yarns and the brilliant tapestry.

He shivered. One hand touched the two heavy links depending from his belt. Still there. Still real. He had dreamed none of it.

"There," Hart said.

With effort, Aidan took his hand away from the links. His palm was damp, but oddly warm, as if the metal had warmed it. The sensation was unsettling. Surreptitiously he wiped his hand against a leather-clad thigh, and looked for what Hart indicated.

At first he saw nothing; then a blot against the dawn. He squinted, trying to distinguish pale blot from new daylight. White wings clove the air in powerful, graceful sweeps, then flattened gently to soar.

"Rael," he murmured aloud.

The dark-eyed hawk was magnificent. White edged with jet, each feather delineated. He swept through the air with deceptive ease and grace, riding the currents of dawn.

Through the link there came a sardonic whisper. Aidan smiled, tilting his head. "*And* there."

Frowning, Hart glanced over. "Where?"

"There." Aidan pointed. "Not so large as Rael, perhaps, but feathered nonetheless. His name is Teel."

Hart looked, smiling. "Brennan wrote me when you received him . . . somewhat out of the ordinary, I think— there has not been a raven *lir* for more than one hundred years. They tell stories about him."

"Lorcha," Aidan agreed. "His *lir* died in the *qu'mahlin*. And as for stories, well . . ." He grinned. "I think Teel will inspire more. If not, he will make his own."

Hart tipped his head back as Teel, following Rael, sliced through the air. Then he looked at Aidan. "How is my *rujho*?"

"Very well—" Aidan began dutifully, then dismissed the platitudes. Hart knew Brennan better than any. "Settled," he said quietly. "The rank is heavy, aye, but he likes the responsibility. You know how he is . . . it makes him feel needed."

Hart's smile was faint. "He would make a good shepherd."

At first he was astounded. Then Aidan laughed out loud; he had never heard his father's competence phrased in quite that way. "Aye, so he would . . . and the flock would prosper for it." He shifted in the saddle, leaning forward on braced arms. "I know what you ask, without asking it." He did. "How does the marriage go? Is my *jehan* happy? Is he content within himself?"

"All of that, and more." Hart sighed, hooking reins over the pommel. The leather cuff rested on one indigo-clad thigh. "He writes, of course, and often—but it is not the same. There was always a private place in Brennan, a place where he went away from everyone."

Aidan was startled. "Even away from you?"

"I think he believed I could not—or *would* not, more likely—understand what he felt." Hart's expression was momentarily ashamed. "And I admit, I was not the most perceptive of *rujholli*. Twin-born, I understood him *better*—but not everything. Brennan and I are different. He was always the shepherd—" briefly, he grinned "—and I always the black lamb wandering too far from the flock."

"And Corin was the dog?"

Hart laughed. "Corin? No, not the *dog* . . . more like the fox in the henyard, making trouble for the cook."

Aidan shrugged. "Well, Kiri *is* a fox."

Hart's tone was solemn, though his eyes glinted amusement. "The gods are always wise."

Aidan looked for Teel, found him; the raven still circled, even as Rael. *Are they?* he asked intently.

Teel's tone was bland. *You know them better than I.*

"So," Hart said, "he and Aileen have made their peace at last."

Pulled back out of the link, Aidan shrugged. "They were never at war."

"No, but—"

"But?" He raised ruddy brows. "Do you want me to tell you things my own father has not told you?"

Hart was unabashed. "If you know those things."

To delay, Aidan plaited mane. He felt odd discussing his parents, even with his uncle. The thing he now knew as *kivarna* made him far more perceptive than anyone else, yet also more intrusive. And now Hart wanted answers to questions Aidan found discomfiting.

"They are content enough," he said finally. "*Jehana* would be happier if there was another son, or two . . . but I am in no danger of dying—at least, not as I used to be—and I think Council is no longer so vocal about the Prince of Homana looking to another princess."

Hart was aghast. "They would have asked it of him?"

"They did. When I was young, and ill for the thousandth time." Aidan sighed and looked across Lestra, frowning in recollection. "No one meant her disrespect, of course . . . they promised a courtesy title and a generous yearly pension, and all the honor due her. I think they hoped she would take herself back to Erinn, so things would not be so awkward—"

Hart's laugh was a curt bark of sound. "Brennan would never stand for that."

"No. Nor did he. And now they know better." Aidan shrugged. "But I know it troubles her. There are things other than a sickly childhood to threaten the Prince's heir. Niall had *three* sons; everyone, I think, would be happier with that."

Hart said nothing for a long moment. The morning was loud with silence. Then, quietly, "It must be especially difficult for you."

Aidan looked at him sharply.

Hart shrugged. "To know so many people crowded around your cradle, fearing you would die . . . and even when you outgrew that, they still attached the *question*—" He sighed and rubbed at red-rimmed eyes. "When they discussed your *jehana*, did no one think of you?"

It was an odd thought. "Why should they think of me?"

Hart looked squarely at him. "I grew up without a *jehana*—a true blood *jehana*—because she was sent away. But it was made clear, at an early age, that Gisella was quite mad. That she had done the unspeakable and tried to give her sons to Strahan. Exiling her was just."

Uncomfortable, Aidan waited.

Hart's voice was very quiet. "But you grew up differently. You had a *jehana*—a true blood *jehana*—more than fit to claim the name. Yet they thought to send her away because she bore only one son. And that devalued you. Surely you must have known it—must have *felt* it."

Surely he had.

Aidan looked away, staring down into the city. After a

moment, he cleared his throat. "No one knew I knew. No one thought about the servants, talking among themselves. I was very young . . . no one knew I was there."

"Did you ever say anything to Brennan?"

"No." Aidan unplaited the mane. "No. What was there to say?"

"To Aileen?"

"No. To no one." *Except to the Lion. And, later, of course, to Teel.*

"No, neither would I." Hart smiled at Aidan's startled glance. "We all of us have our secrets. I will leave yours to you." He shifted in the saddle, resettling himself. "For all they may have believed in the need for more princes, they overlooked the obvious. Niall had two other realms to portion out to extra sons. Brennan lacks the luxury, now that Solinde and Atvia *have* Cheysuli on the thrones. He would find it much harder if there were more boys than you to place, like a hound keeper with a litter much larger than expected."

Aidan smiled back. "As hard as you do with four girls to marry off?"

It hit home. Hart grimaced with a wry twist of his mouth. "Blythe would have been enough . . . but after her there were the twins who died in the summer of sweating fever—both girls—and then Cluna and Jennet. Next, Dulcie." Hart smiled as a wisp of wind ruffled hair. "I would trade none of them—but how *does* a man deal with four marriageable girls?"

"Well, Dulcie is a *bit* young to count as marriageable."

"Not when it comes to royal fledglings." Hart sighed. "You have been very fortunate. The eldest son—the heir—is always the most important in the scheme of who marries whom. My poor *rujho* was betrothed to Aileen before either of them were born."

"And Keely to Sean." Aidan nodded. "There was never any pressure . . . never any discussion—at least where I could hear. Until now." He grinned. "But I am amenable. They have let me have my freedom with never a whisper of duty. Perhaps the time is right."

Hart's stallion stomped and pawed at damp turf. He caught up loose reins with his hand and quieted the horse with a single spoken admonishment. "Well, regardless of common practice, I will not offer Cluna and Jennet even to Homana. They are too young." He laughed at Aidan's expression, part guilt and part relief. "Even if they *were* older. They are hideously willful girls."

Aidan's tone was elaborately mournful. "Which leaves only Blythe, and she is already promised."

"Not promised," Hart said quietly. "As I said, nothing is settled—"

Aidan shrugged, dismissing levity. "It does not have to be. You can see it in their eyes."

Hart sorted out reins, resettled his weight, stroked the black satin neck. Then stared down at his city and sighed his resignation. "It would go far toward healing old wounds."

It startled Aidan. "Why? I thought them all healed with your marriage to Ilsa."

"There was a man," Hart said quietly. "A proud, strong man, dedicated to Solinde. He disliked Homanan usurpers. He wanted the throne for Ilsa, so he could be Consort. So his son could become king. The first Solindish king since Carillon killed Bellam."

Old history. Older enmity. "A patriot," Aidan said.

"A true-born Solindishman of one of the oldest lines." Hart shifted again in his saddle. "I had him executed."

Aidan, who sensed old grief in his uncle as well as a trace of shame, looked at Hart's cuffed stump. "Do you mean the man who cost you your hand?"

"Dar of High Crags; aye. Tevis is his nephew. Son to Dar's youngest sister."

Astonishment overrode caution. "And do you mean to say you will give Tevis Blythe to pay him for Dar's *death?* To wash your guilt away, even though none is deserved?"

"Aidan—"

"The man cost you your *hand* . . . and very nearly your life! It was Dar who gave you to Strahan—do you think my *jehan* has said nothing of it?" Aidan, appalled, shook his head. "He told me all about it. Dar deserved to die. It was the only thing you could do."

Hart's face was tight. "Do you think that is the only reason for this marriage? It is politically expedient, aye—I have learned *something* of kingcraft—but it is not the sole concern. There is Blythe and Tevis also . . . and you have seen that yourself."

Aye, so he had. He had even said so to Hart. "Aye. Aye, *su'fali* . . ." Aidan sighed. "But *my* marriage is politically expedient also . . . Blythe is my age, and half Cheysuli, and

everything else as well—except Erinnish, but *I* have that."
He scraped hair back from his face. "I left Homana to find a
bride. One who would serve the role as well as the prophecy." He slanted a glance at Hart. "Do you blame me,
su'fali? Your daughter is beautiful."

Unease evaporated. Hart's grin was brilliant. "I *thought* it
might come to that!"

"She is." Aidan felt no shame. "What man alive would be
blind to a comely woman . . . especially when he needs to
put a *cheysula* in his bed?" He paused. *"And* on a throne."

Hart frowned a little. "You did not come *expecting* to win
her, did you?"

"I thought my chances good." Aidan smiled disarmingly.
"I am your twin-born *rujho's* only son, the only one there
can be, and heir to the Lion Throne. Part of the prophecy."

White teeth shone in a dark face. "Stooping to kinship
pressure, are we? Thinking to convince me through bloodlink
alone?"

Aidan arched brows. "It was certainly worth the try. And
there had been nothing said of this Tevis of High Crags in
your letters to my *jehan* . . . how was I to know?"

"Aye, well . . . Tevis only came to Lestra four months
ago. He grew up in northern Solinde, high in the mountains
. . . the mountain Solindish are different from the rest of us.
They keep themselves isolated."

" 'Us'?" Aidan echoed.

Hart made an acknowledging gesture. "I am their lord,
after all. And different enough already, as I am often reminded. There is no sense in rousing old griefs . . . this is
my *tahlmorra*, Aidan. And there is Solindish in me as well
as all the other bloodlines."

"Not *all* of them." Aidan grinned, then felt the amusement die. "I thought you told me Tevis *came* to marry
Blythe. If he did not know her already—"

"You did not."

"No." He refused to be turned aside. "But you made it
sound as if they had known one another for years."

Hart reined in a restless stallion, pulling the fine black
head away from the bay Aidan rode. "Did you know this is
Bane's son? I sent the mare to Brennan four years ago for
breeding, and this is the result. I am quite pleased . . . he is
a willful young lad, but worth it."

Aidan liked and respected his kinsman, but something

inside would not allow him to hide from the knowledge Hart was all too human. Although Aidan was, by everyone's reckoning, fully an adult, in his eyes his older kin were above reproach. Yet the *kivarna* showed him reproach was due his elders as much as anyone else.

The *kivarna*, Aidan thought, showed him entirely too much.

Quietly, he said, "You are avoiding the issue, *su'fali*."

Hart glanced at Aidan, then sighed in surrender. "Tevis' *jehan* died ten months ago in a fall. Ilsa, being distant kin as well as queen, sent a letter of personal condolence to the widow. They began to correspond, and soon they traded news of various children, including Tevis and Blythe." Hart shrugged. "It is what *jehanas* do."

Aidan nodded. "And so eventually Tevis was sent in person to win the hand of the princess."

"There was no reason for him not to come. He had bided for many years in the fastness of High Crags . . . he was due a visit to Lestra to see his lord—"

"—*and* his lord's eldest daughter."

Hart's tone was even. "There is nothing to stand in their way."

And you do not want me *to.* Aidan laughed at Hart, lifting hands in surrender. "Aye, aye, I understand . . . no more said of it." He covered a yawn with one hand. "Dawn is done, *su'fali*. Time for me to sleep, before I fall off my horse."

"You are too good a rider, and he too good a mount. You have that of Brennan; the horse has it of me." Hart looked for Rael. "There. Shall we go?"

Aidan nodded after a moment, turning the bay southward to wind back down the hills. Pleasure in the morning was now tinged with empathy. He had seen the brief wistful expression on his uncle's face, the subtle tensing of flesh by blue eyes as Hart looked for and found his *lir*. But he sensed more than wistfulness. He felt more than relief.

Hart wanted to fly with every ounce of his being.

With every fiber of the missing hand that denied him the chance.

Four

Aidan rolled over in bed. Sheets were tangled around him; with effort, he stripped them away. He frowned into unexpected daylight, blinking still-gritty eyes clear. *What am I doing in bed at this time of day?*

And then he remembered. A full night spent over the game, the dawn upon a hilltop. He vaguely recalled falling at last into bed when everyone else was waking.

How long—? He looked at the hour-glass. Four hours abed; barely time to recall his name.

A long, elaborate stretch succeeded in reminding his body it had a purpose other than lying sprawled in bed. Then something moved upon the canopy. Aidan glanced roofward quickly, momentarily startled, then grinned relief and self-derision and relaxed into the mattress once more, rubbing a stubbled jaw. On the canopy frame perched the raven.

So, Teel remarked. *Half a day gone already.*

Aidan yawned noisily. *Not quite half . . . half of a half, perhaps . . .* Yet another yawn. A growl from his belly stopped it; he clapped one hand to flesh. *How long since—?* he began, then remembered the cheese he had eaten while drinking Solindish wine.

And the wine remembers me . . . He rolled out of bed and stood, scrubbing a sleep-creased face. He wondered what he most needed: bath, food, more sleep. And in which order.

No time, Teel mentioned. *The lady has sent for you.*

For one irrational moment Aidan thought his *lir* referred to the Weaver. Then realized what he meant. "Now?" he asked aloud.

The raven contemplated. *Perhaps later,* he suggested, which told Aidan how badly he looked.

He promptly ordered a bath, and food to go with it. *Then* he would see the lady; likely she would thank him.

* * *

Ilsa of Solinde.

Aidan had heard all the stories, the songs and verses extolling her beauty, but such things, he had learned young, were often exaggerated. And when it came to feminine beauty, he knew very well what one man believed was beautiful was often not to another.

Ilsa was beautiful.

Ilsa was *glorious.*

One unwavering glance out of long-lidded, ice-blue eyes, and he was half in love with the woman wed to his uncle. The other half of him felt awkward as a boy in the first flush of young manhood only just discovering women, and what they could do to a body.

Inwardly, he reminded himself, *She is forty years old, or more.*

Ilsa's luminous smile mocked him, as did the fine-boned features. "Aileen had nothing to fear."

Aidan blinked, gathering wits with effort. He was not thinking of his mother, though Aileen and Ilsa were very close in age. Ilsa was not his mother, any more than he her son.

This woman could not be old enough to have borne Blythe or *the twins.*

Her Homanan was flavored with the delicate Solindish accent he had first heard in Blythe. He had liked it in Blythe, finding it attractive. Now he heard the same in the mother. "Wasted years, the worry. The crop stands tall in the field."

He understood her then. "But the harvest not yet begun." He smiled, inclined his ruddy head, gave her the honor rank and beauty were due. *"Cheysuli i'halla shansu."*

"Resh'ta-ni," she answered, though the accent was bad. Ilsa laughed at his expression, much as he sought to hide it. "Hart taught me some of the Old Tongue, but nothing of the accent. Forgive my poor attempt."

He would, as any man, forgive her anything. He very nearly said so, then swallowed it back. It was, he assumed, something she had heard all too often. He wished for once he had a gift for eloquent phrases, the ability to flatter with a smile, a gesture, a word. But he was not a courtier, disliking much of the game. His *kivarna* made him wary of false words when he understood most of the feelings.

Ilsa, still smiling, stroked back a stray wisp of hair from the winged arch of one brow. Her hair, he knew, had always been white-blonde, because they told stories about it. The pearlescent sheen was unchanged, and likely would remain that way. No one would be able to tell the difference, once she dulled into true white. It was a boon others would kill for; she accepted it gracefully. She wore it in two heavy braids bound with thin gold wire. It glistened in the daylight.

That she was abed, he had known; this close to labor, Ilsa took no chances. Hart had said her delivery of Dulcie was not easy, and she was no longer young enough to carry easily. No one wanted to risk the child who might yet be an heir, or the woman who was queen.

The chamber was flooded with daylight. No shuttered casements for Ilsa; she welcomed in the midday sun and granted it the freedom to go where it would. The curtains on the bed were drawn back and tied to testers, looped with gold cord.

Ilsa eyed him critically. "He kept you up all night."

Aidan laughed, smoothing fingers across his jaw. The bath had worked its miracle, as had a shave and food. But Ilsa was too discerning; she had had years of practice. "Aye. But I slept earlier." He did not tell her a lifetime of troubling dreams had accustomed him to less sleep.

Slender, elegant hands stroked the pearl-studded blue coverlet mounded over her belly. Padded bolsters sheathed in satin braced her upright. "I have told him, time and time again, not everyone is as suited to days without sleep," she said, sighing resignation. "Even *he* is not . . . but I have given up remonstrating with him. He does what he will do. I should have known better than to think he would ever change."

There was no bitterness in tone or words. Not even faint resentment. No matter what she said, he knew what she thought. Even without the *kivarna*, Aidan understood very well how strong was the bond that made Hart and Ilsa one.

"But you have," he countered. "I have heard how bad he was as a young man . . . how he refused all responsibility to lose himself in the game. I have seen him with his daughters. I have heard him speak of duty. Regardless of the cause, he is not the same man."

Ilsa smiled. Delicate color crept into her face. "In many ways, he is. And I would have it that way. Why banish what you love?"

He thought of his grandsire and Deirdre. What they shared

was as strong, in different ways, as the thing between Hart and Ilsa. As a child he had been nebulously aware of something intangible linking Niall and Deirdre. Once older, having lain with a woman, he understood more of it. Lust was one thing, love another; the warmth and underlying respect Niall and Deirdre shared made the relationship invulnerable to outside influences. He sensed the same thing in Ilsa and Hart. But never between his parents. That they cared for each other, he knew. And were afraid to admit it.

"Why indeed?" he agreed, thinking of himself. *Who will share my life? Will it be as good as this?*

Ilsa's skin was translucent, pale as a lily. The eyes were luminous. In her he saw the twins, fair-haired Jennet and Cluna; and Blythe, who lacked the fairness, but had the slender, tensile strength with its powerful allure. How had Hart felt the first time he had seen her?

How did I feel the first time I saw Blythe?

One day before. Inwardly, he grimaced; a lifebond took more time. He had grown too accustomed to winning a bedpartner with a warm smile or a gesture. The women of Homana-Mujhar and the city responded readily to the title as well as himself, hoping for various rewards. Before coming to Solinde he had thought of women as pleasant diversions, or an escape from harrowing dreams. This circumstance was different. It was foolish to expect anything more than the first stirrings of attraction.

Although those I admit to freely. Blythe is magnificent . . . but I think Tevis' presence will make things difficult.

Ilsa gestured. "Will you sit?"

Aidan glanced at the indicated chair near the bed, then shook his head. "My regrets, but no. I have no wish to tire you."

She waved a gently dismissive hand. "They have kept me in bed a month. Listening to you speak will not prove onerous."

He glanced at the mound of bedclothes over her belly. She had borne six children, though only four survived. And now bore another to give her lord an heir.

It came out unexpectedly. "What if it is a girl?"

He had not meant it. He had barely even *thought* it. Embarrassment burned his face.

Ilsa's laughter cut off the beginnings of an apology. "No, no—do you think you are the first to ask it? You are only the most recent . . . just last evening one of my ladies asked the same."

"It is none of my concern—"

"It is everyone's concern," she corrected gently. "It has been from the beginning . . . this will be my last child."

He opened his mouth. Then shut it.

"Hart's decision," she said. "And perhaps a little of mine. It was difficult with Dulcie, though I was in no danger. The physicians suggest precautions, so I have taken myself to bed." She spread eloquent hands, then let them rest again on the bedclothes. "Boy or no: the last. And perhaps it is time." Ilsa tilted her head and smiled. "Instead of having children I would rather have *grand*children."

His answering smile was vague. "Blythe."

"And the others, eventually." The light in her eyes faded. "Hart spoke to me earlier. I am sorry, Aidan . . . I wish we had known a half-year ago. Then we might have looked to Homana instead of northern Solinde."

Aidan shrugged. "Hart explained it all."

"But if I do *not* bear a son . . ." A turn of her hand was eloquent. "A grandson could inherit."

Aidan thought of Dar, looking to marry Ilsa to put his son on the throne. Now that son could be born to Hart instead. And the nephew of Dar of High Crags would rule in place of Cheysuli.

He shifted weight self-consciously. "Lady, I will go. I have been asked to stay until the child is born, to bestow the kinsman's blessing. After that, I am for Erinn." There was no sense in staying. Here, Blythe was the only option; now there was none at all unless he looked to Erinn.

Ilsa's smile was kind. "Keely's girl is older than my two fair-haired halflings. And undoubtedly more polite. I think you will do well."

He sensed relief in her, that he did not protest the marriage between Tevis and Blythe. He knew very well a match between Homana and Solinde would solidify the two realms and undoubtedly please the Homanans, while displeasing the Solindish. Hart had been Prince of Solinde in truth as well as title for more than twenty years, and yet it was all too obvious he was not fully certain Solinde wanted him. Ilsa was their queen. For her, they suffered Hart.

Her son they would accept, for her sake. He will have acceptable blood, if tainted with Cheysuli. I wonder if they think to get the throne back someday, when Hart is in the ground and his son—Ilsa's *son*—*sits in the father's place?*

Ilsa was Solindish. He did not really blame her for wanting a Solindishman for Blythe—he might desire the same for *his* daughter, were he a Solindishman—but he wished blood might play a less important role. His own life was ruled by merging the proper bloodlines, and now it also entangled Blythe, who should be free of it. Solinde was *Solinde*—and yet now they made it Cheysuli.

He closed his hand on the two links dangling from his belt. *Perhaps that is the reason for this service. By merging the blood and begetting the Firstborn again, there no longer is any need for dividing up the realms. Four realms become one; six races the same.* Something cold stroked his spine. *And the lir for none of us?*

"Aidan—?" Ilsa began, but the opening of the door cut off the rest of her words.

Cluna and Jennet, of course. Crowding into the room to plead for their mother's attention. Behind them came Hart with a small girl in his arms: black-haired, yellow-eyed Dulcie, Cheysuli to the bone.

Aidan smiled at the girl. Something in him answered the fey look in her eyes. *Blood calling to blood?* He took a step closer. "A lovely girl, *su'fali*."

"My little Cheysuli," Hart declared, pausing a moment to let Aidan look at her, then moving past to Ilsa. "The gods finally condescended to let *one* of us look the part."

Cluna and Jennet were chattering at their mother, both mindful not to press too close. Pale hair, as before, straggled; Ilsa was gently chiding. Hart too stood close, then sat to bring Dulcie down where Ilsa could touch her, stroking fine black hair into neatness.

Aidan found the chamber crowded. He was not accustomed to children, and as unaccustomed to kin. A twitch from deep inside told him what he wanted: the freedom to fly the skies.

Hart, he knew, would understand, requiring no explanation. The others mostly ignored him, but something was due Ilsa.

Aidan paused at the door and looked back at her. Her bed was full of daughters, except for her oldest one. The one he most wanted to see. "May the gods grant you a son."

Ilsa glanced up from her crowded bedside. Her lovely face was alight. "*Leijhana tu'sai*, kinsman. May your words carry weight with the gods."

As Aidan stepped into the hall, he wondered if they could.

Five

He was waiting for her, as she had asked. In shadow, in a chair, hands resting unquietly on the downward sweep of each armrest. A ring glittered on one finger: sapphire set in silver. On yet another, jet, rimmed with delicate gold.

Blythe shut the door quietly, looking at him in concern. The flesh was drawn too tautly over the bones of his face. It made him look almost feral. "It may be nothing," she said. She had already said it twice, on the way to meet him in private.

He did not move at all, not even to agree, or to shake his head. He was angry, frightened, confused, but afraid to admit it. Afraid he had no right. She saw it in his eyes.

She walked slowly across the chamber to stand in front of the chair. The man seated in it did not look into her eyes, but stared as if transfixed at the girdle spanning her waist. Silver chimed as she moved, swinging with her skirts. It stopped even as she did; the silver sang no more.

She could hardly bear to look at him without touching him. It had been so from the beginning, from the very first time they had met. She had put no credence in such tales, consigning them to silly serving-girls dreaming away the hours, but then Tevis had come down from his mountain exile bearing an invitation from Ilsa to spend as much time as he liked. They were of an age, she and Tevis, and like-minded about many things. The instant attraction had flared into something far more physical; and yet the knowledge they dared not fulfill what they most desired increased the tension tenfold. That her parents approved was implicit in Ilsa's invitation; it was, Blythe knew, their way of telling her Tevis was suitable in all the ways that counted for kings and queens.

The last way was hers to decide: could she love and live with the man?

He filled her days and nights. She judged every man against him, comparing the shape of facial bones, the set of eyes, the line of chin and jaw. Even the way hair grew; in Tevis, easy to see because he cropped it short. She thought him everything a man should be to light up a woman's world. The chatter among the serving-girls and court women told her she was correct; he lighted more worlds than her own, or would, had he the chance to stray.

But Tevis had never strayed.

He was a man, even as men judged one another. And yet sensitive as a woman. It was the contradictions in him that appealed to her most: the quietude that spoke of privacy and deep thought; the understated power of personality that, allowed to flare, might consume them all.

Blythe drew in a breath and released it carefully. She put out both hands and locked them into his hair, palms pressing against his head as she threaded fingers tightly. Near-black hair was cropped short, displaying the elegant shape of his head. At the back of his neck it was longer, trying to curl; thick springy waves seduced her.

Slowly she drew him forward. It was a measure of her own apprehension and anguish that she touched him as she did, forcing the intimacy they wanted so badly, but had not shared. Neither of them had dared. Now, she knew, they had to.

His breath caressed the girdle; she pressed him closer yet, turning his face against her pelvis. The arch of his cheek, through the velvet, was hard.

She fought to keep her voice even. "We cannot be certain—"

Lean, long-fingered hands clasped her hips. His words were muffled by skirts, but she heard them. "Aye, I think we can." The hoarse tone was firm, but underscored with despair. "'He has made no secret of it: the heir to Homana has come to Solinde to find a wife.''

She felt the flutter of trepidation in her breast. Her hands in his hair tightened. "If you were to go to my father—"

"He already knows."

Desperation rose. "And have you spoken to him? Have you actually *told* him you want to marry me?"

He withdrew from her sharply, taking his hands from her. A spasm twisted his face. "No. Of course not. How can I? He is the Prince of Solinde, and I am—"

"—kin," she finished flatly, "—to the *Queen* of Solinde."

It was a tangled sovereignty. Hart still used his Homanan title, forgoing the loftier Solindish ranking until his father died, when he would inherit fully. But Ilsa was Solindish, the highest of the highborn, and the Solindish Council had bequeathed her the title when she married Hart. Their petty revenge, Blythe knew; she knew also it did not matter. Her father did not care.

Just now, it might help.

He rose and moved away from her. The room was her own, a private sitting chamber adjoining her personal apartments, and they both knew it unwise. She was allowed great freedom, but only because of trust. She wondered if they would betray it.

He turned. In the dullness of late afternoon, ale-brown eyes were dark. His face was expressionless, but she knew how to peel back the mask and look at the man beneath.

Steadily, he said, "He will make you Queen of Homana."

Blythe lifted her head. "*Will* he, then? Even without my permission?"

The flesh by his eyes twitched. "What woman would not want—"

She did not let him finish. "The woman who would rather live in Solinde, in the high northern fastness of High Crags."

He shut his eyes briefly. Fleeting pain ruined his brow; it smoothed almost instantly. "You are Cheysuli," he rasped. "I have heard of the prophecy."

For a moment, all she could do was stare. Her heritage everyone knew—they had only to look at her father—but it had never been an issue. Not with Tevis. He had come down out of his mountains knowing nothing of her race, and had no reason to fear it.

Nor to remind her of her duty.

She controlled her emotions with effort. "I was born in *Solinde*. I am *of* Solinde. I would rather serve my home than a collection of foreign words."

For a moment, he only stared. And then laughed aloud. "A 'collection of foreign words'!" Tevis laughed again. Blue and black glinted on his hands; the two rings were his only vanity. "Do you know what your father would do if he heard you blaspheme so?"

She felt strangely calm. "I imagine he would be somewhat put out with me. I imagine he might even take it into his head to instruct me in Cheysuli history; certainly I would be told yet again about the *tahlmorra* in us all." Briefly, Blythe grimaced. "But it has nothing to do with me. I am much more than merely Cheysuli."

Brown eyes were black in the shadows. "Much more," he agreed softly, reaching out to touch her face. The fingers barely brushed the curve of her chin. Another step, and he touched her mouth; a third, the sweep of temple meeting cheekbone with a caress that burned her flesh.

Blythe leaned into it. Tension sang between them.

Abruptly he let her go. "I know what I am. Do you?"

She did not soften it. "The nephew of a traitor."

The curves of his face hardened. "They will say it is my revenge."

Blythe smiled. "Perhaps it is."

"You are the eldest," he said, "and there is no male heir."

"Within a week, that could change—"

"And if it does not," he persisted. "If the child is another girl, and the queen bears no more—"

"There will be no more."

It stopped him instantly.

"No more," she repeated. "It has been decided. This is the last, boy or girl . . . if it is a boy, Solinde has an heir."

"And, if not—?"

A bubble of laughter broke. "You said it yourself, did you not? I am the eldest. From me will come the next."

Bitterness pinched his tone. "They will say I *planned* it."

"Does it matter?" she asked. "I must marry someone."

"Then why not Aidan?"

"Because, you *ku'reshtin*, he is not the one I fancy."

Tevis did not smile. "They could force you."

She shook her head.

"If Aidan demanded it—"

"He is too proud to do it."

"Pride has little to do with marriage when a prince desires a wife."

She smiled. "You know nothing about his life. The last

thing Aidan would want is a wife who loves another. Believe me, I *know*."

His hands closed over her shoulders. "If I lost you now—if they took you from me—"

"No." She shook her head.

"But they *could*. Blythe, have you no wits? You are too valuable to waste on a crude mountain lordling when there is a prince in the offing!"

Blythe unclasped her girdle. Silver dripped from her hand, then spilled onto the floor. "Then I will rid myself of value. No prince can afford to marry a woman whose virtue no longer exists."

He caught her hands and held them so tightly she gasped in pain. "Not like this!" he hissed.

"I want it. *You* want it; you would not dare deny it!"

"No," he rasped. "No. You know better than that."

Blythe pulled her hands free and cupped his jaw in her palms. "Then forget everything else. Set everything else aside. Let this merely be *us,* because we want it so much."

"They can execute me for this!"

One wild laugh escaped her. "In this, I will be Cheysuli. I will invoke my heritage."

"*Blythe—*"

"Clan-rights!" she hissed. "I give them freely to you. Now let them argue with *that!*"

Aidan shed himself and flew. Each time he exulted, as he exulted now, in the magic that gave him another form and the chance to ride the sky. He could not comprehend what it was like to be earthbound, tied to the ground with so much freedom all around, and no chance to know it. Even the other warriors, gods-gifted all, were trapped by earthbound *lir.*

He had asked his father, once, what it was to be a mountain cat, trying to understand that a *lir* was a *lir* and none of them better than another. But he had failed. Brennan's explanation had been salient enough—only another Cheysuli could fully comprehend the all-encompassing joy of *lir*-shape—but somehow lacking. No man, Aidan believed, could truly experience freedom without the ability to fly.

What was it like for Hart? Once lord of the air, even as Rael: now trapped forever by the loss of the hand that destroyed his raptor's balance. In human form, merely hindrance; in *lir*-shape, absolute prevention. Too much of him was missing.

Was it one reason, Aidan wondered, he loved Ilsa so? Did he compensate the loss by turning to wife and children?

The denial was emphatic, much as he longed for its absence. Deep in his soul he knew nothing could compensate a warrior for losing the gift of *lir*-shape. Rael lived, and therefore Hart was in no danger of going mad, but the inability to fly must come close to causing madness. He was whole, and yet not. Aidan could not begin to imagine what such torture would be like.

Be grateful, Teel said. *Do not take for granted what the gods give you.*

The raven, he knew, could be referring to Hart's loss and Aidan's wholeness. But he might also be referring to the task set for him, mentioned by the Weaver. A task he could yet refuse.

He had not, since arrival, been troubled by dreams of the chain. He wondered if it had anything to do with holding two of the links. They were real now, tangible evidence of gods; their presence could mean he did have a task, or that he was going mad. Even with a *lir*.

Air caressed his wings. He adjusted them slightly, dropping down through sky to enter another layer of the air that carried him. Tiny muscles twitched and flexed, altering his flight. Beside him, Teel followed.

If I could share this with Blythe—

He cut it off instantly.

Tevis cannot give her this.

He twitched in irritation. Neither could he.

Why would you want a cheysula who wants another man?

Why did his father?

It hurt. It hurt so sharply he stopped breathing. *Lir*-shape, abruptly, was threatened; with effort, he found his balance.

Down, he told Teel.

Aidan stumbled on landing because he took back human form more quickly than usual. Booted feet struck earth and he fell, digging an elbow into turf. For a moment he held his position, awkward though it was, then rolled over onto his back. The day was temperate and bright, the turf immensely comfortable. He was sleepy and disinclined to get up quite yet. So he linked hands across his abdomen and stayed where he was, casually crossing ankles.

"I am a fool," he said aloud. "I set out to look for a wife, and decide I want the first woman I see. I think nothing of asking, because I have never needed to ask: I am, everyone tells me, destined to be the Mujhar of Homana."

Teel perched on Aidan's boot toe, saying nothing.

"She is beautiful rather than plain, which only sweetens the cookpot. I look at her and see a woman I would like to take to bed, which makes her more attractive. And then, in addition, she is a woman I could *like* . . . a woman I *do* like . . ." Aidan sighed deeply. "It is too much to hope for a *cheysula* I could like and love, and a woman who pleasures my bed. Princes and kings only rarely find such things . . . Hart did, with Ilsa, and I assume Keely as well, from what they say of her . . . but what room is there for me? Blythe loves Tevis."

"Blythe loves Tevis." He realized, as he said the words, the pain was already less. It had been foolish of him to care so much, even though that care had been more for finding a woman whose *potential* suited him. Blythe would have been perfect, but Blythe was no longer free. And that, he realized unhappily, had made him want her so much. Had she been free of Tevis, it might not have been the same.

He had wanted the unattainable, which had made him want her the more.

Some men, he knew, would hunt her nonetheless, counting the game much sweeter for her unwillingness to be caught, and the fillip of competition. But that was not Aidan's way.

To Teel, he grinned sardonic amusement. "I want it simple," he said. "Of all the royal fledglings hatched in fifty years, *I* may be the most suited to an arranged marriage. And yet I am left free to choose." He laughed aloud. "How many of my kin would have traded places with me?"

But the amusement faded quickly. He knew at least one: his mother. Left to her own devices, she would have married Corin. And he, born to them, would have been heir to Atvia instead of heir to the Lion.

But I would not have been me. I would have been different— *and therefore my tahlmorra, and the prophecy as well.*

It sobered him. Unsettled, Aidan sat up even as Teel

lifted from his boot toe. He had managed, in contemplation, to remind himself of things too great for him to ignore.

Of Hunters in the woodlands and Weavers at the loom. And gold links on his belt, growing heavier by the day.

Aidan pressed himself up from the ground. Time he went back to Lestra.

He blurred into *lir*-shape. *Time the baby was born, so I can go on to Erinn.*

Six

Aidan knew it the moment he saw them. *Kivarna* or no, he knew. They gave it away in the tiny intimacies of bedmates: a brief, burning glance exchanged, a lingering touch, the small alterations in movement. In Tevis he saw a muted victory, the pride and satisfaction of a man who has won the woman he wanted; in Blythe, the languid, sensual movements of a woman now truly a woman, and the soft new warmth in her eyes.

He sat down at the common table, troubled, and looked at once to Hart. This was no time to speak of it—all kin, save for Ilsa and Dulcie, were present at the meal—but then he was not entirely convinced it was his place to speak of it at all. Nothing official had been said regarding his potential suit, and therefore Blythe's virginity did not really concern him as a successor to the Lion. But as a kinsman, it did.

With a flicker of disgust, he reached for cider. Even as a kinsman it was not his concern; Blythe was a free woman unbound by betrothals and arrangements, as well as a Cheysuli. It was her parents' place to determine the rightness or wrongness of her actions, and even then she remained Cheysuli. Hart would be denying one of the foremost tenets of the clans—that of free choice in bedpartners—if he protested. And Ilsa had made it plain Tevis met the requirements for marriage into royalty. They had done nothing wrong, only precipitated the ceremony.

Cluna and Jennet sat down on either side of Aidan. Warily, he kept an eye on both; they giggled, paid him elaborate courtesies, attempted to play the part—albeit shared—of chatelaine in lieu in Ilsa, whose place it properly was. In Ilsa's absence the role fell to Blythe, but her attention to duties was sorely preempted by Tevis.

Hart seemed oblivious to it all, and there was reason. "Ilsa believes the child could be born tonight or tomorrow—she should know, after six children—so I have set in motion the preparations for a proper celebration. The gods willing, we will be swearing homage to a new prince of Solinde before the week is out."

Aidan raised his cup. "Gods willing, *su'fali*."

Tevis and Blythe, most conspicuously, did not look at one another.

Aidan cleared his throat. "Where is Dulcie?"

It was Jennet who answered for her father. "Oh, *she* cannot come to meals yet. She makes too much of a mess."

"So do you," Hart said mildly. "You have just spilled jam on your tunic."

Jennet, undismayed, scooped it off with a finger. "When are we going hawking?" she asked. "I heard you speaking about it last night."

Hart sipped cider. "I thought after the meal. I have already ordered the horses and hawks prepared." He glanced at his eldest. "I do not mean to rob you of the day, but perhaps it is best if you stayed with your *jehana*. She may have need of you."

Blythe opened her mouth as if to protest, but closed it almost immediately. Aidan saw the glance at Tevis, the dusky color in her face. Had she thought to spend the day in bed with the man?

"Not fair," Cluna put in. "Rael *always* sees the game first, and *always* makes the first kill."

Hart smiled, eyes bright. "Then I will tell Rael not to stoop, and let the rest of you compete."

Tevis, who sat directly across from Aidan, smiled. It was a strangely triumphant smile, full of subtle nuances and knowledge, but Aidan understood it. As Tevis met his eyes, he understood it all too well. The competition for Blythe, though unacknowledged, was over. Whose hawk killed first was of no importance to Tevis, who had already won the hunt.

In silence, Aidan lifted his tankard and slightly inclined his head. Something flickered briefly in Tevis' eyes—surprise? disbelief?—and then he smiled, lifted his own tankard and acknowledged the salute. Beneath the table, Aidan knew, fingers touched, then linked.

In Cheysuli leathers, leggings and linen tunics, Cluna and Jennet were towheaded warriors riding out of the Keep; in this case, the Keep was Lestra. Outdoors, well free of the confines of the castle—and the preferences of their mother— they could lose themselves in the freedom of the Cheysuli half of their blood. Both girls reveled in it, shouting aloud their excitement. Both rode spirited horses, managing them with ease.

Hart, looking after them with Dulcie perched in the saddle before him, smiled as they rode by Tevis to fall into the lead.

"They chafe at walls," Aidan remarked, "though they may not know it yet."

Hart nodded. "The Cheysuli in them. Ilsa often forgets—no one thinks of my shapechanger blood with blue eyes and Ilsa's hair—but I never do. They are as Cheysuli as I ever was; they only lack the color."

Tevis rode abreast. "Will they have any *lir* of their own?"

Hart shook his head. "Unlikely. It is mostly a gift given to warriors, though occasionally a woman can speak with the *lir*, or shift shape. My *rujholla*, Keely, can, but it has yet to show itself in my line."

Tevis' eyes were on Dulcie. "What of the smallest one? She, of all your children, most resembles a true Cheysuli."

Hart laughed. "Aye, she does—even more than Aidan or me. As for the *lir*-gifts, who can say? She is too young yet to show them, even if they are hers."

"Would it matter?" Aidan asked Tevis. "What if Blythe were blessed?"

Tevis did not hesitate. "I do not care what she can do, or what her blood is made of. I do not care who she *is*, only that she be mine." He paused. "Should the Prince of Solinde be willing."

Well, Aidan reflected, *now it is out in the open.*

Hart's left arm was wound around Dulcie, holding her against his chest. Right-handed, he guided his mount. Not Bane's black son, but a quieter, more mannered bay mare. Faintly, he smiled. "It is for Blythe to say."

"But—my lord—"

"For Blythe," Hart repeated. "If you were not worthy of her, you would not be sharing her roof."

Or her bed? But Aidan shook that off; Hart could not know. *And now it is official. If Tevis has been waiting for some sure sign of parental approval, he need not doubt anymore.*

Shrieking, Cluna and Jennet went tearing across the meadow. Aidan nearly winced. "They will scare the game that way."

"Did you come expecting to catch some?" Hart asked in surprise. "No . . . we will see little enough with *those* two riding free. But it is an excuse to get away. No one begrudges it."

Aidan nearly laughed. "Then the walls chafe *you.*"

"Aye," Hart agreed fervently. "I have never become accustomed . . . a holdover, I think, from the days we lived in Keeps. Walls bind our souls . . ." He looked at Tevis, riding quietly beside Aidan. "Do the mountains ever chafe you? High Crags is so isolated . . . do you ever wish for something else?"

Something indefinable flared in brown eyes. Then Tevis looked at the hooded hawk riding quietly on his saddlebow. "Always," he said quietly.

For one moment Aidan's *kivarna* came to life. And then died away to ash, telling him nothing of the man. Tevis was closed to him.

Why not? he wondered sourly. *He has what he wants. What else is there to read?*

"There," Hart said urgently. "Rael has seen something."

The hawk spiraled lazily, then drifted downward. Aidan was about to remind Hart that the hawk was not to hunt first, but a piercing scream broke the air as Rael abruptly stooped.

"*Cluna!*" Hart cried. He caught Dulcie against his chest in one firm arm and set his heels to the mare.

Teel took to the air as Aidan went after Hart. Tevis brought up the rear, though the hawk he carried on his saddlebow screeched and rang jess-bells in protest. They could hear Jennet shouting.

Cluna was huddled against the ground, crying. Close by, Rael drove again and again at the speckled snake, dodging the reptile's deadly strikes. The hawk was too large to be maneuverable, but his attempts distracted the snake from Cluna.

Hart tried to dismount, cursing, but Dulcie's clutching

arms tangled his efforts. Jennet, silent now and white-faced, stood nearby with the horses, too frightened to go closer.

Cluna wailed something in Solindish Aidan did not understand. But he could tell by the way she held her left arm cradled against her chest the snake had bitten her. If they did not kill it and reach her quickly, it could be too late to save her.

Teel, he said through the link, swinging off his mount even as Hart finished dismounting. Tevis, too, was on the ground, saying something in Solindish.

"Wait!" Aidan snagged Hart's arm and pulled him back. "Let our *lir* do the work . . . too many of us might spoil their chance. And there is Dulcie to think of—"

Jennet wailed something, still clutching reins. Hart's head snapped in her direction. "Did it strike you? Jennet—did the snake bite you also?"

Wordlessly she shook her head. Tears streaked her face. "No—no—only Cluna—"

Teel danced around the snake, seducing it this way and that. From behind came Rael, snatching at the place behind its head. Talons sank deeply, locking, and then Rael rose to fly clear of them all, dangling the writhing snake.

"Here—" Hart thrust Dulcie into Aidan's arms.

Even as he did so, Tevis was at Cluna's side. The knife flashed in his hand as he cut into the soft underflesh of her forearm, bisecting fang marks already swollen and discolored. Cluna whimpered but otherwise held her silence, and Tevis set his mouth over the cuts to suck the venom from her arm. The knife, forgotten, fell to the grass.

Jennet deserted her post with the horses and came to Aidan, reaching out to clutch a hand in hers. He felt her trembling through his own flesh; through his *kivarna* he sensed shock, anguish, shame, and a spirit full of fear.

In Solindish, she said something. Aidan put a gentle hand on her blonde head. Hair, as always, straggled out of its braid. "I have a poor grasp of your tongue, *meijhana*. I am sorry."

She gulped a swallow and tried again in Homanan. "I am *afraid*—"

"No need," he told her quietly. "Your *jehan* is Cheysuli, remember? He need only call on the earth magic."

Her face was very pale. "But he only has one hand—"

"*Shansu, meijhana*—I promise, it makes no difference. Your *jehan* is not crippled."

"But he cannot be a warrior. Not a real one, because of his hand. He *said* so."

In the daughter he heard a measure of the father's shame and anguish. Aidan's hand tightened briefly on her head, then slipped to cup a shoulder tightly. "Your *jehan* is as much a warrior as any Cheysuli I know. He is denied clan-rights through old-fashioned ignorance, not a failure on his part. I promise you, *meijhana*, your *rujholla* will be well."

Cluna, crying silently, reached for Hart as he knelt to her. Tevis moved away as the father scooped up his daughter. "Bleeding—" she quavered.

"For the best," Hart told her. "Come, *meijhana*—I will take you back to the castle. There I can summon the earth magic."

"Why not here?" Aidan asked. "I can give you whatever help you need."

"My thanks, but no. It will be frightening enough for her, even as it heals. It will be better done in her own room, where she will feel safer. Tevis has bled her quickly enough . . . the rest can wait that long." He approached the horses, cradling Cluna in both arms. "Jennet?"

She broke away from Aidan, twisting hands into tunic. "My fault," she whispered. "The horse was afraid of the snake. Cluna fell when he sprang aside, and the snake bit her—" She lost her Homanan entirely and slipped again into Solindish, speaking too quickly for Aidan to decipher. But he saw Hart's compassion as he paused briefly by her side.

"No, *meijhana*, it is not your fault. Now mount your horse—you will come back with us." He glanced at Aidan. "Can you and Tevis bring Dulcie?"

"Of course, *su'fali*." Aidan smiled as the girl twisted in his arms to reach a fist in her father's direction. "I would not give her up when I have only just met her."

Tevis rose from where he had knelt to bleed Cluna. "I will bring her horse."

Distracted, Hart nodded and turned to his own mount. He set Cluna up into the saddle and hastily mounted, gathering her in against him as he hooked the cuffed stump around her abdomen. Her head tipped back against his shoulder, displaying a too-pale face. Dulcie, who had held the place first, protested in Aidan's arms.

Hart looked at Jennet. "Hurry," he told her, sending her flying to her mount. In a moment both horses and the great hawk were gone.

Aidan looked at Tevis. "No doubt he will remember to thank you when Cluna is settled. Until then, accept *my* gratitude."

Tevis' smile was faint. "For Cluna, if not for Blythe?"

Aidan sighed. "Aye, well . . . I will not contest it. You know as well as I that if I did, it would make no difference. I am neither blind nor a fool . . . you have won, Tevis. Be proud, but not *too* proud; she is still my kinswoman, and Cheysuli. When you marry one of us, you marry us all."

"If I wanted a red-haired Cheysuli as my kinsman, I would have bedded *you*."

Holding Dulcie, Aidan froze. And then he heard the quiet irony in Tevis' tone as the High Crags lord turned to gather up the reins of Cluna's mount, patiently cropping grass.

He smiled crookedly. *Once I rid myself of regret over Blythe, I may even like the man—*

Something glinted in the grass. "Wait." Aidan bent to pick up Tevis' knife. "Here—you have forgotten." He held it out.

Tevis felt at his sheath, found it empty, put out his hand with a murmured word of thanks. Aidan set the knife into Tevis' outstretched hand, and in that brief moment of contact the *kivarna* flared to life. Tevis was open to him.

Hostility. Pride. Barely suppressed ambition. Impatience that he must wait, when so much was his for the taking.

Aidan nearly gaped. "You *do* want the throne! The throne and everything else!"

Ale-brown eyes were smoky. Tevis did not even bother to ask Aidan how he knew. "Aye," he said harshly. "I want it back. I want *everything* back."

"Back," Aidan echoed. "But it was never yours—"

Tevis cut him off. "Not mine, but it would have been Dar's. *He* was heir to Solinde, even heir to Ilsa . . . but the shapechanger came here and took it, took her, took it all—"

"He *inherited*," Aidan declared, "from his father, the Mujhar, who inherited it from *his* father, who was bequeathed it by Carillon."

"Do you think I care about Homanan history? Cheysuli history?" Tevis stepped close. His hand gripped the knife.

"By all the gods of Solinde, shapechanger, what do you think I am? A young boy content to sit in silence while his homeland is given over to the usurper? We are not so different as that, shapechanger blood or no . . . I know you well enough to say with complete conviction that you would do the same."

Aidan thought it best to ignore the latter, since he was grimly aware how closely Tevis came to the truth. Instead, he focused on what he knew to be patently false. "It was hardly usurped, Solindish. Carillon won it in battle. It was his to bequeath as he wished, and it was to *my* kin it came. Solinde is ours, now."

"Mine," Tevis said flatly. "Or, more like, my son's." He smiled as he saw Aidan's start. "What—did you think I meant to do murder? Do you think I want Blythe merely to serve my own ends? No, shapechanger . . . I want Blythe for Blythe's sake, *and* for the sake of Solinde. The throne is not meant to be mine—I honor my ancestor-kings too much to count *myself* worthy of it—but if the shapechanger gets no son on the queen, then the task falls to me. *I* will sire the heir . . . and in my lifetime, if not Dar's, I will see a High Crags man on the throne."

Aidan held Dulcie more tightly as she squirmed. "And if the queen bears a son? What then, Tevis? Your plan is in disarray."

Lips parted as if Tevis intended a blistering retort. But instead he smiled. It was a crooked, twisted smile, altering his intensity into rueful acknowledgment. "If there is a son born to Ilsa, then my hopes are vanquished. All my ambitions fail." His eyes did not waver. "My lord of Homana, I am neither a fool, nor ignorant. I want what is best for Solinde. So did Dar, even if he was unfortunate enough to go about it the wrong way—"

Aidan's tone was vicious. "He cut off my uncle's hand and then gave him to the Ihlini. To Strahan himself, who nearly destroyed him."

Tevis gestured acknowledgment. "Aye, well . . . that was Dar. I have been told he was impetuous and obsessed—"

"And you are not?"

Muscles flexed briefly in Tevis's face. "I mean no harm to you, or to the man who calls himself Prince of Solinde. There is such a thing as a peaceful revolution, my lord . . . if I marry Blythe and sire a son, the revolution is accomplished without bloodshed. *That* is how I fight."

Aidan shifted Dulcie against his shoulder, focus fragmented by her presence and her pettish discomfort. She wanted her father, not him; Aidan did not blame her.

He sighed. "Then you fight more wisely than your kinsman."

Tevis smiled faintly. "Then perhaps I will succeed where he failed."

Resentment boiled up. Aidan wanted to hit him. He did not. "Did you come here for this? Did you come down from your mountain fastness to seduce a king's daughter?"

And realized, as he asked it, he might ask it of himself, while changing the words a little. It had all been so simple: he would go to Solinde, setting aside the desperation, and find himself a wife. It would satisfy everything: rank, title, body, even the need for escape.

But there was Tevis to be faced. "Did you?" he repeated, more intensely than before. Now it applied to them both.

Tevis turned his back. Fluidly he swung up into the saddle, then looked down on Aidan. "The seduction was accomplished long before I came. It was done in writing, my lord of Homana . . . a courtship between two mothers desiring the best for their eldest children. They made it easy for me . . . I saw my chance, and I took it. Only a fool would have refused."

Aidan felt impotent. "If Blythe suffers for this—"

Tevis gathered reins, then bent to catch Cluna's horse. "She will not," he said flatly. "I am a patriot, Homanan . . . a loyal Solindishman. But I am also a *man*. What man, looking at her, would ever want to hurt her? What man, sharing her bed, would want to drive her from it?"

Aidan could offer no answer. Holding Dulcie, bereft of speech, he watched Tevis ride away towing Cluna's horse behind him.

When he was gone, Aidan sighed and pressed a cheek against Dulcie's head. "Oh, Dulcie-*meijhana*, what do we do now?"

Overhead, Teel croaked. *Go back to the castle,* he said. *There is nothing* to *do, here.*

Disgruntled, Aidan went to his horse and mounted, taking extra care with Dulcie. Then he turned back toward Lestra.

There was nothing *to* do, here. But plenty to do, there.

Seven

Aidan found the castle in an uproar when he rode in with Dulcie. He believed at first it was because of Cluna; he discovered almost at once Ilsa was in labor.

A nursemaid came immediately for Dulcie, releasing him from his unexpected duty. The girl was glad to go, but not before she latched onto a handful of ruddy hair and tugged; Aidan, wincing, carefully peeled fingers away and freed himself, then bent and kissed Dulcie briefly on the forehead.

The nursemaid, smiling, told him he was to go at once to the prince's private solar, where the rest of the family gathered. Aidan took his leave, giving Teel his freedom to do as he wished, and went to find the others.

Hart was in a chair, perched stiffly on the edge with braced legs spread, elbows resting on thighs. Absently he massaged the skin of his forearm at the edge of the leather cuff. He hardly glanced up as Aidan entered. His dark Cheysuli face was taut and biscut-gray.

"What of Cluna?" Aidan asked. Only Blythe, Hart, and Tevis were present.

Hart shifted slightly. "In bed. The healing is done. There is a slight fever, but it will pass."

Aidan closed the door. Though he asked the question of Hart, he looked directly at Tevis. "And the queen?"

Tevis, seated with Blythe standing next to him, said nothing.

Hart abruptly thrust himself deep into the chair, stretching one side of his face out of shape as he scrubbed at it one-handed. "It will be hours, always hours. Blythe was an easy birth—" He glanced briefly at his eldest, smiling absently, then shifted in the chair as if he could find no favored position, "—but the others have been more difficult."

Quietly, Tevis unwound himself from his chair and leaned forward to pour wine. He rose, brought the cup to Aidan, handed it to him. He said nothing, but his gaze was direct and unwavering.

He wonders if I will say anything to Hart. Aidan accepted the cup. *"Leijhana tu'sai."*

If Tevis understood the Old Tongue, he made no indication. He merely waited.

Inwardly, Aidan sighed. Much as he disliked the situation, he saw no reason to add to Hart's concerns at the moment. Imperceptibly, he shook his head at Tevis. Once more he surrendered the war.

Something indefinable entered clear brown eyes. For a moment there was a reassessment, then an odd respect. Tevis smiled faintly. The sunlight slanting through the casements fell fully on his face, limning good bones and fine skin, shining in thick dark hair. He would, Aidan thought, sire handsome sons; the daughters, with Blythe as mother, would be beautiful.

As imperceptibly, Tevis inclined his head in thanks. Then abruptly swung on his heel and went directly to Hart. "My lord, there is something I must say."

Aidan, frowning, watched him closely. He heard the subtle deference in the High Crags dialect. He had never heard it before. Tevis was, he realized, a man of eloquent charm. Aidan began to believe he was capable of anything.

Hart merely glanced at him in distraction. "Let it wait."

"No, my lord. It cannot."

"Tevis?" Even Blythe was nonplussed.

He lifted a silencing finger without looking at her. His eyes were locked on Hart. "My lord, I must admit to you I have not been the man you believed I was. And while it is quite true I love and honor your daughter and wish only to make her happy, there is something more. I will not lie any longer."

Aidan stood very still. *He plays a dangerous game.*

Hart's eyes were steady as he looked into the taut face. "You mean to tell me you covet the throne of Solinde."

Color drained from Tevis. "My lord . . . you knew—?"

From Blythe, a blurt of shock.

Hart merely shrugged. "I have known it for some time." He glanced briefly at Aidan, then straightened in the chair. His voice was perfectly even. "You are not the first, and will not be the last. I have three other daughters."

"My lord—if you *knew*—?"

"—why did I allow you to remain?" Hart looked at Blythe. "Because my daughter loves you. And you, in your way, love her. What sense is there in ending something desired by you both, merely because you are ambitious?"

Tevis smoothed the velvet of his doublet over one arm. "Even if those ambitions could threaten your sovereignty?"

Hart stroked his bottom lip with a finger, contemplating the young man standing before him. Eventually, he smiled. "When you are young, it is quite easy to believe in personal convictions. It is quite easy to be completely committed to a thing, as you are to Solinde. A zealot blinds himself, as he must, in order to succeed. But in that blinding, he cuts off a part of himself that makes the difference between success and failure."

"My lord—?"

Hart smiled. "The key to your strength lies in my daughter. But if you should come against me, she will turn on you. And you will then have nothing, even as Dar did." He paused delicately. "With the same result."

Blythe's face was white. Tevis said nothing.

Hart smiled again. "You can have what you want *without* forcing the issue . . . if the queen bears me no son."

Tevis still said nothing.

Hart sighed. "Do you think I want Solinde to stay mired in internal bickering? I know very well there are still factions who desire me ousted, and who might turn to violence to accomplish it. Executing Dar of High Crags—a known traitor —silenced his followers for a time, but it will not last forever. The peace of this realm rests entirely with Ilsa— unless it rests with you."

"Me," Tevis said numbly.

"A son out of Ilsa is of Bellam's line. *That* line has more claim than any you can muster . . . High Crags is, after all, an isolated mountain domain with geographically limited power." Hart tilted his head. "If she gives me that son, the factions are undone. But if she does *not,* then the succession falls to another. To Blythe, as you well know—through the son she could bear." Hart smiled. "It will not put you on the throne any more than it would have put Dar there . . . but then fathers often gain power through the manipulation of their children."

Blythe was looking at Tevis. Brief hope flickered in Aidan. *If he has lost her with this . . .*

Hart's voice was soft. "If you marry her, you stay here.

You give up your claim on High Crags and become a vassal to *me.*"

Tevis shut his eyes. Then opened them and quietly knelt before the Prince of Solinde. "My lord, I have wronged you."

Hart smiled. "You underestimated me."

The tone was heartfelt. *"Aye."*

"Ah, well, I have spent the last twenty-two years of my life being underestimated by the Solindish. Someday perhaps they will look past the gold I wear—and the hawk who answers my bidding—and see the man instead."

"Aye, my lord. I have no doubt they will . . . if they have not blinded themselves completely."

The dry irony surprised Aidan. But then it was not in Tevis to be completely undone; he was, if nothing else, a survivor. For all his thwarted ambitions, he probably *would* make a loyal vassal.

And a good example for the others. Aidan smiled. *Su'fali, I, too, underestimated you. Perhaps one day your kin will look past the follies of your youth to the king you have become.*

Hart flicked a hand. "Go. There will be another time for the oath. Take my daughter and go . . . I think there are things you have to say to one another—in private."

Tevis wet dry lips and rose, turning to look at Blythe. For a long moment he said nothing. Then, very quietly, "Will you come?"

Color flared in her face. "I am, if nothing else, daughter to my father. Do you think I would allow you to harm him in any way? Do you think I would let you *dare?*"

"No," he answered quietly. "That I have always known."

"Then be reminded of it!" she snapped. Blythe looked at her father, then briefly at Aidan. Color stained her face: shame, embarrassment; Tevis had been unmasked before the man most likely to gloat. She glanced back at Tevis. "Indeed, I will come. And we *will* talk, my lord of High Crags. About *everything.*"

Aidan moved aside as Blythe swept out of the chamber. Tevis followed after a brief bow in Hart's direction. The door thumped closed behind them.

Hart looked at his nephew. "I have had him watched from the beginning. The reason Dar nearly succeeded was because I did not take him seriously, and because I did not know what he was doing. This way, Tevis does nothing without my knowledge."

"Commendable, *su'fali*."

Hart smiled faintly. "But you think I am wasting my daughter when there could be another man more suited to her . . . a man more suitable for the throne."

Aidan moved to the nearest chair and sat down, sipping at last from the wine Tevis had given him. He shrugged. "I will have a throne, *su'fali*. Do I need another?"

Hart laughed. "The Lion has proved most selfish in the past. I doubt it would change now."

In companionable silence, they took up the Bezat bowl set on the table between them and began to play. There was nothing to do, but wait.

Aidan looked at his uncle, whose bowed head as he studied the game pieces hid much of his expression. *We wait,* he reflected apprehensively, *on the future of Solinde.* And then, as Hart drew from the bowl, *Was it this difficult for my parents, waiting to see if I would live or die? If the Lion would have an heir?*

Hart turned over the piece. It was blank on either side.

"Bezat," Hart said quietly. "You are dead."

Aidan put down the winecup. His taste for the game was gone.

He was very nearly asleep when at last the servant came. The hours, as Hart had promised, were many; it was evening, well past dinner, and they had drunk too much wine. Aidan did not have a head for so much, and wanted no more than to go to bed. But Hart had desired company to pass the time, and they had shared the hours in discussion of all manner of things. Aidan could only remember part of them.

He was jerked into wakefulness as the servant opened the door and murmured something to Hart, who was less circumspect. The Prince of Solinde leaped to his feet, moved to buffet Aidan's muzzy head in an excess of joy and emotion, and told him there was a son.

"A son," Aidan echoed dutifully, but by then Hart was gone. "A *son*," he said again, brightening with comprehension, and pushed himself out of the chair.

Most of the family and a few servants gathered in an antechamber near Ilsa's royal apartments. Tevis waited by a deep casment, leaning into the sill, as if trying to hide himself in shadow. Blythe, uncharacteristically, was not with him; instead, she waited nervously by the door even as Aidan entered. Cluna was not present—probably sleeping out the fever—but Jennet was. She, like Tevis, stood very quietly out of the way, half lost in the shadows. Her bedrobe was clutched in two rigid fists.

Aidan knew at once. He crossed the chamber to her. "Come," he said gently, and led her to a chair. She sat down as he asked, then stared blindly at him as he pulled over a stool for himself. Aidan took her hands into his own. "Speaking of it will help."

There was none of the pert forwardness in her manner he had come to expect. Fair hair was loose for sleeping, shining palely in candlelight. She wore a white linen nightrail and rich blue woolen bedrobe, tangled around her ankles. Her hands in his were cold.

Jennet drew in a very deep breath. "I am glad there is a son. A prince for Solinde."

Aidan nodded. "But you believe his coming will make your *jehan* blind to you."

Jennet's mouth trembled. "It will." Another breath. "He has Blythe. She was always his favorite. And now he has a son, and there will be no more room for Cluna and me."

"You have asked him this, of course."

Blue eyes widened. "No!"

He affected mild surprise. "Then how can you know?"

"I just do."

She was not Erinnish. There was no *kivarna* in her, only fear and loneliness. Aidan squeezed her hands. "It is better you do not put words in his mouth or feelings in his heart, unless you know them for fact. It would hurt him deeply if he knew you felt this way."

"But—what if he does?"

"I promise you, he does not. On the life of my *lir*, Jennet—and you know how binding an oath that is."

Clearly, she did. But her misery was unabated.

Aidan squeezed again. "You yourself are a princess, *meijhana*. You are old enough to understand that a realm needs a king, and the king an heir to follow. For too long Solinde has been without that heir. But princesses are important as well. Solinde has need of them also."

Jennet's mouth flattened. "Only because *jehan* can marry us off to men he wants to please."

The bitterness far surpassed her years. Aidan looked at her with renewed attention. "Has someone told you that?"

She shrugged. "I heard Blythe say something like to Tevis earlier." Blue eyes flickered. "She was angry."

Aidan did not smile. "Aye, so she was."

Jennet's worried expression came back. "I do not understand. Blythe has always wanted to marry Tevis. From the beginning."

Aidan could not help himself. "Does she not anymore?"

Jennet shrugged; Blythe was not, at the moment, her concern. "She told him she would . . . that between them they had made certain she would have to." She frowned. "I did not understand that."

"No," Aidan agreed, thinking it was best. "I think you need not worry about such things yet. And I think, when the time comes, you will have even less to worry about—I think *no one* could force you to marry a man you did not wish to." He smiled. "Now, as to the new prince . . . I will not lie to you, Jennet. It may *seem* your father has forgotten you at first, in the newness of having a son, but it will pass. Your *jehan* will never replace you with anyone. He could not; not one else is Jennet."

She studied him solemnly, judging the worth of his words. "Do you promise that on the life of your *lir*?"

She was, he thought, a true daughter of royalty, seeking assurances in everything. He smiled, released her hands, touched her head briefly as he rose. "I promise."

Hart came into the chamber from the adjoining apartments. As he saw them he smiled, eyes alight. "Solinde has a prince," he announced with quiet pride, "*and* a healthy queen."

Jennet threw herself across the chamber and climbed into his arms as he caught her. He laughed aloud; so did Jennet. She shed the burgeoning maturity Aidan had seen and was merely a child again, at peace in her father's arms.

Aidan looked at Tevis and found him looking back. The young lord of High Crags wore an odd expression, and once again Aidan found his feelings masked. The *kivarna* was silent.

Tevis smiled. It was a smile of bittersweet defeat; of comprehension and acceptance. Something glittered in his eyes. A brief, eloquent gesture told Aidan Tevis fully understood the import of the boy's birth; his hopes for the throne, through *his* son, were extinguished. All Blythe could give him now was a nephew, much as he was himself. A royal nephew, perhaps, but absent from the line of succession.

Aidan looked at Blythe. She also watched Tevis, as if judging him even as Aidan did. Her expression was unreadable.

Reflexively, Aidan went into the link to Teel. *Do you think there may yet be a chance?*

But then Blythe crossed the chamber to Tevis, who cupped her face in his hand.

Aidan sighed. *No.*

From Teel there was nothing, who undoubtedly had known.

Eight

In three days' time, Hart called for an official naming ceremony. Cheysuli custom decreed the father must examine the naked infant for physical flaws, after the ancient ways mandating wholeness in a warrior; then, finding him unblemished, name him aloud to the gods and those kin assembled.

But for the newborn prince there was more: according to Solindish custom there must be named a second-father, a man bound to keep the child from harm should anything befall the natural parents. So Hart assembled everyone in a private audience chamber to appease both halves of the child's heritage.

Hart, with Ilsa beside him, stood on a low dais. On a polished perch behind them was Rael, jet-and-white in sunlight. The infant boy was cradled against his father's leather-clad chest in strong, dark arms shining with *lir*-gold. Hart had never looked happier, Aidan thought, as he smiled down into the baby's sleeping face. His pride was manifest, and yet Aidan wondered if the Cheysuli portion of the ceremony would bring unexpected anguish. Hart would be required to examine his son for physical flaws before he could name him, yet he himself was *kinwrecked*, expelled from the clans because of his missing hand. It was a harsh reality once required in times of hardship, yet no longer necessary. Brennan had tried to have the custom changed by appealing to Clan Council, but had failed to sway the men who declared too many of the old ways already had been lost.

It is Ilsa who keeps the pain at bay, Aidan reflected, gazing at the woman who stood at Hart's left side.

One pale, slender hand gently rested on his arm. The trace of fatigue in her face was tempered by a transcendent joy illuminating her already considerable beauty. There was an elegance in the woman unmatched by any Aidan had seen. He was, as always, taken aback by it. Even the glittering jeweled clasps fastening the coils of pale hair to her head could not compete with the brilliance of her eyes as she gazed out upon the people called to witness the naming of her son.

Blythe stood quietly with Tevis; Cluna, mostly recovered, stood with Jennet. Dulcie resided in Aidan's arms, though a nursemaid waited nearby to release him from the duty should the child prove tiresome. For the moment she was fascinated by the torque around his neck; smiling, Aidan unwound thin fingers from it and tried to bribe her with a coin so she would not tug quite so firmly.

Hart smiled brilliantly at them all. "This child is a child of two realms and two heritages, and both should be honored. No man should turn his back on any part of himself, for it is the sum of those parts that makes him what he is. So we have assembled you today to name this child after the fashion of Solinde *and* Homana, so no gods may be offended, and no race be overlooked."

Aidan glanced at Tevis, standing quietly to one side, and wondered how much it chafed the young lord of High Crags to see his hopes dashed so publicly. Tevis' face was expressionless, save for a brightness of his eyes as he looked at his liege lord and newborn prince. He gave nothing away of his thoughts.

Hart's voice jerked Aidan's attention back to the dais. "A Solindish child—and particularly a royal one—must have a second-father. It is not so different from the Cheysuli custom of a liege man in Homana, set to ward the Mujhar from physical threat . . . a second-father also tends the welfare of the child."

Hart settled the infant into the crook of his left arm and carefully peeled back the linen wrappings, unfolding the child from his cocoon. When he was free of the wrappings and entirely naked, Hart counted aloud the fingers and toes, looked into the tiny, flat ears, examined the unfocused eyes and made certain the small manhood was intact. Then he displayed the child to all of them.

"Before the gods of Homana, who are everywhere, I declare this child whole and free of blemish, acceptable to kin and clan. There is no taint in flesh or blood. By this naming he becomes a true Cheysuli, destined for a *lir* and loyal service to the prophecy." He drew in a breath and steadied his voice; even across the chamber, Aidan felt the upsurge of emotion. "I name this child Owain, son of Hart and Ilsa; now known as Prince Owain, heir to the throne of Solinde. I do this with the full blessing of the gods, and can only hope they gift him with a worthy *tahlmorra*." Briefly, he looked at Aidan. "No man may choose his, and certainly not a child."

Aidan turned as the nursemaid came forward and settled Dulcie into her arms. Then he stepped forward to bow his head in brief homage to Hart. Carefully he took up Owain's tiny right hand and kissed it. In his heart he murmured the words of a private kinsman's blessing, wishing health and happiness on the child; aloud he spoke similar words in the Old Tongue, feeling the weight of two gold links at his belt as he did so.

Finished, he inclined his head once again, made the Cheysuli gesture of *tahlmorra*, and turned to face the others.

"This child is a child of the gods. His *tahlmorra* is theirs to impart; their service is his to perform. *Tahlmorra lujhala mei wiccan, cheysu.* May the gods grant this child a perfect service to the prophecy of the Firstborn, and to the people of Solinde, whom one day he will rule."

He waited. The expected response came from those who knew it: *"Ru'shalla-tu."* May it be so.

Aidan smiled. His part in the ceremony was done. He returned to his place, took Dulcie back, waited.

"Leijhana tu'sai," Hart said quietly, eyes aglint, then rewrapped the newly-named Prince Owain. He left one hand and arm free. "It is a second-father's duty to care for this child, should something befall the natural parents. It is his duty to raise this child as his own, treating him as his own, sparing him nothing he would not spare children of his own body, giving him no more or less than he would give children of his own body.

"Upon reaching manhood the child shall go out of the second-father's house and make his own. But he will forever honor that man as his true-father—his *jehan*—with all the honor he would also give to the gods." Hart's face was solemn, but something lurked in his eyes. "The choosing of a second-father is never undertaken lightly. It is an honor bestowed a man who has proven himself strong and loyal. It is a mark of respect and trust, and is never undertaken without the full understanding of its responsibilities."

Hart's eyes rested briefly on Aidan. "A kinsman is often chosen, because there is like blood flowing in the veins and blood binds a man to another man more firmly than anything else. But others are honored as well." Hart smiled. "Tevis, Lord of High Crags."

Clear brown eyes widened almost imperceptibly. "My lord."

"Will you, as second-father, swear to raise Prince Owain as your own? Will you take an oath to serve this child as you would serve the Prince of Solinde, and any child of your body? Will you accept him as your liege lord, caring for his needs as he requires it, never failing this trust?"

Tevis, oddly, was pale. "My lord—you have spoken of a kinsman . . . what of Prince Aidan?"

Hart did not look at his nephew. "Aidan's *tahlmorra* takes him in another direction. We would have you for our son's second-father."

Next to Tevis, Blythe's face was alight. Aidan understood very well why Hart did as he did; it was, he thought, very clever. And undoubtedly would prove extremely fortuitous.

Tevis drew a deep, slow breath. "My lord . . . my lord, I will do anything you require. It will be my honor to serve Prince Owain as second-father."

Ilsa's smile was luminous. "We are honored by your oath."

Blythe pressed Tevis' arm. He approached slowly, head bowed in homage. When he stood before the dais, he knelt so as not to lift his head above that of the infant.

"Rise," Hart said. "Take his hand in yours."

Dazed, Tevis rose and reached out for the tiny hand. He stared at the baby's silk-smooth, fragile skin; the crumpled, sleep-creased face. "I swear," he said quietly. "I swear to raise you as a child of my own body. I swear to serve you. I accept you as my liege lord. I will care for your needs as you require it, and I swear I will never fail your trust." Tevis bent his head and kissed the tiny hand.

Blythe, Aidan saw, had tears in her eyes. Cluna and Jennet were solemn-faced, big-eyed; they understood full well the gravity of the ceremony. Ilsa, still clasping Hart's arm, looked on Tevis with great pride shining in her lovely face; Hart himself wore an expression of many things, not the least of them satisfaction and a quiet, contented triumph.

Inwardly, Aidan laughed. *Oh, aye, su'fali, you know exactly what you have done.*

Hart looked over Tevis' bowed head. His gaze met Aidan's. A new peace entered his eyes.

Aidan nodded acknowledgment. *He has his son . . . his future . . . and his immortality . . .*

Tevis stepped away. He bowed briefly, then returned to Blythe's side. His eyes were strange. He appeared singularly moved, but Aidan sensed no specific emotion through the *kivarna*. The gift, as always, was fickle. It would not be manipulated.

But Tevis, as if sensing Aidan's look, turned. For a moment his face was quite still, and then he smiled a genuine smile.

Aidan smiled back blandly, but inwardly he felt a tremendous sense of relief. *Perhaps, after all, he will be content with this.*

It was evening, in Hart's solar. The light was gone from the day, but candles filled the lack and set the chamber alight. They had succeeded in chasing the women from the room so they could forget the talk of new babies and turn their minds to other things, such as good wine, tall tales, and wagering.

Hart laughed aloud and leaned forward to scoop the winnings into his already impressive pile. Tevis swore mildly, counted what he had left, glanced to Aidan on his left. "Someone will have to stop him, before he robs us all."

Aidan grunted. "Not I. You see how little is left to me—*you* have more than I."

Tevis looked again at his stack of red-gold Solindish coins. It was much diminished, but he did have more than Aidan. He nodded to himself, took up his goblet of wine, drank half down.

Hart pointed. "There is that."

Aidan put a shielding hand over his heavy topaz ring. "This is my signet ring."

"Aye, well . . . it never stopped *me*. A man true to the game does not let such petty things as personal possessions stand in the way of a good wager."

Ruddy brows shot up. " 'A man true to the game'? Do you mean a man who has lost control?"

Hart scowled. "No."

Aidan could not resist it. "A man true to *himself* wagers nothing of importance."

Hart's scowl deepened. "Then what of those links on your belt? They serve no useful purpose."

Tevis nodded briefly. "I had wondered myself."

A hand locked over the links. "No."

"Why do you wear them, *harani*? Not for ornamentation—"

Aidan waved a hand. "I wear them because I want to. Here, if you are so hungry for a wager . . ." He pushed out the few remaining coins he had. "There. That will do. Small, perhaps, but a wager."

Hart sighed and rattled the Bezat bowl. The game was run through; the result, this time, was different.

"Hah!" Tevis cried. "You see? The face of fortune turns at last to one more deserving."

Glowering at the young man, Hart pushed the proper amount of coin back across the table. The sapphire ring on his finger glittered with icy fire; beside it rested the fiery ruby signet of the kings of Solinde. Save for the gold on his arms and in his left ear, the rings were the only jewelry Hart affected. The sapphire's setting matched that of Aidan's topaz, worked with tiny runes, and he recalled with a start that Hart was still considered a prince in Homana.

Aidan glanced at Tevis as he reached out to gather the coin. Like Hart, he wore a sapphire ring; were they fashionable this year? But his was not so massive, and the setting very new. The jet ring looked far older, set firmly in ancient gold.

Hart looked at Aidan intently. "You will have to play again."

"But I lost, *su'fali* . . . and that was the last of my coin."

Hart grunted. "Brennan gives you a light purse."

Aidan laughed and poured more wine. "He gives me all I need. I am not a profligate spender."

"Well?" Tevis asked. "How many in this game?"

"All three," Hart declared. "I will stake Aidan to more gold."

"Just so I can play? *Su'fali,* I swear, it is not that important to me—"

"You are my guest, and you will play." Hart's smile was charming. "I refuse to be the sole loser on my son's naming day."

Aidan dutifully lifted his cup. "To Prince Owain, may the gods grant him a good *tahlmorra*."

Hastily, Tevis raised his as well. "Prince Owain," he echoed absently, looking into the Bezat bowl. "Shall you stir?" He passed the bowl to Aidan.

Thus invited, he stuck two long fingers into the bowl and stirred the contents, rattling etched ivory against the rim. The game had mostly lost its appeal, since he now risked another man's coin, but it was good manners to continue when his uncle had been so generous. He only hoped he could win back enough to cover the loaned coin, since he hated being in debt.

"Here." Hart waited for Aidan to set down the bowl, then dipped in to draw out a piece.

They played mostly in silence, commenting briefly on the draws, or muttering dissatisfaction. Tevis' gaze was fixed on the bowl, but Aidan thought he did not really see it; his eyes had the dazed look of a man lost in thought elsewhere, no longer aware of his actions or surroundings. The skin of his face seemed tauter than ever, as if he was ill or under strain, but there was no other indication of his inattention.

"Tevis?" Hart said.

Tevis twitched on his stool. "My lord?"

"Yours is the next draw. For Aidan."

"Ah." He reached in, dug out the stone, turned it from one side to the other. "Bezat," he said blankly. "The deathstone."

Hart laughed at Aidan's resigned expression. "You lose! Now Tevis and I must play this out—"

The door was flung open. Dulcie's nursemaid stripped loose hair from her eyes. "My lord—you must come at once—"

Frowning, Hart pushed his stool away and rose. "Helda, what is it?"

"Oh, my lord—the *baby*—"

Hart threw down his winecup. It rang against the table even as it spilled a blood-red puddle onto polished wood. Aidan stood up so abruptly he overset his stool, and went after Hart; Tevis, white-faced, dropped the death-stone into the spreading wine and followed.

Aidan arrived in the nursery but a moment after Hart pushed his way through the crowding women. Ilsa was on her knees next to the cradle, clasping the linen-swathed infant to her breast. Her eyes were empty of everything save a harsh, horrible grief.

"Not again," Hart murmured, and then swung frenziedly on them all. "Out!" he shouted to the women. "All of you, *out*. At once."

Aidan and Tevis moved aside as the women departed raggedly. Night-clad Blythe arrived even as they left. "What is it?" she cried. Then, looking past to her mother, "Oh, gods—not *Owain*—"

Ilsa murmured down into the still bundle, seemingly unaware of Hart's presence. It was not until he knelt down and touched her that she raised her eyes.

"*Meijhana*—"

"Dead," she said only.

With trembling fingers, Hart peeled back the wrappings. He touched the face. "Cold," he murmured blankly. "Cold and white as death—"

Blythe's face was as white. "But he was well . . . earlier, at the ceremony . . . he was *well*—"

Hart's hand shook as he cupped Ilsa's head. "Oh, *meijhana*, there is nothing I can say to make the pain softer for you . . ."

What of you? Aidan wondered numbly. *What of your pain, su'fali . . . a son and heir, born and unborn in the space of three days . . .*

Tevis murmured something. Then, more loudly, "He was my son. Mine, too . . . I was second-father."

Blythe reached for his arm, but he withdrew it. Slowly he moved toward the huddled, grieving queen and the Cheysuli who knelt with bowed head, one large hand grasping the tiny fingers of the son who would never rule in his father's palace.

"Oh, no," Blythe said brokenly. "He should not . . . he is not Cheysuli, and does not understand about private grief—"

Aidan did. He moved at once to intercept the Solindishman. "Tevis, no. Let it wait. Come away, for now—" He put his hand on Tevis' arm. "Let the first grief pass—"

Fingers closed, then spasmed. It ran through Aidan like fire, setting bones ablaze even as his blood turned to ice, still and dark and cold, so *cold*—

"You," he croaked. "*You—*"

Tevis' eyes were black. "Put no hand on me."

"You—" Aidan choked.

Even Hart was drawn from his grief by the sound of Aidan's horror. He turned, rising, clearly distracted.

The *kivarna* was blazing within him like a pyre. In that moment Tevis' intentions were clear. "*You* killed the child!"

Blythe's voice was shrill. "Are you mad? Why would *Tevis—?*"

Hart grabbed Aidan's arm and jerked him around. "What are you saying?"

"It was Tevis," Aidan declared. The truth was so clear to him—could none of them see it? Feel it, as he did? "It was *Tevis—*"

The Solindishman's face was white. "I am his second-father. I am sworn to him, to protect him—and you say I *killed* him?"

Hart's voice was harsh. "Aidan, this is nonsense . . . Tevis has been with us for hours."

Aidan was shaking. "I know it. I know it. I *feel* it—" The final shred of disbelief dissolved the remaining vestige of Tevis' shield. "By the gods—*Ihlini—*"

"Are you *mad?*" Blythe cried.

The barriers were gone. Aidan sensed the seething ambition and raw power in the man, the tremendous upsurge of *so much* power, barely bridled; and hatred, so much hatred; *too much* hatred and power and absolute dedication to the service of a god no one else dared worship.

Tevis lifted a hand. Around his fingers danced the faintest glow of flame, cold purple flame; *godfire* at his fingertips, revealing all too clearly what he was. As, now, he intended.

"Wait," he said softly.

Perversely, Aidan wanted to laugh. "Ihlini," he said again, wondering at his blindness. How could he not have known? How could the Cheysuli blood in him not know, or the Erinnish *kivarna?* He of all people—

"Aye," Tevis spat between his teeth. "Child of the gods; child of prophecy—*like you!*"

"He was a baby!" Hart shouted. "A helpless infant! What purpose does it serve to end *his* life?"

"Because I must end *all* the lives," Tevis snapped. "Each and every life I can find—each and every seed—"

"Tevis," Blythe whispered.

"—until there are no seeds left, save ours." Tevis cast a malignant glance at Hart. "Had you left his son unborn, you would not now know this grief. It is your fault, my lord of Solinde . . . to save the lady this pain, you had only to do one thing."

Aidan heard the sluggish distraction in Hart's voice. Shock was starting to distance him from a reality he could not face. "One thing—?"

Tevis smiled. "Name me your heir, my lord. Put me on the throne after you—"

"No!" Blythe cried. "Oh, gods—*no—NO*—"

"Ah," Tevis remarked. "She has only just realized the man she slept with is Ihlini. A Cheysuli and Ihlini, in carnal congress . . . just as the prophecy warned."

Ilsa, forgotten, rose slowly. Her face was ravaged by grief, but it diminished none of her intensity. "Your war has been with adults, Ihlini—always. Why now do you turn to a child? What harm could he do you?"

An elegant shrug. "Now, very little. But it is important to me that no seed survive. Asar-Suti has made it quite clear that if the Ihlini are to regain dominion over the world, we must first destroy the Cheysuli and anyone who serves them."

"How?" Aidan asked. "You were with *us*. How could we not know? How could you touch this child from afar?"

Tevis displayed the sapphire. "A token from your father, my lord of Homana . . . something he gave my aunt many years ago. It has served us very well in the meantime. Anything once worn by man or woman contains an essence of that person—combined with Ihlini arts, we make a shield, so we may walk freely among you and the *lir*. As for touching him from afar, a simple thing to do with an infant. I merely thought on a tiny heart, quite still, and wished it into truth." He smiled. "A fortunate thing, this ring—Brennan should have known better than to give it to Rhiannon."

"Your aunt," Hart echoed. *"Rhiannon?"*

The smooth, urbane expression of a Solindish nobleman faded. Aidan heard Blythe's stifled denial; saw the draining of Hart's face. Tevis was no longer precisely *Tevis*. His features were much the same, but more refined, more feral. In his mind's eye, Aidan made the eyes a lighter brown, almost yellow; the hair a shade darker, now black.

"Oh, gods," Aidan blurted. "Strahan had a *son*."

Blythe's voice was a travesty. "Where is Tevis, then? *Was* there a Tevis?"

"Most certainly," Strahan's son agreed. "I killed him." He displayed the black ring on his other hand. "I killed Tevis and his father in High Crags, when I knew he was coming here. The father's body I left—there was no need of it—but Tevis' I required in order to arrange the proper glamour." He smiled. "Those who knew Tevis, *saw* Tevis when they looked at me. Those who did not, saw me. So, aye, *meijhana*, it was also Tevis you lay down with . . . at least, as much Tevis as remains of him, in this ring."

Blythe, trembling, pressed both hand against her mouth. Her face was ashen with comprehension.

Ilsa took a single step, then stopped. Against her breast she still cradled the murdered child. "I curse you," she said simply. "I am of the oldest House in this realm, Ihlini. With all that I was, I am, and will be—I curse you."

Tevis smiled at her, gently inclining his head. Then he looked at Hart. "I have killed the son," he said. "Now I must kill the father."

Something glittered in his hand. Silver, not purple; the *godfire* was gone. Not a knife, but its edge as deadly. Aidan had heard of the slender silver wafers with curving, elegant spikes. He had also heard the name: Sorcerer's Tooth. It flashed from the man they had known as Tevis and sliced across the room.

"Lochiel," he said softly, "so you will know me as you die."

Without thought, Aidan moved. He meant to knock down the Tooth; to block Hart from the lethal wafer. But he knew, even as he thrust out the hand to catch it, he had made a deadly mistake.

The entry was painless. It sliced into his palm, then through it, severing muscle, bone and vessel as the spikes rotated through the fine bones of his hand and exited the other side. Fingers closed once, spasming, and then vision turned inside out.

Hart caught him as he fell. And as he fell, he recalled the Ihlini forged their Teeth in poison.

Blythe screamed. And then she stopped.

Or he did.

Nine

Where he was, it was cold. So cold he ached with it. He could not move; could not see; could not hear or speak, but his awareness flickered with something akin to life even though he knew he was dead.

Someone had placed him on a barge. He lay on a bier, covered with a silken shroud, and his flesh was dead on his bones.

He floated in perfect silence on a lake of glass so clear he could see the darkness of the depths. He was alone. No one steered the barge. No one held the vigil at his side. No one wailed or keened or grieved, as if his death made absolutely no difference at all to anyone, even to his *lir*.

Teel.

He was alone. He felt a vague distress that his life could have so little meaning that his death would hold even less. He was prince, warrior, child of the prophecy, in line for the Lion; it was as if he had never been. The barge floated silently upon the waters of the glass-black lake, and he was still alone.

Teel.

He heard the ripple in the water. It was faint, so faint he believed it imagination, but the rippling slowly increased until he became convinced it was real. Someone—or something—approached him through the water.

Teel?

He struggled to open dead eyes. And again, this time to move an arm; neither answered. His flesh was still and cold and heavy, so heavy; Aidan began to understand death, and to know the futility and helplessness of a live spirit trapped within dead flesh.

The rippling became a splashing. Aidan, blind still, heard something grasp the edge of the barge. He felt no fear—he was *dead*—but curiosity overrode helplessness. With all the power remaining to him, he snapped open his eyes and looked.

A man. A warrior: Cheysuli. He wore leather and gold, clan-worked all, and his coloring was true. In his planed, feral face was a strange, eloquent sorrow. Softly he pulled himself out of water he did not displace, and then stood upon the barge. Aidan saw he was dry.

Lips and throat answered him. "Did you not swim?"

The other smiled. "I swam. But where I am, water cannot touch me."

Aidan, staring, saw the sword in his left hand. A true, two-handed broadsword of steel and gold, with a massive hilt bearing the rampant lion of Homana. In its heavy pommel, to balance the heavy blade, was a blood-red ruby. Down the length of the blade walked runes.

Two links Aidan possessed. Two Mujhars: Shaine, and Carillon. And now the third before him.

"Donal," he breathed.

The warrior smiled. "Aye."

Aidan looked again at the ruby. Huge and brilliant and *red;* the Mujhar's Eye, he knew . . . and no longer in existence.

Donal saw his expression. "Niall returned it to me."

"But—you were dead. And he threw the sword away . . . he went into the Womb of the Earth and threw it down the oubliette."

The voice was very gentle. "The sword was made for me, by Hale, my grandsire. When I have need of it, it answers."

Aidan wet dry lips; a thing he had believed impossible, on a dead man. With great deliberation he pushed himself into a sitting position. Silken shroud—crimson and black, the colors of Homana—slid down to his hips. He shivered, for he was naked beneath the fine silk. "There was no chain," he said. "I did not dream of a chain. Always before it has been the chain first, and then the Mujhar."

Donal's austere face softened. "Are you so certain?"

Aidan looked. Gold glittered in silk. At his feet, upon the bier, lay the chain. The links, as always, were solid, perfect . . . deadly.

He very nearly laughed. He knew the pattern now. "What have *you* come to tell me?"

"Do I have to tell you something?" Donal gazed across the lake into the setting sun. "No. I will let the others speak for me. The gods have set me a different task."

Aidan shivered, though he was not cold. "What task?"

"You may call me a steersman, for now." Donal moved

to one end of the barge and lifted the sword as a man would hold a staff. Long brown fingers closed on steel; by rights, it should cut.

Astonished, Aidan saw the sword reshape itself. The steel and gold flowed in either direction until it stretched, lengthening, and when it stopped he saw it was no longer a sword, but a golden pole, a steersman's pole, and as Donal slid it into the water Aidan saw the ruby send forth a starburst of brilliant light.

"To ward off the Darkness," Donal explained.

Aidan looked at the setting sun. He believed, in that moment, that his life or death would be decided by what he agreed—or refused—to do.

Quietly, Donal steered. "Your journey has been interrupted. I am here to put you back on the proper path."

"Then—I am not yet dead."

"Not as I know death. But neither are you alive, as the living know it. It is best to simply say you are *elsewhere* for the moment."

Aidan said nothing.

"Men die," Donal said. "Even Cheysuli die. But occasionally the gods see to it that a certain man—or woman— does not, because they have a use for him."

"Use," Aidan echoed. "A weighty word, I'm thinking."

"Most words are." Water splashed softly. "They sent me; therefore I am assuming they have some use for you."

Aidan thought about it. He recalled the things he had been told by the Hunter, by the Weaver, and by the two Mujhars. "And have they given you leave to tell me what this use is, or am I to guess?"

Donal looked at him. The setting sun illuminated his face. It was a face similar to his own, Aidan realized, though the color was much darker and all the angles sharper. The Erinnish in him had softened hue and hardness, redefining the wildness into something more civilized. It was easy to see why the Homanans, seeing a clan-born Cheysuli, had been so willing to name them alien.

This is what I might have been, instead of what I am. Had my line not looked to outmarriage . . .

He touched a strand of ruddy hair. The eyes in his head were right, but certainly not the hair. He did not know whether to be grateful or sorry for it.

Donal's tone was muted. "It would do little good for me

to tell you all the answers, Aidan. Men are men, not gods; they often shun the knowledge of a better way. Men are willful, but the willfulness is what the gods gave them. And so the gods bide their time, waiting to see if the man will follow his proper *tahlmorra*, or turn away from it." Yellow eyes were strangely calm. "What of you, kinsman? Which path do you choose?"

"All Cheysuli follow their *tahlmorras*," Aidan answered automatically, and then knew how foolish it sounded in view of Teirnan's actions, and those of the other *a'saii*. Quickly he asserted, "I intend to follow *mine*."

"Freely, or because you are constrained by blood and heritage?"

"Freely, of course." Aidan spread his hands. "But the choice is hardly a true one . . . what other path is open to me?"

"Many paths are open to you. Any number of them will seem easier than the true path awaiting you. Your life is very young, Aidan . . . do not judge what has gone before as the measure of what will come. You may despise the gods before your time on earth is done."

Aidan disagreed politely. "I think not, kinsman."

Donal arched black brows. "Innocence speaks hastily."

Disgusted, Aidan scowled at him—this meeting with yet another dead kinsman was as obscure as all the others—then marveled that he dared. Donal had been dead for many years. "I have been properly raised, my lord Mujhar. You need have no fear your son has failed in his duty, nor *his* son . . . I will do whatever the gods ask of me."

"And if they ask your life?"

"They asked *yours*," Aidan retorted. "And you gave it."

Sorrow altered Donal's face. He briefly touched a *lir*-band—wrought gold depicting wolf and falcon—then let the hand fall away. "I gave it. But my *lir* were dead . . . I wanted no empty life, no madness. Better to die whole, knowing, than die a *lirless* madman."

Aidan shivered, though he was not cold. Out of habit he moved to pull the shroud to cover his nakedness, and as he did so he heard the chiming of links falling. He stopped himself from touching the chain.

He looked squarely at Donal. "You are my great-grandsire."

"Aye."

"Then I ask a kinsman's boon." Aidan took a deep breath. "Tell me what I must do. Tell me what I must become."

Donal, backlighted now by sunlight, though the barge had not turned, was only a silhouette. Aidan could no longer see his features. But he saw the pole shrink, swallowing itself, until it was a sword in the hand of its master. The point was set through one of the links; lifted, the chain dangled. Aidan stared, transfixed, as the chain was carried closer.

Donal tipped the sword. The chain slid off steel and landed in Aidan's silk-swathed lap. "I cannot tell you what to do. The gods constrain me from that. But I *can* tell you what you must become."

Aidan wrenched his gaze from the chain so close to his manhood to the shadowed face of his kinsman. "Tell me, then."

Donal's eyes were oddly serene. "You must become Aidan," he said gently. "Not Aidan of Homana; Aidan the prince; Aidan, son of Brennan, grandson of Niall, great-grandson of Donal." He smiled. "You must simply become yourself."

"But I *am* all those things! How can I not be?"

"That is your choice."

Aidan put out a shaking hand and touched the chain in his lap. "Is it?" he asked. "Is it my choice . . . or the gods?"

But when he looked up, hoping for an answer, a word, anything, Donal—and the sword—was gone.

He jerked awake with a gasp. His chest felt heavy, empty, as if it had been sat upon for a very long time. He shuddered once, gulping air spasmodically, then opened his eyes and saw Hart's haggard face.

Breath flowed slowly back into his body, filling his chest until he thought he might burst. Then he swallowed forcibly, working his flaccid mouth, and managed to ask a question.

At first, Hart only stared. And then he muttered several things, including a *leijhana tu'sai* Aidan understood was for the gods, rather than for him, which he found oddly amusing. Quietly, he waited.

"Do you know," Hart said shakily, "I had composed it in my head? But the idea of putting it down on paper . . ." He shook his head, then abstractedly pushed silvering hair out of his eyes. "How could I tell Brennan? How could I make the words?"

Aidan smiled faintly. "No need now." He swallowed. "How long, *su'fali*?"

"Four days," Hart answered raggedly. "I thought we had lost you. I thought *both* of you—" He wiped his hand across his face, older now than before. "How could we have been so blind to him? To bring him into our home, into my daughter's *bed*—" He stood abruptly and turned rigidly away, as if he could not face Aidan. His voice was muffled. "Blythe swears she will kill herself."

Shock and revulsion turned Aidan cold. Suicide was taboo.

The dignity was stripped from Hart's voice, leaving behind a father's fear and anguish. "She swears the only way to undo her transgression is to destroy the body itself."

Aidan sighed wearily. "Then she is a fool indeed, and not fit to be Cheysuli."

It jerked Hart around. "How can you say—?" But he understood at once. "Oh. Aye. Perhaps if she looked at it that way . . ." He resumed his seat once more. "I think—I *hope*—once the shock has passed she will be more rational After all, both Ian and Brennan survived—"

"—and Keely." Aidan was oddly light-headed. "*Su'fali*—four days?" It felt like only an hour. It felt like four years.

Hart nodded. "At first I thought the earth magic too weak to destroy the poison. But this morning the fever broke."

Aidan reached for an itchy face and felt stubble. He grimaced in distaste; he detested his propensity for growing a beard. It felt oddly unclean. Or perhaps merely too foreign, evoking his other bloodlines.

Hart's smile was strained. "The Homanan in you. Brennan and I are smooth as a baby—" He broke it off. Only the closed eyes gave away his grief, and then he opened them again. New lines etched his flesh.

Aiden glanced around. He was in the guest chamber allotted to him. The room was empty save for Hart, who sat in a heavy chair beside the bed.

Teel.

Here. The raven briefly fluttered wings; he perched, as always, on the canopy. *Rest yourself, lir . . . I am here.*

Awareness reasserted itself; Aidan looked sharply at Hart. "The Ihlini?"

"Gone. Blythe's scream brought servants . . . Tevis—no, *Lochiel*—dared not remain. Too many Cheysuli." Hart's tone was grim. "He took his leave as so many of them do: in smoke and purple fire."

Aidan was, abruptly, in the audience chamber, holding a tiny infant only barely named. He recalled the insignificant weight; the crumpled, sleeping face; the hope for continuity.

He recalled also the look of pride and peace in Hart's face as he had named Tevis second-father.

The pain was greater than expected, because it was two-fold. The *kivarna* gave him that; he experienced his own grief while also echoing Hart's.

Aidan drew in a deep breath. He could think of no words worth the saying. So he said the obvious ones. "I am sorry, *su'fali.*"

"I know." A slight gesture closed the topic. A right-handed gesture, since he had no left.

And suddenly Aidan's fear and anguish was for himself. He thrust his left hand into the air, staring at it fixedly. It was swathed in bandages. He remembered, with unwanted clarity, the vision of steel piercing flesh, slicing too easily through skin and blood and muscle, dividing even bone.

"Is it whole? Oh, gods, *su'fali*—is it whole?"

Hart drew in a deep breath. "Whole," he said, "but damaged."

"How damaged?" All he could see was the old pain in Hart's eyes whenever he spoke of a clan no longer his. Would he share it, now? "Will I have the use of it?"

"I cannot say."

Aidan struggled upright. "Cannot, or will not? Are you trying to save me grief? Trying to save me the realization—?"

Hart's face hardened. "I told you the truth, Aidan. No one knows. The hand is whole, but damaged. You may or may not recover the use of it. I promise you nothing at all."

"A maimed warrior has no place in the clans," Aidan quoted numbly.

Pain and anguish flared afresh in Hart, with such virulence that it smashed through Aidan's awareness like a mangonel stone. "No," he agreed.

Aidan slumped back against bolsters. Strength and fear and comprehension spilled out of him like a bag of grain emptied. He had not wanted to pass the pain to Hart yet again. Ihlini poison had left him weak. "But," he said quietly, "I am still a prince, as you are, with a place at the Lion's side, with a hand or without."

When he could, Hart smiled. "Aye."

"The gods will have to be content with me as I am—*they* gave me the burden." Aidan's eyes drifted closed. "Where are my links?"

"Your links?"

Eyes remained closed. "The links on my belt." He was naked beneath the coverlet, as he had been on the bier.

"They were put away. Do you want them?"

"No. Just to know they are safe." *Because there will be a third to come. There must be; I met Donal.*

"Aidan."

All he could do was grunt.

"Shall I arrange to send you home once you are feeling stronger?"

It made sense. He wanted to go. He had very nearly died—he would like to see home again, and all of his kinfolk—

—but his great-grandsire Donal had come to set him back on the proper path.

"No," he managed to whisper. "There is Erinn yet to see."

So, Teel observed, *you did not lose all of your wits.*

Sluggish irritation. *Only the use of a hand.*

Teel, to do him credit, did not respond to that. He merely tucked his head under a wing.

Blythe came, as he expected. She came as he put the last of his possessions into his saddle-packs, and stood just inside the door. Even in her bleakness, he thought her beautiful.

Right-handed, he closed the flap on the saddle-pack and looped the thong loosely through the buckle. Then he looked at Blythe.

Her hands, in skirts, were rigid. He wished he could do the same. "They said—" She stopped. "They said it does not move."

"The *hand* moves," he corrected. "Even the thumb, a little. But the fingers are mostly useless." Aidan forbore to look. He knew what it was, under the bandages. He had examined it most carefully when it was clear the healing was done.

She lifted her head a little. "Will it make you *kin-wrecked?*"

It took everything he had to answer casually, so as not to display the fear. "Probably."

Color flared in her face. "How can you sound like that—as if it makes no difference? As if you hardly care? You have only to look at my father to know what it means . . . the pain he has to live with—all because of a gods-cursed ancient custom in a race too blind to see that a man can be a man even *if* he lacks a hand—"

"I know," he said tightly.

"Then how can you stand there and shrug so elegantly,

wearing all your gold, when you *know* what they might do—and to the man who will be Mujhar!"

"I know," he said again.

Tears glittered. "Know *what?*"

"How badly it hurts."

Blythe had cut her hair. She clawed at it now; it barely touched her shoulders. "He told me what you said. That I was not fit to be a Cheysuli. Not worthy of the taboo."

"No. Only a *lirless* man can accept the death-ritual, or there is no honor in the death."

"Honor!" she snapped. "What honor is left to me? I have been *defiled*—"

Aidan shook his head. "All you were, was tricked."

"I lay with an Ihlini!"

"Do you know who he is?"

Blythe blinked. "What?"

"Do you know who he is? The man you believed was Tevis?"

Clearly, she did not have the slightest idea what he meant. "Of course I know who he is. He told us: Lochiel."

"Strahan's son," Aidan said, "who is nephew to Rhiannon, who is our great-uncle's daughter."

"What?" Blythe snapped. "What has this to do with anything?"

Aidan shrugged. "I thought I spoke clearly enough."

"But none of this makes *sense*—"

"Does it not?" He shrugged again. "I thought I had just named off a generation or two of our birthlines."

"Aidan—"

Sympathy dissipated. "By the gods, Blythe, you are not the first Cheysuli—*or* the first of our line—to lay with an Ihlini! Ian did it first. Then Brennan, my father . . . then Keely, my aunt. And *all of them tricked,* Blythe. D'ye hear what I'm telling you?"

She shouted back at him. "Do you expect me to *like* it? Do you expect me to be *proud*? Do you expect me *not to care?*"

"No," he said softly. "I expect you to survive."

She swallowed painfully. "He wanted me for the throne."

"And for a son," he told her. "I know, Blythe—I know it hurts to realize you have been tricked, been *used* . . . but it could have been much worse."

"Worse?" She was aghast. "He killed a three-day-old baby!"

"But not you. Not Dulcie, or the twins. Not your mother

or father. Think again, Blythe . . . it could have been much worse."

"He would have killed us all. You were there. He wanted my father first—"

"Because he was discovered." Aidan sighed; he still tired easily. "Had I not uncovered who he was, Owain's death would have been remarked as a sad, tragic thing—no true-born heir for Solinde. But Hart made it clear there was an alternative—*your* child, Blythe . . . your son by Tevis of High Crags. Lochiel did not come here planning to murder everyone for the throne, but to *marry* for the throne."

Her lips were pressed flat. "Is that supposed to please me?"

Aidan picked up the saddle-pack. "Perhaps not, just now. Perhaps all you can see is the humiliation you feel because you bedded an Ihlini."

Anger flared forth. "Save your compassion, Aidan. You do not know what it was like."

"What it was like?" He threw down the saddle-pack. "I'll tell you, then, so we'll *both* be knowing about it: you bedded him willingly. It was probably your idea, so you could be putting an end to the unwanted suit of an unwanted kinsman come from Homana to find a bride. And *that,* my highborn Solindish, is why you're so angry now!"

Color peeled away. White-faced, Blythe stared as the tears ran down her face. Her chin trembled minutely. "I am ashamed," she whispered. "Oh, gods—so *ashamed!*"

For the first time since he had arrived, Aidan touched Blythe. And the *kivarna* remained silent.

"I know," he said as softly, as she moved into his arms. "*Shansu, meijhana*—I know."

"I want to die," she whispered. "Oh, gods—I want to *die*—"

He stroked her ragged hair. "Your parents have lost three children. Are you wanting to steal another?"

A shudder wracked her body. "I want it back the way it was. The way it was before he came."

"The Wheel of Life has turned."

With a quiet, deadly vehemence, "Then the gods are very cruel."

Aidan looked over her shoulder at the hand that would not work. "Sometimes," he agreed sadly.

Thinking of the Weaver, who let so many die so the Wheel could turn again.

PART III

One

He rode westward, bound for Andemir on the wild coast of
Solinde battered by the Idrian Ocean. There he would take
ship to Kilore, where the Aerie of Eagles perched upon the
white chalk cliffs of Erinn, overlooking the Dragon's Tail.
He had heard much about Kilore from his mother and from
Deirdre; he wondered if it would fit.

Teel flew overhead. *Will you not marry the girl?*

Aidan frowned skyward, but thick trees screened the raven. The plains were far behind; all he could see was forest
and the track stretching before him, sheltered by foliage.
*Blythe? No. At least, not just now. There is the possibility of
a child . . . all of us agreed it would be best to wait.* He
paused, thinking of Blythe as she had been, alive with love
for Tevis, and the Blythe he had seen at the last, devastated
by Lochiel. *She needs time. The worst thing for her would be
to enter into a marriage just now. She associates me with
Lochiel. Once I am back from Erinn, and if there is no child,
then we might think of marriage.*

Are children not desired?

Aidan wondered how he might explain things to a raven,
whose understanding of human things was not always perfect. The *lir* were very wise, but not omniscient.

Finally he gave him an answer. *Preferably my own.*

There is the prophecy, Teel said lightly. *Two magic races
united . . .*

Ruddy eyebrows ran up under hair. *Are you saying I
should marry Blythe, even if she bears an Ihlini halfling?* It
was the last thing he expected a *lir* to advocate.

Should, or should not, Teel said, *is your choice to make.*

As always. Aidan scowled in the raven's general direction. *Why should that change now?*

Teel made no answer to his *lir's* irritation, though smugness thrummed through the link.

Aidan thought about it. Two magic races, indeed. How else to merge the bloodlines than by bedding an Ihlini?

Inwardly, he quailed. For all he had offered solace to a frightened, angry cousin, he did not wish what had happened to her to be a thing *he* faced.

"That gods-cursed ring," he said suddenly. "I should have gotten it from him. Somehow. Some way. That gods-cursed ring of my *jehan's* has been the bane of us all."

He looked down at his left hand. He wore no rings on it, because he saw no sense in ornamenting a useless finger. No longer bandaged, the hand was obviously a hindrance rather than a helpmeet. The fingers had begun to curl as severed tendons died, but not all equally. The Tooth had sliced through vertically, so that the cut ran across his palm from fingers to heel. He had partial use of his thumb, and a bit in the smallest finger, but the other three were too damaged. Each day they twisted more tightly. Eventually what had been a hand would become an awkward claw.

Aidan tucked the hand into one thigh, trying to ignore it. But his belly squirmed unpleasantly. The fear he had fought back since learning of his injury rapped yet again at tightly sealed shields.

I am not so brave, he thought hollowly. *All my studied nonchalance when Blythe shouted at me was nothing but affectation. I* do *care, almost too much—I do not want to be kin-wrecked. I do not want to be Hart, left outside the clans. I lack his kind of courage—*

Almost against his will, he tried to fist the hand. All it did was spasm and send pain the length of his arm.

"I cannot go home," he said aloud. "If I do, they will know—*everyone* will know . . . and then they will take my name off the birthlines in Clankeep. A *kin-wrecked* man, I'd be—what kind of Mujhar is that?

Lir, Teel asked, *do you ever plan to stop? Or will you ride through the night?*

"Through the night!" Aidan snapped, then cursed himself for a fool. What good would it do to rail at his *lir?* Teel knew as well as he how helpless he felt, how frightened he was of being *kin-wrecked.*

Lir. Teel again. *The sun is going down.*

So it was. The woods were alight with sunset, gilding trunks and trappings. If he did not stop soon, he would lose all of the light and be left to make camp in the darkness, in a wood he did not know.

Aidan sighed. "All right, *lir*. Your point has been made. Go off and catch your meal—I will make a camp."

But once he had settled on a sheltering thicket of saplings, Aidan discovered how he had taken for granted things such as two whole hands. It was nearly impossible to unsaddle his horse, and he realized it was the first of many things he would be unable to do well one-handed. The acknowledgment came painfully. At first he tried to ignore it and go on as he always did; in the end, completely defeated, he swore at intricate buckles done up for him in Lestra, cursing thoughtless horseboys; then humiliation followed. So much depended on *two* hands, on *eight* fingers and two thumbs; he offered one of the latter and only four of the former.

He could not undo the final buckle. Frustration welled up. Its power stunned even Aidan. "Is this some kind of test?" he shouted, staring up at the tree-screened sky. "Or merely ironic coincidence, something worth laughing about?"

There was no answer save the clattering of gear from a horse only half unpacked. Aidan's ruined hand dropped away from the trappings as he leaned against the horse, brow pressed into saddle. Frustration and fear and futility were suddenly overwhelming. He felt very much as he had facing the Lion as a child, railing at a chain that existed only in dreams.

"Why?" he murmured into leather. "Why did it happen to *me*? What did I do to deserve this?" He knew, even as he asked them, the questions were unworthy. They were also selfish and petulent, but at that moment he did not care. He was angry and very frightened, and very much a child.

Aidan squeezed his eyes closed. "Oh, gods—I will be *kin-wrecked* . . . I will have to go before Clan Council and tell them what happened, and display my infirmity . . ." Humiliation writhed deep in the pit of his belly. "They will do all the things they did to Hart—" He sucked in a deep, noisy breath, trying to ward away panic. "Unless—unless I *insist* . . . I am not Hart, who was meant for Solinde . . . I will be Prince of Homana, and one day Mujhar—if I *insist* they change the custom—" Aidan pressed himself from the horse, new resolve hardening. "I will insist. I *will*. How can they deny me? One day I will be *Mujhar*—"

But even as he said it, Aidan felt the infant resolve waver.

To stand before Clan Council and denounce one of the oldest traditions of his race was not a thing he wanted to do. His father had asked, had petitioned; had even, he had been told, shouted at Clan Council, but it had changed nothing. Even for the Mujhar's middle son, the tradition could not be altered. Too many things had been changed. Now the older warriors, abetted by *shar tahls*, hung on to the old customs to keep new ones at bay.

"Fools," Aidan said aloud. "Blind, arrogant fools . . . what use is it to waste a warrior now? We are no longer hunted, no longer at war . . . they would do better, all those *shar tahls*, to look to the future instead of to the past."

The horse shook his head. Still saddled, he was unhappy. It renewed Aidan's anger. "Fools, all of them . . . had I any influence, I would change things."

Teel's tone was severe. *Questioning your tahlmorra?*

Was hunting so bad you are back already? Aidan abruptly drew his long-knife and cut the strap in two. "Why not question?" he asked aloud. "If they did not mean us to, they would not have given us words with which to ask them."

Cutting that will not help you when you pack the gear tomorrow.

No. Anger spilled away. "Too late," Aidan muttered, dragging saddle and packs free. Teel was right, of course. Teel was usually right.

But then if you went in lir-shape, buckles would not matter.

Aidan stopped moving. He had been afraid to ask; now he knew he had to. "Do I still have recourse to *lir*-shape?"

You did not lose *the hand. It merely changed its shape.*

The answer made him weak with realization. He released a gusty breath, mixing laughter with heartfelt relief. "*Leijhana tu'sai*, for that."

Teel uttered a croak. *And for other things as well.*

Aidan grinned and settled the gear, then tended to the horse. He felt better already, knowing he still could fly. Being *kin-wrecked* was bad enough, but not being able to fly—

Aidan put it out of his mind. Instead he thought of his grandsire, Niall, who lacked an eye. He bore scars worse than Aidan's. No one called *him* half-man, or a failure. All knew better.

If he could become like Niall—

"So," he said aloud, "if I do not think myself crippled, I will not *be* crippled."

Much better, Teel remarked. *You are bearable now.*

Aidan knelt to lay a fire. "*Leijhana tu'sai*, again." Couched in exquisite dryness.

Fix enough for two.

Aidan stopped moving stones, peering through twilight at the raven-shaped shadow perched in a nearby tree. "Was hunting *that* bad?"

Not for me—for him.

Aidan dropped the rock and spun, moving from knees to feet in one quick motion. He hand was on his long-knife, but he forbore to draw it.

"Wise," the man applauded. "At least you are not overhasty."

The prickles died from his flesh. "If you do this often, *someone* will be."

"Oh, no . . . I think not. The others do not hear me as a man. They hear me as the wind, or an animal, or something else offering no threat. You see?"

The stranger moved out of the sheltering trees. His gait was awkward, ungainly; he leaned upon a crutch thrust under an arm. His right leg was missing from below the knee, yet he moved almost noiselessly. He sounded nothing like a man.

Aidan took his hand away from the knife. "I have enough for two."

"You see? Being crippled is not so bad . . . it softens another man's soul."

Aidan stared as the stranger made his way out of darkness. He was old, though not truly ancient, with a fringe of white hair curling around his ears. The top of his head was bald. The rest of it was a face comprising the map of Homana; Aidan cut off the impulse of looking for landmarks he knew. The stranger deserved better, and *he* was better mannered.

Dark brown eyes glinted from under bushy white brows. "A fine young man," he said. "Well-mannered . . . and well-born?" He nodded to himself before Aidan could give him an answer. "There is the look of a fox about you: red hair and yellow eyes . . . would a fox be your *lir?*"

Only a flicker of surprise; Cheysuli were no longer strangers. "No," he said, "a raven." He thought of his other uncle. "Though a kinsman claims a vixen."

"Oh, aye; of course." He wore rough woolen homespun tunic belted over equally rough-made trews, and a single brogan shoe. The half-trew on his right leg was knotted beneath the stump.

Uneasily, Aidan thought of Tevis who was not Tevis at all, but Lochiel in disguise, using subterfuge to bring down a king. This was Solinde, after all; the homeland of the Ihlini. But his *kivarna* told him nothing, and neither did his *lir*.

The stranger levered himself down and sat beside the fire that was not, yet, a fire. He smiled up at Aidan. "You did say food, did you not?"

"Aye." Aidan knelt to resume his work. When the ring was built and kindling laid, he drew out flint and steel.

And realized almost at once it would take two hands to light.

The heat of shame set his face ablaze. He gritted his teeth tightly and refused to look at the man. He thought briefly of asking him—the stranger had two hands—but then realized it was folly. He would not always have someone to help. He needed to learn what to do.

Eventually, he managed. A twist of useless hand, pressure from new sources, careful concentration. The fire was lighted at last. Sighing, Aidan turned, wiping dampness from his forehead, and saw the stranger nodding.

"The patience will come," he said gently. "So will the acceptance." He gestured to his stump.

Helplessness spasmed. "When?" Aidan blurted. "All I can think of now is what I was before!"

"Natural, that. I have done it, myself." The old man slapped the palm of his hand against one thigh. "The bitterness will fade, along with the helplessness. There are worse things in this world than lacking a bit of flesh."

Aidan's grunt was politely noncommittal as he added fuel to the fire.

Dark eyes glittered. "Do you count yourself less than a man?"

Aidan, piling on wood, wanted not to answer. There was no way he could fully explain what it was to a man like himself, warrior-born and bred. But a glance at the stranger told him the man wanted an answer.

Do not blame him . . . do not punish him, either. Aidan

sighed and schooled his tone into patience and tolerance.
"You are not Cheysuli . . . it is difficult to explain, but our
law forbids a maimed man from remaining part of the clan.
The warrior is expelled, cast out . . . in Old Tongue, he is
kin-wrecked."

"Why?" the stranger rasped. "Why throw away a warrior
because he lacks a useful hand?"

Aye, Aidan agreed. But retreated from bitterness into an
explanation. "In the old days, when we were hunted, it was
necessary that each warrior be able to fight. If he could not,
he could not protect his kin, or his clan . . . he ate food
better given to someone who could."

The stranger scratched at his stump. "A harsh law, that.
But there are times in a man's life—or in the life of his
people—that hard decisions must be made. When it comes
to survival . . ." Again he gestured at the stump.

Aidan's mouth twisted. "I am less sanguine than you.
This is but two weeks old."

"Then I will ask it again: do you count yourself less than a
man?"

He was, at first, angry: who was this old man, this stranger,
to ask him such a thing? But then anger spilled away. He
knew he spoke the truth, though part of him tried to deny
it. "No. *This* is not me. Not a hand. Not a leg. What I am
comes from somewhere else . . . somewhere in here." Aidan
touched his breast.

The stranger nodded. "But you would rather have it
back."

Aidan thought of Hart, and quailed. "Who would not
want it back?"

"And what would you give up to have it?"

Aidan looked into the eyes. They were expressionless in
the darkness, but oddly purposeful. He no longer doubted
the stranger was more than merely a stranger, come upon
him by coincidence.

Not here. Not in Solinde. Not where Lochiel yet roams.

His hand went to his knife. He thought again of Hart,
offered reattachment of his still-whole hand at the Gate of
Asar-Suti, in the depths of Strahan's fortress. He had heard
the story. The cost was service to Strahan. The cost was the
weight of his soul.

Resentment faded. So did bitterness. Certainty replaced

both, and an unexpected resolve. "It is only a hand," he said clearly. "Not worth the price you want."

"But to be whole again . . . a true warrior . . . not to be *kin-wrecked*—"

Aidan laughed at the man. "Not for any price will I risk my *tahlmorra*."

Firelight made the old man young. His eyes were dark as pits. He sat upon his rock with his good leg stretched before him and the crutch at his side. He rubbed the knotted stump. "Think again," he suggested. "Think twice, or thrice, or more."

Aidan shook his head.

The old man smiled. Once more he touched his stump, save now the leg was whole. "Come here," he said.

Aidan knelt down before him.

"Give me your ruined hand."

Aidan offered the god his hand. "What are you called?"

"In this guise, I am the Cripple." He studied Aidan's hand, examining curled fingers, the two-sided scar. "He struck well, the Ihlini. But it was not at you he struck."

"No."

"You took what was meant for someone else."

"He was a kinsman. And a king."

"Kings are men, too. Men die; kings die. How do you know it was not his *tahlmorra* to die?"

He had not thought of that. "But—I had to. I could not let him be struck down. I *had* to. There was no choice."

"Perhaps it was *tahlmorra*. Perhaps it was *yours*, Aidan."

He dared a glance at pit-black eyes. "Was it you who sent Donal?"

"I sent him. I could not allow you to die just yet, even as you could not allow your kinsman to be struck down. And so you live." He shrugged. "For now."

Aidan shivered. He tried to suppress it; could not. "Can you tell me what you intend for me? Am I always to travel blind? I will serve you willingly, if you only give me the chance."

"No." The Cripple's tone was cold. "No man accepts everything willingly. Sacrifices must be made. Too often a man *knowing* the sacrifice would never be willing to make it, just as you were unwilling to let the Ihlini kill your kinsman."

"But—"

"You will know what you must when the time is come. Now, as for this . . ."

Aidan looked down. The twisted hand was still cradled in the hands of the god, but liquid spilled out. At first he feared it was blood, but it was rich and gold and heavy.

"Open your hand, Aidan."

A part of him wanted to laugh. But he knew better, now. He no longer thought to question.

The fingers, tendons reknitted, answered his bidding. The liquid congealed, then formed itself into a shape. Across his unscarred palm lay a heavy rune-worked link perfectly matched to the other two.

The god smiled on him. "You sacrificed no portion of your *tahlmorra*. The price for your hand was honesty; that, you gave tenfold."

"Donal," Aidan said, staring at the link.

The god did not answer. The Cripple, with his crutch, was gone.

Aidan laughed. He wanted to cry. But he thought the laughter best. When he was done, he looked at the link. Then he looked at his hand, perfect and whole and unblemished.

"Why?" he asked of Teel.

The shadow that was his *lir* fluttered feathers briefly. *He asked you questions. You answered them. I think you might be wise to assume you said what he wanted to hear.*

"But what do they *want* from me?"

They are gods. Who can say?

Futility possessed him. "Teel—please—help—"

When at last the raven spoke, his tone was more gentle than Aidan had ever heard from him. *I do what I can. It is all a lir can do, certainly all I can do . . . the gods made us, too. And even the lir cannot predict or explain a tahlmorra that is still on the loom.*

Aidan gripped the link. "Why me, Teel? What do they see in me? Why do they come to *me*?"

Through the *lir*-link he heard a sigh. *I cannot say*, Teel answered. *No one has told me, either.*

Two

Crying out, Aidan awoke abruptly, thrusting himself upright into the dawn. For a long moment he did not know where he was, only that he was *somewhere* . . . and then he realized he was not in the Great Hall of Homana-Mujhar, trying to touch a chain in the lap of the Lion; nor was he in Lestra, staring in shock at a hand sliced nearly in two by poisoned Ihlini steel.

"Agh," he said aloud, "they *are* starting again!"

Teel, in a tree, fluttered. *What are starting again?*

"The dreams." Aidan rubbed his face, stripping dew-dampened hair out of gritty eyes and being glad all over again he could use both hands for the motion. He lowered his recovered hand and examined it critically again, as he had every morning since meeting the Cripple. Five days, now. The relief had not passed.

Neither had the dreams.

He wore three links at his belt, rather than two. They chimed as he rode, reminding him constantly of dreams and gods and tasks. He slept poorly and woke too often during the night, trying to banish the dream-chain long enough to get a proper night's sleep. He could not recall a time when he had felt so confused, so disoriented. At least before the gods had come to him, he had believed himself merely fanciful. Now he believed himself mad.

Sighing, Aidan peeled back blankets and kicked legs free. "Time to go, *lir*. Erinn gets no closer while I lie here in skins and wool, thinking about dreams."

It gets no farther, either.

Aidan forbore to answer and commenced packing his horse. He had long since learned commenting on Teel's remarks made no difference. The raven was cleverer than he; his best wager was to ignore him altogether, because then there was no clear-cut victory.

Of course, it meant the contest continued.

But it was better than nothing at all.

When he came across the wagon with its bright-painted canvas canopy, Aidan gave it a wide berth. He was ready to pass it by and forget about it, as travelers usually did on the road; often, it was safest. But the woman on the seat was so vivid she caught his eye and turned his head quite literally; Aidan nearly stared.

Her answering smile was so warm and guileless he could not simply ignore it—not if he desired to name himself a man for he rest of his life. He slowed his horse at once and waited for her team to catch up, then fell in beside her. His greeting was in accented Solindish; hers in the same tongue, though flawless. Much as he had expected.

Black hair fell in tight, tangled ringlets all the way to a narrow waist. She wore a chaplet of bright gilt dangling with false pearls that framed a heart-shaped face, and copper hoops in both ears. Black eyes were bold but also shy, as if she longed to be a bawd but had not yet learned how to do it properly. She was not truly beautiful, not as Ilsa was, but she had a burning liveliness of spirit that put Aidan in mind of his mother and Deirdre.

He glanced beyond her shoulder to the closed canvas canopy. "You should not be traveling the road alone."

"No," she agreed gravely, though her eyes were bright with mirth. "It would be a very bad thing. And it is why I do not do it." Her hand parted the bright canopy, baring the face of a young man so remarkably beautiful Aidan thought it might do better on a woman.

"A very bad thing," the young man said, crawling through the canopy to take his place on the seat beside the woman. "But then we know better than to allow Ashra to go anywhere alone . . . there are men who would stoop to stealing her to share more than she might care to."

And men who would steal you . . . But Aidan's manners would not allow him to say it.

Like Ashra, the young man had black hair, though he lacked her length or ringlets. The bones of his face were truly beautiful, and the skin smooth and dark and unblemished. Something in his expression and the assemblage of bones reminded Aidan of his own race, though he had never seen a Cheysuli with such magnificent purity of features, or green eyes. And yet there was something else as well. He was most like Ilsa, Aidan decided finally, though dark instead of light. His suppleness bespoke exceptional grace, and his speaking voice was firm, yet melodious.

Green eyes assessed Aidan. "I am Tye, singer by trade. Ashra dances. And the old man, Siglyn, is a magician." He gestured toward the canopy. "Travel is harsh on old bones; he will be well enough, but he requires rest." Briefly he eyed Aidan's saddle-packs, the travel-stained brown cloak drawn over both shoulders. "Where are you bound?"

"Westward to Andemir."

Ashra laughed. Her voice was low and, to Aidan, attractive. "Andemir for us, also. Perhaps we shall be road-partners."

"Ashra," Tye said quietly, with a quick warning gesture from one hand.

She laughed again, tossing back ringlets and shrugged a supple shoulder. "Your turn to drive, Tye. I will question this stranger, since you are so mistrustful."

"With reason," Tye said grimly, as she handed over the reins. "Which you know as well as I."

Obligingly, Aidan gave them his name, though omitting his rank. He had learned if a man truly wanted to know what others thought, he would do well to keep quiet about heritage and titles. People spoke more freely if they believed themselves of a kind.

He meant to ask them more about themselves, but Teel interrupted by alighting on Aidan's left shoulder. Ashra cried out in delight. "A tame raven!"

Aidan grinned. "Only sometimes."

"And other times?" she challenged.

Tye flicked her a warning glance, which she did not see. Aidan frowned. "For a troupe of players making a living off the road, you seem uncommonly wary."

Tye's austere expression—far too restrictive for the fluid lines of his face—relaxed, but only slightly. "With good reason, stranger—we were accosted three days back by a band of brigands who took what little coin we had. The old man was injured—struck on the head—and I have since learned to be suspicious of everyone." He looked at the raven. "But none of *them* had a bird, or the likelihood of wanting one, so I doubt you are one of them. Forgive my bad manners."

A line knitted Ashra's black brows. They were heavy and

oddly straight, but Aidan found the look exotically attractive. "If the raven is tame only *some* of the time, as you say,
what of the other times?"

"The other times he is most annoying," Aidan answered
truthfully. "But to be fair, he is not tame . . . Teel is a *lir*."

Black eyes widened. "*Lir* are blessed of the gods . . ."
She looked more sharply at Aidan. "But you are not Cheysuli.
What are you doing with one?"

He felt a brief flicker of surprise that she should know
anything about who did and did not consort with the *lir*, but
answered her question easily enough by throwing the cloak
back from his shoulders to display the gold weighting bare
arms. A hooking of hair behind left ear brought the raven-
shaped ornament into daylight.

Even Tye frowned. "A *red*-haired Cheysuli?"

Aidan smiled. "My mother is Erinnish. This is her legacy
. . . left to my own devices, I might have preferred black."
He affected a negligent shrug. "But I do have my father's eyes."

For confirmation, Tye looked. And nodded, patently unimpressed. "Yellow as a beast's—" He grinned. "Aye, aye
. . . no insult intended. I only tease, shapechanger."

Ashra raised level brows. "He would make a most handsome beast."

Tye grunted. "You are a woman. Women are often overly
imaginative."

She stroked back a ringlet, retucking it under the chaplet.
"Solinde is ruled by a Cheysuli."

"The usurper," Tye agreed, then laughed as Aidan stiffened. "Have you no sense of humor? I *tease,* shapechanger
. . . does the animal in your blood keep you from enjoying
the quips and jests of others?"

"When they are at my expense." Aidan smiled blandly.
"Too often such words are meant, Solindish . . . do you
mean yours?"

Tye sighed. "If I meant them, I would not now allow you
to ride with us to Andemir." He paused. "If you desire to
ride with us."

"He might if you sang," Ashra suggested.

Tye flicked her a quelling glance. Aidan began to wonder
if they were brother and sister, or husband and wife. He
hoped it was the former.

"When do we stop?" called a querulous voice from within
the canopy. "Or will you rattle my bones into dust?"

Teel departed Aidan's shoulder, slapping his face with one wing. Aidan, muttering, rubbed at a stinging eye as Ashra laughed.

Tye nodded. "We stop, old man. Soon." He shot a quick glance at Aidan. "Will you share our food?"

He blinked the sting away and nodded. "My thanks. I have wine."

Ashsra's boldly charming smile flashed out again. "So have *we*."

Camp was established off the road in a cluster of sheltering trees. The sun, sliding down the line of horizon, painted slats of light and shadow across the canvas canopy. Aidan thought it much like the pavilions at Clankeep, bright blue painted with equally vivid figures: a dancer dressed in red and green and gold; a singer with wooden lute; a magician conjuring smoke and fire from the air. The wagon itself was of dark wood, but its wheels were painted red, lined with yellow on inner rims and spokes. Altogether it provided a most tempting—and visible—target to brigands.

Tye tended the horses as Ashra assisted the old magician from the wagon and escorted him to the patchwork cushion by the fire Aidan had laid. He was a very old man dressed in gray wool robe over time-faded indigo linen draperies. A plain leather belt with tarnished silver buckle snugged a narrow waist. The robe hung loosely, swirling a half-torn hem about swollen ankles. His feet were shod in crushed leather slippers. He scuffed through turf and fallen leaves as if movement were very painful.

Aidan went to him at once, offering a second arm. A pair of rheumy blue eyes fixed themselves on his face, weighing him against some inner measurement. But they were proud eyes, and freely disdained Aidan's arm. The thin mouth tightened as his grip on Ashra increased.

Aidan relinquished his offer at once, stepping away with a slight inclination of his head. Ashra helped the old man sit down on the cushion, then pulled his robe closed.

"Siglyn," she said softly, "his name is Aidan. He is bound for Andemir, as we are."

"What is that on his arms?" the old man asked harshly. "He carries enough wealth to bribe all the brigands in the world away from us."

"Hush," she chided gently. "He is Cheysuli, from Homana. That is the *lir*-gold a warrior receives when he becomes a man." Black eyes flicked in Aidan's direction, silently apologizing. "He is not a brigand come to rob us, or a man offering unwanted charity. Look at him again; you will see what he is, merely by looking into his eyes."

"Faugh!" The old man glowered as she bent to make certain he was comfortable on his cushion. His hair was white, very thin, very long. A matching beard straggled down the front of his robe. But his eyes, for all their agedness, were sharp as he glared at Aidan. "Come, boy," he ordered brusquely.

Aidan bit his tongue. Never in his life had he been treated so rudely or disrespectfully. Nevertheless he did as ordered and moved closer. He stood quietly, unwilling quite yet to bow, though undoubtedly it was what the old man wanted.

Siglyn eyed him. "Shapechanger, are you?" The flesh of his face creased. "Aye, perhaps you are, for all the fire on your head . . . you have the look in your eyes."

Aidan blinked. "The—look?"

"The wildness, boy! The feyness. Arrogant as an eagle, in its aerie above the world . . . and a wolf at bay betimes, mistrusting the selfsame world." Siglyn bared yellowed teeth. His fingernails were clean, but cracked; idly, he chewed them. "I've lived a long time, boy. I've seen many things. Not so long ago your race and mine were at war."

Aidan smiled; the old so often shortened time. "Long enough."

Siglyn frowned and removed fingers from mouth. "I fought in the wars with Carillon . . . you lack the accent, boy."

Ruddy brows rose. "Which one?"

"The one I heard, when we took prisoners." Nastily, the old man grinned. "You speak it differently."

Aidan shrugged. "I am from Mujhara. There are dialects—"

"Hah! Mujhara is the king's city." Siglyn sighed thoughtfully. "Never been there . . . never been out of Solinde. Been to Lestra, though, and *she's* a king's city." Blue eyes sharpened once more. "Why are you come to Solinde?"

Inwardly, Aidan sighed. But he had been taught to treat the elderly with great respect, regardless of the treatment received in return. "I am on my way to Erinn. To Kilore. I will take ship from Andemir."

Siglyn gifted him with a malignant stare. "You could have done *that* from Hondarth. Why are you come to Solinde?"

Aidan cleared his throat, maintaining a neutral tone. "I have kin in Lestra."

Tye came back from hobbling and graining horses. He pushed an arm through thick black hair and dropped down to tend the fire Aidan had been called away from. "Lestra," he said lightly, as if tasting the word. "*Shapechanger* kin in Lestra." He fed in a length of wood, then slanted a glance at Ashra and the old man. "Not many can claim that."

"A few." Aidan, glad to turn from Siglyn, knelt also and added wood.

The old man had not given up. He raised his voice preemptorily. "How is the *Mujhar?*"

Aidan laughed and dropped another faggot on the flames. "The last time I saw him, he was quite well. But you will not trap me like that, old man . . . I am not in hiding. You have only to *ask*, instead of wasting your time—and mine—hinting."

The magician laughed unpleasantly. "I *like* hinting," he said. "Not much left for an old man's nights."

Ashra knelt down next to Aidan and put a hand on his arm. "Who are you?" she asked. "Siglyn is not usually so bad . . . are you someone he knows?"

Aidan laughed once. "Only someone he *thinks* he knows, because he is a busybody." He looked at Ashra. In firelight, her bold features were softened. "I am grandson to the Mujhar."

Her mouth slackened slightly. Then she threw back ringlets with a toss of her head. The hand was gone from his arm.

Tye grunted. "I thought you looked too soft for a man of honest blood . . . and yet you ride with no servants."

Aidan sighed in resignation. "We do not *all* move about the countryside with great trains of servants in our wakes." Although his mother would have liked it. "It is not a Cheysuli custom to be dependent on others."

Tye laughed, one winged black brow rising. "Is that so? Well, I am surprised. I had thought all of royal birth had blood so thin they required propping up by the labor of others considerably less blessed."

Aidan grunted. "There speaks ignorance. Had you met your own lord, you would never say that."

Tye's tone was dry. "People such as we only rarely meet his like."

Aidan's tolerance was gone. He rose, wrapping the cloak

around his arms. "I offered you wine; you may have it. But perhaps you would be more content without my company."

Ashra was at his side instantly. "Oh, no!" she cried. "Forgive him, my lord . . . Tye is often overhasty when he speaks, but never when he sings. Only wait, and you will hear." She cast a glance at the magician. "As for Siglyn, he is old. He forgets what he says. Bide with us the night."

The old man, thus invoked, stirred testily. "Don't speak for me when I have a tongue yet in my head! I say what I wish, and to *whom* I wish, no matter what they like."

Ashra grimaced, then smiled tentatively at Aidan. "Will you stay? You would be safer with a group . . . and we would no doubt be considerably safer with a Cheysuli."

Tye grinned. "Prove to us I am wrong. Show us you are worthy of our respect."

Aidan opened his mouth to refuse, but Teel was in the link. *Why not?* he asked. *It might prove less tedious than a night without argument.*

I have you for that.

One bright eye glinted. *A lir is many things, but a lir is not a woman.*

Aidan very nearly laughed aloud, but good manners kept him from it. It was discourteous to stay in the link any longer than was necessary, with the unblessed around.

He looked at Ashra. He thought about Teel's comment. And smiled. "I will stay."

When Aidan discovered the Solindish entertainers had little enough to eat, he offered to share his own rations in addition to his wine. The offer was accepted only after a brief discussion—in Solindish—that Aidan barely followed because of the dialect: Tye was uncertain they should place themselves so heavily in a stranger's debt, while Siglyn muttered about brigands who starved an old man by stealing food from his mouth; Ashra, who was hungry, said both of them were fools and *she* would eat shapechanger food even if they would not.

Scowling, Tye gave her leave to accept the offer. Ashra thanked Aidan prettily, black eyes flashing beneath lowered lashes as she dipped a graceful, if unstudied, curtsy, but it was Siglyn who ate more and faster than any of them. Aidan wondered idly where it showed itself on the old man, for he was thin and stringy almost to the point of emaciation.

When the food was gone, the wineskins were passed more frequently. Siglyn had his own and was disinclined to share, saying the vintage was a personal favorite, but Tye was companionable enough as he handed his skin to Aidan. Ashra drank sparingly, but high color came into her face as she stared transfixed at the fire.

Tye settled himself more comfortably against a rolled blanket thrust beneath his neck. "What is it like?" he asked, when he was done swallowing wine. "What is it like to take on the shape of an *animal*?"

Having done his share of damage to a wineskin, Aidan was not irritated by Tye's disrespect. He lay propped against his saddle and smiled. "You are asking the wrong man. There are others better suited to explaining the *lir*-shape, which is very personal—and others better suited to understanding."

For a long moment only the crackle of flames broke the heavy silence as Tye considered the irony. Then he smiled, lifted a wineskin in wry tribute, nodded his head at Teel, perched atop the wagon canopy. "Try to explain. I will *try* to understand."

Aidan shrugged, vaguely discomfited. He did not quite know where to start.

Tye frowned. "Do you not change? Do you not become *him*?"

Answering was easier. "No, not *him*. I become another."

"But a raven."

"Aye, a raven. That is how you know the shape we become: by the *lir* who accompanies us." He shrugged. "No matter what the stories say, we are not free to become anything—or any*one*—we desire. We are not monsters, or creatures of darkness. The gods made us, Tye . . . and they made the *lir*."

Ashra's tone was detached as she stared transfixed into the flames. "Why did you choose a raven?"

"The choosing was not mine. It is never the warrior's choosing . . . there is more to it than that." Aidan squirmed into a more comfortable position, hugging wineskin between elbow and ribs. "When I was fourteen I fell sick—the *lir*-sickness, we call it—and knew only a great and terrible need. There is no cure for the sickness, no relief for the need, except to go out into the forest and find a *lir*. And so I did."

Tye's doubt was manifest. "Alone?"

Brief irritation flickered. "Of course alone . . . it is not a thing for another to share."

"They let a fourteen-year-old-boy—one who would one day be king—go out alone into the forest?"

" 'They,' as you call them, are also Cheysuli. No one would stand in my way, least of all Cheysuli kin."

Tye frowned thoughtfully. "And so you found *him*."

Aidan shrugged. "Teel and I found each other. For the *lir* it is much the same: they know a need, and they fill it. A Cheysuli with no *lir*—and a *lir* with no warrior—is incomplete. Once linked, we are whole.

"With the ability to shift your shape."

Aidan nodded. "But only into whatever shape the *lir* represents. If I had two *lir*, as did my great-grandsire, Donal, I would then be able to assume two different forms. But I have only Teel . . . the gods are sparing with gifts."

Tye's laughter mocked. "The gods, when they do anything at all, are sparing with everything. Especially good fortune. Only the bad flows generously."

Aidan grunted mild disapproval. "They will hear you."

Tye made a derisive sound of dismissal. "The gods hear nothing. Why should they? Do you think they care? Do you think they pay the slightest attention to any of us?"

Ashra stirred. "Hush," she said quietly. "You offer offense to our guest."

The singer put out a hand to touch Ashra's arm. She sat close by his side, and Aidan had decided, with regret, they were not brother and sister. "You have already told him I am overhasty when I speak," Tye reminded her. "Why should I hide it now?"

She slanted him a glance from the corners of her eyes. "Offense should never be given a guest. Think what you like in private . . . there is no need to speak it."

Aidan waved a hand. "No need to bother yourself, Ashra—I think Tye and I will never be reconciled about much of anything."

Siglyn spoke for the first time since the meal. "Do you think only you are right, then, in what you believe? Because of your birth?"

Aidan sighed heavily. "My birth means nothing at all. Why do you dwell on it? In the clans only the blood matters, and its continuation, not in what flesh it flows. Do you see? I am Cheysuli first: child of the gods. I am then a warrior, and I honor my *tahlmorra*. I am a prince last of all."

"That," Tye declared, "is not possible."

Aidan, sliding into an Erinnish cadence, fixed him with a baleful eye. "I'd be venturing, my pretty lad, 'twould be far easier for me to shed my royalty than for the likes of you to *gain* it."

Ashra laughed, not in the least taken aback by Aidan's verbal attack on Tye. "Well said!"

"Indeed," Siglyn agreed morosely.

Tye, unaffronted, merely grunted. "Most probably. But I have no wish to be a prince."

Aidan nearly laughed; his *kivarna* bespoke the lie. "No man *never* wishes he were a prince, Solindishman. Had you the chance—"

"—he would accept it instantly," Ashra finished. "And you *would*, Tye."

Tye grunted again. "But it is bootless. There will be no chance for me to find out. I am only a singer, and a poor one."

Ashra was instantly outraged. "Poor! You are the best I have ever heard!"

Tye grinned at her. "And how many have you heard?"

Color stained her cheeks. "Enough," she said softly, touching fingers to his face. "Enough—and more—to know."

The old man tightened his robe around thin shoulders. "What magic do *you* claim, shapechanger?"

Aidan, considering, recalled Siglyn's trade was in magic, and fashioned his answer to suit it. "Nothing to rival yours, old man." He smiled disarmingly. "All I claim is *lir*-shape."

Siglyn grunted. "Nothing more? No more than that?"

Aidan shrugged, making light of his answer. "We can heal, when required."

Rheumy blue eyes narrowed. "And?"

Aidan put off answering by unplugging the wineskin and drinking, then carefully squeaking the cork home. "Some say there is a third gift," he admitted frankly. "But it is only rarely used. We do not care for what it does to a man's soul."

The old man smiled. It was not a pleasant smile. "And what does it do to a man's soul, that you would quail from it?"

Aidan's gaze did not waver. "It takes," he answered

flatly. "It overpowers. It sucks away a man's will and leaves him with nothing at all save what the other tells him."

Siglyn's eyes shone. He grunted approval, as if vindicated. "I thought so. I've heard it said many a time the Cheysuli have he power to be demons, if they choose."

Aidan's tone was clipped. "We do *not* choose," he declared. "We understand too well what compulsion can do to a man, and we choose otherwise. The power to be demons is reserved by the Ihlini. It is what they practice."

Tufted white brows jerked upward. "*Do* we?" Siglyn asked. "Is that what we practice?"

Even as the purple flame shrouded the old man's fingers, Aidan was on his feet. The knife was in his hand, but Ashra was at his side instantly, touching his wrist.

"No," she said softly.

Siglyn laughed. It had a rusty, creaking sound, as if only rarely used. "I have taken you by surprise."

Aidan, whose immediate testing of the *lir*-link told him there was no interference, frowned at the old man. "Aye," he said abstractedly. "But—I can reach my *lir*. And he said nothing—"

"Does it matter?" Ashra asked.

"He should have warned me. A *lir* always gives warning of an enemy."

Her fingers turned the knife downward.. "That should tell you something."

Aidan barely heard her. He stared across the fire at Tye, whose green eyes were odd in the flickering light. "And you?"

Tye smiled. "I am, as you are, many things. Solindish: aye. Ihlini as well. But also a singer. My teacher was Taliesin."

"Taliesin has been dead for more than twenty years!"

"I am older than I look." Tye sat upright, setting aside his wineskin. "You are not a fool, Aidan of Homana. Why act like one now?"

Bitterness welled up. "Am I a fool to be wary of the enemy?"

Siglyn glared. "How quick you are to assume the worst of us. Aye, you are a fool! You have not wit enough to *ask* your bird if we mean you any harm. And yet only moments before you condescended to inform us a prince is no different from any other."

Teel? Aidan asked. *Why was I not warned? You should*

have told me . . . and I should have sensed the interference in the link— His belly tightened. *—unless they also have something of a Cheysuli for use in making shields—*

Teel sounded disgusted. *Are you so blind as that? Or have you become a lackwit?*

I am no lackwit because I prefer to know *who my enemies are—* Aidan broke it off laggardly, belatedly comprehending. *Is that it? Solindish, Ihlini, or no—they are not my enemy?*

In the link, Teel sighed. *There is hope for you yet.*

Irritated, Aidan glared again at the old man. "Do you blame me for being dubious? Our blood has been at war for centuries. You *yourself* fought—" He frowned. "And if you fought Carillon, it means you fought *with* Bellam."

"Of course it does," the old man snapped. "I was a loyal Solindishman—"

"—a loyal *Ihlini*—"

"—and dedicated to my land." Siglyn glared. "You are rude. You have no respect for the aged—"

"You have no respect for *me*—"

"Because we fooled you?" Siglyn grinned, baring old teeth. "You fooled yourself. Because *we* did not declare our race, as you do with all your barbaric, ostentatious gold—" he made a rude gesture all too dismissive of the *lir*-gold "—then we are obviously tricksters out to spill your blood." Siglyn indicated the knife still clutched in Aidan's hand. "Of course, *you* have the weapon . . ." He sighed, glancing at Tye. "The Cheysuli spend much of their time telling gullible Homanans that we are all demons and servants of Asar-Suti, the Seker—without once considering our feelings."

"Your *feelings!*" Aidan was astounded. "You are the enemy—at least, some of you are . . ." He scowled blackly at the old man, disliking the morasss he was, from all appearances, walking into on his own. "*Too many* of you are. Do you know how many of my race—of my *kin*—your kind have killed? Do you know that Strahan's son only weeks ago murdered a helpless infant, and then tried to kill your lord?"

"What baby?" Ashra asked. "We have been long on the road, and news travels slowly . . ." A vertical line drew heavy brows together. "What baby, Aidan?"

"My cousin," he answered curtly. "Lochiel murdered him in his bed without even so much as touching him."

She exchanged a glance with Tye. Neither of them spoke, but Aidan sensed they were not pleased by the news. Ashra squeezed his wrist briefly in a gesture he interpreted as sympathy.

Siglyn shifted on his cushion, clearly annoyed. "Strahan was a puffed-up, arrogant fool with delusions of godhood . . . must you judge us all by him?"

"It is a bit difficult *not* to, when he has been so dedicated to destroying my race. And now his son as well—"

"But we are not his sons, or his daughter," Ashra said quietly. "We are merely Solindish-born Ihlini, trying to make a living in a land gone mad from war." She sighed, removing her hand from Aidan's wrist. "Strahan has done more damage to his race than any other, save for Tynstar. It was he who *began* it all."

Siglyn grunted. "You know nothing about Tynstar, girl. I knew him personally—" But he broke it off, waving a hand at Aidan. "Sit down, sit down. If you are to hear the truth, you should do it with cloth beneath your rump and good wine close to hand." Tufted brows rose. "Sit *down*, boy!"

In the link, Teel suggested it might be wise. No sense in standing when one could sit and be more comfortable.

Aidan sat. But was not comfortable.

Three

"First," he said, before any of them could speak, "I want to know how. *And* why."

Ashra, who added fuel to the fire, cast him a puzzled glance across one slender shoulder. Ringlets writhed. "What do you mean?"

"I should have known you. All my life I have been told a Cheysuli can tell when an Ihlini is near, because of the interference in the *lir*-link. And the *lir* always forewarns—" Aidan grimaced, not looking at Teel, "—*usually* forewarns." He sighed, shifting the wineskin in his lap. "None of us knew Lochiel because he had a ring once worn by my father. It has been bespelled for years, ever since he gave it, unknowing, to an Ihlini witch. Rhiannon." He dismissed her with a gesture. "Lochiel has the ring now, and he used it. Is that how Teel and I did not know you? Have you a like item?"

Tye shook his head as he settled down against his rolled blanket. "Have you met none of us before?"

Aidan nearly smiled. "No Ihlini has come into Mujhara—or Clankeep—for many, many years."

Ashra was clearly startled. "And you have been nowhere else?"

Her unfeigned astonishment at first puzzled him, until he realized she had most likely spent her life on the road, and could not comprehend a man who lived only in two places.

And then he considered how that sounded, even to him: he had been nowhere in the world save Mujhara and Clankeep. Even though one day he would rule a realm it took weeks to ride across.

Tye grinned. "All unknowing, she strikes true." He squirted wine into his throat, swallowed, then plugged the opening. "You did not know us because there was nothing to know."

"You are Ihlini—"

"—and kin." Tye's green eyes were odd in the light. "Without your gold and your *lir*, would another Cheysuli know you as Cheysuli?"

Aidan gestured. "I may lack the color, but—"

Siglyn cut him off. "Answer the question."

Aidan waited a moment, marshaling his courtesy, then did as Siglyn ordered. "Without my gold and my *lir*, it is possible he would not . . . but if you knew how to look for other things—"

Tye sighed in disgust. "He will not cooperate."

"Aidan." Ashra's voice was soft. "You did not know we are Ihlini because we are kin. It is true all Chyesuli bear certain similarities in color and shape of bones, but past that there is only what resides in here." She touched one breast. "We are less obvious than Cheysuli, lacking a uniform color and the *lir*, but our hearts are the same, and our blood."

Aidan avoided her eyes, looking instead at his healed hand. There was no scar, but he remembered all too well the pain, the shock, the acknowledgment of Lochiel's intent.

Siglyn's voice was harsh. "It's an easy enough answer, boy: we did not drink of the cup. We are uncommitted

Ihlini—save to our land—and therefore Asar-Suti is not in us. Our blood is ours, not his . . . have you or any of your kin ever known a hostile Ihlini who was not one of the Seker's?''

Aidan, who had known none at all, could only think on the stories he had heard. His uncles had known Ihlini, but all had served Asar-Suti. Keely's contact had been with Strahan and his minions, all sworn to the Seker. There was Rhiannon, but she, too, belonged to the Seker. Every Ihlini, save for one, had meant his kin harm.

Then he stirred, recalling. "There was Taliesin."

Tye shook his head. "Taliesin repudiated the Seker. It was why Tynstar made him drink of the blood, so he would live forever knowing what had been done in the name of his race . . . and it was why Strahan destroyed his hands.''

Aidan stared into flames. "Then I have never known—or known *of*—a hostile Ihlini who did not serve the Seker."

"To drink of the blood is to bind yourself to Asar-Suti," Siglyn said. "The bond, once forged, cannot be broken, save by death. Taliesin eventually was cast out—but an uncommitted Ihlini always knows one of the Seker's, just as a Cheysuli does."

Tye's lips peeled back. "There is a stench," he said clearly, "that clings to everything they touch."

Aidan drew in a breath. "And so you are saying they are different from you?"

Ashra smiled. "They have always been different."

He found breathing difficult. He wanted to laugh, but there was nothing to laugh *at,* save the memories of lessons taught so carefully in Clankeep. Lessons all Cheysuli learned, believing implicitly, because the *shar tahls* said so. If it was said by a *shar tahl*, it was so: everyone knew that. The *shar tahls* were the guardians of the prophecy, of the old ways, making certain tradition remained untainted and the service continued unbroken.

"Untainted," Aidan murmured, "by such things as the altering of a custom called *kin-wrecking*, even though the need is gone."

"What?" Siglyn snapped; the old man, regardless of revelation, was unchanged.

Aidan swallowed painfully. "What if they are wrong? What if, after too many years, it has become *habit* to hate Ihlini—*habit* to name them enemy, suitable only for killing?

Do you see? We are taught it very young: to hate, and fear, and kill . . ." He shut his eyes and rubbed wearily at his face. "The prophecy says we must unite two magic races, and yet the *shar tahls* tell us time and time again we should have no congress with Ihlini, because Ihlini want to destroy us."

"*They* do," Ashra explained. "Those of the Seker *do*— but not the rest of us."

Tye's tone was oddly gentle. "Teachings can become twisted. There may be no intent, but it occurs . . . and eventually the twisting becomes unchanging tradition."

Aidan stared at them all. "Are we wrong? Are all the teachings twisted?"

A glint showed in Tye's eyes. "Why ask us? We are Ihlini. The enemy. And this is merely a clever game played to cause you grief, confusion—and doubt." He smiled crookedly. "Ask your *lir*, Cheysuli. Ask your other self."

Aidan did it through the *lir*-link, because there was no interference. Because he could, in spite of Ihlini presence. Because he was afraid not to, as if asking aloud cheapened the *lir*-bond his kind revered so much.

Tell me, he said. *Are all the teachings wrong?*

Teel did not answer.

Tell me, Aidan repeated. *Are we blinded by the very thing that all Cheysuli serve?*

The *lir*-link quivered briefly. Teel's reluctance to answer was manifest.

Aidan forsook the link. "Tell me!" he shouted. "I have conversed with *gods* . . . do I not deserve an answer from the *lir* they gave me?"

Teel's tone lacked his customary acerbity. *The times demand harsh truths*, he said at last. *And sometimes harsher falsehoods.*

Falsehoods. Aidan clamped his teeth shut. *Are you saying all of it is a lie?*

They have taught what had to be taught.

Why did it have *to be taught?*

Ignorant men do ignorant things.

Such as ignoring prophecies.

After a moment: *Aye.*

And ignoring the prophecy results in no Firstborn.

Feathers were fluffed. *Aye.*

You have us, Aidan said intently. *You have us, and the Ihlini. Are we not enough? Why must there be the Firstborn?*

Because they were firstborn . . . and the gods want them back.

Suspicion roused itself. *Firstborn—bestborn? Is that what it is? The gods gave us self-rule, and the bloodlines fragmented because of Ihlini ambition. So the only way of restoring the balance—of regaining the bestborn children—is to make them out of the bits and pieces culled from all the lands.*

Not all. Teel sounded himself again. *Not all—only four. Four realms and two races.*

Aidan felt rage building. With effort, he damped it down. *If they want them so badly, why not simply* make *them? It was what they did in the first place!*

Teel sighed faintly. *They gave their children self-rule. Self-rule perpetuates itself . . . none of you are what you once were, and the gods can force nothing. They can only ask, and suggest, and guide—*

Gods are gods! Aidan cried. *Gods can do anything!*

Even create a being greater than themselves.

Greater—?

There is nothing a god can do that you cannot do.

But there is—

All that a god can do can be done by the children. Only the ways and means are different.

Teel—

The raven sighed. *There is intellect, and freedom, and skills beyond belief. They gave you everything. They made you what you were—you* made *you what you are.*

I do not know what I am, anymore.

Amusement touched the link. *Child of the gods. What more is there to be?*

It was too much to contemplate. Aidan withdrew from the link and sat motionless near the fire, staring sightlessly into flames. Light burned first into his eyes, then into his brain.

"Times have changed," he murmured. "Everything has changed."

No one said anything.

"It was a means." Aidan stirred a little. "A means, nothing more. A way of communicating. Too often one man will not listen to another, no matter how wise he is . . . but if a *god* says it—" *Oh, gods.* "—if a god says it, one or two may listen. Then one or two more. Until eventually a grouping becomes a clan, and a clan becomes a people." He sighed heavily. "We serve a collection of words. And the words have become twisted."

Ashra's voice was soft. "Then set them straight," she said. "You have it in you, Aidan."

His laughter was bittersweet. "I have nothing inside me now save a profound emptiness."

Green eyes glinted. "Fill it," Tye suggested.

Aidan sighed and slung aside the wineskin. "I need sleep. I need a true sleep, not this pale mockery filled with too many dreams . . ."

"Everyone dreams," Tye said.

"Not like this. Not as I do." Aidan spread his skins. "Not so vividly, or so unsettlingly."

Ashra was very calm. "Siglyn speaks dreams."

"He *speaks*—?" But Aidan shook his head. "No insult intended, but I do not need a road magician's tricks—"

"And I'll give you none," snapped Siglyn. "I speak truths, not falsehoods."

Truths and falsehoods. Much as Teel had mentioned. Aidan looked across the fire at the old man. Shadows and firelight warred in his face, making planes and hollows and creases. The rheumy eyes were bright. The challenge in them implicit.

Aidan nodded once. "Speak my dreams," he said. "Divide the falsehoods from the truths."

The old man smiled. "First there is Tye, and Ashra. Then I will speak your dreams."

Four

Tye brought his lute from the wagon and seated himself on his blanket across the fire from Aidan. The instrument was delicate, of a pale blond wood with ivory pegs and inlay. In firelight, fragile sinew strings glowed gold.

Slender hands caressed the wood and strings though no sound was emitted. The lute waited. "Will you hear me, Homanan?"

Not Cheysuli. Frowning, Aidan nodded.

"Will you *listen*, Homanan?"

He wanted to protest; did not. He nodded yet again.

Notes ran from the lute like water, clear and cool and sweet. It sang of tenderness and joy, love and dark hatred, astonishment and acceptance. The sounds pinned Aidan to his skins, then flayed him until his spirit vibrated with the richness of its song. And then the lute-song, dying away, became nothing more than accompaniment to the human instrument.

Tye sang in a true baritone almost at odds with his beauty, for Aidan had expected a tenor. But the baritone was clear and effortlessly eloquent, swinging down to caress the top range of a skilled bass, then soaring upward to drift across the sweet register of the finest tenor. Tye's magic was manifest.

Aidan stared into the fire until it burned away his sight. He saw colors inside his head. And then a shadow crossed his vision, blotting out the fire, and he saw Ashra begin to dance.

She wore bright layered skirts of green and red and gold, and a snug black leather jerkin that displayed full breasts and narrow, curving waist. She knotted slender hands in tangled ringlets and lifted them until they cascaded down her shoulders and back. She tipped back her head, baring an exquisite throat, and Tye's song abruptly turned from the

grace of illusion to the driving notes of seduction. When
Ashra danced, the Wheel of Life stopped turning.

Aidan found he could not breathe. A brief, warning tickle
touched the back of his consciousness, reminding him Ashra
was Tye's woman, but he was vividly aware of a new and
perverse side of his nature promising him he could brush
Tye aside like a gnat. He had been intrigued by Ashra from
the first, from the *very* first; he had respected the bond
between singer and dancer, but that respect was coming
undone as he watched her now. He could not help himself:
he wanted Ashra badly.

She came to him. Hair hung to her waist, tumbling as she
moved, clinging to breasts and hips. She bent, touched him,
took his hands into hers. Her touch set him afire.

Black eyes promised him all he wanted and more. Ashra's
smile was for him, for him alone; Tye no longer mattered.
And when she drew him up, first to his knees, then to his
feet, he allowed it; he wanted it; *needed* it.

"Come," Ashra whispered.

She led him from his pallet of skins to the bare earth
before the old magician. Dully, Aidan stared down at him;
he wanted, at this moment, nothing to do with Siglyn or his
dream speaking. He wanted only Ashra.

"Come," she said again, and took him to the ground. He
knelt there willingly, because she requested it.

The old man's eyes were very bright. "Sit you there," he
said. "Do nothing, save what I tell you."

Aidan, still lost in lute-song and lust, merely nodded.

Ashra withdrew. The old man put his hands on Aidan's
head, cradling his jaw as one might a child's, or a woman's.
The palms were rough-textured from age, but the wiry fingers were strong. Aidan stared into rheumy blue eyes, because he had no other choice.

"Son of the forests, son of the cities, son of the sunlight
and darkness," Siglyn said softly. "Warrior and prince, skep-
tic and adept. You are more than many, and less than what
you must be. And you dream . . ."

Aidan sucked in a sudden breath, because he had forgotten. He was aware the music had died, and Ashra no longer
danced. She stood behind him, while Tye sat silent as stone
upon his blanket, holding the moon-bleached lute.

"You dream of chains," Siglyn said. "Chains that bind a

man; chains that set him free. Bound, the life continues; broken, it is freed. Which do you seek?"

"It breaks," Aidan blurted. "Always. I have only to touch it—"

"Do you wish it to break?"

"Wishing makes no difference. It simply *breaks*—"

Siglyn's hands tightened. "Chained warrior; chained prince; chained raven. That is what I see."

Aidan swallowed painfully. "If I broke it . . . if I broke the chain, would I be free?"

"That is not for me to say."

"But you said the life is freed if the chain is broken."

Siglyn removed his hands. "Did I say such a thing? Or did you perceive it?"

Aidan's blurted laugh was hollow. "I could not even begin to tell you."

"But I can begin to show you. And if you wish it, I will."

Aidan's head came up. "What is the cost?" he demanded. "There always must be a price."

"Of course there is," Siglyn agreed. "Nothing is gained without risk; nothing is learned without cost; nothing is given without a price. The gods exact a heavy toll."

"And you, old man? What do you expect?"

The old man laughed. "Paying the price without knowing the cost is a part of learning. The choice—and the risk—is yours."

Aidan knelt in dirt with the fire—and Ashra—at his back, conscious of an almost overpowering sense of futility. He could not deal with this; could not comprehend the riddles he was expected to anticipate and answer. He could only sit helplessly before an old Ihlini magician and shake his head.

"Tell me," he rasped. "Show me. I will accept the cost."

Blue eyes narrowed. "Willingly?"

He drew in a deep breath and blew it out as quickly. "It is a part of my *tahlmorra*. I am required to do it willingly."

"Tye," Siglyn said, but his eyes never left Aidan's face.

Tye rose, set down his lute, and crossed the fire's shadow. He knelt at Aidan's side. Briefly he worked at his belt, a snake of hammered links lying flat against his hips, gilded by firelight. He gave it into Siglyn's hands.

The belt was of poor workmanship. Aidan, looking at it, saw where the hammer had crushed a link too flat, beveled another too crooked, crimped the gilt entirely. Even its gilding was false, shedding itself in Siglyn's hands.

But the old man smiled. He lifted the belt and threw it into the fire. "Fetch it out," he said.

Aidan blinked. "Out of *there?*"

"You agreed to do as I said, no matter what the cost."

"And this is the price? I am to burn the flesh from my bones?"

"Do as I say."

The vestiges of distrust rekindled. "How do I know this is not an Ihlini trick?"

Siglyn's teeth showed. "You do not."

Aidan glanced at Tye, who knelt next to him. The smooth dark face was expressionless, the green eyes averted. Tye merely waited.

Ashra moved from behind Aidan and walked to Siglyn's side. Like Tye's, her face was curiously blank, but her eyes were not averted. They bored into Aidan's. They did not beseech, but he knew himself seduced.

Briefly, he considered *lir*-shape. A raven might slip into the flames quickly and retrieve an object without risking much of himself, but Aidan knew the belt was too heavy. The only way he could fetch it out, as Siglyn required, was to reach into the flames and lift it.

He turned, and knelt on one knee by the fire. It was not so large a fire that it might threaten his life, but nonetheless it would hurt. If he were quick enough, he might singe only the hair on his hand and arm, but the hot metal would surely sear his hand. And he had only recently gotten back the use of both.

I was told there was a task. Perhaps this is it.

Aidan set his jaw so hard his teeth ached. Then he reached into the fire.

He plunged his left hand down through the flames into coals, grabbing for the belt. His fingers found the heated links and caught them up, dragging the belt from the fire. He spun around and dropped it in the dirt in front of Siglyn, nursing his hand against his chest.

"Are you burned?" the old man asked.

Aidan opened his mouth to shout of course he was burned—and then realized there was no pain. He held out his hand and saw unblemished flesh. He had not singed a single hair.

Siglyn nodded. "You put your hand into the flames, fully expecting it to be burned. It matters little the flames were not real . . . only that you *believed* them real—and still performed the task." He nodded again. "There is some hope for you yet."

Aidan stared at Tye's belt in the dirt. The cheap gilt paint had burned away, leaving base metal bared. It was, he thought bitterly, analagous to himself.

Siglyn reached down and lifted the belt. He took an end into either hand, stretching it, then snapped the links flat. Metal cracked, then flaked away. In silence, the old man tied knots in the cheap metal belt. Four of them. And as he snapped the knotted belt a second time, the knots became joined links of purest, flawless gold.

Aidan nodded. Of course.

"Chained warrior; chained prince; chained raven." Siglyn smiled. "Your choice. To break it, or make it whole."

Aidan unbuckled his leather belt and slid the three matching links into his hands. A brief examination told him they were of the same making as the joined links in Siglyn's hands.

"How? he asked. "How do I make it whole?"

"That is your choice?" Siglyn asked.

"Aye: to have it whole."

"Be certain of it."

He smiled. "I am. I would have it whole."

Siglyn's eyes were very still. "Give one link to Tye. One to Ashra. The last to me."

Aidan did so.

"Name them."

Aidan looked at the link in Tye's hand. "Shaine," he said quietly. "Shaine the Mujhar."

"And?"

"Carillon." He looked into Ashra's emotionless face. "Carillon of Homana."

The link glittered in Siglyn's hand. "The last?"

"Donal, who was Cheysuli."

Siglyn nodded once. "The links are distributed. The chain is for you. The joining is for you."

Slowly Aidan knelt in front of the old man. From him he took the chain of four joined links. He touched the one he had named Donal to the single link Siglyn held, and in the snapping flash he squinted, knowing the joining complete.

He repeated the ritual with Ashra, then Tye. Four links were joined to three: the chain at last was whole.

Aidan waited, staring fixedly at the fifth link. Waiting. When it remained unbroken, he smiled joyously at Siglyn. "Whole," he exulted. "*Not* shattered. *Not* broken. Its name is not Aidan!"

Relief was overwhelming. Aidan cast a glance at Tye, at Ashra, looking for some sign of acknowledgment, but they gave him nothing more than silence. It did not matter. Aidan laughed at them all, then yawned a tremendous yawn into Siglyn's face.

"Forgive me" he said, when he could. "I did not mean to do that."

"Magic does tire a man," the old Ihlini said gravely. "But not so much as dealing with gods." His hand was on Aidan's head. "Sleep, child of the Firstborn . . . and dream your dreams in peace."

He slept dreamlessly, knowing peace for the first time in too long. When he awoke he fully expected to be alone. But the wagon still stood by the tree, and Ashra sat by the fire.

Memory rushed back. Aidan sat up, pushing a hand through tangled hair. "I thought—" But he broke it off raggedly, no longer certain what he thought.

Ashra smiled. "You thought you would be deserted. No. Not yet."

He looked beyond her and saw Tye with the horses, hitching them to the wagon. Siglyn was absent; probably *in* in the wagon. Teel, perched on the canopy, croaked a morning greeting.

Aidan looked back at the girl. "Why?" he asked roughly. "What was all of it for?"

"You should know, by now." Ashra tossed her head and sent ringlets flying. Copper hoops in her ears flashed. "It is because of you we are here."

Certainty increased. "But you are not gods."

"No." Her smile was sweet. "We are what you see: Singer, Dancer, Magician. But we are servants of the gods, as you witnessed last night. We do their bidding."

Aidan recalled too well what had occurred the night before. "Are you real?"

"As real as can be, as the gods made us." Ashra's bold eyes were bright, full of unself-conscious awareness of what her body had promised. "We are as you wish us to be. It remains for you to decide."

The image of her dancing rose before his eyes. He recalled her supple, seductive movements; the bright promise of her eyes. And the burning of his flesh as she put her hands upon him. "Real," he said hoarsely. "I want you to be real."

Her smile enveloped him. "Then I am."

His traitor's body betrayed him. "And if I said I no longer wanted you to share Tye's bed?"

Ashra laughed aloud. "I have shared Tye's bed since before you were born. Since before your father was born, and his. I think it very likely I will go on sharing his bed."

It hurt. "Then there is no hope for *us*—"

"No," she agreed solemnly. "That is what dreams are: wishes, and the illusion of reality. And truth. If you lay with me, you would never know if it were real or false. And that would not satisfy you."

A dry irony shaped his tone. "For a while, it might."

She laughed again and rose with the supple motion of a born dancer. The chaplet in her hair gleamed against black ringlets.

"Wait." He put out a hand to delay her. "If none of this is real, why did you let it go so far? Last night . . ." Shrugging, he let it go. "I am not a celibate man, nor a boy misinterpreting a woman's intent. I have seduced women myself, and I have been seduced. You lured me last night with promises of coupling. Why, if you meant nothing of it?"

A graceful hand swept across breasts, then down to touch curving hips. So easily she seduced him, though her eyes were serious. "Because you *are* a man," she said, "and a man must recognize his own mortality, his own weaknesses and flaws, before he can set them all aside. Desire is one of the strongest of all emotions. A man cannot always control it. He cannot always set it aside when it must be."

He thought of countless times he had allowed himself to lose control. Much of it had been genuine desire. But *as* much had been the need to lose himself in something to forget what drove him so.

"I have slept with many women . . ." It was a statement of truth, not a boast. He had never been that kind. Women to him were special, because of the *kivarna*. He knew what they felt in his bed. It deepened his own pleasure, to know what it was for the woman. But he had *used* the women . . .

though very considerate, he had not looked for anything more.

Ashra's exotic face softened. "I did not tease you out of cruel perversity. I did it so you would see how easily it is done, so it would not lead you into misfortune. You are a man, not a god, and you must know it always. Even when you might believe yourself more gods-blessed than most."

He grunted skepticism. "Am I?"

Her smile was slow, serene. "You are many things, Aidan. But you must be only *one*, before you understand."

Tye came up beside her, slipping an arm around her waist. "How fares the lesson?"

She smiled and squeezed him briefly. "He does not yet understand."

Tye nodded. "The learning will come of its own time and place. We have done as much as we dare . . . it is time we moved on."

"Siglyn?" she asked.

"In the wagon." Tye kissed her on top of her head. "Go and see to his comfort, while I bid our prince farewell."

Ashra moved away. Aidan looked at Tye, bitterness lacing his tone. "Have I amused you?"

Tye's face was solemn and inexpressibly lovely. It was not womanish after all, Aidan decided, merely the work of a master's hand. "The struggles of a man never amuse me," Tye said quietly. "I have seen too much to laugh at anything. Ashra, Siglyn and I have been about this for a very long time . . . you are not the first, and certainly not the last. But for now, as you travel toward your *tahlmorra*, you will feel yourself quite alone. Quite apart from the rest. But never think yourself *better*." His green eyes were level. "Do you understand?"

"I think I understand nothing," Aidan admitted truthfully.

Tye laughed. "It will come." He briefly inclined his head. "Nothing is done without purpose. Remember that, Aidan."

Aidan watched the singer walk toward the wagon. Tye climbed up onto the wide seat and took up the reins. Beside him sat Ashra, chaplet glinting in the dawn. The wagon jolted into motion as Teel lifted from the canopy. As it trundled away, the mists closed around, muting the canopy's brilliant colors. In a moment the wagon was gone.

Aidan looked down at his pallet of skins and wool. The

chain lay there. A whole, unbroken chain, as he had made it the night before.

He knelt down and touched it. Took it into his hands. And knew, for the first time, the journey he undertook would lead him to different roads, and to choices rarely offered.

It was up to him to make them.

Five

The first thing Aidan noticed about Kilore was the scalloped line of chalk cliffs thrusting upward out of the seashore like a mailed, white-gloved fist. Atop the fist, he knew, perched the Aerie of Erinn, where all the proud eagles were hatched. His own mother had been. It seemed odd to think of it, so far from Homana. But this was Aileen's home. Homana was his.

The second thing Aidan noticed about Kilore was the pungent smell of fish. Its pervasiveness was oppressive; he grimaced quiet distaste as the ship was carefully docked. He deserted it at once, walking hastily onto the dock, and promptly tripped over a tangle of net and kelp as he twisted his head from side to side in a bid to see everything.

He made an effort to recover his balance with some show of aplomb; nevertheless, he was embarrassed. He was half Erinnish himself, with sea-blood in his veins. Surely it meant something.

But no one seemed to have noticed; if they had, no one cared. The day was nearly done. Fishing boats were coming in brimming with the day's catch. No one had time for him.

Aidan left the docks and went into the city proper, a tumbled collection of buildings clustered between ocean and cliffs, meticulously avoiding dray-carts and baskets full of fish and effluvia. He soon found himself in the markets where the catch was fully displayed. Here the stench was worse.

"I come from this stock," he muttered. "I had best get used to it."

Why? Teel asked. *Are you planning to live here?*

Aidan laughed. *Not if I can help it.* He paused, looking around. *How do I find the road to the castle?*

Easier done from up here.

Aidan glanced up. Teel, in a flock of seabirds, was black against cream and white. *Where do I go?* he asked. *Your view is better than mine.*

Teel agreed benignly. *You might try going up.*

Aye, but I meant which road— Aidan grinned, comprehending. *Aye, lir "up."*

He went up, and up again, reveling in *lir*-shape and the ability to fly. He might have stayed an hour or two longer, drifting about the fortress, but it made no sense to do so when his business was within. Regretfully, Aidan took back his human shape at the head of the cliff path, and walked the rest of the way across dampened ruts to the massive gates of Kilore.

Unlike Hart's castle, Sean's was properly guarded. Aidan was required to show his signet as proof of identity, then was taken at once through the baileys into the fortress itself. Dark stone was wind-scoured smooth, even on the corners, giving the blocky fortress a soft, rounded appearance Aidan knew was deceptive. No one had ever taken Kilore. The fortress was unbreechable, perched on its clifftop aerie all warded about with stone. The walls were spiked with iron.

A servant escorted him to a private chamber and gave him leave to enter. Aidan at first thought it odd that he would be so summarily sent in to face his aunt and the lord of Erinn—Liam, Aidan's grandfather, had died four years before—but the servant merely smiled and opened the door. Aidan stepped in.

A man stood just inside of the door. His broad back was to Aidan; he leaned on a longsword, nodding from time to time. As he heard the door shut he glanced back briefly, showing a strong-featured face, then returned his attention to the other occupants.

It was a practice chamber, Aidan saw in surprise. Not the private chambers of a lord and his lady, but a chamber reserved for learning the use of weapons. Racks filled the walls, full of swords, spears, pikes, halberds and other deadly things. The room itself was plain, with no illumination save for torch brackets set high in the walls, spilling light into the chamber. On steel, it ran like water.

Two people sparred in the chamber, scuffing across smooth stone. Aidan paid them little notice as he quietly shut the door, then stepped up next to the man just before him and made the mental adjustment to change languages. He had learned his Erinnish from Aileen and Deirdre and spoke it passingly well, but with a Homanan accent.

"My lord?" he began diffidently.

The other barely glanced at him. "A moment," he said briefly. "They'll be done soon enough."

Aidan looked. A man and a woman. To himself, he smiled: he knew without even asking who the woman was. Only Keely knew the sword, and was so steadfast in its art.

But nothing in their sparring led him to believe she and her teacher would be done any time soon. They seemed well matched, and neither in any hurry to end the bout. They led one another into traps, parried expertly, patiently began again. Faces were flushed and breathing was loud, but both were obviously supremely fit and not in the least winded.

This might last all day . . . Except the man at his side— Sean, he assumed—had said it was nearly done. Aidan glanced sideways at the big man by his side. "How can you tell?"

The other smiled. "I'm the sword-master. I'm supposed to be knowing these things."

Surprise stole diffidence. "*You* are the sword-master?"

The man grinned, showing a gap in one side of his upper teeth; an eyetooth was missing. "Aye. Did you think I was the lord?"

Aidan slanted him a glance. No, now that he knew better. He was too rough, too worn for lordship. And certainly too old; Sean was, he knew, closer to fifty than to forty. This man was older yet.

Intently, he glanced back at the couple. "Then *that,* I take it, is Sean."

"Aye. And yon woman the lady." The sword-master grinned. "If he's not careful, she'll have him. And then we'll be hearing all about it for at least a seven-day."

"He's too big," Aidan protested instantly, with no prick of reproval for discounting Keely so quickly. "*Much* too big—how could a woman beat him?"

The older man cast Aidan a considering glance. "You're

not from Erinn, lad, in spite of your Erinnish—or you'd be knowing the answer."

It stung. "I am *of* Erinn. That woman is my aunt—your lord is my uncle."

The sword-master grunted. "The House is a large one . . . I'm not knowing which one you are."

Aidan blinked. "Homana," he answered. "Grandson to the Mujhar."

It earned him another glance, but this one was equally unimpressed. "There's another of those here."

Aye, so there was: Keely's son, Riordan, if Aidan recalled correctly. "Aye, but—" He broke off, staring. "She *will* beat him!"

"Aye. She has before." The sword-master grinned. " 'Twill be a noisy meal."

Aidan was astonished. He had heard of Sean's legendary size and prowess from his mother and others. He had expected to find Sean smaller in fact, since stories were often wrong, but this time it was the truth. Sean of Erinn was a very large man of very obvious strength . . . and yet Keely was beating him.

Until Sean hooked her foot and dropped her like a stone.

"You *ku'reshtin*!" She glared up at him from the floor. "It was to be a true bout, not a wrestling match!"

Sean grinned down at her. "I wanted to win, lass. To do it, I'll be doing whatever I must. So will any man with a bit of a brain in his head."

"*Ku'reshtin*," she muttered, more quietly. She hitched herself up on elbows, wincing elaborately. "I would have had you, and you know it."

"I know it," Sean agreed cheerfully, leaning on his sword. "Why d'ye think I cheated?"

"A Cheysuli would never have done—"

"A Cheysuli most likely wouldn't have a sword in his hand in the first place." Sean reached down. "Here, lass, catch hold—I'll not leave you on the floor."

"But you'll *throw* me there." Keely caught his hand and let him pull her up. She wore snug Cheysuli leathers and soft, supple boots mostly suited for household use. Blond hair was braided back from a face no longer young, but striking for its spirit. She was tall, slender, fit. She was also past forty, but age sat lightly on her. She moved like a young woman as she bent to pick up the fallen sword. "So," she said, "you win. Next time will be different."

" 'Twill always be different—next time." Sean cast a glance at Aidan, thick eyebrows sliding up beneath a tangle of curly hair. He was blond, bearded, brown-eyed, with shoulders fit for a plow. "So, lad, you're here. Are we to know who you are, coming so freely into our home?"

Aidan smiled faintly, displaying his heavy signet. "I was brought here properly. And I did pass the test."

Keely studied him. A frown knitted brows. "You have the look and the eyes . . . but that is *not* Cheysuli hair."

"Erinnish," he agreed with resignation, wondering how often he would have to explain himself. "Aileen's hair, though darker; Brennan gave me something."

Keely's eyes widened. Aidan found it briefly amusing that *she* should remark on color; she was fair-haired, fair-skinned and blue-eyed, and no gold on her arms. He more than she had the right to invoke their race.

"Not *Aidan*," she said. "You were a sickly child . . . Aileen said you had outgrown it, but I did not expect this!"

Aidan nodded gravely. "I am better now. Instead of dying today, I will wait until tomorrow."

Sean laughed aloud, sliding his sword back into a rack. Keely did not smile, though a spark in her eyes kindled. She studied Aidan closely, much as she would, he thought, a horse. "Brennan's son," she mused. "Are you as stuffy and pompous as he is?"

Aidan sighed aloud, though inwardly he laughed. She was everything they said; probably more. He was looking forward to it. "He was hoping marriage had forced you to grow up . . . I'll be telling him the truth: you're obviously as bad as you ever were."

Keely scowled. "Don't be giving *me* that Erinnish cant, my lad . . . you've never been here, boyo, and I've lived here very nearly longer than you've been alive."

She had gained her own share of the cant. Aidan, grinning, offered her the courteous bow she would, he knew, scorn. It was why he did it. "They tell stories of you," he said. "Would you like to hear them now?"

Sean's big hand closed on Keely's shoulder. "Not now, lad—we'll be due some wine and ale. Come into the hall with us; Keely will mind her tongue."

"Then I will be disappointed."

"Ku'reshtin," she said calmly, handing her sword to the man still waiting by the door. "Well? He beat me."

"He cheated," the big sword-master said equably. " 'Tis the only way he can win. I've taught you that much, lass, in the years since you've come."

Keely laughed and slapped a corded arm. "Aye, so you have—but perhaps you should look to a new lesson that teaches *me* how to cheat."

Sean shoved open the door. " 'Tisn't in you, lass . . . you've too much Cheysuli honor." He waved her through impatiently, eyeing Aidan with great good cheer. "Have ye come for long, lad?"

Aidan followed Keely. "Long enough to find a wife."

His aunt stopped dead in her tracks, swinging to face him abruptly. "A wife," she said softly. "And would you be meaning my girl?"

Aidan smiled blandly. "I wouldn't be meaning your boy."

It was not, perhaps, the best way to put himself in Keely's favor, but then he had not come to give her the kindnesses and false courtesies she had, from all reports, always despised. He knew enough of her history to be fully aware she would be less inclined to consider his suit than Sean, who was, his sister said, a reasonable, intelligent man. Aileen had also said Keely was much the same, but could be difficult. Aidan did not yet know if marriage to Shona would be suitable, but there was no sense in lying about the reason he had come. Especially to Keely.

Even now, as Sean led the way into the central hall and waved him into a chair and handed down a cup of Erinnish liquor, Keely's expression was stiff. "Does Brennan want this?"

Aidan sipped, blinked surprise at the bite of the liquor, then raised the cup in tribute to Sean. All as he looked at Keely. "Not this *particularly*," he said, "but he wants me married, aye."

A faint line etched itself between her brows. " 'Not this particularly,' " she quoted. "An odd thing to say. Does that mean my oldest *rujholli* argues against my daughter?"

Sean snorted. "I doubt he'd be such a fool. 'Twould be a good match." He ignored the black glance Keely cast him and contented himself with settling his large body into a rough, iron-bound chair. Blond beard parted slightly to exhibit white teeth. "You married into Erinn, and Erinn into Homana. He'd hardly be a man for saying the lass isn't worthy of it."

Keely, who remained standing very near Aidan's chair, tapped a booted right foot briefly. "No," she conceded. "All right, then, kinsman—what is your meaning?"

Aidan did not answer at once, distracted by his surroundings. Kilore was not a place of much refinement. Certainly nothing like Homana-Mujhar, or even Hart's castle in Lestra. It was, first and foremost, a fortress. The casements were tall but very narrow, more like arrow-loups than windows, and the cavernous ceiling was broken up only by greenish, studded beams as big around as a man. Illumination was negligible, save for the blazing fire in the massive fireplace.

"Well?" Keely prodded.

Recalling her question, Aidan smiled. "He merely said he wants me married." The smile stretched into an ironic downward hook. "It is suggested the Lion might be happier with one more male in line to plant a rump in the wooden lap."

Keely's mouth twisted. "How like him," she said lightly, then turned away from Aidan. She took up from a nearby table the cup Sean had poured her, then perched herself on the edge. "And does Aileen say the same?"

"She says I should have more time." Aidan shrugged. "I doubt it will make a difference. The Mujhar is in good health, and my *jehan* is young enough to rule for decades after. If I take a *cheysula* now and get a son on her, or wait ten more years, I doubt the Lion would notice."

Keely's gaze was steady. Pointedly, she said. "And yet you are here."

Sean stirred in his chair. "Lass, the lad's not a child. Could be he's *ready* for a wife." Brown eyes warmed. "Though perhaps he'll think better of it once he's met our lass."

Aidan smiled back. He liked Sean very much. "Is she much like her *jehana*?"

Sean's brows rose. "Like us both, lad . . . a full plate, you might say."

"She has a mind of her own," Keely declared. "No daughter of mine will ever sit behind a man when her place is *beside* him."

Sean nodded blandly. "No daughter of yours would dare such a thing, with you to set her straight."

Aidan laughed into his cup. "Aye, well . . . I did not set out for Shona. I went to Solinde first—"

"Blythe," Keely said at once. She nodded consideringly. "There has been a Solindish-born Queen of Homana before . . . but very long ago." She frowned faintly. "Though there was grief of it—Electra betrayed Carillon by becoming Tynstar's light woman."

"*And* bore him a child. Strahan." Aidan sighed, thinking of Strahan's son. "It does not matter so much any more . . . Blythe is not at the moment ready for marriage, to me or to anyone else." He frowned consideringly into his cup, then sorted out his words. Quietly he told them the story of what had happened.

Softly, yet with a great malignancy, Keely cursed Lochiel when Aidan was done. And the man who had sired him.

"So," she said viciously, "this time they strike at *Solinde*. If they cannot take Homana directly, they will try another way." She slammed down the cup. Wine sloshed over the rim. "To murder a helpless infant . . ." Three long, stiff strides carried her toward the fireplace. All Aidan saw was her back, and its eloquent rigidity. After a moment she turned. "It will be worse for Blythe."

Neither man spoke, transfixed by her intensity.

"Worse," Keely repeated. "For me, it was force. But Blythe bedded him *willingly*—" Keely's face spasmed. "She will hate herself for that."

Sean stirred, stretching out a hand. "Lass—"

Keely shook her head. "You were right to leave her, Aidan. She will want nothing to do with marriage for now. Perhaps for some time to come. And if there is a child—" The lines of her face altered. She looked older, and tired. "She will have to make her choice, just as I did. Although, in the end, the gods saw to it themselves . . ." Keely sighed and thrust splayed fingers into her hair, stripping loosened loops back from her cheeks. "If Hart has any sense, he will show her the proper way of performing *i'toshaa-ni*."

Aiden smiled faintly. "Hart has sense." He shifted forward in his chair. "Aye, I came to speak of Shona and marriage; even so, I am not *convinced* she is the only alternative . . . if we do not suit, I will not insist on it." He thought of his parents. "I know better."

Keely's expression was odd. "I thought that long finished. In her letters, Aileen says they do well enough—"

Aidan, who had no desire to bog himself down in a convoluted discussion of the feelings between his parents, interrupted smoothly. "Let us say I would prefer a match well-suited from the beginning. As yours was."

Keely and Sean exchanged glances. Sean grinned crookedly, but swallowed more liquor rather than say anything. Keely's manner was brusque. "Aye, well . . . it speaks well of you that you are willing to consider Shona's feelings instead of politics. Aileen's doing, I'd wager; Brennan thinks too much of the Lion."

"A common curse, among our kin." Aidan relaxed back into the big copper-bound chair, hooking the foot of his goblet over his belt buckle. He was weary from the journey, but it was a good weariness. What he felt most was a deep, abiding contentment. It came, he sensed, from Kilore herself . . . and the couple who lived with her.

Keely smiled for the first time since he had met her. "You look more suited to Kilore than Homana-Mujhar, or even Clankeep. There may be more of Erinn in your blood than Homana."

He smiled back, unoffended. "My *jehana* has said that once or twice . . . until I come back from Clankeep, and *then* she says I am naught but Cheysuli, prickly pride and all."

Sean grunted. "I am in a better place to judge, I'm thinking, not being biased." He ignored Keely's skeptical grunt. "And 'tis too soon to know . . . how long d'ye plan to stay?"

Aidan opened his mouth to answer—he thought to stay until he and Shona knew if there was a chance, or no—but was interrupted by a treble voice piercing the hall as the big door, opened by a servant, disgorged an angry boy.

" 'Tisn't *fair!*" he cried, marching across to hall to stop in front of his father. " 'Tisn't fair *at all*. She hasn't the right to be ordering me around, this way and that—and *no right at all* to take the bow away!"

He was blond, like both his parents, and his eyes were Keely's blue. His skin was very fair, as Sean's must have been before wind and time had weathered it. If there was any Cheysuli in him, Aidan could not see it.

"The bow," Sean said blankly.

"*My* bow," the boy declared, and then had the grace to look abashed. "At least, 'twould be my bow if you saw fit to let me have one." He slanted a blue-eyed glance at his mother. "Shona has a bow."

Keely nodded gravely. "Shona is somewhat older."

"But she's a *girl*," Riordan declared.

Sean grinned. "A lad with eyes in his head, is it?" He sat forward in his chair, shifting a body much larger than that of his son's. Aidan wondered fleetingly which branch of the Houses Riordan would emulate: the broad bulk of his father's, or the slender fitness of his mother's. "When you're a mite older, lad, you'll be having your own bow. If Shona's told you no, 'tis because she tends your welfare."

" 'Tisn't," Riordan retorted. " 'Tis because she thinks she's *better*."

Keely sighed. It was, somewhat obviously, an old argument. "A Cheysuli warbow is not something a boy should play with, Riordan—"

"I wasn't playing with it," he declared. "I was trying to shoot at a target, just as Shona does—just as *you* do—but she caught me at it and took the bow away." He sighed aggrievedly. " 'Tis bad enough already . . . now they'll be saying I'm a coward afraid of his sister."

"*Who* will?" Sean asked.

The small face was downcast. "All the other boys."

Sean and Keely exchanged a glance. The interplay was subtle: Sean's arched brow, Keely's lifted shoulder.

" 'Tis something we should be tending to, then, I'm thinking," Sean said quietly. "Tomorrow we'll see to finding you a bow—a boy's bow, Riordan, not a Cheysuli warbow—and we'll set out to learn the proper way. I'll not be having them say you're a coward, but neither will I be having a boy too small for a warbow chance hurting someone else."

Riordan, who had been all set to argue, saw he would lose even that much if he protested. So he did not. He merely grinned at both his parents, slanted a briefly curious glance at Aidan, then headed out of the room. His posture was one of irrepressible exuberance.

"Nine," Keely said, before Aidan could ask. "And spoiled near to rotting by a much too permissive *jehan*."

Sean sat back in his chair, smiling blandly. "Aye, well . . . I *am* the Lord of Erinn. Who is there to stop me?"

Aidan watched the door thump closed. "Nine," he mused. "Too young yet for *lir*-sickness, or any signs of it."

Keely's mouth twisted. "He may never require a *lir*. The Erinnish blood, I have discovered, is thicker than our own . . . Shona has none of my gifts, and Riordan may miss as well." She flicked an unreadable glance at Sean. "But as it is Erinn he will inherit, there may be no need."

Aidan did not answer. Keely had schooled her tone into a negligent matter-of-factness, but his *kivarna* told him the truth. She had hoped Shona would share her own unique gifts, thereby asserting the Cheysuli portion of her heritage. The girl had not; now Keely hoped—and probably prayed— Riordan would make up the difference. It was true that in Erinn the need was not so great as in Homana—Aidan's grandsire, Niall, had gained a *lir* so late it made his claim to the Lion tenuous in the eyes of the clans—but undoubtedly Keely wanted to leave the mark of their race in Erinn's history. It was a natural desire; he felt it in himself. But for Keely, the need was stronger.

She recalls too clearly what Strahan did to her . . . and the child she might have borne him. Dishonored, as Ian was— giving Erinn a Cheysuli lord will mitigate her guilt—

He broke it off. It was not his place to delve into Keely's feelings. They were private. *Kivarna* or no, he should respect them.

Sean combed his beard with two fingers. "Shona is out on the headlands, with the dogs. 'Twould not be a bad thing to see her alone, rather than cluttered up by a household."

Keely shot him a sharp glance. "She is not a woman for games." She turned the gaze on Aidan. "Tell her the truth of why you have come."

Aidan smiled blandly. "If you like, I will wear a placard."

His aunt scowled darkly. "I have good reason for what I say. Too many men tease and twist a woman. I'll not have it done with Shona."

Aidan set down the goblet. "*Su'fala*, the last thing I would do is tease and twist a woman. I promise, I will be honest with Shona—I see no reason to play games with a woman I might marry—but I will not blurt out my reason for coming before the proper moment. What chance would I have then? If she is anything like you, she prefers honesty to lies, but there is room for diplomacy. Also courtesy."

Keely's eyes narrowed. "Brennan taught you that."

Aidan smiled calmly. "My *jehan* has taught me many things, aye . . . but I am no more my father than you are your mother."

It was a telling stroke, as he meant it to be. Keely's mother—his granddame, Mad Gisella—had earned only contempt by her conduct with the Ihlini. The last thing Keely wanted was to be thought anything like her.

Keely raked him with a sulfurous glare. Then her mouth twitched. *"Ku'reshtin,"* she said calmly, flicking a hand toward the door. "Go. I will let Shona deal with you—you will find her a worthy match." Another dismissive flick. "On the headlands, as he said. Amidst a pack of hounds."

Six

The turf was lush, thickly webbed, excessively green. None of the nubby rugs in Homana-Mujhar approached its thick texture, nor even the bear pelts in his own chamber, so far away. Erinn was much damper than Homana, and its flora responded with a vigorous, unrestrained growth. Everywhere he looked was *green;* even as he glanced back at Kilore, falling behind, he thought the mottled gray stones acquired a greenish hue, as if to blend in with the turf and trees and storm-gray skies.

So far from home, he thought vaguely, feeling the brief pang of regret flutter deep in his belly. He had not, as he had so belatedly realized in Ashra's company, ever been anywhere. It had never seemed odd to him—he was sufficiently satisfied with life in Mujhara and Clankeep—but now he knew himself incomplete. There were places in the world he could not go, and therefore places in himself he would never know. A man who chained himself to his home drew a curtain over his eyes, blinding himself to all the majesty of the world.

And yet he proposed, one day, to chain himself to a beast. The Lion of Homana, acrouch in Homana-Mujhar.

Is that so bad? Teel's croak emanated from overhead; Aidan glanced up. *A man could have a worse tahlmorra than to be Mujhar.*

Aidan was not disposed to argue. *He could.*

Are you wanting dogs?

He frowned briefly, momentarily nonplussed, then followed the raven's change of topic. *More to the point: do I want the woman with them?*

Teel angled back toward Kilore. *Meet her and find out.*

The raven departed swiftly. Aidan, laughing quietly, looked ahead. The headlands were flat, a green flood of turf edging toward the sea—except that the edge was sharp as a blade, dropping off to a chalky cliff. Somewhere along here, Aidan recalled, his grandsire had ridden a horse off the edge of the world, intent on escape. Deirdre had bidden Niall do it, to keep his honor intact; he had broken another part of his honor as he had broken his parole to Shea, Lord of Erinn, but the circumstances had required it. Had he not gone . . .

Aidan smiled. *Had he not gone, he would never have married Gisella of Atvia, nor sired four children on her, including my own jehan—*

In the distance, something barked. And again. And Aidan, knowing how to read the nuances of such sounds, stopped walking and held his ground.

The river, in full spate, poured across the turf. Ash-gray, smoke-gray, storm-gray, even palest silver. A handful of hounds—no, *more*—nine or ten; he could not count them all. But they clearly counted him, ranging themselves around him. None of them barked, now; the warning had been given. They waited.

Bitches, most of them. Two or three half-grown males, still pups, awkward and gangly. And one huge male who stood hip-high to Aidan, massive shoulders tensed. Hackles bristled on neck, shoulders, rump; deep in his chest, he rumbled.

How many men would test that? Aidan wondered in detachment. *How many men would dare?*

Not he. He was no fool.

The pups, he saw, were less interested in domination than in seeing who he was. But the big male—their sire, undoubtedly—was in no mood to allow anyone closer to Aidan, or Aidan closer to them. And the bitches—how many were there, again?—would not allow a stranger to harm their young.

Impasse. Aidan sighed, wondering how long it would take Shona to release them. He *could* take *lir*-shape and escape this travesty, but he wanted to meet her as a man, on her terms; taking *lir*-shape would lend him an advantage he did not, just yet, want to display.

Then he saw her. Distant yet, but approaching, striding along the edge of the cliffs with no apparent thought for her nearness to danger; hummocky turf curling over the edge could give and send her to her death. But Shona strode on easily, smoothly, without haste; could she not call to them? Or whistle?

No. He realized that as she came closer yet. She was blatantly unconcerned with any discomfort or anxiety engendered by the wolfhounds. What concerned her were the hounds themselves.

She came into their midst as one of them, a hand touching here, there; thick long tails waved. But none of the hounds moved, save to flick an ear, or thump her hip with a tail.

Her language was Erinnish, as expected. Her tone cool, quiet, unhurried. *He* could wait as long as it took. He saw it in her eyes.

Aidan assessed her. Tall. *Very* tall; she was, he thought in shock, at least as tall as himself. While he did not match the elegant height of most Cheysuli, he was easily six feet. So was Shona.

And big-boned to match her height, with broad, level shoulders. There was no delicacy in her, or fragility, or anything approaching femininity. She was, quite clearly, Sean's daughter. Keely, next to Shona, would be shorter, slighter, leaner.

A true-born Erinnish, big of bone and stature . . .

Incongruously, he thought of Blythe. Slender, elegant Blythe, very much a woman. And while there was no doubting Shona's gender—no man would dare—there was nothing at all in her reminiscent of feminine Blythe. Whom Aidan had thought beautiful.

No, he thought wryly, *that is not in Shona's purvue.*

But something was. In movement, in posture, in expression, Shona's gift was *presence*.

She was blonde, like Keely and Sean. A wild, unruly blonde, had she worn her hair cut short. But she did not, and so the curls were tamed. The long, heavy braid—thick around as his forearm—hung over her left shoulder, dangling to her hip. She had tied it off with a leather thong ornamented with amber beads. Their color matched her tunic; her trews were dusty ocher.

Sean's daughter indeed: brown eyes observed him calmly. Her features, though perfectly regular, were not those he might have chosen, given leave. They lacked the elegant aquilinity of Blythe's. There was no delicacy. It was a strong, almost masculine face, devoid of beauty or elegance. Its statement was one of strength. And of unremitting power.

Something tickled his belly. *This woman was born for a throne . . . it shines out of her like a beacon—*

He wondered what Teel would say.

He wondered what Shona would say.

"Enough," she said softly in a low, smoky voice.

For one odd moment he thought she meant him; that she knew why he had come and was giving him his dismissal. But he saw the hackles go down; the male wolfhound's tail waved.

The growling stopped. Aidan blinked. The sound had been so low, so infinitely soft, he had not truly heard it. But with its absence, the silence was absolute. The threat was dissipated; he felt himself relax.

"So," she said, "you're here. What are ye wanting from me?"

To marry you, he said. But only to himself.

Blonde brows arched. "Are ye mute?" she asked.

Until this moment, no. Aidan cleared his throat. "Handsome dogs," he said; the inanity amazed him.

Shona considered him. "They'll do," she allowed gently. " 'Tis what I do, d'ye see? I bred the boyo myself, and all the lads and lasses . . . but not *all* the bitches, of course. The line must not get too tight, or the blood will ruin itself."

Aye, he agreed fervently. *Much like our own.*

Shona gestured briefly. "That one, d'ye see, came from over-island. And that one from Atvia . . ." She shrugged. "They're not known for their wolfhounds, there, but 'twas a line I admired. I brought the bitch in to shore up what was *here*."

Why are we discussing dogs? Aidan smiled weakly. "I like that one there."

Shona glanced briefly at his choice. Her contempt, though fleeting, was manifest. Her smile was barely polite. " 'Tis a judge of wolfhounds, is it?"

"No," he demurred.

Eyes crinkled. "Good; the man admits it. He's the worst of the litter, that lad. A bit crooked in the rear to run down a pack . . . but you'll be knowing that, I'm sure."

"No," he said again. "I know nothing about wolfhounds."
And less about myself; this is not a woman I would look *at,
in Homana—*

Shona laughed aloud. It was a full, hearty laugh, more
like a man's than a woman's. "So, it knows what it doesn't
know—not so many men will admit such a thing, and fewer
to a woman. You must be worth the knowing." She tilted
her head a little. "*Are* you worth the knowing?"

"Some days," he agreed.

Shona smiled. It set her face alight. And then she turned
to the wolfhounds, said a single word, and Aidan was
engulfed.

"There," she said, "they're free. And so are you, if you
like; they'll none of them harm you now."

Not intentionally, perhaps, but ten or twelve wolfhounds—
even some only half grown—were enough to drag down a
man even in polite greeting.

The pups, of course, were uncontrollable, but the others
were only slightly more reserved. Aidan found his elbows
trapped in gently insistent mouths, and his manhood endan-
gered by whipping tails thick as treelimbs. He did what he
could to protect himself—something deep inside laughed to
consider Homana's future unmanned by a pack of dogs—
then one of the hounds reared up and put both front paws
on Aidan's chest.

Off-guard, Aidan stepped back, felt the paw beneath his
boot and heard the anguished yelp; sought to move, and
did: landing full-length on the turf.

"Agh, get off the man . . . let the man *breathe*, d'ye
hear—?" Shona waded in, slapping at hips and shoulders.
Eventually the knot parted; Aidan saw sky again, instead of
a forest of legs.

He was laughing. He could not help himself. He had
grown up with only cursory attendance by dogs—Cheysuli,
having *lir*, did not keep pets—and knew little enough about
the subtleties of unblessed animals kept as companions. He
had known Homanans who trained dogs for hunting, or
kept cats to kill the vermin, but he had never thought about
what it was like. There had been Serri and Tasha in his
childhood, and eventually Teel. *Lir* were very different. A
man could *reason* with *lir;* now, in this moment, all he could
do was laugh and fend off exuberant hounds.

Shona urged them back, giving Aidan room. Eventually

he sat up. He did not at once stand, thinking it might be easier to keep his balance on the ground. The dogs milled around him, snuffling at ears and neck. Noses were cold, damp, insistent; Aidan pulled up his cloak and snugged it around his neck.

Shona laughed. "They're meaning you no harm. 'Tis their way of welcoming you."

Incongruously, he thought of another welcome. The welcome of a woman for a man, home from hunting, or war. He saw Shona standing before a rude hillcroft, wild hair and homespun skirts ravaged by the wind, waiting for his return. He saw Shona bedecked as a queen, receiving foreign envoys who were agog at the height and bearing of Homana's queen; at the overwhelming strength that blazed within her spirit. And he saw Shona kneeling in soiled bedding, sweat- and blood-smeared, gently aiding a wolfhound bitch as she strained to pass a leggy pup into the world.

He took no note of the milling wolfhounds. Only of Shona, in their midst; of the sudden excruciating acknowledgment that pinned him to the turf.

This is what it is to recognize a tahlmorra—

Smiling, Shona reached down a hand. "You'd best come up from there, or they'll be making a rug out of you."

Fingers linked, then hands. And Aidan, moving to rise, felt the power blaze up between them.

Deaf. Blind. Mute. Flesh rolled back from his bones, baring the Aidan within. His body pulsed with a tangle of emotions so alien he felt ill.

Shock . . . astonishment . . . denial . . . anger . . . fear . . . an odd recognition—

—awareness, sharp and abrupt, of intense, painful arousal—

And comprehension so acute it cut like a knife.

Shona.

And then she tore her hand from his. The contact was broken. The clarity, the empathy, the comprehension was cut off, leaving him sweating and shaking and ill, bereft of understanding. All he knew was an unpleasant incompleteness.

Much like a *lirless* warrior.

Vision cleared. He found himself still half-kneeling on the turf, splayed fingers rigid. His breathing was ragged, noisy, as if he had fought a war and lost.

Shona's face was white as the chalk cliffs. Like Aidan, she shook. "Who—?" she blurted. "Who *are* you—?"

He tried to speak and could not. Unwittingly, his free hand groped for hers.

Shona lurched back a step. *"No—"*

The wolfhounds growled.

"Wait—" he managed to croak.

Three more steps. Then she whirled, braid flying, and ran.

Seven

He lay supine, heels, buttocks, and shoulder blades pressed into cool turf. A mounded hummock pillowed his head. Wind blew down the headlands, rippling the folds of the cloak he had snugged across his chest. Hair teased his eyes, but he let it alone, ignoring it, until it crept between lashes. Then he stripped it away limply and tucked the hand back into woolen cloak.

He did not know why he lay on Erinnish turf so close to the chalk cliffs, defying the vigorous wind, except that it brought him an odd sort of numbness. Not a true peace, for that required a contentment in spirit, but a certain detachment, a distance that allowed him to push away the acknowledgment of what had happened.

He smelled salt, sea, fish, and a pervasive dampness. The rich earth of Erinn, supporting webby turf. But most of all he smelled emptiness, albeit in his mind. And a blatant futility.

"I should go home," he said aloud.

He had thought it several times since Shona had left him. But he had not said it, until now; now it took on the trappings of resolve. He *would* go home—

"Lad."

It took Aidan a moment. Then he realized the voice was quite real, not a figment of his currently turbulent thoughts, and he sat up. He intended to stand, but Sean waved him back down. The Lord of Erinn, wind-blown, wind-chafed, joined Aidan on the spongy green turf and, as Aidan, stared out into the sky beyond the edge of the cliffs. Sean had changed out of the plain woolens worn for swordplay into more formal tunic and trews of very deep red. Silver bands the width of Aidan's forearms clasped formidable wrists, worked with intricate knots of wire and thumb-sized bosses.

Aidan drew in a breath, then sighed. "She told you."

Sean continued to stared into the sky. His voice was a rusty baritone. "She told us a stranger came, giving her no name. And that when he touched her—when she put out her hand to help him up—the world fell into pieces."

Aidan gritted teeth. "Not so much the world, for me. *I* fell into pieces."

Silently, Sean put a hand to the turf and uprooted a plot with gentle violence. Then, as if realizing what he had done, he replaced it and tamped it down with broad, deft fingers. And laughed softly, acknowledging the fruitlessness of his repair.

Aidan waited. He still felt empty, and numb, and bereft of something he had only briefly begun to understand, in that instant of physical contact.

Sean's laughter died. His face was a good face, full of strength and character undimmed by nearly fifty years. The gods had been kind to him, gifting him with strong but well-made bones, and a spirit to match them. Aidan had heard stories of how Sean had come from Erinn to win Keely's regard, knowing full well if he lost he lost everything. He had won, in the end, but the battle had been duplicitous and dangerous. He was not, Aidan knew, a stupid man, or a fool; Sean of Erinn was an ally well worth having. And Aidan had hoped, for a very short span, Sean would also become a father.

It was Shona's face, Shona's eyes, Shona's hair, underscored by masculinity. And it hurt with an intensity he had not believed possible.

Sean frowned. "There is a thing of Erinn, my lad, very hard to explain. 'Tis a thing of the blood, much as your *lir*-gifts are . . . with something of the same price to be paid, in certain circumstances."

Recognition flickered sluggishly. "Do you mean the *kivarna*?"

Sean's eyes sharpened. "What are you knowing about it?"

He shrugged. "Only that it exists, and that it gives some

people the ability to understand how others feel." He paused. "And that I *have* it."

Sean sighed heavily. "How long have you known?"

"That it had a name?—a few months, no more. My *jehana* told me when she realized I had the ability . . ." Aidan's mouth twisted. "I thought it was something everyone had. I never even *asked*."

Sean shook his head. "Not everyone, lad. 'Tisn't so prevalent as it once was—even then, 'twas mostly limited to the Aerie. We intermarried too much, in younger days . . ." He squinted into the sky. "Shona has it from me."

Aidan frowned. "But even if she *does*, what difference does it make? Why does the *kivarna* have anything to do with what happened when we touched?"

Sean did not look at him. He stared down at his hands, assiduously pulling up turf and shredding it. "When I came to manhood," he began, "I was no better than a rutting boar. What woman I wanted, I took, if she was willing . . . and she was. She *always* was: I was the Prince of Erinn." He looked at Aidan briefly, sharing the common knowledge of rank and title. "I was taught very young about *kivarna*, so I understood why I found it distasteful to pursue an unwilling woman, and why I was not a bully, and why it hurt me when someone else's feelings were hurt. 'Twas a difficult thing, as a child—but then, you'd be knowing that." His smile was crooked. "They say I sired half the bastards on this island, but no. There was the Redbeard, too . . . perhaps *between* the two of us, we accounted for half."

Aidan, frowning, wondered why Sean was telling him the story of his youth. It was none of Aidan's business how many bastards Sean had sired, or that he had sired any; and it had nothing whatsoever to do with his *kivarna*.

"My lord—"

Sean lifted a silencing hand. "What I'm saying, lad, is I was very lucky, because I took care to be so. I knew I would one day be marrying the Princess Royal of Homana, and that if I was *not* very careful, I alone could turn the future of Erinn—and possibly Homana—into a travesty."

Aidan's frown deepened.

"*Kivarna*," Sean said softly, "has its own sort of price."

Aidan reined in impatience. "My lord—"

"A man who has *kivarna* is blessed in bed," Sean said bluntly, "because he knows what the woman feels. But that same man, lying with a *woman* who has the gift, seals himself to her forever. As she seals herself to him."

Aidan stared at him, recalling all too clearly the results when he and Shona had touched.

Sean drew in a breath. "Had I lain with a woman who had *kivarna*, I could never have lain with Keely. D'ye see? 'Tis a *mutual* binding . . . you may know up here you should lie with another woman, a woman who lacks the gift—" he tapped his head "—but the body says otherwise. The body refuses."

"Refuses?" Aidan echoed.

Sean's expression was odd. "There are more ways to geld a man than with a knife."

"But—" Aidan stared at him blankly. "Are you saying so long as I lie with women who lack *kivarna*, I am in no danger?"

"Aye, lad. And I'm assuming you've found that out already." One of Sean's brows arched sardonically. "Have you not?"

Impatiently, Aidan waved a hand. "Aye, aye . . . I was never a rutting boar—" He stopped. "Perhaps I was, a little—but the *reasons* were different . . ." He saw Sean's private smile; he scowled and went on. "So, you are saying that Shona and I share this *kivarna*, and if we slept together we would be bound to one another."

"Forever," Sean affirmed.

"But you do not share this with Keely."

The Lord of Erinn grinned. " 'Tis your way of asking if I'm faithful, is it?" Then, as Aidan tried to protest, Sean shook his head. " 'Twas never an issue, lad. She has no Erinnish, and no *kivarna*, but it doesn't matter. Keely is more than woman enough for any man, even a reformed boar." Then the humor faded. "D'ye understand what I'm saying?"

"Aye." Oddly, jubilation welled up. Now he understood. Now it had a name. Now it had a *purpose*. Aidan smiled. "What is the problem? I came to Erinn to see if Shona and I would suit one another. Obviously, we do."

Sean's expression was solemn. "Do you?"

"Aye! Even this *kivarna* says we do."

Sean nodded after a moment. "Aye. But there's something you're forgetting."

Aidan spread his hands. "What?"

"Shona. She's wanting no part of you."

* * *

She paced, because she could not stand still. Back and forth, back and forth—until the dogs began to whine. Until her mother, rather more calmly than expected, told her to stop.

Shona swung around. "Stop!" she cried. "You tell me to stop? 'Tis the only thing keeping me whole—"

Keely's contempt, though subtle, displayed itself nonetheless. "There is no sense in allowing yourself to become so overwrought."

Shona's eyes blazed. "And would *you* not be overwrought?"

Looking at her daughter, Keely sighed. She had bequeathed the girl her own stubbornness and outspokenness—Shona disdained such things as polite diplomacy when bluntness would do, and she had little patience for convoluted courtesies. She was, Keely reflected, exactly as she had made her . . . and now her mother must live with it.

But so must Shona. And just now it was impossible.

They were in the central hall, where Shona had announced her arrival by slamming open the door before the startled servant could do it for her, with less drama. Shona's flamboyant arrival, complete with eleven wolfhounds, nonetheless was quickly forgotten in the shock of seeing brown eyes gone black in confusion and shock, and the pallor of her face. She had blurted out what had happened. Sean had at once dispatched himself to find Aidan; Keely dismissed gathering servants and shut the door personally, telling her daughter of Aidan's reason for his visit.

Now the girl paced before the fireplace. The hounds, sprawled here and there as living, breathing carpets, watched her worriedly. Keely, lacking *kivarna*, nonetheless shared a portion of their anxiety. But she would not let her daughter see it.

Shona turned on her heel and paced back the other way. "Married, is it? They might have warned me. They might have *written*. Even *he* might have; was he thinking I'd welcome him?"

"Undoubtedly," Keely answered. "We give welcome to all our guests."

Shona cast her an impatient scowl. " 'Twasn't what I meant . . . I *meant* he might have been thinking how I'd react, meeting him like that."

"I doubt he anticipated the *kivarna*," Keely said dryly.

"Aileen said nothing of it to me in any of her letters, and it was the last thing I expected. We all forget he is half Erinnish . . ." She sighed and chewed idly at a thumb. "And for all you were taken by surprise, I'm thinking he was, too. Are you so selfish to think only of yourself?"

Shona had the grace to look abashed. She stopped pacing and threw herself down into a chair. It was her father's favorite, and engulfed her. Her expression altered slowly from fierce outrage to something akin to compassion. She smiled lopsidedly. "He was no more prepared for it than me. You should have seen his face . . ." Shona slung one muscled leg over the chair arm, settling into its depths. "I felt everything he felt, when we touched—it mirrored what I felt, throwing it back at me . . ." She frowned, squirming uncomfortably. " 'Twas not something I'm wanting to repeat . . . gods, but he was so *open*—" Shona laced fingers into her braid and tugged, as if to distract herself. "And I knew, when he touched me, he was wanting me—*needing* me—"

She broke off with a muttered curse, clearly embarrassed as well as frustrated. Keely waited, trying to sort out her own welter of emotions.

Shona sat upright abruptly, unhooking the dangling leg and planting both booted feet on the floor. She leaned into her elbows and hid her face behind both hands. Her words were muffled, but the raw helplessness of the tone was undisguised. "Gods help me, but 'twas what *I* was wanting too—every bit of it, I wanted . . . I could not *help* myself—" She drew her hands away and cast an anguished plea at her mother. "What was I to do? I couldn't bear it, all that nakedness of feelings, all the knowing what he wanted, *and* me . . . all I could do was run away! Like a child, a wee bairn fleeing—" Self-contempt was plain. "And me knowing all the while if I gave in, it was over . . . if I even *wavered*—" She shut her eyes. "Gods, I feel so helpless . . . it made me feel so *helpless*—"

Keely drew in a deep breath, trying to still her voice. "It was the *kivarna*—"

Shona rubbed violently at her brow. "I'm knowing *that*, well enough . . . I just never thought—" She broke it off, rose, began to pace again. "How can I marry him? We're strangers to one another, knowing nothing about our habits and interests . . . how could he think I might be willing?"

Keely lifted one shoulder in a shrug. "The way anyone

thinks a man might be willing, or a woman, when they first meet."

Shona stared blankly at the dogs, sprawled on the stone floor. Eventually she sat down by one of the bitches and began to stroke the narrow, wiry head. One of the pups came over and collapsed as near to Shona as possible, burrowing her head into her lap. Absently, Shona petted both hounds.

" 'Twasn't that way for you and father."

Keely grunted. "You know that story. I've told you."

"So has he." Briefly, Shona grinned. "But you loved one another before you married. You've *both* said so."

"Your *jehan* and I had less in common when we met than you and Aidan. There was no *kivarna* for us."

Shona's cheeks reddened. "I'm wanting more than what we felt. That was little more than two children setting a broomstick alight—and having the rafters catch!"

Keely smiled. "Aye, well . . . there is something to be said for passion, and something to be said for peace. Sometimes one outdistances the other, but eventually they catch up."

Troubled, Shona continued to stroke the wolfhounds. "But I know the cost of *kivarna*. I'm knowing what it means. If we married, Aidan and I, and he died, I'd be left alone. Forever. With no man to love, or love me back." She looked at her mother. "What would you do if father died?"

Keely drew in a long, painful breath, then released it. "Go on," she answered quietly. "He would expect it of me."

Shona's eyes were steady. She was too much like her father; Keely found it difficult to answer that face. "What would you expect of yourself?"

After a moment, Keely smiled. It was ironic and bittersweet. "Once, I would have told you no man is worth the loyalty of a woman, or her soul. That no man is so important his passing would leave a woman bereft; she has strength of her own, and worth, and should go on very well without him." She stroked a strand of hair back from her face. "But I have learned that a woman need not subjugate herself to live with a man, nor give up any part of her beliefs. A woman is free to love as she will, and therefore free to grieve." She looked at her daughter's intent face. "If your father ever asked me to do something I was adamantly opposed to, I would refuse. No one has the right to expect another to compromise personal beliefs simply to accommodate the other. If he asked me not to grieve, I would laugh into his face. But if I thought he expected me to end my life when he died, I would leave him instantly.

"Even if you loved him?"

"I will always love your father. But I would leave him. And he knows it."

Shona's face was grim. "It would be more difficult if there was *kivarna* between you."

Keely gestured. "Perhaps. But *because* we had it between us, it might never come to that. Perhaps if more men and women shared a mutual *kivarna*, there would be less contention between them."

The tone was argumentative. "So, you think I *should* marry him."

Keely smiled calmly. "I think you should make the choice for yourself, and then live with it."

Shona scowled. "That is easy for you to say."

Keely laughed aloud, "Is it? Oh, my foolish lass, you're knowing nothing about it. Nothing at *all* about it."

Shona looked affronted. "How can you say that? You're not in my position—"

Keely stood up, tugging her jerkin back into place. "We all make choices," she said, "Man, woman, and child. And then we must live with them."

Shona's voice rose as Keely approached the door. "But your choice isn't like mine. It never was. You *loved* my father. You're not knowing what this is like."

Keely was at once swept back years to the bleakest portion of her life. To the hardest decision she had ever faced. To the knowledge that the child she carried was a child of rape, both physical and emotional, and the product of her most hated enemy. Knowing the child, if born, might have equal access to magics more powerful than any presently known, and that he or she might use them for evil.

Swept back to the decision that she could not, would not bear the abomination, and would do whatever she could to miscarry it. Because it was, to her, the only answer. The only alternative.

Keely drew in a breath. "There are people in this world who want to make decisions for you. Some of them even do it out of misintentioned goodness, of well-meant kindness.

They believe wholeheartedly they are doing you a service when they take away your freedom of choice, in the name of their morality. Who am I to take away *your* right to choose?" She spread her hands. "I will answer any question you have, and I will give you all the advice you want, but I will not make the decision for you. That is for you to do."

Shona opened her mouth to protest. But she did not, and after a moment, she smiled. "Aye, so it is. And for that freedom, I should be grateful."

"Aye," Keely agreed, thinking of Brennan and Aileen, who had known no freedom.

And of their son, and her daughter, whose unexpected "gifts" might rob them of their share.

Eight

Aidan stood beside his borrowed bed, contemplating his baggage. One set of saddle-pouches, carrying changes of clothing, preserved food, a few other oddments. A servant had been sent to unpack for him, but Aidan had thanked him and dismissed him. He was not yet certain he was staying long enough to unpack anything.

Teel, perched upon a bedpost, fluttered blue-black wings, *The least you can do is stay to the evening meal. Why run away on an empty belly?*

Aidan grimaced. *I am not running away. Why stay where I am most obviously not welcome?*

The woman is the daughter, not the lady . . . let the others determine your welcome.

He had left the door open. Someone stepped through. He knew before she spoke exactly who it was; the *kivarna* told him plainly. "So," she said coolly, "I'm thinking there's something to be settled."

Aidan did not turn. "Aye. And I am settling it this moment."

The smoky voice was curt; she did not understand his reference. "What?"

He turned. She was everything he recalled: long of limb,

broad of shoulder, impossibly strong of will. She blazed with
determination. "Am I to go, or stay?" He gestured idly
toward the unpacked saddle-pouches. "I have only to throw
them over my shoulder and walk back down to the city.
There will be a ship. And I can go home."

Shona's assessive eyes narrowed. "You give in easily."

"Give in?" He loaded the words with elaborate surprise.
"I did not know we had even gotten *that* far."

Now her tone was glacial. "We got nowhere at all, *I'm*
thinking, except to recognize the *kivarna*." Her feet were
spread, legs braced; she was poised for war, Aidan thought,
in one way or another. Her jaw was tightly set. "Did you
know what would happen?"

He made a sound of disgust. "I know as much about
kivarna as you do about having a *lir*." Abruptly he paused,
thinking of Keely. If Shona were like her mother, his last
comment bore no meaning at all. "You have no *lir*, have
you? Or recourse to *lir*-shape?"

Muscles flexed in her jaw. "No."

The *kivarna* flared briefly. He had touched a nerve. It
was plain to him: Shona displayed no physical characteristics
of her mother's race, nor the magic of the Cheysuli. What
she was, most obviously, was Erinnish, complete with Erinnish
kivarna.

And she feels diminished because of it.

Aidan shook his head, answering her more kindly. "No, I
knew I had it, but not what it was. Nor what it could do."

It seemed to mollify her. And he realized, with an unpleasant jolt, that the extra sense he relied on to tell him what
people felt was *her* gift as well. Shona could read him as well
as he read her.

He was not certain he liked that.

Unexpectedly, Shona laughed. "Aye," she agreed, "unpleasant. Unsettling, I'm thinking—*and* you. D'ye see what
we'd be dealing with, day in and day out?"

Rebellion flickered. "There is more to it than that."

Derision was blatant. "Oh, aye. There's this, too. I'm
thinking." And she strode across the room to catch both of
his hands in hers, grasping tightly. "This, too, my boyo. D'ye
think we can deal with *this?*"

It flared up between them as strongly as before, but the
emphasis was different. There was less of pure, driving need
and more of anticipation, of promised pleasure, of warmth

and exhilaration; of a certainty of completeness. There were layers, Aidan realized, even to physical need, buttressed by the spiritual and emotional. What lay between them was far more than a desire for mere physical gratification. With Shona, there was a future beyond a single night—or hour—in bed.

Once, it might have frightened him. But now it was what he wanted.

This time, Aidan broke contact, to show her that he could. Even as she tensed, intending to release him, he pulled his hands from her grasp.

Aidan pointed at the bed. "There is more to life than that. And I *want* more."

Color stood high on her face. This time there was no fear, no flight, no denial. This time there was comprehension, and control. And yet clearly she was as shaken as he by the *kivarna*. "I want—" Her voice was hoarse. She swallowed heavily. "I want the freedom to choose."

"You have it."

"Have I?" In the light, her features were harsh. "If we face *this* every time we touch, what choice is that? That, my lad, is helplessness—"

He cut her off. "The first time you sat upon a horse and it ran away with you, that was helplessness. The first time one of your wolfhound bitches whelped you a dead puppy, that was helplessness. But you still ride, do you not? And you still breed dogs."

Her face was very white. "I'll not be bound by this. I'll not give up my freedom to a whim of the gods, who no doubt find this amusing."

Aidan very nearly smiled, thinking of the Hunter, the Weaver, the Cripple, but she would not understand. Instead, he appealed to her taste for confrontation. "Then prove yourself stronger. Vanquish it." Aidan turned to face her squarely. "If we believe a falsehood, it gains strength. So challenge this *kivarna* to a duel. Find out which of you is stronger."

Level brows knit. "Why?" she asked. "You saw me but hours ago, and now you argue a commitment to something that could well destroy us. We're not *required* to marry . . . we're neither of us betrothed. 'Tisn't like your parents, or mine. We're bound to nothing at all." She shook her head. "How can you be so willing to set aside personal desires and chain yourself to a stranger in the name of *kivarna*?"

He shrugged. "Because this *kivarna* may well be linked to my *tahlmorra*. Which is part of the prophecy . . ." Aidan sighed, scratching idly at his neck. "I am somewhat accustomed to doing what is expected, by gods and by parents."

Shona grimaced. "*Tahlmorras*, prophecies—" She looked harshly at Teel, still perched upon the bedpost, then shook her head with an expression of impatient tolerance. "Oh, aye, my mother told me all about such things . . ." Tolerance faded abruptly. Shona turned away and took two paces toward the door before swinging back. "D'ye really believe such blather? I know my mother does; do *you*?"

Aidan's right hand closed around the chain threaded onto his belt. "Aye," he said. "I do."

She stared at him, judging his commitment. When she saw he meant it, her tone was incredulous. "And because of these beliefs, you're willing to pay the price of the *kivarna*? That if one of us should die, the other is sentenced to a life of abstinence and loneliness?"

Aidan shrugged. "Considering the cost of the *lir*-bond, I find the *kivarna's* demands rather tame."

Her tone was venomous. "And you're a liar, my lad."

"Am I? I?" Aidan laughed at her. "You should know, *my lass*. Use your accursed *kivarna*."

Brown eyes were nearly black. Her strong chin was thrust upward in challenge. "How am I to know you can't lie with it? 'Tis only a matter of *feelings*, not words. And even then I'm not knowing *everything* you feel—"

"Words lie," he told her. "Feelings, even those well-hidden, tell only the truth."

Shona swore. "Full of sweet words, are you? Forgive me if I don't swoon, but I'm not that weak a woman."

"Good," he said flatly. "I am a man who wants a companion, not a serving-girl."

Shona's contempt was plain. "Don't forget whose daughter I am. They neither of them raised a fool."

Aidan scooped up his pouches. "Not a fool, " he agreed. "Just a stubborn, blinkered mule." He slung the pouches over his shoulder and walked by her through the door.

Lir. Are you coming?

Teel's tone was amused. *I will go out the casement. The air is clearer, out of doors.* He flew from bed to casement sill, then slipped out the narrow slit and into the sky beyond.

Aidan turned to the right, heading toward the spiral stair leading down to the bottom floor.

"Aidan. *Aidan!*"

He continued walking.

"Come back here, you *skilfin.* D'ye think I'd be letting you walk out of here like this?"

His pace did not slow.

She came up behind him. "What would my parents say if they thought *I* was the cause of you leaving without a proper welcome or guest-gift?"

"You are," he answered briefly, into the corridor. "You may as well face them with the truth . . . or are you a coward?"

"I'm not afraid of them. They give me no cause."

"No. What you're afraid of is the *kivarna* itself." Aidan went down the winding staircase, attuned to her nearness. Her steps did not flag as Shona followed him down.

For several moments all he heard were her footsteps, echoing his own. And then strong fingers caught in the wool of his cloak, clenching through to the leather jerkin. *"Stop,"* she commanded.

He stopped, even as she jerked her hand away, and turned. She stood two steps above, which made her tower over him. She braced either hand against the staircase walls, as if to hold herself in place. Loose cuffs fell away from her arms, baring strong wrists and sinewy forearms more suited to warrior that woman. The thick braid fell across one shoulder, dangling past her breast, her waist, and hip to brush the top of her wool-clad thigh. In the dimness of the narrow staircase much of her expression was muted, but he saw the set of her jaw; the fierceness of her eyes; the upward slant of cheekbones too blunt for Cheysuli elegance, yet striking all the same. The sheer power of her personality, reflected in expression, stature, spirit, stripped the words from his mouth; all he could do was stare.

Shona came down one step. Palms scraped against the walls. "I *am* afraid," she admitted. "But you're knowing that. You have only to use what *I* use, when I want to know the truth of a person." One more step; her head was level with his. "I know the sword and the bow and the knife. I am more content with men's things than with women's—I have that of my mother . . ." Briefly, Shona smiled. "But there's more to me than that. There's another woman inside me, one who wants a man the way other women do . . . the way they dream about. The one who wants a man to love her, and to love him back—" She lifted a staying hand as he opened his mouth to speak. "No. D'ye hear? D'ye *feel?* What I'm saying is the truth: I want all of it, Aidan, the way the stories promise. A man and a woman meet, and they fall in love, and they marry . . ." Her mouth jerked briefly. "You give it to me twisted. You give it to me empty."

After a long moment he nodded. "I never meant it to happen this way. I came so we could meet, to see if we suited one another, as friends first. I never meant to pressure you, or make you feel trapped. I promise you that. But when you reached out and took my hand, the choice was taken from me. The time the stories promise was stolen from us both—"

"I know." Shona drew in a deep breath and released it heavily. " 'Tis a capricious thing, the *kivarna;* you're knowing that as well as I." She caught hold of the braid and flipped it behind her shoulder. "D'ye see? 'Tisn't right for either of us. You'd do better with a woman not so bound up by *Erinnish* magic—a Cheysuli woman, perhaps, or a Homanan—and I'm thinking I'd do better with an Erinnishman, a big, brawling islander who has no *kivarna* at all, so we neither of us will suffer."

Which us? he wondered. *You and your brawling islander? Or you and me?*

"Aidan."

It was not Shona, who stared past him in open curiosity, but her father, who waited at the foot of the stair. Aidan turned. "Aye, my lord?"

Sean's face was solemn. "You'd best be coming with me."

How could they know already I intend to leave? He frowned faintly, trying to find the proper words. "My lord—"

"Aidan, come with me. It has to do with Gisella."

For a moment, the name was alien. Aidan stared at Sean. "Gisella—?" And then he knew. "My granddame?"

Sean nodded. "Corin has sent word from Atvia. Gisella is dying."

Keely's face was a travesty, a mask made of stone. Only the eyes were alive: blue and bright as glass, glittering with emotions. There was anger, shock, resentment, even hatred. But mostly there was a cold and abiding commitment to feel nothing at all, no matter how much she wanted to.

No matter how much she *had* to.

She waited as they came into the hall: Sean, Aidan, Shona. She stood rigidly by one of the chairs, but did not sit; nor did her posture indicate any intention to sit. A folded, crumpled parchment lay discarded on a nearby table. In her hands she gripped a silver goblet. The pressure of her fingers against the metal turned them white.

"So," she said, "it comes. Too many years too late, but at last it comes."

Sean did not go directly to her. Instead he moved by her as if to sit down in the chair she disdained, and then paused. One big hand settled upon her right shoulder. A moment later the other shoulder was also engulfed. Very gently, he squeezed, and Aidan saw the tension of Keely's fingers relax almost imperceptibly. Now the goblet shook.

Aidan looked at her face. *Is it comfort he offers her? Or restraint?*

"So," Keely repeated. "Gisella is dying, and wants to see her kin."

It startled him. Slowly Aidan sat down, conscious of Shona drifting toward the fireplace. His senses chafed at the distance, but he studiously ignored them. If this was what *kivarna* was, this strong physical tie, he was not certain he wanted to obligate himself to it. Understanding the feelings of others was bad enough.

Aidan cleared his throat. "Will you go?"

Keely's astonishment was blatant. "I?"

"Aye. She is your *jehana*. If she wants her kinfolk, surely she means you."

Keely laughed once, mirthlessly. She gulped from the goblet, then thunked it down upon the table. "Whether she means me or not makes no difference. She gave up any claim to me more than forty years ago, when she tried to hand my *rujholli* over to Strahan." Keely's face hardened. "I renounced her in life. Now I renounce her in death."

Sean's hands remained on her, gently working the taut tendons stretched between neck and shoulders. "Lass, 'tis Corin you should be thinking of. 'Twill dishonor him if no one goes."

"Corin will understand." Keely's eyes were hard as stone. "I thought perhaps Aidan might go."

"Me!" He stared at her in surprise. "I have never even seen her. Gisella is nothing to me . . . *Deirdre* is my granddame, if only in name." He shrugged, feeling uncomfortable. "I have no desire to see a dying old woman."

"Her blood is in your veins," Keely said. "It is what makes you a part of the prophecy, Aidan—" But she pulled free of Sean and strode away from them all, turning back awkwardly when she had gone three paces. "I cannot go. I cannot *make* myself go, even if I should. I have spent a lifetime hating that woman . . . she is old and sick and dying, and *mad* . . ." Wearily she rubbed her brow, stretching the flesh out of shape. "Someone should go, for Corin's sake if nothing else . . . and for Gisella's. But not me. I would look at her, and see the woman whose actions nearly destroyed me, and I would hate her. And no one, dying, deserves hatred. She deserves forgiveness—" Keely's face was frozen. Tears glittered briefly. "There is none of that in me."

Sean's voice was quiet rustiness as he looked at Aidan. "She's seen none of her grandchildren, lad. I've no doubt she's a lonely old woman, now—it might ease her passing if she saw you."

"I know, but . . ." Aidan sighed, giving up. "Aye. I understand. If nothing else, I can carry word home to my grandsire that the Queen of Homana is dead . . . it might be best from a kinsman, rather than a messenger." He pulled himself out of his chair. "I will go."

"Wait." It was Keely. "If you go, there is something you must do."

Aidan nodded, willing.

Her gaze remained steady. "You must leave your *lir* behind."

"Leave Teel! Why? How can you even ask it?"

Sean's voice was placatory. "There is reason, lad."

"I cannot leave my *lir* behind"

Keely shook her head. "You must, Aidan, or risk losing him. In Atvia, ravens are death-omens. They shoot them whenever they can, so the birds cannot bear tidings of death to the next one meant to die."

It was unbelieveable. "But *Corin* rules. He is Cheysuli. Surely he has taught them what a *lir* is."

"They understand," Keely told him. "But Kiri is the only one they know, and she is a fox. For centuries the Atvians have killed ravens. That sort of habit is not easily overturned, even by a king—especially a foreign one . . ." She sighed. "Is it worth taking the chance? Leave Teel here."

He shook his heat. "If he remains here, I have no recourse to the *lir*-gifts. No shapechange, no healing—"

"Will you need either, there?" Keely put her hand on his arm. "Stay a week. A ten-day, at the most. Then come back—" she cast an enigmatic glance at her daughter "—and do whatever you must do to settle your affairs."

Aidan looked at Shona. For a long moment their gazes locked. Then she turned her head, staring into the fire resolutely, and his reluctance to go to Atvia evaporated. Perhaps the best thing for them at this moment was to part, to put things in perspective. To better understand precisely what the *kivarna* meant, without feeling its presence so tangibly.

Aidan looked back at Keely. "First I will speak to Teel, Then I will go."

Sean's smile was faint. "No need to *run*, lad . . . stay the night while we feast you. I'll see you fetched across the Dragon's Tail first thing in the morning."

Aidan nodded. Shona turned on her heel and strode out of the hall.

Nine

Clearly, the Atvians had expected Keely, or someone of her household. When only Aidan arrived, a stranger unattended by even a single servant, or a message from the Lord and his Lady, they displayed polite bewilderment, then belatedly mustered the appropriate courtesy and ushered him into a chamber. To wait, he was told, for a proper personage.

Aidan, left to ponder the wisdom of his coming, idly walked the room. Rondule was, much like Kilore, a fortress built to defend Atvia, not a dwelling designed to offer excessive comfort. There were chairs, tables, benches; three pelt rugs; a newly lighted fire. The beamwork was rough-hewn, hacked out of massive timbers, and left purposely crude. Not much like Homana-Mujhar's fine, silk-smooth beams, arching in graceful waves beneath the dark stone groins.

Aidan sighed and halted by the fireplace, warming morning-chilled hands. The brief voyage across the Dragon's Tail had been accomplished with speed and skill, but he had a landsman's belly. He was pleased to be aground again.

Over the mantel hung a massive wooden shield bossed with brass. The shield was obviously quite old, with an honor all its own; gouges pocked the dark wood and the brass was dented in places. Pieces were missing here and there, displaying the dark outlines of the original ornamentation beneath. Aidan knew better than to believe it a keepsake brought by Corin from Homana; more likely it was left over from the wars between Atvia and Erinn.

It seemed odd now to think of it. But the enmity between the two island realms, separated only by a narrow channel, had forged a bitter rivalry into ongoing hostility, so that two peoples who might otherwise be much alike had spent generations killing one another. Now they were united in a peace forced by Corin's assumption of the Atvian throne and a treaty first with Liam, then with Sean, but Aidan knew better. People did not change their ways so quickly. Only twenty years or so before Alaric had ruled, pure Atvian of the old line, a man dedicated to making Erinn part of his domain. Corin, his grandson by Gisella, had ended that ambition by inheriting on Alaric's death; Sean, married to Corin's sister, had no wish to continue the battles that had, until Liam's time, stolen away a portion of Erinn's manhood every year.

The door swung open. Aidan turned, expecting Corin; instead, it was a woman.

She paused, then entered the room and shut the door behind her. Small hands were clasped together in the folds of her deep russet gown. The color was most flattering against dusky skin. Dark brown hair was braided neatly back from delicate face and slender neck, then netted in gold and pinned to the back of her head. A rope of dark garnets bound her waist, then dripped down to the hem of her skirts. The dyed brown toes of slippers peeped under the hem as she moved toward him, smiling exquisite welcome.

She was, most obviously, not a serving-girl. Aidan revised his greeting instantly and offered a courteous inclination of his head, explaining who he was and why he had come in place of Keely or Sean.

Huge eyes reflected momentary surprise. Then, still smiling, she gathered swirling skirts in deft, graceful hands and swept into a curtsy. Garnets rattled briefly; then she rose and placed one flattened hand over her heart, dipping her head in eloquent acknowledgment. Beneath lowered lashes,

Aidan saw brown eyes rich and expressive. The mouth, curving slightly in a delicate, fragile face of quiet loveliness, made no move to speak.

She was thin, very thin, but with a tensile grace that belied the fragility of her body. The long, slender neck, set off by the netted hair, was exquisitely elegant. He thought of Shona, so tall and broad and strong, and realized next to this woman the Erinnish princess would resemble a sturdy kitchen wench, albeit one with a royal pedigree. But this woman's strength did not require a body so much as it required eyes; looking at her. Aidan found himself understanding her disability, and why it made no difference.

The door swung open again. The woman turned, skirts swinging out, and Aidan realized she was only mute, not deaf. He saw her delicate face light up as the man entered, and then she went to him and took his hand, drawing him through. Her smile was luminous as she turned to Aidan, still grasping the man's hand; she put out her own, gesturing gracefully, and seemed to say everything necessary with that single motion.

It was, of course, Corin. Aidan knew it at once. There were few men in the world who so strongly resembled the Mujhar, though Niall's stamp was somewhat diluted by the other blood in Corin's veins, and the Lord of Atvia was much younger. He was tawny-haired and blue-eyed, but bearded, like Sean. He also lacked Niall's tremendous height and weight, built shorter and slighter, though no one would name him small. He was, Aidan thought, at least as tall as Brennan and Hart, perhaps even a bit taller. He wore traditional Cheysuli leathers, which Aidan found unexpected in light of Corin's realm. There was gold on his arms and in his left ear, glinting through thick hair. He was nothing at all like his brothers, Aidan realized. But like his sister, aye. Keely was in his face and smile.

Corin nodded thoughtfully, assessing Aidan rapidly. His tone was very dry. "Not so much of a weakling after all, are you? Was it Brennan's righteousness, or Aileen's stubbornness that made you defy all the doomsayers who predicted your death?"

Aidan smiled politely. "And were you one of them?"

White teeth flashed. "Hardly! You forget, *harani*—I know your *jehana*. I never believed for a moment a son with Aileen of Erinn in him would give up so easily."

Aidan had expected more. Sadness. Resentment. Perhaps bitterness, even after so many years. Instead what he sensed was pride, and an undercurrent of approval. It was almost as if Corin looked on Aidan as his own son, and was pleased with what he saw. It was not the reception Aidan had expected.

"She is well," he offered quietly, looking for reaction. "She sends her greetings."

"So does Brennan, no doubt." Laughter glinted in Corin's eyes. "I know what you do, *harani*. Doubtless all the servants fed you the tales . . . well, I imagine the follies of our youth *do* make good telling. He shrugged, smiling warmly down at the woman at his side. "But old wounds heal, Aidan. I loved her once, very much; now it is a pleasant, if bittersweet, memory." One hand guided the slender woman forward. "Pay your respects, *harani*. This woman is Atvia's queen." Corin's brows arched slightly. "In the Old Tongue, my *cheysula*. Her name is Glyn."

Aidan opened his mouth, then shut it. He wanted to protest that of course the woman was not Corin's wife, because no message had ever arrived announcing the wedding. But who was he to argue? And why? It was well within Corin's power to marry whomever he chose, publicly or privately—and yet Aidan was left feeling oddly flat. After so many years and so many stories, he had come to believe Corin would never marry, because Aileen had married Brennan. It was almost as if Corin had betrayed his mother.

He swallowed heavily and stepped forward, accepting the woman's fragile hand and bestowing the kiss of homage. Her warm smile and eloquent eyes soothed him immediately, dissolving the remaining resentment, until he smiled back at her.

"Had I known, I would have brought a bride-gift." Delicately, he offered Corin reproach, and a chance to explain himself.

Corin, unruffled and unrepentant, shrugged. "It was a private thing. I did not wish to share Glyn with anyone." His tone was very quiet as the woman returned to his side. "Few would have understood the Lord of Atvia taking a woman who could not speak."

Perhaps not at first. But Aidan felt Glyn's muteness beside the point. One had only to look at her expression, as she gazed at Corin, to know what her world was made of.

Corin's beard hid much of his crooked smile. "When a man stops railing at his *tahlmorra*, often the gods repay him with more than he deserves. After too many years of solitude, they sent Glyn to me. I have learned to leave the past behind, living instead in the present." A gesture dismissed the subject. "Now, I am assuming Keely refused to come."

Aidan nodded. "She said you would understand."

Corin grimaced. "I do. I wish she did . . ." The dismissive gesture was repeated. "Do you know, I think if Gisella had tried to give her daughter to Strahan as well as her three sons, Keely would be less bitter. But Gisella did not. Keely was dismissed as entirely unimportant, because she was a girl." He smiled faintly. "That is the definition of Keely, *harani*: she would rather be caught in the midst of some Ihlini vileness than be left *out* of it merely because of her sex."

"And Shona is very like her," Aidan sighed ruefully, then set the topic aside. "You sent word Gisella wishes to see her kinfolk. Will I do?"

Corin's expression was odd. His tone odder still. "That is the wrong question. It is not simply will you *do*, but whether you will survive with your dignity intact." He gestured toward the door. "Come with me."

The room lay deep in shadow, for the casement slits were shuttered and only a handful of candles illuminated the bedchamber. The commingled scent of beeswax and death filled his nose as he entered. The door thumped shut behind him as the serving-woman went out, leaving him alone inside the chamber. Corin had said Gisella was not strong enough for more than one visitor at a time. Aidan, lingering uneasily by the door, was not certain *he* was strong enough to visit.

He had never been so close to death before. He had learned to fight, as he was expected of a man who would be Mujhar, but he had never been to battle. His kin were vigorous and strong; he had never watched the aged wither away until their spirits left them.

He had not anticipated the smell. He had not expected the emotions. He faced the dying woman with a horrified fear of what he would see and feel, because he thought his *kivarna* might be the undoing of him.

When his eyes grew accustomed to the gloom, he saw the faint outline of her body beneath the silken coverlet of the canopied bed. The fabric was a deep, heavy indigo, nearly inseparable from the dimness. Only after a moment of concentration could Aidan see the differentiation between coverlet and shadows. Gisella seemed to wear it like a shroud.

She was propped up by bolsters and pillows. At first he could only barely see her face, blending with the dimness, then he saw the shine of eyes. Pale, feral eyes, like his own, fixed on him—on the intruder—with a fierce intensity.

Gods—I see now why the unblessed fear us so much when they see us for the first time— Aidan swallowed painfully and wet dry lips.

Her hair was mostly gray, dark, mottled gray, but her face was outlined by silver-white. She wore it loose over thin shoulders; twin ropes of cord against indigo silk. Her skin, once Cheysuli-dark, had yellowed with age and illness, her face was all of hollows. Aidan, unsettled, wondered what illness would take her to the grave. Mere age only rarely ravaged a Cheysuli so virulently. Generally his race died gracefully.

Aidan stopped at the foot of the bed. *She is mad*, he reminded himself. *A sick, dying, mad old woman—*

The pale eyes did not so much as flicker. "Which one are you?"

The flat tone was colorless. Aidan did what he could to put life into his own. "Aidan," he told her. "Aidan of Homana; Brennan's son.'"

Gisella smiled. Her teeth were displayed in a feral clenching. "Yet another son I have not seen."

He was careful. "You have Corin."

Her voice rasped. "Who?"

"Corin." Aidan drew in a breath. "Your third-born son. Corin, now Lord of Atvia—"

"My father is Lord of Atvia. Is Corin my father?"

Oh, gods— "Corin is your son."

Querulous, now. "Who are you?"

"Aidan." He began it yet again. "Aidan of Homana—"

"Brennan's son; I *know*." Teeth showed briefly. "They tell me things, all of them . . . and then tell me again and again and *again*—do they think I am a fool?"

"No." Aidan briefly sought a chair out of the corner of his eyes, then dismissed the impulse immediately. He did not wish to remain with Gisella that long. He wanted to leave as soon as he decently could.

"And will *you* be Mujhar?"

It snapped his attention back. "Aye. One day."

Pale eyes glittered. "But Niall still lives. Still rules. *Niall* still rules . . ." Gisella put thin fingers to her mouth and stroked withered lips, as if recalling all too graphically once she had shared a man's bed. "Niall," she said softly.

"My grandsire." Aidan surreptitiously glanced back toward the door. "Perhaps I should come back another time—"

"Come here. Come *here*. Come closer. Come *here*."

Against his will, he responded.

Gisella stared up at him. He stood there, letting her look, and fought down the impulse to run. His *kivarna* was afire with the confused welter of her emotions, so tangled and black and incomprehensible. She was mad, all too obviously mad, but there was more to her than that. Underneath the layers of confusion was the girl she might have been, once, had Lillith not twisted her. A childlike, innocent girl, trapped in a woman's body, but nonetheless innocent. She was not and never had been fit to be queen. But neither had she deserved the meticulous, deliberate reshaping of her spirit. Lillith had destroyed the innocence. Lillith had destroyed Gisella in a quest to destroy Homana.

Gisella pointed to him. "You."

He waited.

"Cheysuli," she said. "They told me. Lillith. My father. They *told* me—" She smiled. "Cheysuli, Atvian. Erinnish, Solindish, Homanan. All necessary to complete the prophecy."

She was, uncannily, lucid. Aidan stared at her.

"They bind the Houses and mingle the blood—my blood, *your* blood, *their* blood . . . to make the proper child. *The child.* The boy who will become king over all the lands; a man combining the blood of two magical races and—and—" She tilted her head, frowning faintly. "Peace."

Aidan nodded. "The prophecy, granddame. Two magical races and four warring realms, united in peace."

"*Tahlmorra,*" she murmured.

Again Aidan nodded. "We each of us have one."

Her eyes sharpened. "Do you?"

"Of course."

Slowly, she shook her head. "No. No. No."

"Granddame—"

Gisella glared at him. "Lillith told me about it . . . a *tahlmorra* is nothing more than a binding made up long ago by men calling themselves the Firstborn so they could make people think them greater than everyone else."

"Granddame, Lillith lied—"

"Give them a prophecy, she said. Give them a fate and call it *tahlmorra*, something to bind them so strongly they will never break away . . . something to turn them into nothing more than servants, but leave them their pride so they will believe themselves better, *better* . . . better than everyone else so they will *keep* themselves bound—"

"No granddame—"

"Lillith told me," she said plainly. "She told me the truth of it: the Cheysuli have been made what they are by the connivance of the Firstborn, who saw the power of the Ihlini and feared it. So they fashioned themselves an army—Lillith *said*—but called it a race, to use the Cheysuli as their weapons. They turned warrior against sorcerer; child against child—"

Aidan overrode her. "Granddame, *she lied.*" He waited until she stared at him, outraged. More quietly, he went on. "You are ill and angry and confused . . . granddame, Lillith did naught but lie to you, all these years ago—"

"You are lying to me now."

"No." Aidan sighed. "Granddame, I have a task, and a *tahlmorra*. Repeating lies Lillith told you will not turn me away from what I have to do."

"The throne will never be yours."

It stopped him in his tracks.

Gisella smiled, tilting her head to one side. "Never."

"Granddame—"

"It denies you." She saw his shock, his recoil. "The Lion. I *know*, Aidan" She gathered the coverlet in thin, sharp fingers and leaned forward. Her voice was very soft; in its quietude, Aidan heard conviction, and the cant of prophecy. "Throneless Mujhar. Uncrowned king. A *child*, buffeted by fates he cannot understand . . ." She slumped back against the bolsters. "Touched by the gods, but ignorant . . . a man so touched, so claimed as one of their own, can never know peace as a king." Gisella smiled warmly, yellow eyes slight. "You will never rule Homana."

Aidan blurted the first thing that came into his head. "Are you saying I will die? Granddame? Am I to *die?*"

In a tiny, girlish voice, Gisella began to sing.

Ten

He awoke near dawn, haggard and shaking and frightened. His chambers were cold with the light of false dawn, but even yanking the covers up in a convulsive gesture did not warm him. Aidan sat upright and cursed, rubbing viciously at grainy, burning eyes.

Teel?

But almost at once he recalled the raven was not with him. Teel waited for him in Erinn, near Shona; a sick, uneasy loneliness curled deeply in Aidan's belly. He was quite alone, *too* alone, even though his own kinsman slept within the fortress.

So did his grandmother.

"Another dream," he muttered in disgust, but this one had been much different.

He recalled only bits and pieces: himself, seated on the Lion Throne in the Great Hall of Homana-Mujhar; himself, dead in the Lion, with blood running from mouth and throat; himself, mourned as a throneless Mujhar, an uncrowned king. No proper monarch, Aidan of Homana; merely a nameless prince all too soon forgotten.

He stripped tangled hair back from his face, purposely pulling too hard, as if the discomfort might alter his memories. It did not. "A witch," he muttered. "An Atvian witch, trained to treachery by an Ihlini . . ."

He was empty. Unwhole. Teel was too far even for the *lir*-link.

And Shona too far for the *kivarna*.

He needed one or both of them. He knew it with perfect clarity as she sat huddled in bed, shivering. Teel for the *lir*-link and all its gifts; Shona for the physical, the spiritual, the emotional. They were each of them tied into his *tahlmorra*, into his life; if he neglected either, or dismissed either, he destroyed a part of himself.

Into his head came Gisella's declaration. He heard it

again so clearly as if she stood beside his bed, bending over him as a mother over a child; as a grandmother over a grandson badly frightened by nightmares.

But Gisella offered no comfort. Gisella offered fear and self-doubt. *"You will never rule Homana."*

Aidan tore back the covers and climbed out of bed hastily, finding and pulling on fresh leathers, boots, his belt, a dark blue cloak. Then he paused by the saddle-pouches, reaching into one to draw out the chain of gold. The links were massive, perfect, heavy. Six of them he could name: Shaine, Carillon, Donal, Niall, Brennan, himself. But the others he could not. Undoubtedly one belonged to his son, and the others to the Mujhars after him.

Aidan put a finger on the sixth link, his own, and wondered what sort of king he would be.

And then wondered if he would be a king at all.

Almost viciously, Aidan whipped off his belt. He threaded the leather through the links and put it on again. He could feel the weight and curvature of each link. A man would kill for such a fortune; Aidan pulled his cloak over the belt and left the chamber, pausing in the corridor just long enough to tell a servant he was well, but required air. He had sat up late with Corin the night before, trading news, drinking wine. No one would question a morning ride; likely he needed one.

Without Teel, he was half a man, a shadow. He felt his spirit cut free from his body like a boat loosed from its moorings. It made him snappish and impatient; the horseboy, startled out of sleep, hastened to ready a mount even as Aidan apologized. When the horses were ready, he swung up quickly and rode clattering out of the bailey, intent on shedding the residual unease and bad temper as soon as possible. It was the dream, of course; he knew it. Since the chain had been made whole in Solinde, he had suffered none, sleeping soundly each night. But the nightmare he had experienced but a half hour before filled him with a nameless, increasing dread.

Aidan left the city as soon as possible and rode up into the hills, skirting the headlands overlooking the Dragon's Tail. Below him the city was quiet. Smoke threaded its way from chimneys and spread a thin haze over the rooftops, but he could see little other activity. Just before dawn, he was truly alone atop the ramparts of the city, riding the backbone of Atvia. The castle itself perched atop a jagged, upthrust stone formation. The knobby dome was called the Dragon's Skull.

He saw the crumbled headland tower in the distance. It stood alone at the edge of a cliff, sentinel to the sea. Morning mist wrapped itself around damp gray stone, but the rising sun changed silver beading to saffron, altering the pitted, grainy texture to smooth ocher-gold.

Aidan contemplated it, then shrugged. *I have nothing better to do . . .*

He thought it a shell, until he rode closer; then saw the bench by the low door and the windows shutters latched back to let light into the tower. It was a curious dwelling. Once it had served as a vanguard against the Erinnish enemy's approach; now it was little more than a crofter's incongruous hut. Aidan, hungry, dismounted and threw reins over his mount's head. He left the horse to graze and went across the hummocky turf to the tower, hoping its inhabitant would share his morning meal.

The door stood open, much as the shutters did. Aidan called out but received no answer; after an indecisive moment he ducked beneath the low lintel stone and went in. He had coin. He did not know a crofter alive who spurned good money, even from a stranger too hungry and impatient to wait for an invitation.

The tower was round. So was the room. The walls were bare of tapestries, but whitewashed. Kindling had been laid in the rude fireplace, but the fire had gone out. Aidan, with flint and steel in his belt-pouch, knelt to tend it properly.

In the gray light of dawn there was an air of desertion in the tower, and yet signs of habitation belied the feeling. A narrow cot was pushed against the curving wall. A table with only the merest slant to its legs stood in the center of the room. A stool was tucked under it. A rickety bench leaned against the wall by the door; on the other side was a twist of stairway, leading toward the upper floor, and the roof.

Aidan heard a step in the doorway. Still kneeling, he turned. He thought the posture less threatening to the man who lived in the tower, especially with flint and steel in his hands rather than knife or sword. But the anticipated man resolved himself into a woman, Aidan rose anyway, hastily, and tucked the implements away.

Mist was behind her, and sunlight. It clung to her roughspun gray cloak, shredding as she moved, dissipating as she smiled. Her unbound hair, snugged beneath the cloak, was black and glossy as a raven's wing. Something about her reminded Aidan of someone—black hair, wide black eyes; a vivid, alluring beauty.

The thought came unbidden, shredding the residue of his fear. *She could give me escape. She could give me release.*

So many women had. And this one expected it. He had learned to judge the eyes, the subtleties of movement.

She can give me ease . . .

He smiled as she came into the tower, and took the bucket of water from her hands. Their fingers touched briefly.

Kivarna—and other things—told him the truth. *She wants it as much as I.*

He set the bucket on the table, hoping the weight did not prove too much. The table held. So did her gaze, locked on his face. Her own was enigmatic. She did not question his presence in her tower; she did not appear frightened or dismayed by finding a stranger in her dwelling. She merely dropped the cloak from her shoulders and tossed it across the table, next to the bucket, and smiled.

Her gown, incongrously, was crimson, bright as new-spilled blood. It was cut loose at the shoulders, loose at narrow waist. He saw that her hair, now freed of cloak, was completely unbound, falling nearly to ankles. Loose gown, loose hair; moist, smiling mouth. Aidan, drawing a difficult breath, felt the powerful response deep in his belly.

He thought of Shona. Of Ashra. Of Blythe. Of women he had bedded, and women he had wanted to. Before *this* woman, all of them paled to insignificance.

She will give me heart's ease, and banish Gisella's words.

Black lashes were long, and eloquent. She knew how to use her eyes, her face, her body. Her tone was langourous. "Were you sent?" She paused, stroking back a strand of hair with a negligent, silver-tipped nail. "Or did you come?"

"I—came."

"Ah." She moved past him to the fire, loose grown swirling, loose hair swinging, and put out elegant hands. A curtain of silken hair fell forward across her right shoulder and hid her face from him. "My thanks for the fire, my lord."

The earring was hidden by hair, the *lir*-bands by his cloak, as was his belt. There was nothing about him, he thought, worthy of attaching rank to him. "Why do you call me that?"

Still her face was hidden. "You wear it like a crown." She turned, black eyes alight. "Do you know who I am?"

Mutely, he shook his head. He did not really care.

She laughed softly: a husky, seductive sound. "I am a woman and you a man. Perhaps that is all you need to know." Her smile was enigmatic. "I am a whore, my lord—or so *they* would have you believe."

His voice was rusty. " 'They'?"

"The castle folk." She waved a graceful hand, indicating the distances beyond the door, the mist, the morning. "Your kind, my lord."

"Are they? Are you?" He knew he did not care. Not in that moment. She was the most striking woman he had ever seen. She burned with a flame so bright he could feel it in his own flesh, creeping through to bones.

She lifted both hands and threaded fingers into hair, pulling it up from shoulders, from neck, from face. It cascaded through slender fingers, defining the shape of her face and the elegant line of her spine. "Do you want me, my lord?"

Aidan wanted to laugh, but could not. She was blatant in her actions, but he found he did not care. "If I lay with you, lady, it would mean what the castle folk say is true."

More hair slipped through her fingers. "Do you care?"

No. No and no. "What payment, lady?"

Black eyes narrowed. As she took her hands away, hair curtained the sides of her face. "You could not pay it, my lord. And you might be grateful for it."

Her thought not. He also thought she lied. A glance at the narrow bed, too narrow for two people, confirmed it. He did not know what she played at, or why, but he was tired of it. "I came in because I was hungry. I hoped to bargain for food . . . but I will leave, if you prefer it."

It was the hardest thing he had done, when he wanted to stay so badly.

She laughed. "No. I prefer no such thing. Your cloak, my lord . . . and I will give you food."

He slipped it and gave it to her. Her eyes, marking *lir*-bands, widened briefly. Something else came into her eyes as he saw the links threaded through his belt. Something akin to avarice, and comprehension. Uneasily, Aidan began to wonder if she were a whore after all, and counting her price in advance.

She fed him on barley bread and eggs, and when he asked where were her chickens she smiled and said she required none. He drank milk but forbore to ask about the cow, because he feared she might say she had none. She seemed to have very little, and yet gave it all to him.

When he was done she took his hand and let him to the narrow stair behind the door, and took him up to her bedroom.

No narrow cot was shoved against the curving wall. In the center of the chamber stood a wide bed draped with fine linens and lush pelts. There was nothing else in the room. Slanted light from a single wide casement illuminated the bed.

He looked at her. He could not call her whore. Something in her eyes kept him from it, though he understood her now. She needed no cow, no chickens, no stock. She needed nothing but the continued attentions of any man who could pay her price.

Surely *he* could. He would be Mujhar of Homana.

"Can you banish dreams?" he asked. Then, more intensely, "No—can you banish nightmares?"

The woman's smile gave him his answer. He put out his hand, and she took it.

He awoke to the chime of gold. It rang repeatedly, as if someone counted coin; as he listened more closely he realized it was not coin at all, but links. And he sat upright in the bed.

She was wrapped in his cloak. Bare feet and ankles showed at the hem; the rest was flung carelessly around the slender, magnificent body he had so thoroughly enjoyed. Her hair flowed to the pelt coverlets and pooled, blue-black on indigo.

"Where is your *lir*?" she asked.

He stared at her. Then her eyes moved from the chain to his face. Very softly, she repeated her question.

"In Erinn," he said at last. "Does it matter?"

Her lips parted in a glorious smile. "I think it might." She dangled the chain from one hand. It glowed in slanting sunlight. "How did you come by *this*?"

He did not care for her manner. He altered his own to

match it, hoping the answer might startle away her arrogance. "A gift," he said, "from the gods."

"Ah." She nodded musingly. "I thought so," Once again the chain flowed back and forth from hand to hand, chiming. "Indeed, I thought so."

Frowning, he asked her the question he was beginning to think he should have asked at the very beginning. "Who are you?"

Something moved in her eyes. Something dark and dangerous and infinitely *amused*. "Lillith," she told him gently. "Lillith of the Ihlini."

He felt his belly cramp, and something much deeper. Fear. Denial. Disgust. And comprehension. A terrible comprehension.

Lillith's black eyes glinted. "I could not believe it would be so *easy*. I thought surely you must know me. I thought it was why you had come, to vanquish the sorceress . . ." She smiled. "Corin banished me, of course, and for a while I went . . . but Valgaard grows tedious without my brother, and Lochiel saw fit to go to Solinde to try his own workings . . ." She shrugged an elegant shoulder. The cloak slipped, baring satiny flesh. "So I came back here, to Atvia. For a while. To see, from afar, how Corin dealt with Gisella." Lillith smiled. "Poor, addled Gisella—has she begun to plague *you*, yet?"

He could manage one sentence. "Gisella is dying."

"Is she?" Lillith considered it. "Ah, well, it is the price of remaining entirely human . . . I, of course, serve Asar-Suti, and have an advantage." Her eloquent eyes assessed him. "Do you know how old I am?"

Aidan drew in a tight breath. "Old enough to know better."

Lillith laughed. The sound was free, unconfined, and it frightened him. "Aye," she agreed. "But how old am I *really?*"

He had heard stories, of course. Lillith was Tynstar's daughter. Tynstar had been dead nearly a hundred years, and had sired Lillith hundreds of years before his death. And yet, looking at her, Aidan knew very well he could not believe the stories. She was young, beautiful, and infinitely deadly.

He ignored the question, and asked one of his own. "What do you want from me?"

Lillith thought about it. "Oh, a child, I think."

Aidan recoiled.

She nodded. "A child, such as the one I bore Ian. Rhiannon. To be used for Ihlini purposes." She looked at him consideringly. "Your prophecy rushes you toward reestablishment of the Firstborn. The Cheysuli may even succeed in accomplishing it . . ." Frowning slightly, she tapped a silver-tipped nail against one link. "We have, heretofore, failed to stop you. Perhaps it might be best if we *aided* you—only with a twist." Lillith's smile widened as she made a fluid gesture of explanation. "If we control the Firstborn, we control everything. One way to control them is to make our own." The faint smile dropped away. Her eyes bored into his. "You, my lord, are very important to me, and to all of us. *You*, my lord, have the proper blood. You are everything: Cheysuli, Homanan, Solindish, Atvian, Erinnish. All you lack is the required *Ihlini* blood." Tilting her head, she made another graceful gesture. "Do you see? A child conceived between Aidan of Homana and Lillith of the Ihlini would *be* a Firstborn. The prophecy would be complete . . . only it would be *on Ihlini terms*."

For a long moment all he could do was stare. Her explanation was so clear, so precise. With unsettling matter-of-factness, she spelled out the doom of his race.

Worst of all, for him, was the knowledge she could do it. In part, it *had* been done; first Ian, by siring Rhiannon; then Brennan, by siring gods knew what on Rhiannon.

And what might *he* sire?

A shudder wracked Aidan's body. "You make me vomit," he declared, knowing he as much as she was to blame for this situation.

Lillith smiled. She put out a hand, drew a rune, and a chamber pot appeared on the floor beside the bed. "There, my lord. You need not soil the covers."

The hollowness in his belly began to knot painfully. He knew very well she could do whatever she threatened. But he would not admit it to her. "Will you resort to rape?"

Lillith laughed. "Rape, my lord? You only recently proved yourself more than capable of responding to me . . . and as for repeating the act, need I remind you your *lir* is in Erinn? You are, as Ian was, *lirless* and therefore powerless. You will do or say whatever I require." She shifted forward onto her knees, moving close to him. The cloak slipped, pooling across her heels. "You are quite helpless, Aidan—need I prove it?"

She said the last against his mouth. He tried to pull away, to strip her arms from his body, but something kept him from it. She was pulling him down onto the bed, rousing him, taking away his control and sanity.

She made him respond, taking him to the edge but no farther, even as he hated it, and then withdrew, laughing as he cursed himself, and her. She lifted the chain before his face, letting it drip from both hands. "*Lirless* man," she taunted. "Child of the gods, are you? More like child of the earth, of *me*—"

His eyes fixed on the chain. Heavy links gleamed as she cradled it. He thought of the Hunter, the Weaver, the Cripple. He thought of himself, on his knees before the Lion, sobbing aloud as he put out his hands for a nonexistent chain. And yet here it was before him, whole, unbroken, untarnished, joined by his own hands in the ceremony presided over by Siglyn, witnessed by Tye and Ashra.

Ashra, who had warned him a man might lose control of himself if a woman's arms proved too beguiling.

I am a child of the gods . . .

"No," he said aloud.

Lillith laughed. "Ian said the same thing, many times. But that spell is weak. The binding always fails."

"I said NO—"

The chain moved in her hands. Aidan, transfixed, watched it coil upon itself. Lillith uttered a single cry of shock and tried to throw down the chain, but it clung to her arms like shackles.

Godfire leaped from the tips of her fingers, then sputtered out. The chain wound itself around her right arm and began to work its way toward her shoulder.

"Stop it!" Lillith hissed. "*Stop* it!"

Aidan lunged from the bed and stumbled against the wall, feeling cold stone scrape against bare buttocks.

"Aidan!" she cried. "Make it *stop*—"

The chain crawled beyond her elbow. In the light from the casement, it glowed.

"*Aidan!*"

The chain burrowed through hair and wrapped itself around her throat.

Lillith gave up her entreaty of Aidan and resorted to a

tongue he did not know. She shouted, hissed, chanted; calling, no doubt, on the noxious god she had served for so long. But the chain ignored her grasping, desperate fingers and settled snugly around her throat, cutting off her voice entirely. All Aidan heard was a throttled inhalation.

White teeth showed in a rictus grin. Lillith staggered up from the bed, clad only in hair and gold, and turned toward Aidan, pleading soundlessly. Her color was deepening. Black eyes protruded slightly.

Aidan, unmoving, stood next to the casement. Lillith stumbled toward him, still wrenching at the chain, clutching at hair and flesh and metal.

She saw the answer in his eyes. Comprehension convulsed her briefly. Then she turned from him, took two steps, and flung herself through the casement into the skies beyond.

When he could move again, he dressed. Slowly, because he still shook. He waited, sitting slumped on the wide bed, and when his strength began to return he thought he could manage the stairs. Carefully he went down, taking up his cloak from the crooked table, and went out to find her.

She lay sprawled on thick green turf, awkward in death as she had never been in life. He had thought she might have aged in death, showing her true features. But she was still Lillith. Still young, still beautiful—and still very dead.

Her hands were locked around the chain. Distaste stirred sluggishly, but numbness replaced it. Aidan pulled her hands away and freed the chain, then unwound it from throat and black hair. He set it aside and shook out his cloak.

When she was covered, save for the curtain of hair fanned out against the turf, Aidan walked out to the edge of the cliff. The chain dangled from one hand. He considered, for an angry moment, throwing it into the sea so far below, but did not. The anger dissipated. The chain was his, fashioned expressly for him by the gods themselves. It was so infinitely a part of him it even answered his wishes.

Or did the gods?

Aidan stared blindly across the turbulent Dragon's Tail to the clifftop Aerie of Erinn. And nodded his acceptance.

"Resh'ta-ni," he murmured. *"Tahlmorra lujhala mei wiccan, cheysu. Y'ja'hai."*

Eleven

When Aidan, still somewhat shaken, returned to the castle, he was met by a servant who said he must go to Gisella's chamber at once. Foreboding swept in from the distance he had built brick by brick in his soul as he rode down from the headlands, and he realized the delicately nurtured equanamity was nothing more than a sham. He understood the gods—or himself—no more than he had *before* Lillith's death, and now Gisella commanded his presence yet again.

Corin met him just outside the chamber. His face, beneath the blond beard, was excessively stiff. Only the eyes gave him away. "She wants you," he said harshly. The physicians say there is very little time . . ." He passed a hand over bloodshot eyes. "I think they have the right of it, no matter what she believes." His mouth flattened as he took his hand away. "She said she could sing to herself until you came."

"Gods," Aidan blurted. "How have you stood it so long? She is mad, completely mad—how can you bear to look at her and know she is your *jehana?*"

Corin shrugged awkwardly. "I learned years ago it was easier if I thought of her as someone else. Deirdre has always been my *jehana*—" He saw the expression on Aidan's face, the concurrence, and sighed, nodding. "Deirdre has been many things to very many of us. While Gisella has been—Gisella." He gestured. "Go in, Aidan. It will be the last time." A muscle twitched high on his cheek, beneath an eye. "This time I come, too."

Aidan went in. He was aware of Glyn's presence almost at once, which somehow soothed him. She sat very still in a chair beside the door, keeping vigil. A queen, even cast off, deserved whatever honor could be offered at her death. And word must be sent to the man she had married so many years before.

Glyn did not smile, though she looked up at him. Her

eyes, so large and eloquent, seemed to offer strength, which he needed. He nodded gratitude almost imperceptibly, the moved slowly toward the bed.

Gisella's breathing was audible. It caught, was throttled, then rasped raggedly in her throat, as if expelled from lungs too tired to function. Her color was a sickly grayish yellow. Her eyes were closed, but as Aidan stepped noiselessly to her bedside, they opened.

Gisella smiled. "Do you know the story?"

Wary, he said nothing.

"The story," she repeated. "How I came to be mad."

Oh, gods . . . Aidan swallowed tightly. "I have heard it."

Her voice was thready, but unyielding. "She was a raven, my mother . . . not knowing it was a bad thing. Not knowing here, in Atvia, ravens are killed whenever they can be. They are a death-omen, you see." The cords stood out in her throat, like knotted wire. "My father saw her—saw a raven—and shot her out of the sky. Not knowing it was Bronwyn in *lir*-shape. Not knowing she fled him, meaning to go back to Homana . . . he shot her down. And as she died, she bore me." The yellow eyes were unflinching, untouched by the tale. "They say it is why I am mad."

She did not sound it. She sounded perfectly lucid. Perfectly normal. And Aidan, looking at the fading old woman, wondered if Lillith's death had somehow broken through Gisella's addled wits to another woman beneath. To the *real* Gisella, sane as anyone else, and worthy of wearing a crown.

Gisella's breath rasped. "The chain is broken."

He twitched. "What?"

"The chain. Lillith told me about it. She said she would break it. Destroy it. So the prophecy would die."

Aidan frowned. "When did Lillith tell you this?"

Gisella's face folded upon itself as she thought. "Days? Weeks? Perhaps months." She looked past him to Corin, who approached quietly. She forestalled his question. "*He* said he sent her away, but she came back. Lillith always came back. She *loved* me."

Aidan nodded perfunctorily, unwilling to argue that Lillith's attentiveness had nothing at all to do with love. "Granddame—"

"She broke it."

The chain again. Aidan reached for patience. "No."

"She *said* she would."

"The chain is not broken ." He put his hand on one of the links. "Do you see?"

Feral eyes stared at the gleaming links. Gisella attempted to push herself up in the bed, but failed. And Aidan, much as he longed to help her, could not bring himself to touch her.

Gisella's mouth opened. "She said she would break it! She *promised!*"

"She failed." Aidan glanced sidelong at Corin. "Lillith is dead."

Gisella's eyes stretched wide. "*No—*"

"All of them are dead. Tynstar. Strahan. Now Lillith. Do you see, granddame? Their time is finished. The prophecy is nearly complete. Everything Lillith told you was a lie. The chain is whole. I am alive. And the prophecy *will* be completed."

"No." She glared up at him, trembling. "Throneless Mujhar. Uncrowned king—"

"Granddame, it is over."

"I talk to gods," she whispered.

Aidan's belly knotted.

"I talk to *gods,*" she repeated.

Corin murmured something beneath his breath. Something to do with madness, and dying. But Aidan knew better. Perhaps she *did* talk to gods.

He drew a careful breath. "What did they tell you? That I am to die?"

Her eyes lost their focus. "You are not to be Mujhar. The Lion wants someone else."

It chilled him clear to bone. Aidan suppressed a shudder, shutting one hand around a link. For all he knew, it was his own; for a moment, it did not matter. "Granddame . . ." It took all his strength to sound very calm. "Lady, if that is true, then surely the gods will tell *me.*"

Gisella gazed at him. "The broken link . . ." she whispered.

Aidan marked the bluish tint of her tips, the weakening of her voice. "Granddame—"

But she no longer looked at him. Her grandson was forgotten. Now it was her son she tried to reach, third-born of Niall's children. "Strahan never would have slain you," she said in a poignant appeal. "He only wanted to *use* you. He needed you. He needed me. He needed all of us." The cords of her neck tautened. "I needed to be needed. What I did was not so bad."

Corin's posture was impossibly rigid. "What you did cursed you in the eyes of your children forever," he said hoarsely. "You must decide if it was worth the sacrifice."

Her eyes were fixed on his face. As the last breath rattled in her throat, she whispered something no one in the chamber could hear.

When it was certain she was dead, Corin called in a servant from the corridor and ordered arrangements for the news to be carried throughout Atvia. Then, as the servant departed at once, Corin walked slowly back to the bed. He leaned down, shut the withered lids, then sat down upon the edge. From the bedside table he picked up a twisted gold torque.

He gazed at it steadily, turning it over in his hands. Aidan, looking at it, recognized the workmanship as Cheysuli. He had several similar torques of his own, though none such as this. It was, he knew, a Cheysuli wedding torque, signifying the bond between warrior and wife.

Corin's voice was odd. "He gave it to her before he had a *lir*. Before he knew what she was, and what she meant to do." He sighed heavily, frowning. Aidan sensed anguish, regret, sorrow, and more than a little confusion. No doubt Corin had expected to feel relief. But relief was slow in coming; what he felt mostly was grief. "She was Cheysuli, once. But they never gave her the chance to know what it meant."

Aidan damped the *kivarna* purposely, giving Corin privacy. "I would not presume to speak for Hart and my *jehan*, to say if they would or would not have forgiven her. I know Keely did not." He paused. "What of you?"

Corin's mouth twisted painfully. "She never asked. I doubt she knew how."

"And if she had?"

Corin looked at Glyn for a long moment. Tears stood in his eyes. "I think," he said finally. "I would have, had she asked. Had she *tried*."

Aidan looked a final time on the woman in the bed, then turned to go. But Glyn, rising from her chair, stopped him at the door. Her hands were on his bare left arm, delaying him. He glanced at her in surprise and saw a deep compassion in her eyes. She did not have *kivarna*, perhaps, but her own measure of empathy was plain.

"Wait," Corin said. He rose from the bed.

Aidan wanted nothing more than to leave. Glyn's hands on his arm seemed to burn into his flesh, reminding him how easily he had succumbed to Lillith's power. He had wanted the Ihlini woman the moment he saw her, and while he believed any man, in his position, might feel the same, it grated within his soul to know he had been so malleable.

"Come into the corridor." Corin's hand on his shoulder guided Aidan out of the room as Glyn pulled open the door. She shut it behind them, staying within, throwing up a barrier between the dead woman in the bed and two men who owed their lives to her, if not respect and honor and love.

Aidan, dreading the question, stared resolutely down the corridor, as if his express *dis*interest might dissuade Corin's interest.

But if Corin saw the unspoken wish, he did not honor it. His voice was harsh. "You said Lillith was dead."

Aidan shut his teeth. "She is."

"We have been fooled before, *harani*, and to our detriment. Are you certain—"

Aidan's tone was clipped. "Quite certain."

Corin's expression was grim. "I hope you will understand if I insist on knowing how. Lillith has plagued us at all too many years—"

"I killed her."

"*You*—" But Corin broke it off. No doubt he was recalling his own sister had been responsible for Strahan's death. He relaxed. "Then we all owe you our gratitude. *Leijhana tu'sai, harani.*"

Aidan shrugged. What had happened was too personal, too unsettling for him to share with anyone. He recalled too clearly the power that had risen at *his* command. While he himself had not laid hands upon her, it had been at his behest that the gods had come to his aid. She was as dead as if he himself had twisted the chain around her throat and thrown her from the tower.

That sort of power, that sort of *influence*, terrified him.

"Aidan—"

"You would not understand."

"I might." Corin sighed. "I know very well what that

woman was. But let it go. What matters is that she is dead."
His gaze went to Aidan's waist, to the gold threaded through
by leather. "Gisella spoke of this. She said Lillith meant to
break it."

"She said a great many things." Forboding made him
curt. "*Su'fali*, forgive me . . . there are things too personal
to speak of. Let it suffice that Lillith is dead, and Gisella,
and the chain is whole."

"And what Gisella said of you?" Corin's hand clasped a
bare arm briefly. "You know better than to give credence to
a madwoman on her deathbed. She was babbling—talking
to gods?" He shook his head. "Let us go down to the hall.
There are preparations to be made—"

"No." Aidan felt the apprehension rising. He recalled
with distressing clarity that Gisella had not been the first or
only one to tell him he would never hold the throne. There
had been Shaine, then Carillon. Even the gods themselves
seemed to be preparing him for something else, something
more. And the Lion, time and time again, had repudiated
him.

He knuckled dampness from his brow. The biting edges
of comprehension made him queasy. "I have to go." He
heard himself: a half-choked, unsteady voice. "Teel is in
Erinn. I have been too long without my *lir*."

"Aidan." Corin's hand closed on him again. Now his tone
was commanding, granting no room for compassion. "Gisella
was mad, and a tool of the Ihlini. Whatever she said to you,
whatever her babbling meant, let none of it bear fruit. She
was *mad*."

Aidan looked into the steady blue eyes so much like his
grandsire's single one. He wanted to give in and agree, to
laugh and jest and suggest they go to the hall, as Corin
wanted, but he could do none of those things. He could find
no words to tell Corin that Gisella had not been babbling.

That she was not the first to warn him of his ending.

That he was very much afraid.

Twelve

Wolfhounds gathered around her. Muscles tensed, tails waved, dark eyes brightened expectantly. Shona held the stick: the dogs were prepared to chase it until she forfeited the game.

It was a good throwing stick: long as her arm, gnarled and rounded, bent just enough in the middle to distribute the weight properly. It was their favorite, and hers; toothmarks scored in the wood dated back five generations. Shona pulled it behind her head and hurled it with all of her strength. An ocean of dogs gave chase.

It was a game she generally enjoyed, laughing aloud and calling encouragement as the winner then fought off a pack of usurpers, intent on snatching the stick from his jaws. But today, this morning, she neither laughed nor called out. She simply threw the stick again and again, methodically, until at last even the strongest of the pack retired to sprawl on the turf, huge tongue lolling freely. The stick lay at her feet, where the big male had spat it out.

She felt no worse, nor better. Perhaps *she* should have chased the stick.

"Shona."

Her mother. Shona shut her eyes a moment, then turned. "Aye?"

Keely's faint smile was neutral. "I thought you would be *glad* to see him go."

Shona bent and picked up the stick. "I am."

"Are you?"

"Of course. We said what there was to say, I'm thinking . . . what good in beating a dying horse?"

Keely sighed. The wind snatched at braided hair, trying to undo the plait that dangled over one shoulder. Like her daughter, she wore woolen tunic and trews, belted with Erinnish copper. "There is something to be said for speaking your mind honestly, instead of hiding behind diplomatic falsehoods. You are much like me: you say what you think.

But there is a price for such openness, Shona. That sort of forthrightness makes it difficult to hide your feelings even when you most want to."

Shona hurled the stick. The dogs, still sprawled on turf, merely watched it fly, then fall. None of them went to fetch it.

She made a gesture of futility encompassing dogs and herself. "What am I to do? I meant to send him from me, brideless . . . then Corin's summons saved me from explaining more than I already had: that I'm refusing to surrender control of my life to something so binding as the *kivarna*. 'Tisn't *fair*." She broke it off, grimacing bleakly. "But it gives me no choice, now. 'Tis in my blood, and his . . . and we've had a taste of it." Glumly, she stared at the dogs. "Like a newborn pup on a nipple: give me more—and more—and *more*."

Keely sighed heavily. "Gods—how could we have foreseen? Your *jehan* and I put off having a child immediately, because of many things . . . and when at last we knew I had conceived I made him promise, if you were a girl, you would have all the advantages a boy has, growing up—if you wanted them. Among them was free choice in marriage partner . . ." Keely's bleak expression mirrored her daughter's. "And now because of this, that choice is stripped from you."

Shona shrugged. "I could still refuse. 'Tis difficult now, but once he's gone and the memory of the *kivarna* dies away . . ." She laughed abruptly. "Perhaps what I'm needing is to find an islander with *kivarna* . . ." But that, too, trailed into silence. "No. 'Tis too late. I'm lying if I deny it." She pressed both hands against her face and scrubbed violently at her brow. "Agh, what I *should* have done was go to bed with someone. If I knew what it was already, perhaps I could fight off this *kivarna*." She took her hands away and smiled ruefully at her mother. "But right now all I'm thinking about is how I felt when Aidan touched me. And how I'm wanting *more*."

"Like a newborn pup on a nipple." Keely smiled crookedly. "I come from a race ruled by *tahlmorra*. I am perhaps not the best person to offer advice. But it seems to me if the gods touched his blood *and* yours with this 'gift'—and then brought you together—perhaps there was a reason."

Shona snorted inelegantly. "The easy way, I'm thinking—let the gods make the choice."

Keely shook her head. "*You* must make the choice. And then you must live with it."

Shona shook her head. "No. 'Tisn't a question of living with the choice. 'Tis living with the *man*."

Keely looked past her daughter to the wolfhounds, rousing from their rest to fetch the stick once more. "There are worse to be had than Aidan."

"And he *is* half Erinnish." Shona grinned lopsidedly as she took the stick from the big male. " 'Tis something in his favor—that, and the hounds like him."

Keely sighed resignation. "I suppose there are worse ways to judge a man."

"None better," Shona said, and hurled the stick skyward.

Aidan stepped off the ship onto the docks at Kilore and stopped dead in his tracks. The *lir*-link meshed even as he sent the preemptory call to Teel.

Relief as the link flared anew washed through him with such abrupt violence he nearly fell. Trembling, he draped himself against the nearest stack of crates and lost himself in the reaffirmation, conscious of odd looks from strangers and not caring in the least. All that mattered was Teel. Only Teel.

Lir.

Eyes snapped open. *Where are you?*

Here.

Aidan looked up intently and saw the dark speck in the sky, rising over the fortress atop chalky palisades. The smile hooked one corner of his mouth and then both, widening to a transfixed expression of relief and exhilaration.

Slowly the speck enlarged, and wings became visible. Aidan sighed deep contentment. Muttering his thanks over and over again, he gripped the crate and waited for the physical contact. As Teel settled onto his left shoulder, Aidan grinned fatuously into the sunlight.

After a moment, he laughed. *Has it been like this for you?*

Teel did not answer at once. When he did, the characteristic acerbity was missing. *We belong together. They made us for one another, you and I.*

You were *the one who said I should go.*

But I did not say we would enjoy it. Teel paused. *Will you fly?*

Aye, Aidan said fervently. *I have been too long on the ground.*

Teel lifted off the shoulder and flew. Aidan, not caring one whit who saw the shapechange, with or without warning, lifted both arms, snapped up hands, give himself over to the change.

The void was swift and powerful, filling him with familiar exultation. As always, he walked the edge of pain, but it was a sweet, comforting pain, filling every portion of his being with triumph. He would not trade this for anything, anything at all.

Muscles knotted. Bones reknitted. The heart, pumping blood, sought and found new avenues. Aidan, shouting aloud, heard the human voice altered even as he cried out, and knew the change complete.

He did not go at once to the fortress, but lingered over Kilore with Teel, sweeping across the ocean, then angling back again. He was not a hawk, to soar, or a falcon to plunge in stoop, but a raven. He flew as a raven flies, glorying in the freedom, but knew it only delayed what lay before him. So he flew to the fortress gates, took back his human form, and gave polite greeting to the astonished guard contingent.

Aidan smiled blandly. "Surely you have seen the Lady do similar things."

One of the men cleared his throat. "Aye. But she always warns us, first."

That did not sound like Keely. But then perhaps she had changed, during her years in Erinn; after all, he had not known her at all. She had sailed from Homana when he was but a few months beyond a year. He did her a disservice if he gave credence to *all* the tales.

He was admitted at once and went immediately into the fortress, looking for Sean and Keely. He found them in the central hall, occupied by guests. He paused in the doorway, thinking another time might be better; Keely saw him, put something down, rose and called him in. Sean, bent over a gameboard with another man, looked up, saw him, pushed away his stool.

Aidan acceded to Keely's invitation solemnly, the peace regained in *lir*-shape dissipating too quickly. He felt the eyes on him, all of them, and glanced briefly at the visitors as he made his way to Keely. And realized, as he looked at the man with Sean, he was among kinfolk. There was only one man in the world who claimed all of Sean's size and more, as well as the flaming red beard.

"Well?" Keely's voice was sharp.

He saw no reason to soften the truth, or belabor it. "The Queen of Homana is dead."

She was very still. Then she drew in a deep breath, released it, nodded once. *"Leijhana tu'sai."*

Aidan felt a flicker of unaccustomed hostility. "Are you giving me thanks for the news, or to the gods for answering your petition?"

Keely's mouth opened. Blue eyes were wide and astonished, outraged by his presumption, and then he saw the flinch of comprehension. Keely turned from him rigidly and sought her chair, sitting down with exceptional care. She took from the table the thing she had held as he entered; he saw it was a sword. Now it rested across her knees, as if she meant to continue polishing it, but she made nb move to pick up the cloth. Both hands were on the blade, dulling the shine; he saw the tension in her fingers as she closed them, and he wondered if she intended to cut herself so the physical pain would keep the emotional at bay.

"Jehana," Keely said numbly. No one made a sound, not even Sean, who watched her compassionately, or the blonde woman nearest her with a young child in her lap.

The moment lasted a year. Then, with renewed resolution, Keely shook her head. "No. That was Deirdre—" She looked at Aidan, blinking away unshed tears. "There are kinfolk for you to meet."

Aidan smiled. "I know. Rory Redbeard, is it not?" He nodded a greeting, glancing at the huge man.

"And your *su'fala,*" Keely continued steadfastly, as if introductions might delay the acknowledgment of Gisella's passing. "Maeve. And four of five cousins."

Courtesy kept him in the hall. He greeted all of them— the blonde, green-eyed woman very much like Deirdre, her mother; the red-haired boy of sixteen, so obviously Rory's; the blonde girl of fourteen or so, and another perhaps ten, both sweet-faced and shy; the last a very young child in Maeve's arms—but he wanted only to find Shona. There were things he needed to say to her.

"Where is—"

Sean was the one who answered. "Outside, with Riordan. And Blais." His brown eyes were steady. "On the south side of the wall, shooting arrows."

Aidan nodded absently and turned to go at once, only vaguely aware he should stay to talk, to exchange news, but to do so would drive him mad. He had renewed his link with Teel; now there was Shona.

"Aidan."

Irritated, he turned back. Keely rose, holding the sword. "I want you to have this. I had it made—'tis a woman's blade."

The Erinnish lilt nearly made him smile. "I thank you for your generosity, *su'fala*, but what use is a woman's blade to me?"

"Not for you. For your daughter. For Shona's—" Keely broke it off, scowling fiercely at the blade. "I want no milk-mouthed granddaughter in Homana-Mujhar. Give her a sword, Aidan—and give her the means to use it."

Keely set the sword into his hands. He appraised it carefully, marking its superior balance, the perfect weight and excellent quality, and grieved that he would dishonor the giving as well as hurt Keely. But there was nothing else for it. He would not lie to her.

Aidan handed back the sword. "Keep it," he said softly. "And give it to *Shona's* daughter."

The emphasis was deliberate. As he turned away he heard her indrawn breath of shock, and knew she understood what he intended to tell her daughter.

He found them, as Sean had said, on the south side of the fortress wall. Three of them: Riordan, Shona, and a stranger. Their backs were to him as he approached. Shona's thick blonde braid divided her back in half, dangling to her thighs, and Riordan's unruly shoulder-length hair tumbled in the wind. But the stranger's hair was very black, also long—though not nearly as long as Shona's—and also braided. For a moment Aidan believed the stranger a woman, until he looked beyond the hair and saw height, shoulders, stature.

He wore Erinnish clothing: long-sleeved wool tunic, dyed dark green, with copper-bossed leather bracers snugged halfway up his forearms; leather over-tunic, belted with copper platelets hooked together by copper rings; and green woolen trews tucked into low-heeled calfboots. Although most Erinnish were light- or red-haired, Aidan had seen some with near-black hair. But there was no doubting the stranger's heritage, regardless of where he was or what he wore. His eyes, when he turned, were pure Cheysuli yellow.

Aidan's *kivarna* tingled. Recognition, acknowledgment; his blood knew perfectly well even if *he* did not.

The stranger smiled. The hair, though braided back in an Erinnishman's warrior plait, looped through with cord, was also held from his face by a slender leather thong.

This man looks more Cheysuli than I do, even without the gold . . . It was an unsettling thought. Aidan did not know him. Neither did his *kivarna*.

But then Shona turned, and Aidan forgot all about strange Cheysuli warriors. So, clearly, did she; her color drained away, leaving her gray as death, then rushed back to splotch her cheeks and set brown eyes to glittering with a vibrant intensity. In loud silence, she held the bow. A compact Cheysuli warbow once refused to her brother.

Now apparently not. Riordan, deaf and blind to the sudden tension—which betrayed the absence of *kivarna* in Sean's son—impatiently tapped the bow. "Shoot it, Shona—or let *me* shoot it!"

Aidan approached steadily, taking care with each step. He was not purposely delaying the moment, but his nerves screamed with acknowledgment of her nearness. He refused to give into emotion, or physical sensation, merely to please a gift he did not fully understand. His *kivarna* needed training. He was prepared to instruct it.

Riordan now tugged at the bow, but Shona was unmoved. She clung to the weapon with steadfast determination, ignoring her young brother's muttered threats. She was as intense as Aidan; he wondered if she, too, fought the silent battle with her senses.

He meant to speak to Shona. But the stranger, standing beside her, beat him to it. "Aidan, it is?" he asked. "They said you'd be coming—but not so soon, I'm thinking . . . unless Gisella died."

Distracted, Aidan spared only a quelling glance for the stranger. His world was alive with Shona's nearness, and yet something about the stranger snared his attention as well. It was more than a little astonishing to hear a Cheysuli warrior speaking pure, fluent Erinnish with a broad Erinnish accent.

His command of the tongue and its nuances was expert enough to mark him islander-born, except that he was so blatantly Cheysuli.

And then Aidan knew. Not islander-born, but almost. As close as one could come, while drawing first-breath in Homana. "Blais?" he asked tentatively, recalling Sean's brief mention.

The other nodded, grinning. "Half-cousins, we are. Maeve is my mother. And the Redbeard, well . . ." Blais shrugged, gesturing oddly. "In spirit if not in blood, Rory is my father."

In spirit *only.* Aidan recalled, with unsettling clarity, precisely who Blais was.

Yellow eyes narrowed assessively. "If you're not minding, cousin, I'll be sailing back with you."

"Back?"

"To Homana." The faint smile was ironic. For all his accent was Erinnish, Blais' attitude was Cheysuli. "You *will* be going back, I'm thinking . . . who would turn his back on a throne like the Lion?"

Who indeed? Certainly not Teirnan, Blais' true father. Teirnan still fought *for* the throne, with his treacherous followers.

Blais' eyes glinted. In fluent Old Tongue, he said, "I think it is past time I met my *jehan.* I have a *lir,* but no gold, no Ceremony of Honors, no proper *shu'maii.* I am as Cheysuli as you, cousin . . . do you not think I am due what other warriors are given?" He paused delicately, then added in Homanan, "A warrior should know his own bloodline. It is easier for the gods to keep track of us."

A well-schooled tongue . . . But Aidan, looking from Blais to Shona, forgot his kinsman almost at once.

"Now, then." Blais, smiling privately, switched back into Erinnish as he took the warbow from Shona. "We'll be letting *me* show the boy, while you two take a walk."

Shona made no protest. She walked to Aidan, then by him toward the headlands, out beyond Kilore.

She stopped at last, pausing on an overlook above the Dragon's Tail. Wind whipped them both, dragging at Aidan's hair, but Shona's was safely confined in a network of complex braids, small ones wrapped around big ones, then joined into a single thick plait that hung like rope from her head. She still wore trews and tunic, but the wool was very fine, the pale yellow dye very good, the embroidery exquisite. Her throat was naked of ornaments. Aidan longed to touch it, to put a torque upon it in the shape of his own *lir*.

Or one perhaps incorporating a wolfhound as well, to show they *shared* the bond.

Shona's voice was tight. "I thought you would stay there longer."

It was not quite what he had hoped for. "She died yesterday, at midday."

Shona shrugged slightly. "I thought you might stay with Corin, for whatever ceremony is due her." She paused. "She was my granddame, too."

He had not thought of it. "Did you ever see her?"

Shona's laugh was a blurted, breathy exhalation. "My mother would never let me. But then, I never asked." At last, she looked at him. Something flickered in her eyes. " 'Tis sorry I am, Aidan. For you, if not for her . . . my mother never allowed me to think of Gisella without thinking of what she did, but 'twas probably different for you. Your father likely didn't hate her so much."

"My father only rarely spoke of her. There was no hatred of her—just an absence of thought." Discomfited, Aidan shrugged. "Deirdre was there. No one wanted to dishonor her. So no one mentioned Gisella."

"And now the Mujhar is free . . ." Shona smiled a little. "D'ye think he'll marry her now, and make her a queen at last?"

Aidan laughed. "The moment he hears the news, the Mujhar will summon a priest." Then the humor died. "No, perhaps not—Gisella *was* the queen, and there are proprieties . . ." He sighed. "Deirdre will have to wait. But she has already waited so long, I doubt this will disturb her."

"And Maeve will be a princess, true-born and legitimate." Shona laughed. "A bit too late for my mother . . . she said she resented Maeve's bastardy for a very long time, since it made Keely of Homana something to be prized for other than she was. She told me if Maeve had been true-born, *she* would have had more freedom."

"And likely she would not have married your father, and you would not be here." Aidan paused. "I am going home to Homana."

Shona nodded. "I know."

"Alone."

Her color drained. *"Why?"*

"Because I am going to die."

Anger. Resentment. Her *kivarna*, and his, was ablaze. "How can you know?" she snapped. "How can you think such a thing? And how can you be such a *fool* as to think I will believe you?"

"Shona—"

"If you're not wanting me, say it. Stow this blather about dying, and say it. I'm not needing lies made up to hide the truth, merely to spare my feelings." Her brown eyes were nearly black. "D'ye think I can't tell, with the *kivarna*? D'ye think—" And then she broke off, eyes widening. "By the gods of all the oldfolk, you *do* believe you're to die!"

Aidan turned from her. He could not bear to look into her eyes and see the shock, the comprehension, that reinforced his own. Shona more than any might understand how he felt, and that doubled comprehension frightened him even more. He could, when he tried, ignore it, shunting aside the gnawing fear, but Shona brought it back. Shona deepened it.

"Aidan."

He walked rigidly to the edge of the cliff and stared down at the turbulent sea.

"Aidan—" And then she broke off, muttering in swift, disgusted gutter Erinnish he could only barely understand, because his mother had never taught him.

"Go back," he said roughly. "Blais might suit you better."

The muttering stopped. Shona's voice was dry. "Blais is sailing with you." She came up and stood beside him. Wind whistled across the headlands, curling over the lip of the cliff. "Why are you dying?" she asked.

Deep inside, something knotted. "Because I think I have to."

"*Have* to! Why? What man *has* to die, except when he's grown old?"

He did not know how to start. "There is this prophecy."

"I'm knowing *that.*"

"And there are gods."

"That, too."

"And then there is *this.*" He gripped the chain on his belt.

Shona did not answer.

Aidan clamped folded arms across his chest, to hold himself together. From head to foot, a shudder wracked him. "I killed a woman," he hissed, "without even touching her!"

She reached out to him. This time it was Aidan who pulled back, warding away intimacy.

"No." Shona closed cool fingers around his forearm. "You're needing it, Aidan. Who am I to look away? I'm selfish betimes, when I like, but I'm not cruel. You *need* me, just now . . . who am I to shut my eyes to your pain? What reason is good enough?"

He could think of one: *kivarna.*

But then she touched him and the *kivarna* blazed to life, shocking them both with its intensity, and he was babbling, telling her what had happened and how, except he did not *know* how, only that it had; only that *he* had, in his idiocy, in his maleness, allowed himself to be lured and seduced by an Ihlini witch who had done it before, even though he had been warned against it; an Ihlini sorceress who had seen him, seen his lust, seen a way to additional power through him, through his body, and through the child he would give her. He had been warned by Ashra, who was a tool of the gods almost but not entirely human; had been warned by Carillon himself, and Shaine; had been warned by Gisella— mad, dying Gisella, claiming she talked to gods—and who was *he* to argue? *He also* talked to gods, and with them, face-to-face. They told him things, he said, clinging to her hands so tightly he feared he might crush them. They told him things, and expected things of him, and he did not think he had the strength to do what they wanted him to.

Shona's voice was uneven. "And what is it you're thinking they want?"

"Me to die." He expelled it spasmodically. Then squeezed his eyes tight shut. "Gods, Shona, d'ye see? Do you see what I am? I lay with her even though I had been warned, without even giving it thought, and when I knew what she was and what she could do—what she *intended* to do—I killed her. I called on the gods, and they answered. Because *I asked them to.*" He could not stop shaking.

Shona stepped closer. He tried to back away, but she held him, slipping close, wrapping arms around him in a hug intended to offer comfort. And it did, but something more; something he hoped she would not recognize.

Her smoky voice was soothing. "Hush, my lad, my boyo— you're not knowing what you're saying . . . you're all bound up inside and out, knotted to death with gods and dreams and uncertainties . . . 'tis no wonder you hurt so. D'ye think I can't feel it, with or without the *kivarna*?" She sighed heavily. "And you not knowing a thing at all, I'm thinking . . . ah, Aidan, how can you be so foolish as to think it's *death* they want? How can you know they don't mean you for something else?"

He gave way and hugged her hard, glad of her closeness, grateful to her for staying with him, for touching, for talking, for simply being *there*, so he was not so terribly alone.

He had been very alone for most of his life, even when in a throng.

But not with her. Not with her. *Never alone with Shona.*

Aidan clung to her with all his transitory strength. This moment, he needed her very badly. "Why not for something else?" He threaded fingers into the complex weavings of her braid. "Because of the dreams, and the things I have been told . . ." He was aware, suddenly, how close to the edge of the blade they walked, so tantalizingly near. If they slipped, if they allowed their attention to wander, they could be cut. Even killed. "Gods, Shona—don't—"

"D'ye think it matters?"

He was lost, and knew it. "I cannot take the chance. I will not punish you . . . I will not sentence you to a life of loneliness and abstinence . . . I will not marry a woman only to die, and make her a prisoner of the *kivarna*—" He pressed her against him, rocking, rocking, trying to assuage the pain, the longing, the need. "I will not do this to you."

"Aidan—"

He set her back, lifting a staying hand between them. He pressed air again and again, keeping her from touching him. "No. No. I am going back. Alone. If I am to die, I will do it without hurting you."

"And if you're *not*?" she shouted. "What *then*, ye *skilfin*?"

"No," he said. "No." And then turned from her stiffly, striding back toward Kilore.

Thirteen

She came as he lay awake in the darkness, wracked by self-doubts and contempt. Who was he to think he was an instrument of the gods, carefully selected for some specific purpose? Who was *he* to think himself different from everyone else, when each man and woman alive knew doubts and fears and confusion?

But who was he to deny it when he had proof in the form of a chain of flawless gold, heavy and substantial?

Who was he at *all?*

She came, pulling aside the bed hangings, and he knew her instantly.

He heard the robe slipped off her shoulders. He slept, as always, with no candle lighted; he required no illumination. In daylight or in darkness, he would know her anywhere.

Deep inside, he quivered. And then the *kivarna* awoke.

She climbed up into the bed. Her fair, free of plaited braids, rippled over shoulders to twine against the bed pelts. She was naked, but for hair; save for anguish, so was he.

The pain was exquisite; the knowledge bittersweet. Shona knelt beside him, then slowly placed a cool hand upon his chest. Beneath flesh and bone beat his heart. His breathing ran ragged.

"Ah, no," she whispered. "Don't let it be in fear. Let it be in joy."

His voice sounded rusty. "You know the truth, *meijhana.*"

"Do I?" The hand drifted upward to touch his throat, his chin, his mouth. "Do you?"

Every sense was alive as she touched him. His body rang with it.

Shona's smoky voice was soft. "If 'tis myth, we'll have shared naught but a night's pleasure. If 'tis truth, then we'll by sharing *more* of these nights, I'm thinking."

Against his will, he smiled. And took her into his arms.

* * *

Two months later, at dockside, Keely put a sheathed sword into Aidan's hands. "There," she said firmly. "What excuse do you offer *this* time?"

He laughed. "No excuse at all. Aye, *su'fala*, I will see to it you have no milk-mouthed granddaughter in the halls of Homana-Mujhar. She will have this sword, and the means to learn its use."

Keely looked beyond him to the ship. Then turned abruptly away, as if she could not bear to look at the vessel that would carry away her daughter. Fiercely, she stared back toward the cliffs. "Where is Shona?"

"Bringing the dogs," Aidan said dryly.

Even Keely was startled. "*All* of them?"

Aidan smiled crookedly. "The big boyo himself, as well as the bitch from over-island, and the one from Atvia, and the two in whelp, and the one she got last year from the fawn bitch who died, and the pups from the last litter . . ." He sighed. "Ten or twelve, at least. We will repopulate Homana-Mujhar."

Keely inspected his expression. "Do you mind? She is headstrong, aye—I made her so—but she knows what she is doing. She loves those hounds . . ." She sighed. "I think it is compensation for having no *lir*-gifts."

"Or perhaps she simply loves dogs." Aidan grinned. "Here she comes now—and Sean. And Blais."

"And dogs," Keely muttered. "There will be no room on the ship."

"Not once those two bitches have whelped. Ah—here is Riordan, also."

They made their way to the dock, trailing hounds and servants with baggage. Blais strode down the dock first, accompanied by his ruddy wolf, who walked unconcernedly ahead of the pack of hounds bred to kill her kind. She had, as *lir* were required, made her peace with unblessed animals. Or else she had put the big male in his place, and he the rest in theirs.

Aidan glanced at the ship. High in the rigging, perched upon a spar, Teel preened himself.

Sean himself directed the loading of Shona's baggage, calling out orders in his rusty voice. The hounds milled around, getting in everyone's way; Shona's remonstrations did nothing in the midst of such confusion, for half the dogs were too young to have learned proper manners. But when at last the loading was done, Shona sent the dogs up the plank onto the ship—and discovered none of them would go.

"Agh, gods," Sean muttered, and scooped up one of the bitches. Without further delay he carried her up the plank and onto the deck.

"There," Shona said. "d'ye see? Will you walk on all your legs, or be carried like a meal sack?"

The huge dark male, eyeing the ship balefully, leaned against her hip. Shona staggered and nearly fell.

Aidan fished her out of the pack and pulled her away from the water. "He will go when you go. Get the others on board—we can tend him later."

One by one the rest of the dogs were led up the plank and onto the deck. When at last only the big male remained, Sean himself knelt down to look him in the eye. " 'Tis a fine, bright boyo you are, my lad, and 'tis sorry I am to see you go. But we've others here—though none as fine as you—and the lass will be needing you. Tend her well, my braw, bright lad, and come back whenever you like. The lasses will be mourning."

So was Sean. Shona went to him and hugged him, clinging to his big frame, then let go and turned away, putting her hand on the hound's neck. With no more urging required, he climbed the plank to his pack.

Aidan, looking at Sean and Keely, felt inadequate. He was taking Shona away from a warm, loving family who had instilled her with courage, spirit and determination, along with pride and a powerful loyalty. He could not predict if she would find the same in Homana, or even if they could make it. For one horrible moment he believed he was taking her to a doomed future.

Sean shook his head as Aidan glanced at him. " 'Tis something every man feels," he said, "and something every woman faces." His brown eyes were warm and bracing, and Aidan realized the *kivarna* lived in Sean as strongly as in his daughter. "You'll do well enough, my lad. And so will my lass."

Blais came out on deck, leaning against the rail. "Are we sailing *today?*"

"*Skilfin,*" Shona muttered, then turned abruptly to embrace her mother.

Aidan climbed up the plank. The big male wolfhound

greeted him with a whine. "She will be here in a moment."
He patted the narrow head.

"Or two days from now," Blais amended.

Aidan glared at his cousin. "She has every right to take as
long as she likes. Erinn is her home . . . *and* yours, I'm
thinking."

Blais grinned. "An Erinnishman, is it? Aye, well—let her
take her time. 'Tis indeed her home she's leaving . . . while
I'm going to mine."

Aidan was surprised. "You intend to stay in Homana?"

Blais shrugged. " 'Twill depend on many things."

"Such as your father?"

Yellow eyes flickered. "A man has every right to seek out
his *jehan*."

Aidan smiled coolly. "A Cheysuli, is it? After all this
time?"

Blais sighed. "Aye. It is. And you should walk in my
boots, cousin . . ." He thrust out one booted foot. "I have
the hair, the eyes, the color, the *lir*—but no one in Erinn
truly understands."

"Keely might."

"Keely does. 'Twas she who suggested I go."

Aidan frowned his doubt. "Even knowing—"

"—what my father is?" Blais shrugged. "She said that
while *she* bore no affection for Teirnan of the *a'saii*, she was
not blaming a son for desiring to know his *jehan*."

*Perhaps because she never desired to know her jehana, and
felt guilty because of it.* Aidan nodded. "A man has a right
to know his father. But he may not like what he meets."

Blais's expression was serious. "My mother never lied to
me. I know what he did. I know what he wants to do. But
I'm thinking 'tis only fair I hear *his* side of the story."

Aidan granted him that. But he did not think it would
last.

Shona at last broke away from her kinfolk, hugging Riordan
a final time, and walked straight-spined up the plank. Her
expression belied nothing of what she was feeling, but Aidan
knew. For all they promised to return as soon as was decently possible, such plans often changed. Keely herself had
been home twice in twenty-two years, and not for fifteen of
them. She knew as well as any the likelihood of seeing
Shona any time soon was negligible.

Blais still leaned against the rail. Like Shona, he stared

down at the dock. Rory and Maeve and their children stood beyond Sean and Keely, with Rory dwarfing all but Sean; both sisters were crying. Of all the women, only Maeve's eyes were dry.

Blais' jaw was taut. "She's not wanting me to go."

Shona shrugged as the ship was secured to sail. "None of them *wants* us to go."

"She less than most. She thinks I'll be joining my father."

Shona's tone was hard. " 'Tis your decision, I'm thinking. To be a fool, or not."

Blais looked at her. "He's not softened your tongue, has he?"

Shona displayed her teeth. "He knows better than to try."

Aidan lifted a hand as the ship slipped her mooring. On the dock, the eagles waved, from the shadow of their aerie.

PART IV

One

By the time the ship reached Homanan waters, eleven wolf-hounds had become twenty-four. Blais spent much of his time secluded with his *lir*, locked away in private thoughts. And Shona and Aidan, reveling in the wind and the freedom and the magic of the *kivarna*, were almost sorry to see the end of the voyage draw near. They had come to prize the isolation of the vessel, knowing all too soon Aidan would face the increasing responsibilities of his title. They had spent weeks learning one another's likes and dislikes, in bed and out of it, and were not quite prepared to lose the privacy.

And yet as the ship sailed into the harbor, it was Shona who clung to the rail and pointed to the mist-wreathed island so close to Hondarth. "Is that it?"

"The Crystal Isle? Aye." Aidan leaned close to her. "The *shar tahls* teach us it is the birthplace of the Cheysuli; that the Firstborn appeared there, then went to Homana."

Shona's expression was intent. " 'Tis where he took her."

"Where who took—? Oh." Aidan clasped a rigid hand. "Aye. And where she killed him."

Restless, Shona pulled away and paced two steps, then turned back, braid swinging, toward the island. "Strahan made this place over into an Ihlini domain. She said so."

"For a time. No one lives there now . . . it was and always has been, save for two brief occupations, a significantly Cheysuli place."

"Significantly," Shona muttered. "That's something I'm not knowing, with so much Erinnish blood . . ." She sighed, transfixed again by the mist-wreathed bump of land. "For so many years I prayed to be as my mother, able to talk to *lir* and take on any shape . . . but there was nothing. All I had was the *kivarna*."

Aidan laughed. " 'Tis enough, I'm thinking."

She flicked him an impatient glance, though a tiny smile acknowledged his purposeful lilt. "Could we go?"

It startled him. "Now? But we are so close to the mainland—"

"I'd like to go, Aidan. I know so much of what happened to my mother . . . and yet I've never seen any of the places I've heard so much about."

Blais appeared from the bow of the ship, flanked by his ruddy wolf. Like Shona, he stared hard at the island. "If 'twas here we were born, as the *shar tahls* say, we *all* should see the place. 'Tis history, and tradition . . ." He flicked an ironic glance at Aidan. "Or are you so secure in your heritage you're needing no reminding?"

Aidan understood very well the pointed jibe. Of them all, Blais had less reason to see the island. His Cheysuli father had turned his back on such things as tradition and heritage, forging his own renegade clan out of malcontents disturbed by too much change within the existing clans; yet if Blais wanted to go to the Crystal Isle, it indicated he at least wanted to weigh matters before deciding on a side.

Something to be said for our arrogant kinsman . . .

Aidan, giving in, turned to call the order to the captain, who in turn passed the orders along to his men. The ship heeled off of Hondarth and sailed toward the island instead.

Curving white beaches stretched in either direction, blinding the eye in sunlight. Shona, Aidan, and Blais, accompanied by adult wolfhounds and appropriate *lir*, strode off the ship onto the crushed white shells. A path wound away from the beach toward the wooded interior. Through the trees they could see the glint of white stone here and there, bleached brilliant by sunlight.

Shona directed the dogs up the beach, laughing as they romped, but then turned her attention to the path and its destination. "Where does it go?"

"Undoubtedly to the palace." Aidan gestured toward the white mass only vaguely visible behind foliage and forest. "It was a true palace for decades, serving the Firstborn, but later fell into disuse. Carillon restored it as a prison-palace for his exiled queen, Electra, and then Strahan lived in it for a time, in hiding . . . but other than that it has not been truly inhabited for many years."

"Why wait?" Blais asked lightly, and headed up the path toward the palace.

Shona looked back to the hounds. All but the two bitches with litters and the new pups were present, splashing through surf and leaping upon one another. Seawater glistened on wiry coats, silver-gilt in the sunlight.

"They have noses," Aidan reminded her. "They will find us if they get lonely."

She gifted him with a sour scowl. "They were bred for sight, not smell."

"Does it matter? If you like, I will have Teel keep an eye on them."

She gave the pack of hounds another judicious look, considering, then struck out after Blais, leaving Aidan to catch up.

The path to the palace was mostly overgrown, since it had been more than twenty years since anyone had tended the island, but Aidan and Shona found it less tedious than expected. Here and there a vine or branch was broken, testimony to Blais' earlier passage, and the white shell-and-stone path was layered with years of dirt, deadfall, and the unintended scatterings of animals. But it was easy enough to follow, and led directly to the big wooden gates in the bailey wall.

"Here," Shona breathed. "She said she climbed up the gate, and over . . ." Slowly she walked through the opening left by a yawning gate leaf. "D'ye see? She said the iron studs allowed her purchase for bare feet."

Aidan, following, looked at the gate. He would not want to climb it, himself. That Keely had, in the midst of a raging storm, to escape Strahan only underscored her determination.

"And somewhere here is where Taliesin died. He got her free of the palace, and used his sorcery to keep Strahan at bay for a little . . ." Shona glanced around. "They must have come from there. D'ye see? A side door, mostly hidden . . ."

Aidan, distracted, nodded. Something was impinging on his awareness. Something *tugged* at him, like a child on his father's tunic, trying to get his attention.

"And then across here, to the gate . . . she got over and ran into the trees."

Again he nodded. He was only vaguely aware of Shona's observations.

"Do we go in here? Or in the front?"

Aidan twitched shoulders. Something cool tapped his spine. "Wherever you like, *meijhana*."

"Here, then. The way she came, with Taliesin." She paused. "Are ye coming, then?"

Troubled, Aidan nodded and followed her across the cobbles to the narrow side door, little more than a wooden slat in the thick stone wall. Its hinges were rusted stiff, but Shona simply grasped the latch and tugged, undeterred by anything so tame as twenty years of disuse and neglect.

Rust crumbled. So did hinges. The door fell away from the wall.

"Agh—" Shona caught it, then grinned as Aidan swore and sucked at the ball of his thumb. His instinctive grab for the falling door had resulted in a shallow slice. "Wounded, are you?"

He shrugged it away and levered the door against the wall as Shona peered into the interior. She sniffed. "I smell sorcery."

"You smell mold and dust and dampness—and perhaps a cousin somewhat interested in annoying us."

" 'Twasn't through here he came. The door was whole . . . besides, d'ye think he'd ever go in the side when there's a *front* way all the grander?"

Aidan looked inside the entrance. "Probably not."

"Go," she suggested, fisting him high on the shoulder.

Teel? Aidan appealed.

The raven's tone was amused. *Mold and dust and dampness. And, somewhere, a cousin.*

But nothing more?

Not here.

It was not nearly as comforting as Aidan anticipated. 'Not *here?*' What did that mean?

"Will you go?" Shona asked. "Or d'ye want me to go first?"

Aidan sneezed. Mold and dust and dampness. "No," he muttered glumly, and went into the narrow corridor.

It intersected with a wider corridor running in either direction. The floors were floured with dust. Heading deeper into the palace were two sets of footprints: man's boots, and a wolf's pawprints.

"This way," Aidan suggested, and followed the marks in the dust.

Eventually they reached a wide doorway that opened into a massive hall. The ceiling arched high overhead, intricately fan-vaulted, pale and delicately textured like an elaborate spun-sugar cake. The hall itself was rectangular, with arched windows cut through white stone high in the walls. Below each arched embrasure hung a faded banner. Window upon window, banner upon banner, dripping down lime-washed walls. The colors were muted by time, but the patterns remained discernible. Aidan, who knew his clan history, realized the banners were not of Cheysuli making, but of a much later time.

"Carillon," he murmured. "He must have had them put here."

"But would Strahan *leave* them here?"

"As reminders of his victory? I think so." Aidan moved further into the hall, abreast of Shona, who walked with her head tipped back, throat stretched, so she could see the vaulted ceiling.

Then she stopped. "Look at the columns!" Her voice echoed oddly. "All twisted into spirals—and the *runes*—"

Aidan looked as she touched the nearest column. It was, as she said, twisted, spiraling up to the fan-vaulting. On either side of the ridge that marked the upward sweep of the spiral, runes had been chiseled deep into stone.

"Can you read them?" she asked.

Aidan studied the nearest chain of glyphs winding its way from floor to ceiling, higher than he could see. "Some of them," he said at last, reluctant to admit he knew too few of the symbols. "Something to do with asking the blessing of the gods, and the birth of the Firstborn—" Aidan, broke off, shivering. The flesh stood up on his arms.

" '*Tis* cold, " she agreed. "All this stone, and no fires—"

"Not that," he muttered, then moved farther into the hall. "I imagine there were pelts, and furniture—" He broke off yet again, staring.

"*Aidan,*" Shona gasped.

They had moved from behind a column, angling into the hall. Now the dais came into sight. They stood far to one side of it, nearly behind it; from their view all they could see was one side of dark wood, sweeping forward like haunches, and the upward curve of the back. It arched up, then over, forming a wooden canopy.

"The Lion," Aidan blurted. And then, in relief, "No. No. This one is smaller, less elaborate . . ." He drew in a deep breath of relief. "Even the head is different. The jaws are not open—" He laughed, moving closer. "How could I—"

And then he stopped dead, for there was movement in the throne.

He thought, improbably, of yet another dead Mujhar, come to take him to task, to upbraid him for his failings. But there were none left. He had met with all he knew, those in his immediate ancestry. Those before Shaine did not matter, save for knowing their histories. Shaine had been the one most responsible for the plight of the Cheysuli, and for furthering the prophecy by *forcing* the Cheysuli to act.

Shona laughed. The sound rang in the hall and blotted out the darkness. " 'Tis *Blais*—oh, gods, we should have known." And she took Aidan's hand and pulled him around the side of the dais.

Blais, slumping negligently against the scrolled back, hooked a muscled, trew-clad leg over an armrest to dangle a boot. He arched one raven brow. "It suites me, I'm thinking."

Shona made a derisive sound. "No more than *me*, ye *skilfin*."

Aidan loosed his hand from Shona's and took two paces closer. The dark stone dais was low, barely raised above the floor, and the throne itself a much smaller version of the Lion in Homana-Mujhar, but it spoke to him nonetheless of majesty and magnificence; of power too long forgotten. Of things he needed to know, while knowing none of them.

"D'ye want it?" Blais asked lightly. "Will you fight me for it?"

Dimly, Aidan knew his cousin only jested. Blais was, for all his arrogance, a decent man, if uncommitted. Undoubtedly he jibed for the fun of it, no more; but to Aidan, transfixed by the throne, it whispered of heresy.

He climbed the dais. Blais, so casually ensconced with his *lir* at his other foot, did not move. Not even when Aidan paused and put out a hand to touch the armrest.

Its shape was a lion's foreleg, with a downward-curling paw forming the place for a hand. It was very like the Lion Throne in Homana-Mujhar in appearance, and yet Aidan was conscious of an entirely different presence. *That* throne had repudiated him. This one, somehow, did not.

Blais uncoiled himself and stood. "There. 'Tis yours. You've more right than I, I'm thinking—at least, until I settle things with my father."

Distantly: "Your *jehan* is a traitor. A heretic. He is *kin-wrecked*; do you wish to become tainted yourself?"

Blais' tone hardened. He spoke in Old Tongue to match Aidan's unexpected change of languages. "My *jehan, leijhana tu'sai*, does not even know I exist. My *jehana* never saw fit to tell him she had conceived, *or* that she had borne me, before sailing off to Erinn with Rory Redbeard." He slipped back into Erinnish. "I'll do whatever I choose, *kin-wrecked* or no. 'Tis due the both of us."

The wood was satiny. Aidan's *kivarna* spoke to him of tasks yet undone; of knowledge yet unlearned; of a people yet unborn. "Aye," he said quietly, answering Blais, and then took his hand away. He turned to face Shona. "Will you stay here? There is something I must do."

She stared. "Now? Here? But—"

"Will you stay?"

Shona and Blais exchanged glances. Eventually she nodded. "I'll wait. Blais and I can argue about which chamber was used for what . . ." Her voice trailed off. "Are you well, Aidan?"

"I have to go," he said.

Shona pointed. "There is the door. And *that* way lies the ship—if you take too long, I'll be there."

Grinning, Blais resettled himself in the throne. "And I'll be *here*. This beastie suits me well."

"Skilfin," Shona muttered, but Aidan walked away from them both and heard nothing more of their wrangling.

TWO

Aidan walked out of the palace through the front doors, though hardly conscious of it. And then directly across the cobbled bailey to the open gates, thinking nothing of Keely's escape or Taliesin's death or even Strahan's defeat. Instead he thought of the flicker of awareness that guided him. It was not precisely *kivarna*, nor was it the *lir*-bond that gave him access to the earth magic. It was something older, something stronger . . . something rooted more deeply in the fabric of his life—and countless lives before him—that drew him out of the old Cheysuli palace, where another lion crouched, into the forested depths of the Crystal Isle.

He heard a fluttering in the trees and glanced up to see Teel settling onto a branch. The raven's tone was almost too quiet for Teel. Too *gentle*.

Are you certain this is the way you wish to go?

Aidan stopped. *This is the way I have to go.* Something skittered out of his awareness, whispering of apprehension. He appealed to Teel at once. *Should I go back?*

I did not say that, nor did I suggest it. I merely asked: are you certain this is the way you wish to go?

Aidan drew a steadying breath and looked around. A path lay before him, though little more than a twisted, narrow passage through the trees and thick foliage. No one had passed for decades, and yet he made his way easily enough, even through snagging creepers and sweeping boughs. But he saw no reason not to go. He had felt no premonition of danger, and surely Teel would warn him if what he did might prove deadly.

He released the breath evenly. *It seems the thing to do. A thing I should do.*

The raven studied him a lengthy moment, as if weighing his worth. His eyes were bright and black. *Well enough*, Teel said finally, and flew away into shadows.

Aidan went on. He rounded a curve in the twisted path and saw the ruins before him: tumbled, rectangular stones that once had stood upright in a meticulous circle, warding a chapel. The stones leaned haphazardly upon one another, or lay fallen in the dirt. The doorway was shallow and lopsided, its lintel stone cracked. The stones themselves had once been a uniform gray; now they were pocked and stained with age, wearing green lichen cloaks to hide blackened pits and scars.

He approached slowly, peeling aside foliage. He was very much alone. Teel was gone, the link suspiciously empty. Aidan knew the raven was within calling distance if he chose to summon him, but obviously he was intended to go on without benefit of company. Not even that of a *lir*.

A single stone stood three paces from the door. Aidan passed it, paused, then ducked beneath the cracked lintel and went in.

The interior of the chapel was even worse than the exterior. Rotted beamwork had fallen like tossed rune-sticks in a fortune-game, hiding much of the floor. The place was little more than a shell, but Aidan felt the power. It was a tangible presence.

The altar leaned crazily to one side like a drunken man, propped up by fallen brothers. Sunlight penetrated the gaps between the standing stones and slanted deep inside, stripping the altar gold and gray. Worn runes were dark against the stone, nearly indecipherable, but they snared Aidan's attention and drew him to the cracked plinth and tilted altar like an infant to the breast.

He found himself on his knees. He could not recall when he had knelt, or if he had fallen; he knew only he felt dampness seeping through his leathers. His hands were pressed against the altar stone as if he worshiped it; he began to think he did. Or that he must.

"Gods," he whispered hollowly.

Did he pray? Or did he merely express awe, as so many did, not thinking at all of gods? Aidan could not answer. He only knew he hurt deep inside. Wracked with doubt, contempt, confusion, he was exquisitely certain he was insignificance personified.

He knelt before the altar of his ancestors, and cried. Because of anguish, of doubt, of uncertainty. Because he was so unworthy. Because his color was so dull within the tapestry of the gods; his link so weak, so fragile, so very sure to break. He was Aidan, and he was nothing.

"You are what you wish to be."

Aidan jerked upright and spun on his knees, one hand slipping instinctively to his knife. But the hand fell away as he saw the man. The Hunter.

He tingled unpleasantly from subsiding shock. With effort, he managed to speak. "Will you give me my answers now?"

"If you ask the proper questions." The Hunter came into the chapel and found a stone on which to seat himself. The incongruity struck Aidan; here was a god for whom the chapel had been built, perched upon the wreckage with perfect equanimity.

Aidan shook his head. "How do I even begin?"

The Hunter smiled warmly. "You began quite some time ago. As a boy, in fact. The dreams, Aidan . . . all those turbulent dreams that troubled your sleep."

"I have them no longer. Not since I sailed from Erinn."

The Hunter's mouth quirked. "Aye, well . . . women often have the ability to make a man think of things other than troubling dreams." The smile widened. "Enjoy your peace— and sleep—while you may. You have spent much of your life with neither." He paused. "Are your knees not growing numb?"

They were. Aidan took the question as an invitation to rise. He stood slowly, unsticking damp leather from knees, and fixed the Hunter with what he hoped was a compelling gaze. "Why are you here? Did I summon you?"

"In a way, but not through any prayer or muttered invocation." The Hunter's tone was dry. "I came here because it is time for you to know more. To answer all those questions you have had, and no one of whom to ask them."

"Good," Aidan said, before he thought about it.

The Hunter—the god—laughed. "Men believe we move in mysterious ways merely to confuse the issue. No. We have reason for what we do. If we wrote it in stone, most men would forget to read. If we showed ourselves to everyone the way we have to you, we would therefore become common- place, and consequently of no importance. Gods must main- tain some portion of mystery here and there, or the awe and honor recedes, and nothing is ever done."

Aidan had never thought about it that way.

The Hunter picked a daub of mud from his leathers. "There are men and women in the world who consider the gods little more than figments of imagination—for we gave you that, as well—and little more than a mechanism by which some— those quicker of wit and large of ambition—control others. It is a simple explanation, and effective. There are also people in the world who lay everything at the feet of a natural progression, denying our power, our presence, our *existence*." He shrugged. "They are welcome to disbelief."

"But that is heresy," Aidan protested.

"Ignorance," the god corrected. "They are afraid. Puffed up with self-importance because they believe strength lies in *not* requiring gods. They believe they have discovered Truth, and that it lies elsewhere. Not in the palm of the gods." Smiling, the Hunter made the Cheysuli gesture denoting *tahlmorra*. "But it was we ourselves—gods, Aidan—who *gave* man self-rule and the ability to think for himself; therefore we also allow him his petty heresies. It is an individual's personal decision which afterworld he prefers—or none at all."

Aidan felt battered. "But I have always believed."

"We know that. And now you will benefit from it." The Hunter glanced away from Aidan a moment, then smiled. A woman came through the low doorway: a small gray-haired woman with magical eyes and a weaver's callused hands.

"Aidan," she said kindly, "you have been patient far beyond most men's capabilities."

Shame flared. "I have not. I have doubted, and feared, and railed. I have questioned."

The Weaver was unruffled by his admission. "Naturally," she agreed calmly. "Men must always question. We gave them curiosity, and impatience, and anger, and the need to know. You are a man; you are no different. But you still have been very patient."

Aidan felt on the verge of a great discovery. And he felt afraid. "So—now you will tell me everything?"

"We will give you the means with which to make your decision."

The response was swift. "There is no need. I will do whatever you ask."

She smiled, hands folded in a multicolored skirt woven of colorless yarn. "We do not require blind obedience, though often it seems that way . . . and some would go so far as to argue we do." She shook her head. "No. We require sacrifice and hardship, but given and undertaken freely, because learning is not accomplished without either."

"Have I learned anything? Or nothing?"

There was a sound at the tumbled entryway. "Surely you have learned *something*," remarked the Cripple as he crutched into the chapel. "You have learned how easily a man can be steered from the proper path by a woman."

Aidan stared fixedly at the old man, marking again the creviced face, the shiny pate, but mostly the missing right leg. It was as if the god had chosen to show himself in the guise Aidan had seen first.

He swallowed heavily, pulling himself back with effort. "Do you mean Shona?" Dread rose up like a wave. "Are you saying I should *not* marry her?"

The Cripple's dark eyes glinted. "We are saying no such thing. She has the blood your House requires."

"Then who do you—?" Heat bathed him. "Lillith."

The old man leaned on his crutch. "Ashra warned you," he chided gently. "She gave you good warning, and you chose not to heed it."

The response was swift. "I was *lirless*."

"An excuse."

"But the *truth*. She used sorcery."

"No. You *believed* she did, because you stopped believing in yourself." The Cripple shook his head. "Lillith, though indeed powerful, used nothing more than herself. With you, it was sufficient."

Shame suffused him. He was hot and cold at once, unable to look any of them in the eye.

The Cripple's tone softened. "But I will warrant you learned something from it."

"*Aye.*" The single word was heartfelt. "You answered me. When I called. When I asked your intercession. The chain." He filled his hands with heavy gold. "You answered my petition."

The Cripple was silent. The Weaver also said nothing. Aidan looked sharply at the Hunter, trying to suppress apprehension so violent it knotted muscles and belly.

The brown man's tone was infinitely quiet. "Think what it means," he suggested, "when a man can say he summons the gods at will."

Aidan had no answer.

The Hunter's eyes were steady. "Does it make *him* a god?"

"No!"

"Think, Aidan. Surely it means something."

"It means——" Sweat dampened his temples. Aidan wet dry lips. "It means they have chosen him for something."

"And does that make him better than anyone else?"

"No."

"Perhaps—different."

Resentment shaped his tone. "You *want* me to claim myself different, so you can shame me. So you can enforce humility."

The Hunter laughed. "We are not *that* cruel, Aidan. Answer truthfully."

"Do I think myself different?" Aidan looked from one to the other, to the other. "Aye. Because I *am*."

The Hunter idly inspected a cracked thumbnail. "And what will you do with your difference?"

Suddenly infinitely weary, Aidan sat down on a fallen stone. He could think of nothing to say that would please them, or satisfy their convoluted examination, and so he said nothing at all.

The Weaver's blue eyes were bright. "At least you do not speak before you know how," she observed dryly. "That is something."

"Something," the Crippled echoed. "I think he has become weary of us. I think he is exercising his impatience."

"What do you expect?" Aidan snapped. "You batter me with words and innuendos, hinting at tasks and undertakings . . . do you think I will sit meekly by waiting *forever* while you decide if I am worthy for whatever new game you have developed since the last time we spoke?" He glared at them. "What is the sense in bestowing self-rule upon us, and curiosity, if we are not to use either?"

"Some people do sit meekly by forever." The Cripple said mildly. "Everyone—and everything—has its place in the Wheel of Life."

Aidan, who had had this conversation with the Weaver, glanced at her. She did not smile.

"Chained warrior," the Hunter murmured.

"Chained prince," added the Weaver.

"Chained raven," ended the Cripple.

The Hunter took it up. "Chains that bind a man; chains that free a man."

The Weaver nodded once. "Bound, the life goes on. Broken, it is free."

The Cripple smiled. "Which do *you* seek?"

Aidan touched the chain. "I made it whole."

Dark eyes were fathomless. "The choice was made freely?"

"Aye. I chose it."

"Who are you?" asked the Weaver intently.

"Aidan of Homana." He looked at each of them. "Prince of Homana, after my *jehan*, who will be Mujhar. A warrior of the clan. Cheysuli." He paused. "And very, very confused."

The Hunter laughed. "The last is obvious. As for the others . . . well, your road yet lies before you. You have not come as far down it as we had hoped."

Fear flickered to life. "Not—?"

The Weaver's voice was gentle. "There is still the task to be done."

Aidan was on his feet. *"What task?"* he shouted.

"And the sacrifice to be made," agreed the Cripple, ignoring the outburst. "But I think, when the time comes, he will make it freely."

Aidan, angry and afraid, opened his mouth to ask another question. But he was all alone in the chapel.

And no wiser at all.

Three

In Hondarth they had purchased horses for themselves, and made arrangements for Shona's baggage train to follow at a more sedate pace. Now, having covered the distance between the port city and the crossroads near Mujhara, Blais looked at Aidan

"Which way?"

"East. That way." Aidan gestured. "Mujhara is west, but a few leagues up the road. Clankeep, from here, will take you half a day."

Blais shrugged. "I've waited twenty-two years to see it. Half a day won't tax me."

Shona shook her head. Around her mount, wolfhounds milled. "You should come with us to Homana-Mujhar. There are kinfolk, and the Lion . . . can't you wait a day or two before haring off to look for Teirnan?"

" 'Tisn't just that," Blais said quietly. "There's the Ceremony of Honors, first, to celebrate my *lir* and warriorhood Cheysuli fashion, and to receive the gold I'm due." He slanted a smile at Aidan. "*Then* I'll be 'haring off' to look for my father."

Aidan frowned. "Forgive me if I offend, but who will be your *shu'maii*? You know no one in the clans . . . unless you mean to name me."

"No." Blais grinned cheerfully. "And I *do* know someone —a *shar tahl*, in fact. His name is Burr."

It took Aidan a moment to remember. When he did, he stared hard at Blais. "Burr is from the north, across the Bluetooth. I have spoken with him . . . how do *you* know him?"

"I wrote to Clankeep." Blais's patience was exaggerated for Aidan's benefit. "Burr wrote back, telling me what he could of my father, since no one else would." His face hardened. "Is it they're afraid I'll do the same? Without even knowing me?"

The question made Aidan uncomfortable. "I cannot answer for Clankeep . . . I only know that Teirnan's rune was erased from the birthlines. He was *kin-wrecked*, Blais—that means he no longer exists in the eyes of the clans."

The feral set of Blais' facial bones was more pronounced as he stared back at Aidan. "*Kin-wrecking* one warrior should not be passed on to his son, if he's done nothing. They're not knowing anything about me, least of all whether I'll be following my father. Why not judge me for me?"

Aidan shifted in the saddle. "He repudiated everything. The clans, the prophecy, the Lion—*everything*. He took with him warriors, *lir*, women, and children. Do you expect Clan Council to look kindly on a man who turns his back on everything our race stands for?"

Blais slipped into Old Tongue. "No. I expect them to look kindly on a son who is not guilty of the *jehan's* crime."

Aidan looked at his cousin. He could not really blame Blais for his bitterness. He was not certain *he* would feel so sanguine if he were judged by the actions of a kinsman he had never seen. It was unfair, he thought; but then he had come to believe there were several things about Cheysuli tradition that were unfair.

"Go," he said quietly. "Burr is a good man—a *shar tahl* with insight—and he will aid you. He will make a good *shu'maii*. But if you need me, send your *lir*. Or come yourself. You will be welcomed in Homana-Mujhar."

Blais laughed. "That is something, I'm thinking." He glanced at Shona. "Be careful with the boyo, lass. Homanans are more fragile than Erinnish."

"Blais—" She steadied her horse. "Blais, give thought to whatever you do. 'Tisn't always your greatest strength—" she smiled "—and sometimes your greatest failure. Take the *time*, my lad, to be certain of what you do."

"Did you?" Blais inquired. " 'Twas *you* who brought all those wolfhounds." And then, as Shona glared, he lifted his arm in a farewell wave and took the eastern road. His wolf loped beside him.

* * *

Outlying crofts, cradled in troughs between hills, soon gave way to villages and then at last to the proper outskirts of Mujhara herself, until Aidan and Shona clattered through narrow cobbled streets toward the rose-hued stones of Homana-Mujhar, deep in the heart of the city. Shona spent much of her time whistling and calling back her wolfhounds, who wanted to investigate—or challenge—everyone, and Aidan was much relieved when the massive bronze-and-timber gates finally jutted before them.

"Homana-Mujhar?" Shona asked, leaving off remonstrating with the big dark male.

"The front gates." Aidan drew rein and leaned slightly downward, offering his signet ring as identification, but the men on the gates knew him and called out vulgar greetings, until they spied Shona and found a better use for their tongues.

Aidan, laughing, waved her through, counting wolfhounds, and was relieved as the last of the great dogs slunk through. The two bitches with litters had been left with the baggage train, so that he and Shona had not been slowed by puppies.

First the outer bailey, then under the portcullis that gave entry into the inner bailey and to the palace itself. Shona muttered something beneath her breath, staring in awe at the curtain wall, parapets, and ramparts. Homana-Mujhar lacked the crude, overt strength of Kilore, Aidan thought, but its sprawling magnificence could be denied no more than its defenses.

" 'Tis no wonder it never fell," Shona breathed.

"But it did," he told her. "Once, to Bellam of Solinde—with the help of Tynstar the Ihlini." He jumped off his horse and threw the reins to a horseboy, then turned to lift Shona down.

She was having none of it. Trews precluded the encumbrance of skirts and she jumped down herself, slanting him a scornful, amused glance, then gathered her hounds close. "What of the lads and lasses?"

"We have kennels, of course."

She nodded pensively. "But—now? Can they not come in with us first?"

He blanched, envisioning giant wolfhounds racing through the corridors of Homana-Mujhar. "All of them?"

"We can put them in our chamber."

"It will not be 'our' chamber, not at first. The Homanans

are somewhat bound up in proprieties . . . we will have to have separate chambers until after the ceremony."

Shona's eyes widened. "We've been sharing a bed for months! We've never kept it a secret."

"The Homanans—"

"—are *skilfins*, " she muttered. "Well, then, if we're to have separate chambers, I'll be putting the hounds in mine." She turned on her heel and marched toward the steps, thick braid swinging.

Aidan, following, tried to compromise. "It does not mean we have to sleep alone, Shona—only *live* in separate chambers. No one has to know who sleeps where . . ." Except they would. Everyone knew such things. Common gossip had a nefarious power when it came to making the rounds. "Never mind," he said. "Put them wherever you will . . . but if any of them bites me when I come in at night, 'tis out to the kennels for them all."

Shona slanted him a glance. "Perhaps."

"Or you could come to *my* chamber."

She arched a brow as they reached the top step. "If the Homanans are so persnickety—I'd be thinking *you'd* have more right to be sneaking about the castle at night than me."

"But I do not keep fourteen dogs on my bed."

"Eleven," Shona corrected pointedly. "And for now there are only *nine*, until the two bitches and the puppies arrive."

Aidan sighed. "Does it matter?" And then signaled the door to be opened. "This is the formal entrance. There are other, less conspicuous ways in—"

"My lord." A servant bowed briefly. "My lord, you are to go at once to the Mujhar's chambers. By order of the Prince of Homana."

"Go to—why?"

The servant was not forthcoming, except to repeat the need for haste. "At once, my lord."

Blankly, Aidan turned to Shona. But before he could say anything, she spoke to the wolfhounds, dropping each with a gesture. A command to hold kept them in place; Shona turned back to Aidan. "They'll not move to trouble anyone."

Another time he might have argued with her—his experience with dogs did not lead him to believe they would stay where they were put—but just now he was not even slightly concerned with whether the wolfhounds stayed or wandered.

He merely nodded absently and led Shona through torchlighted corridors and up two winding staircases to the Mujhar's sprawling apartments on the third floor.

Two men in the crimson tabard of the Mujharan Guard flanked the largest entrance. The door itself stood open. As Aidan arrived with Shona, both guardsmen bowed. He nodded absently at them, then went in with Shona at his side.

He knew the truth when he saw Deirdre. She sat in a chair at Niall's bedside, very still and pale. Her eyes were fixed on the bed's occupant.

Ian stood at one of the casements, his back to the doorway. All Aidan could see was his silhouette, but nothing more was required. The rigidity of Ian's posture bespoke the measure of his grief.

It was Brennan who came across the room to Aidan. His gaze rested briefly on Shona's stricken face, then he turned to his son. "He will wish to see you. Come."

Aidan was cold. Cold and sick. He did not want to be present. He wanted to turn and walk out immediately, to go somewhere no one could find him, because if he was gone the dying could not be accomplished.

But he did not turn and walk out. Slowly, numbly, Aidan moved toward the canopied bed. Aileen was there as well, seated on a stool near Deirdre. Curled at Niall's side was the ruddy-brown wolf, Serri.

Niall lay beneath silken bedclothes. But his face was uncovered still, displaying the ravages of the thing that would claim his life. The patch over his eye did not hide the loose downward slant of the right side of his face, or the drooping of his mouth. His flaccid flesh was waxen.

"Jehan," Brennan said quietly. "Aidan has come home."

For one horrible moment Aidan feared his grandfather was already dead, but then he heard the ragged, shallow breathing and saw the single eye crack open. It was clear, unclouded by pain; Aidan's *kivarna* abruptly flared to life, bringing him the unwelcome and painful awareness that Niall knew precisely what had happened and precisely how long he had.

Niall's right arm lay slackly across the wolf, not hugging Serri because he could not, but touching him, maintaining the physical contact as well as the mental. Serri's head rested very gently on Niall's chest. Incongruously, Aidan thought of Shona's wolfhounds. And then was ashamed.

A lir is nothing like a dog . . .

He was, oddly, perfectly calm. He stood beside the bed, beside his father, and looked down on the wreckage of his grandfather.

"Take his hand," Brennan said softly. "He cannot reach for it himself—and he would want it."

Dully, Aidan knelt down and reached for Niall's hand. The flesh was cold and lifeless. "Grandsire. I am come home."

The single eye remained open. The lips twitched, then twisted. Niall's speech was slow and halting, but he made himself understood. "The girl?"

Aidan nodded, turning slightly to stretch out a hand to Shona. "I have brought her home, grandsire. All the way from Erinn. Keely's girl, grandsire . . . and Sean's."

Shona moved across the bedchamber slowly, lacking her natural grace. Aidan sensed her grief and shock and abiding regret: she looked on her grandsire the Mujhar for the first and last time, for it was quite clear Niall would not live to see the sun rise.

She stopped beside Aidan, but did not kneel. She was very tall in a chamber full of tall men, and incredibly dominating through sheer force of personality. Aidan, sensitized to her, still felt the tingle of her strength, and smiled in bittersweet acknowledgment as he saw the recognition in Niall's eye.

Shona wore, as usual, Erinnish tunic and trews, belted and booted. The heavy braid of intricate double and triple plaiting hung over her shoulder, dangling against the bedclothes. There was nothing even remotely feminine about her, or subdued. She burned like a beacon.

"Keely's girl," Niall slurred. "Ah, gods, but I knew she would bear one worthy of the blood and trust and truth . . ." He swallowed with difficulty. "You must wait your turn, my bright, brave Erinnish lass, but one day you will grace the halls even as my Deirdre . . ."

Aidan twitched. "Grandsire—"

Brennan touched his shoulder. "Not now, Aidan. Later."

But Aidan knew better: there would not be a later.

"Grandsire, I bring news from Atvia." He cast a glance at Deirdre, so white and still in her chair. "What would you most desire in the world?"

Niall was visibly weakening. "I have what I most desire."

"No . . ." Aidan caught Deirdre's hand and pulled her

from the chair, onto her knees beside the bed, then placed her hand atop the Mujhar's. "No, there is more. There has always been more."

The dimming eye flared. "Is it true? Gisella—?"

Aidan swallowed down the painful lump. "Aye. In my presence." Then, knowing it would require a formal declaration in front of kinfolk as witnesses before being accepted by the Homanan Council, he raised his voice. "The Queen of Homana is dead."

The cold fingers twitched. Aidan took his own hand away and left Deirdre and Niall to share the handclasp. Niall's voice was deteriorating, but he managed to give the order. "Have the priest fetched at once."

Deirdre was shocked. "Niall—*no* . . . let it wait—"

He summoned waning strength. "If I do nothing else before I die, my proud Erinnish princess, I will make you a queen."

Aidan, at the doorway, dispatched one of the guards for a priest. Then he waited beside the door, not wanting to intrude on the Mujhar and his *meijha*.

The marriage ceremony was necessarily brief. Niall struggled to say his vows. Deirdre answered quietly but firmly, and when it was done she bent to kiss his ravaged mouth.

"Queen of Homana," he whispered. "It should have been yours from the first."

Deirdre, dry-eyed, shook her head. "I never was wanting it," she answered. "All I ever wanted was you. The gods were kind enough to allow it . . . but oh, my braw boyo, the years have been so short . . ."

Niall's eye did not waver as he gazed at Deirdre of Erinn, now Queen of Homana. "Better than none . . ." he whispered. "Better than none at all . . ."

She was queen for the space of a breath. As Niall ceased to live, the title passed to Aileen, and Brennan became Mujhar in his father's place.

It was Ian who executed the custom. Slowly he went to the bed and took Niall's hand in his, easing the heavy black seal ring from the still hand, and then he turned. To Brennan.

"My lord," he said formally, "you are the Mujhar. Will you accept this ring; and with it, my fealty?"

Brennan's mouth barely moved. *"J'hai-na,"* he said. *"Tu'halla dei, y'ja'hai . . . Tahlmorra lujhala mei wiccan, cheysu. Cheysuli i'halla shansu."*

Ian waited until Brennan put out his hand, and then he stripped from it the glowing ruby signet of the Prince of Homana. He replaced it with the black ring etched with a rampant lion.

Brennan, stark-faced, nodded. *"Y'ja'hai."* He took back the ruby ring from Ian, and turned.

Aidan, still standing by the door, abruptly realized the ceremony included him. Panicking, he backed up a step, met the wall with his heel, and stopped.

Brennan took Aidan's cold hand into his and eased the topaz ring from his right forefinger. The ruby went on in its place. *"Tu'jhalla dei,"* Brennan said formally. "I declare you Prince of Homana, heir to the Lion Throne."

Aidan felt empty. He stared at his father, seeing a stranger; feeling a stranger himself, defined by a single sentence that did not, he felt, accurately sum up anyone, least of all himself.

"Tu'jhalla dei," Brennan repeated. Lord to liege man; they all of them were liege men now, if by definition different from the Cheysuli custom. That had been Ian's place. And Brennan did not, Aidan realized in shock, have a true liege man.

He swallowed heavily. *"Ja-hai-na."* he whispered. *"Y'ja'hai, jehan. Leijhana tu'sai. Cheysuli i'halla shansu."*

He heard Aileen's quiet tears. Saw Deirdre's bone-white, bone-dry face. Saw the rigidity of Ian's posture; the grief and comprehension in his father's eyes. Sensed Shona's tangled emotions as painful as his own.

Something moved. He looked to the bed. Serri sat up, amber-eyed in the shadows. Then he jumped down and trotted out of the chamber.

Aidan moved.

"Let him go," Brennan murmured.

"But—*Serri*—"

"Serri is a *lir*."

It was, Aidan knew, enough. Sufficient to explanation. And as he nodded, acknowledging, he heard, as they all did, the single distant mournful wail keening through the corridors.

In chorus, the wolfhounds answered.

Four

In the pale, still hours of dawn, Aidan found himself in the Great Hall. The firepit coals were banked. Only the merest tracery of first light crept into the hall through stained glass, muting the colors into unaccustomed pastel softness. The dawn did not yet illuminate anything below the intricate beamwork of the high ceiling, losing itself in scrollwork.

Aidan stood for a moment just inside the silver doors, listening to the silence, and then he began to walk.

He looked at the walls as he walked: at the faded tapestries generations old; at the brighter, richer ones worked by Deirdre and her ladies. He looked at the intricate patterns of weapons displayed on the walls: whorls of knives and lances, brass bubbles of bossed shields, the gleaming patina of blades. Even the floors now were not so stark; carpets imported from foreign lands softened the hard bleakness of stone. Once Homana-Mujhar had been little more than a fortress, a stone shell; now it was the cynosure in all its magnificent splendor, the seat of Homana's power. And the font of that power was the Lion itself.

Aidan at last looked at the throne, thinking of the smaller version on the Crystal Isle. But this one was different. This one was filled. This one housed a Mujhar.

Aidan stopped dead. He felt betrayed, his intention usurped. It did not matter that he knew the man, or that he was flesh of the man's own flesh, only that he had come to summon his grandsire, and his father had stolen the chance.

Brennan watched him with eyes devoid of expression. He sat slumped in the throne haphazardly, arms and legs askew. He wore black, as was his custom, and faded into the dim hollowness of the crouching Lion.

Kivarna flared. Aidan sensed grief and anger and sorrow and pain; the acknowledgment of a new task. And the desire to abjure it altogether, if it would change the present.

Aidan walked. And then stopped. He stood before the Lion and the Mujhar it now protected.

Brennan did not stir, except to move his mouth. "Men covet thrones," he said quietly. "Men conspire and kill and start wars and destroy cities, all for the winning of a throne. But rarely do they think of what it means to *sit* in one . . . or to acknowledge the consequences, the cause of the change in power."

Aidan said nothing.

"The firstborn sons of kings know they will inherit, one day," Brennan continued, "but they never think about how they will get it. They consider only what they will do when they are kings in their fathers' places, and what changes *they* might make, and how they will conduct themselves . . . but never do they consider how thrones pass into their hands."

It seemed to require a response. "How?" Aidan asked softly.

"A man *dies*," Brennan said, "to make another king in his place."

Aidan purposely damped down the blazing of his *kivarna*. He had no desire to intrude on his father's anguish; and even less to let it intrude on his. "He would not have wanted to live forever," he said evenly. "Especially like that. You know that, *jehan*. His time was done. Yours was come."

"Too glib, Aidan."

"But the truth." Aidan glanced behind, judging the coals, then sat down on the rim of the firepit, balancing carefully. "When did it happen?"

"Two days ago. At midday." Brennan scrubbed a hand across his weary face. "He was with Deirdre, in her solar . . . they were discussing the need for refurbishing guest chambers. Nothing of any consequence . . ." He sighed, expression bleak. "One moment he was fine, the next—as you saw him."

Aidan nodded. He had heard of it before, though he had never seen the results.

"We were not at war," Brennan said. "And most likely never to go to war again, so that he could die in battle . . . but somehow I always thought it would come upon him another way."

Aidan thought of something he had heard once, and

repeated it, hoping to soothe his father. " 'A warrior can predict his death no more than his *tahlmorra*.' "

Brennan grimaced. "Too glib, again. But then you have always had smooth words when everyone else had nothing." He moved, putting order to his limbs. "Why did *you* come?"

Aidan, hunched on the rim of the firepit, stared blindly at the dais through eyes full of unshed tears. "I wanted to bring him back."

Brennan said nothing at first. And then he released an uneven sigh that bespoke the grief and understanding. "I wish there were a way—"

"There is." Aidan's face spasmed. "I have done it before . . . with other dead Mujhars."

"Oh, Aidan—"

"I *have*."

Brennan hooked rigid hands over the clawed handrests and pulled himself forward, from under the Lion's maw. "Now is neither the time nor the place to speak of dreams—"

Aidan was on his feet. "But I *do* speak of them—because they are more than dreams!" He took two long strides forward, stopping at the first of three dais steps. "*Jehan*, you have no idea how it is for me—how it has *been* for me—"

"I have every idea!" Brennan cried. "By the gods, do you think we have not stayed awake at nights? Your *jehana* and I have spent countless days and nights discussing you and your dreams, trying to make sense of seemingly senseless things . . . Aidan, have *you* any idea how it has been for us?" He clutched the dark wooden throne. "And now you come on the night of your grandsire's death to say you can *summon* him!"

"*I can*," Aidan whispered.

Silence. Brennan's eyes were ablaze with grief and something akin to frustration. "We all loved him. We all would like him back. But none of us concocts a story—"

" 'Tis *not a story!*" Aidan shouted. "I have spoken with dead Mujhars: Shaine, Carillon, Donal—why not with *Niall* now?"

Brennan's face was ashen. His hands shook on the throne.

"I can," Aidan repeated.

Brennan closed his eyes.

I will prove it to him. I will prove me *to him*—Aidan

clutched the links on his belt. *If I cannot prove this to him, he will never trust me again. This is necessary.*

"No," Brennan croaked.

Aidan twitched, staring. He had begun to concentrate.

"No," Brennan repeated. "You will not do this thing."

"If I do not—".

"He is dead. Let him be dead."

"The others have come, *jehan*—"

"I said *let him be dead!*" Brennan leaned forward. "I do not know what—or *who*—you are . . . for the moment I would like you simply to be my son." His face worked a moment. "I need you to be my son."

Stricken mute by the magnitude of his father's emotions, Aidan could only stare. And then, when he could, he nodded. He took his hands from the links.

Eventually, Brennan eased himself back in the throne. His posture was less rigid, his tone less intense. He smoothed the fit of his jerkin with a deft, yet eloquent gesture. "So, you have settled on Keely's girl."

Aidan understood very well what Brennan did. The change in topic was intended to change also the knowledge of what they had only just shared regarding Aidan's congress with dead Mujhars. Neither would ever forget it, but Brennan wanted it set aside so he need not deal with it.

Aidan shrugged. "Neither of us 'settled' on one another. The gods took an interest . . . there was no other choice."

"She is not much like Keely . . . more like Sean."

Aidan smiled faintly. "She is very like Keely on the inside. On the outside—well, there is Keely there as well. Once you get past the Erinnish height and stature, and Sean's coloring . . ." He smiled more broadly. "Shona is mostly Shona."

"You realize the wedding will have to wait," Brennan warned. "There is the Homanan mourning custom for a deceased Mujhar . . . they would look askance on any wedding, even a royal one, so close to the Mujhar's passing."

Aidan shrugged. "Then we will wait. It does not matter. Shona is not a woman much taken by ceremony . . . it will hardly blight her life if we wait a while longer to have a priest mumble the words."

"A woman with sense." Brennan smiled faintly. "Of course Aileen will attempt to change her mind . . ." He let the words trail off. He could not avoid the topic he had tried diligently to close. "Those things you said to me . . . things you have said before."

Aidan waited.

"Are they true?"

He was tired, confused, grieving. But no less than his father. "Did Ian say anything when he came back from the Solindish-Homanan border?"

Brennan frowned. "Say anything?"

"About me." Too clearly he recalled the Weaver's storm and Ian's shattered hip. "About anything that happened."

"Only that you and he felt it best you go on alone." Brennan shrugged. "I did not argue. Ian would never have left you had he believed there might be danger, and you have never been the sort to seek it out." He paused. "Why? Is there something he should have said?"

"No. He left it to me." Aidan scrubbed wearily at gritty eyes. He had tried to sleep, but could not. "*Jehan*—I told you once before about speaking with gods."

The recoil was faint, but present. "Aye." Brennan's tone was guarded.

"What if I said there was more to it than that? That I met with them personally?"

Delicate objectivity; *kivarna* stripped it bare. "As you have with the Mujhars."

"Aye. With all of them."

Brennan sighed deeply, giving in. "I would say perhaps you are putting too much weight in the things you dream."

Aidan smiled. "I have always dreamed. I have never dreamed about talking to gods, or with *meeting* them."

Clearly unsettled, Brennan shifted in the throne, looking infinitely older. "Men do not talk *with* gods, Aidan. They talk *to* them, through petitions and prayers. For the *shar tahls*, it may be different . . . but even the Homanan priests say they serve out of faith and belief, not because of personal contact."

Aidan's mouth hooked down in irony. "I am not a priest, *jehan* . . . I cannot say *what* I am, other than to agree the circumstances are quite unusual."

Brennan's black brows met. "Aidan, this is not possible—"

He said it matter-of-factly. "Then I must be mad."

It stopped Brennan cold. He stared fixedly at his son, trying to read the truth. "But—with *gods*, Aidan?"

"Only three of them. They assumed human form for it, so

as not to frighten me senseless. And they spoke—they speak—in riddles, telling me there is a task I must perform, and sacrifices, and the fashioning of a chain." He paused. "That much I have done."

Brennan stared blankly at the heavy chain depending from Aidan's belt. What he thought was clear: Aidan could have bought it, or had it made. That was the only explanation.

Aidan sighed. "The task remains. But I wanted you to know, so you and *jehana* could stop worrying about me."

"*Stop* worrying!"

"I am not cursed after all; rather, I am blessed. Chosen for some specific purpose."

"*What* specific purpose?"

Aidan shrugged. "They have not shown or told me yet."

Brennan struggled with comprehension. Objectivity lost. "You will be Mujhar one day," he growled. "That, I should think, is task—and blessing—enough. As for a special purpose, how many men are born to inherit a throne, least of all the Lion?"

Aidan shook his head. "There is more. They know very well I am in line for the Lion—they made it so, did they not?—and yet they have made it very plain there is something else I must do."

Slowly Brennan shook his head. "How can a Mujhar rule a realm when he converses with the gods as if they were mortal men?"

"I would think it is something far out of anyone's ken," Aidan answered. "And perhaps a beneficial thing. If a man *knew* he acted with the blessings of the gods . . ." He shrugged, scratching an eyebrow, dismissing implications to increasing weariness. "It is so vague a thing . . ."

"*Aye,*" Brennan agreed heartily. He stared pensively at his son, clearly concerned as well as baffled. "How is it Aileen and I got you? You were never what we expected, not from the very first."

Deep inside, something twisted. "And are you disappointed?"

Brennan sat bolt upright. "No! Never *that,* Aidan—you are everything a man and woman could desire in a son. But you *are*—"

"—different?" Aidan smiled, thinking of the last discussion with gods he had had. "But I have been clearly advised that it does not make me *better.*"

Brennan sighed and sat back in the Lion. He rubbed both eyes wearily, stretching the flesh out of shape. When he looked at Aidan again, dawn etched lines and shadows where there had been none before. "There will be more responsibility for you now. You are Prince of Homana. Men will seek you out, asking your opinions on all manner of things, and asking you to plead their cause before me. They will hound you night and day . . ." He smiled crookedly. "All the honor will be yours, but also the weight of it. And there are times it grows so heavy . . ." His hand closed over the massive black ring he now wore. "You will never again know the peace you have experienced up till today."

Aidan thought about the "peace."

"Things will never be the same. Prepare as best you can."

Aidan stared hard at the ring glowing bloody on his hand. *"Tahlmorra lujhala mei wiccan, cheysu."*

Brennan shook his head. *"Cheysuli i'halla shansu."*

Five

With meticulous precision, Aidan crossed his bedchamber to the chair beside the bed and sat down, settling himself slowly. The candle on the table was too bright; squinting, he leaned over and pinched it out.

Shona closed the door. Mutely she went to him and reached down two-handed to remove the gold circlet he wore. "Here," she said calmly. " 'Twill ease the ache, I'm thinking."

It did help. With the tight metal band gone, the tension lessened slightly. He sighed, slumping against the chair; sighed again as Shona set the circlet on the table and began to rub his temples. "A long two months," he murmured.

" 'Tis over now," she said. "Niall has been laid to rest with all due ceremony . . . 'tis time the rest of you were able to breathe again."

He had not thought of it like that. He had known only that the Homanans required daily ceremonies of passing for a full sixty days to honor the dead Mujhar; duly honored, Niall was formally interred in Homana-Mujhar's mausoleum, his dressed-stone sarcophogus resting beside Carillon's. There was none for Donal, who had given himself over to the Cheysuli death-ritual following the deaths of his *lif*, but Niall's passing had not required adherence to the stringent Cheysuli custom. His had required only multitudinous ceremonies designed to honor his memory, after the fashion of Homanans.

But it was done. The sixty days, save for several hours, were now passed. And he could breathe again.

Already his head felt better. Smiling, Aidan reached up and caught Shona's competent hands. "Now perhaps we can think about *our* ceremony."

Shona shrugged, turning to perch on the arm of the chair. Because of the ceremony, she wore skirts instead of trews, and a gem-encrusted girdle spanning the width of her hips. "I'm not needing one of *those* to know we're bound."

"No. But the Homanans prefer such things." He threaded idle fingers into the weave of her braid. "And it will give Deirdre something to do."

The archness left Shona's tone. "Aye. Poor Deirdre . . . gods, what grief she feels, and yet she tends to everyone else. First to Brennan, who is a ship without a rudder; then to Ian, who tries to close himself off to what we're *both* of us knowing is a horrible emptiness."

"He was the Mujhar's liege man."

"Liege man, brother, boon companion—d'ye think the titles matter?" She pulled herself up and sat instead on the bed, but three paces away, tugging at the fit of her loose-cut gown. "He has spent his life serving our grandsire, according to love and to custom, and now that service is ended. What d'ye think he'll be doing?"

Aidan rubbed a temple. The headache was receding, but a residue remained. "'We have been his whole life. He has neither *cheysula* nor *meijha* . . . I think he will stay with us, to give us whatever help he can."

"And himself, as well." Shona sighed pensively, idly resettling the girdle. "But there is Deirdre, still. Will she stay? Or will she go?"

"Back to Erinn?" Aidan shook his head. "Homana is her home. She has been here most of her life."

"But Niall is dead, and her only daughter—and all of her grandchildren—live in Erinn."

"Except for Blais." Aidan frowned. "I wish he had come. The Mujhar was *his* grandsire, also . . . and yet he did not come to any of the ceremonies. You *know* he must have heard—word has been carried throughout all of Homana."

Shona's mouth hooked down sardonically. "Blais is not a man to do what others expect, or desire. 'Tis a stubborn *skilfin* he is—likely he heard, but chose not to come."

"He would have been welcomed."

"Would he? He is the traitor's son."

Aidan shifted restlessly. "Likely he would find less welcome among the Cheysuli than the Homanans. The Homanans care little enough about Teirnan—what did he do to them? His heresy has to do with his own race. It is a Cheysuli concern."

"Aye, well . . . likely Blais had his reasons." Shona eyed him attentively. "Your head is better."

"Aye."

"Good. Then you won't be minding a walk."

"A walk?" Aidan frowned. "It is late. I thought we would go to bed."

"We'll do that after," she said. "There's something I want to see. Before, I didn't ask because 'twasn't fitting, in light of Niall's death. But now there's nothing to hinder it." She stood expectantly, tugging at rucked up skirts and the binding of the girdle. "I want to see the Womb."

Aidan's brows rose. "The Womb of the Earth?"

Shona nodded. "I've heard all about it. My mother told me, and others . . . about the oubliette beneath the floor of the Great Hall, and all the marble *lir*."

Aidan looked at the bed a moment, thinking about sweet oblivion and an end to a nagging headache. But Shona was due an introduction to her heritage on any terms she liked, and he saw no reason to refuse. His head *was* better; nodding, he rose and gestured her out of the room.

"No dogs," he warned.

She cast him a dark look. "I've left them all in *my* chamber."

"Good. If you want to meet the *lir*, you can do it without dogs."

Shona shouldered open the door. " 'Tis only because they like *me* better that you resent them."

"I do not resent your dogs. Only that there are so many—do you know how little room there is left to me when they try to sleep on my bed?"

Shona preceded him out the door, kicking skirts aside. The change in attire did nothing to hide long-legged strides. "They sleep on *my* bed, boyo, since you've banished them from your chamber."

"They come anyway, whenever they can. Just yesterday four of them had nested—"

" 'Tis because they smell me there. But if you like, I can sleep in my own bed." Shona headed down the staircase, yanking skirts out of the way.

"No. But we do have kennels."

"They'll fight with your hounds."

"I have no hounds. They belong to Homana-Mujhar." Aidan followed a step behind, taking care not to step on her heels or the hem of her skirts. "I know you love them, *meijhana*—"

"Aye." Her tone was final.

"—but could you perhaps treat them as dogs? The servants are complaining about the hair, and bones always underfoot, and the *other* things underfoot."

"The pups are near to broken."

"And do you intend to keep them all?"

Shona continued down the stairs in silence. When she reached the bottom, she stopped, waiting for Aidan. "No," she said at last. "But 'tis hard to give them up."

"I know, but—"

"They'll go,' she said fiercely. "Not all, but some of them. 'Tis what I breed them for . . . to improve the lines, and to sell them. Already I have offers."

"For all of them?" he asked hopefully.

Shona's scowl was black. "For *some* of them," she said. "Some of them I'm keeping."

It was a beginning. Aidan let it pass and gestured her to continue. "The Great Hall," he said. "The entrance is there."

When they reached the silver doors, Aidan took a torch down from one of the corridor brackets and carried it within, spilling haphazard illumination across the floor. Only hours before, the hall had been full of kin and high-ranking Homanans, all gathered in Niall's name; now the hall was emptied of life entirely, except for themselves.

Shona paused inside as the door swung shut. " 'Tis different." She glanced upward. "They've taken down all the black banners—all the wreaths." Slowly she turned in a circle. "They've taken away *everything* of the mourning ceremonies."

"The mourning is concluded." Aidan fell silent, then amended the declaration. "The *official* mourning is concluded; now begins the reign of a new Mujhar."

Shona peered the length of the hall. "In this light, the Lion is malevolent."

"In any light," Aidan muttered, then carried the torch toward the firepit. "The one on the Crystal Isle was much more *ben*evolent."

"D'ye think so?" Shona followed. "Blais and I decided it was naught but a bit of wood, fashioned for vanity. There was no life to it." She watched as Aidan mounted the rim of the firepit and began kicking aside coals. When he handed her the torch, she took it amenably and held it so he could see. "Do you know, they might have made it a *bit* more easy to reach the stairs . . . why did they bury the opening *here*?"

Aidan continued to rearrange the contents of the firepit, waving his hands at drifting ash. "Originally the firepit did not extend so far. Cheysuli built Homana-Mujhar centuries ago—at that time there was no need for hiding anything. But when they decided to give the Lion back to the Homanans, the firepit was extended to cover the opening to the staircase." He paused, modulating his tone carefully. "It was thought wisest to obscure the *Jehana's* Womb, so no defilement was possible."

"D'ye think—?" She broke it off. "Aye. They would have. My mother has told me how bloodthirsty were the Homanans in the days of the *qu'mahlin*." She moved as Aidan gestured her aside, then marveled as he caught hold of the iron ring attached to the hinged plate set almost flush in the floor. " 'Tis no wonder they never found it, is it? Buried like this . . ."

Aidan gathered every ounce of his strength and levered the plate up, then eased it down against the firepit rim. Stale air rushed out of the opening, causing the torchlight to gutter and dance. But after a moment it stilled, and flame bloomed afresh.

"Safe," he murmured, and took the torch back from

Shona. "Stay close behind me, *meijhana*. If the stairs are damp, they can be dangerous."

Shona's tone was dry. "Aye. I'd not be knowing aught of such a thing, island-born as I am."

"I meant because of your skirts. You're not knowing much about *them*." Aidan cast her a bright glance, then started down the shallow stairs, thrusting the torch before him. The staircase was cut directly out of solid stone, pitched steep and narrow. He had been told the stairs numbered one hundred and two; for the first time in his life, he counted.

"Gods," Shona breathed "how deep do we go?"

Her voice echoed oddly from behind. "Not so deep," he answered. "Not so deep as the Womb itself."

Shona said nothing else until they reached the bottom. The ending was abrupt and without warning, in a small closet, until Aidan found the proper keystone and pressed. A portion of the wall grated on edge, turning; blackness gaped before them.

Torchlight spilled into the vault, caressing veins of gold and the smooth ivory silk of polished marble. From out of the shadows *lir* leaped, breaking free of marble bonds, tearing wings and beaks and claws out of stone. Wolf, bear, mountain cat; hawk, falcon, eagle. And countless other *lir*, twisted this way and that, as if once they had lived to walk the earth or ride the skies.

"Gods—" Shona breathed.

"*Lir*," Aidan responded.

"Look at all of them . . ." Shona leaned forward, edging toward the vault. "Can we go in?"

"Aye. Beware the oubliette."

She looked. In the center of the vault, half-shrouded in distorted torchlight, spread the nothingness of the Womb. A flawlessly rounded hole, rimmed with rune-scribed marble, dropping straight down into the depths of the earth itself. The oubliette was three paces equidistant from the four *lir*-worked walls.

She was in awe, but not fear. Shona took two steps inside the vault, then turned back. He saw comprehension in her eyes, and a vast, abiding acknowledgment. She was, as he was, Cheysuli, child of the gods, born of the earth and the wind and the sky; born to pride and power and magic.

Shona smiled. She put out her hand, and he took it. Two steps and he was beside her, within the vault housing the

Womb; together they gazed on the *lir*, marveling at the artistry that made them so alive, so vibrant within the stone. Even the ceiling was worked with *lir* of all shapes and sizes, struggling to burst free. In the distorting torchlight, all of them seemed to lean toward the open door, as if longing to exit the vault. As if they *could,* given leave. Given the power to do so.

Aidan shivered. Shona laughed softly and squeezed his hand. "Aye. I feel it, too. D'ye see? Each of them means to go."

He felt curiously distant. "One day, each of them will."

"What?"

He shook himself. "What?"

"What you said, Aidan. 'One day, each of them will.' " Shona stared at him. "What were you meaning by that?"

"I said that?"

"Just now." She frowned. "Have you forgotten already?"

He shivered again, glancing around. "It is this place. I feel it in my bones. A cold, deep darkness . . ." He peered over the edge of the oubliette without moving so much as a toe. "There is a story that one of our kinsmen threw himself into the Womb."

She was properly horrified. "Down *there*?"

"Aye. Carillon."

"But—Carillon was Mujhar." Shona's tone was puzzled. "If he threw himself into the Womb, how did he become Mujhar? Did he not die?"

"Not then. Supposedly he became Mujhar *because* he threw himself into the Womb." Aidan frowned, peering around the vault. "They say at one time it was how a true Mujhar was judged worthy. He went in a child and came out a man; went in a prince, came out a king. He was born of the *Jehan*." Aidan looked at her, marking her expression. "It is one of the *stories*, Shona. I doubt there is truth to it."

"My mother never told me *that*."

"Aye, well . . ." He shrugged. "There are hundreds of stories about our ancestors, *meijhana*—and doubtless one day there will be as many about us."

Shona arched a brow. "And children to tell them to?"

He grinned. "One day."

She touched the knotted girdle. "Sooner than that, I'm thinking."

He opened his mouth to question her, but the *kivarna* flared up even as she laughed. While he could not sense the presence of the child, he knew the truth without a doubt. Shona's emotions were to easy to read.

"Gods," he blurted, *"when?"*

She smoothed a hand over the girdle, rattling its weight of gems. In the torchlight, colors flashed. "Did you truly not guess?"

"No." He looked. "Not even now. Are you certain?"

"Oh, aye." She made a face. "To me, I'm showing—see how the gown barely fits? And how short the girdle is tied?" She sighed, twisting her mouth. "I meant to hide it, so I could tell you closer to my lying-in . . . but Aileen and Deirdre saw it too soon. They sent the midwife to me." She grinned. "Three months, my lord . . . and we'll have us a wee bairn of our own."

"Three months—"

She nodded. "I'm so tall and wide, the babe is spread all over. If I were a smaller woman, there'd be more bairn here." She put a hand to her belly.

He was not thinking of that. "But that would mean . . ." He paused, counting back. "That would mean we were still in Erinn."

Shona nodded. "And, by the days, 'twas that first night together." She laughed. "You're a potent one, I'm thinking."

Aidan frowned. "I thought it was the Homanan food."

"So, you *did* notice!" She scowled fiercely, though without much sincerety. "Too polite to mention you thought I was getting fat?"

He colored. "There are more flattering things to discuss."

"Aye, well . . ." Shona grinned. "Does it matter? 'Tis a bairn, not too much Homanan food—will it be a lad, d'ye think?"

"How am *I* to know?" Aidan slid the torch into a bracket by the door and turned to pull her close. "And does it matter? If not, there will time for us to make a lad."

"Six or seven," she agreed, and then blurted out a garbled sound of shock. "Aidan—*look*—"

He swung from her, alerted by the very real alarm in her tone, and saw the shadow stretching down into the door. And then the man who wore it, stepping into guttering torchlight to stare blindly at them both.

Silvering black hair was long and unkempt, tangling on his shoulders; leathers were stained and tattered, fitting his frame too loosely; bare arms were naked of *lir*-gold. But the

marks of armbands remained, graven into flesh. As much as
the loss of them—and his *lir*—were graven into his spirit.
Teirnan of the *a'saii* was well and truly mad.

Foreboding swept in. Aidan touched the hilt of his knife.
"What do you want?"

Teirnan stood framed in the doorway. His tone was an
odd amalgam of detachment and intensity. "What I have
always wanted."

He felt rather than heard Shona's movement behind him.
Instinctively he put out a shielding hand, thinking of the
unborn child. "How did you get in?"

Teirnan's smile was a travesty. "Such a thing to ask a
Cheysuli."

Aidan swallowed back increasing trepidation. He had never
met the man, knowing him only by reputation; that reputation made him an enemy. "Your *lir* is dead," he said. "Spin
me no tale of *lir*-shape, kinsman. You are *kin-wrecked* and
lirless, and you have no place here."

Torchlight limned his intensity. "But you have just called
me kinsman. And I *am*." He stared past Aidan to Shona.
"Are you Keely's daughter?"

Her voice was level. "Aye."

He nodded. "Blais described you. And the others . . . but
none of them matter. Even *you* do not; you are not of my
flesh. You are not of my bone." Yellow eyes burned fiercely
in the torchlight. "And most certainly not of my spirit."

There was Blais in him. Aidan could see it, even beyond
the harshness of age and privation. They were of a like
height and stature, in addition to coloring. Maeve had given
her son nothing.

Unless it be her good sense. Aidan drew in a breath.
"Very few are of your spirit," he retorted. He looked more
closely at the warrior, looking again for Blais, or something
of Maeve, and marked the lines etched so deeply into the
flesh beside his eyes, the hollows below arched cheekbones.
Teirnan's self-exile had not been an easy one. But Aidan
thought the emptiness of his spirit had more to do with
lirlessness than with a life of privation. "So, you have met
Blais. What do you think of your son?"

Muscles ticked in the ravaged face. "He is not my son. He
is *hers* . . . Maeve made a Homanan out of him—an
Erinnish—" Teeth showed briefly in a feral clenching. "Left
to me, he would have been a warrior. Left to *her* he is

nothing, a shadow-man, a soulless halfling with no understanding of the truth."

"Ah," Aidan said. "He repudiated you."

"Wise man," breathed Shona.

"He came to me and said he was my son—*my* son, whom she kept from me all these years . . ." Again the feral grimace. "She should have left him to me."

"So you could twist him? So you could take him into the deepwood and feed him on lies?" Aidan shook his head. "Maeve knew what you would do. It is why she left Homana."

"He was *my* son, once—"

Aidan overrode him. "He is a warrior. Clan-born, blood-born . . . no matter what you say, Teirnan, he is a true-born Cheysuli, with the right to choose. The gods gave us that right. Even you have profited from it—if you call the travesty of your life profitable." Aidan shook his head. "You were a fool, kinsman. There are other ways of undoing things. Quieter ways of accomplishing change."

Teirnan was too thin, too tense, too *unbalanced*. He had voluntarily shed the anchor of his life by renouncing the prophecy and everything it stood for; the death of his *lir* had stripped him of everything else. There was nothing left to Teirnan save the fanaticism that had driven him from the clans, and even that was stretched too fine. Without a *lir*, he was nothing. A void stood before Aidan clad in human flesh shaped in the likeness of a man.

"Why did you come?" Aidan asked.

"For the Lion," Teirnan rasped. "Niall is dead. Now it is mine."

Aidan shook his head. "The Lion has been claimed."

"By Brennan?" Teirnan laughed. "That is an old conflict, kinsman . . . it began even before you were born. Brennan and I are old enemies and older rivals, both pursuing the Lion." His smile was a rictus. "If he thinks it is for him, tell him to come down *here.*"

Aidan frowned. "What do you mean?"

"Tell him to come down here. *Here,* in this vault. With the door *shut,* and the Womb of the Earth to receive him."

Aidan felt Shona's nearness. Also her puzzlement; the unasked questions: what did Teirnan want? What did he expect?

Teirnan touched marble *lir.* "Tell him to come here be-

fore the Womb, and ask the blessing of the gods in the *old*
way. The way Carillon did, wanting to be Mujhar.''

Apprehension became fear. ''Why?''

Teirnan's eyes burned. ''Because he will not. Because he
is *afraid;* do you not know the stories? Brennan of Homana
is afraid of places like this. Because he *knows* the Womb
will swallow him whole and never give him up.''

''That has nothing to do with it.'' Aidan knew very well
his father would not enter the vault, but it had nothing to do
with fear of the Womb. It was a fear of enclosed places; it
had always been Brennan's weakness. ''He *is* Mujhar,
Teirnan. The Homanan Council says so, Cheysuli Clan
Council—''

''Only the gods matter.''

Aidan nearly laughed. ''I know something of *that*, kinsman. As for you? You turned your back. You took your
a'saii and went away from everything, repudiating your heritage. How do you expect to convince anyone—even your
own son—you are worthy to be Mujhar?''

''How?'' Teirnan took one step into the vault, then another. ''By being born, kinsman . . . as the old Mujhars
were born.''

Comprehension blossomed. ''Teirnan—*no*—

He stood on the brink of the Womb. ''She will give me
back,'' he said. ''She will. I am a child of the gods. Child of
the *Jehana*. I will go in the man and come out the Mujhar.''

''Teirnan—'' Shona blurted.

''She will give me back,'' he repeated. ''Hers is a fertile
Womb. She gave Carillon back. She will give me back a
Mujhar, so my son will not renounce me. So *no one* will
renounce me. I will be Mujhar, blessed in the old way, the
way of our ancestors.'' He lingered on the edge. ''I see it in
your faces; you think she will not do it. You think my way is
madness.''

''Don't,'' Shona whispered, one hand splayed across her
belly. ''Gods, man, *don't*—''

Teirnan's face spasmed. ''I must. It is the old way. Too
much of the old ways have been lost—too many of the
customs discarded in the name of the prophecy . . . do you
not see? If I am made Mujhar, I can change things back. I
can make us what we once were.''

''Teirnan.'' Aidan took a single step toward the oubliette,

and the man. "This will not win back your son. This will not win you the Lion."

It was a litany. "The *Jehana's* Womb is fertile. She *will* make me Mujhar, just as she did Carillon." Teirnan's laughter echoed. "*I*, at least, am Cheysuli."

"No," Aidan said. Twofold denial: of the act, and of the claim.

Teirnan smiled and stepped off the rim.

This time the Womb was barren.

Six

The assumption of power by a new king was done with very little fanfare. Brennan considered it unseemly under the circumstances; even though the two-month mourning period was over, sorrow lingered. Niall had ruled Homana for nearly fifty years. Neither his presence—nor the honor and affection—would fade immediately.

The new Mujhar received messages of condolence from other kingdoms with good grace, remarking privately to Aidan that no one was laggard in also wishing Niall's successor a lengthy, peaceful reign, and set about exerting his own power over the Homanan Council without delay. And though Brennan had spent most of his life preparing for the moment, Aidan knew he did not enjoy it.

Although the changes were not immediately evident, it became quite clear Brennan was arranging the governing of Homana to suit his personal tastes. His policies were more assertive, though not overtly aggressive, and the kings of Caledon, Falia, and Ellas found long-standing trade treaties in the throes of renegotiation. Brennan wrote long letters under official seal to Corin and Hart, informing them they now ruled their realms autonomously, as Niall had always intended they do once he was dead. But he involved them in his new plans for Homana as a way of insuring Solinde and Atvia followed suit. The prophecy would not be served if the realms remained divided by more than distance. If they were to insure four realms were to unite, politically the three brothers had to think as one.

That left Erinn, under Sean's rule. Though married to Keely, Sean was neither Homanan nor Cheysuli, with nothing owed to the prophecy. But he did owe the Mujhar; Niall had wisely forced a trade alliance that improved Erinn's economy so that separation would prove detrimental. With Keely's presence—and influence—Sean agreed to a new alliance that extended the old treaty. Erinn would not lose; neither would Homana.

Aidan watched his father's machinations with a sense of wonder tinged with amusement. He had always known Brennan was the most serious of his kinfolk; now he saw why. The Prince of Homana was never allowed to forget his place; never allowed to think of himself as independent of the Mujhar; never allowed to think for himself; never given the opportunity to know freedom from his future. The Prince of Homana, named Mujhar, stood the highest in three realms. And Aidan was next in line.

It was brought home with perfect clarity the day Brennan called him into his private chamber and said they should consider opportunities for betrothing Aidan's child.

Aidan, perched on a casement sill, stared. "It is not even *born* yet!"

Brennan, slumped deep in a chair, gestured impatiently. "We can discuss possibilities regardless of its gender."

"Why *should* we? Let the child be born."

The Mujhar sighed and rubbed a hand through silvering hair. "You know as well as I we none of us have the freedom to wait so long. *You* had more than most, but there was me between my *jehan* and you. Now I am Mujhar and you the Prince . . . we should look to insuring your hold on the succession."

Aidan sighed with forced tolerance. "No one is going to wrest my grasp from the succession, *jehan*. Teirnan is dead. There is no one else in all of Homana who wants to change the order now."

"We cannot be certain of that. Now that Teirnan is dead, the *a'saii* appear to have fallen into disarray—but how are we to be sure? There is Blais, after all."

"Blais repudiated him. That is one of the reasons Teirnan threw himself into the Womb." Aidan eased himself back into the deep-cut casement. "Just because Blais refuses to come to Homana-Mujhar does not mean he plots against the succession. Blais is *stubborn*, and he came to be a

Cheysuli, not an ambitious kinsman desiring more than his due."

"We will discuss it anyway."

Aidan eyed his father. There was a new note of authority in Brennan's tone. Their dealings before had been courteous and circumspect with a mutual regard, but there had always been a generalized affection that lightened parental orders and commands. Now Brennan spoke as a king to his heir. Aidan began to see the taut web that the title wove around him.

Since his father had no intention of dismissing the topic, Aidan chose a diplomatic tone of voice. "Cousins have wed cousins for years, *jehan*. Is that what you desire? Or do you think we should look elsewhere?"

Brennan's scowl deepened, but it was not directed at anything—or anyone—in particular. "A part of me agrees with the first, for we have mixed linked bloodlines to form closer kin-ties. It was required to strengthen the gifts. But we are so *closely* tied . . ." He sighed. "Perhaps it *is* time we looked to other realms."

Aidan nodded thoughtfully. "We are now too close to Erinn."

"And to Solinde."

"And Corin's Glyn is barren." As his father looked up sharply, Aidan shrugged. "He told me before he left. He does not care, he says—he did not marry her for children."

Brennan scowled thoughtfully. Then sighed, shrugging. "If we look to other lands, there is Ellas, Falia, and Caledon."

Aidan raised a single brow. "But Homana has never married into those realms. Finn's daughter came the closest by marrying the youngest son of Ellas' High King—" he paused "—how many generations back?"

Brennan waved a hand. "It does not matter. That is old history, and we are speaking of new."

"Aye, well . . ." Aidan thought it over. "I am not so certain I like the idea of marrying my daughter into foreign lands."

Brennan smiled. "But if she is a son, he will remain here. And the princess come to *him*."

"As Shona has?" Aidan arched a brow. "*While* we are speaking of weddings, what of mine?"

Brennan gestured. "I thought you might wish to wait.

Even though official mourning is ended, it would not be seemly to hold a large wedding celebration within a year of the Mujhar's passing."

"Then we will hold a small one." Aidan shrugged. "As I have said before, Shona is not a woman for ceremony. And I myself do not care. I only thought it might be wise in view of the imminent birth. There are only two months left, *jehan*. And you know the Homanans."

"Aye, so I do." Brennan stroked a temple. "I could speak to Aileen. Together, she and Deirdre could fashion a ceremony. And it might be good for Deirdre."

"It might be good for us all." Aidan slipped off the sill. "I will speak to Shona. I promise, *jehan*, she cares little for ceremony. She will not insist on splendor.' He grinned. "All she insists on is for the two months to pass, so she can rid herself of the burden."

"So did your *jehan*." Brennan smiled briefly. "I will speak to Aileen."

"There *is* one thing."

Brennan eyed him warily. "What is it?"

Aidan was amused; was he so unpredictable? "I want to take her to Clankeep. To bear the child there."

Raven brows rose. "Why? Would she not prefer Homana-Mujhar?"

Aidan shook his head slowly. "She has grown up ignorant of her heritage, except for what Keely taught her. Shona has a great need to know her ancestry, to understand the history of our people. She is empty of us, *jehan*. She is empty of the knowledge. There are *shar tahls* to learn from, and clansmen to meet." He shrugged. "I think she longs for a thing of which she has no understanding."

Brennan sighed. "*Lir*-sickness, in a way. After all, she is Keely's daughter. Who is to say what needs burn in her blood?" He looked at his son. "Take her wherever she wishes. She is Cheysuli, too. Nothing is closed to her."

Aidan nodded. "I will tell her to plan for a wedding. Then we will go to Clankeep."

"You might *ask*," Brennan suggested. "Telling is not always wise."

Aidan grinned. "You forget, *jehan*. There is the *kivarna* between us. She will know the truth of things the moment we see one another."

Something glimmered in Brennan's eyes. "Then I would say it is fortunate you are not a habitual liar."

"Nor *any* kind of liar." Aidan crossed to the door. "I think it is time I put up my own pavilion in Clankeep. As a gift to the child."

"No," Brennan said quietly, as his son swung open the door. "As a gift to yourself."

Aidan paused, staring. He sensed regret commingled with a desire to alter things of the past. *"Jehan?"*

"As a gift to yourself," Brennan repeated. "You will lose too much in the years to come. The Lion will swallow you up, as well as the Homanans. It is how things are, and not necessarily *bad* . . . but I might wish for another way, had I to do it again."

"What would you change?"

Brennan's gesture encompassed the chamber. "This. Walls bind me, Aidan . . . they bind every Cheysuli. But I cannot very well order the Lion taken out of the Great Hall and dragged off to Clankeep, to crouch amidst the trees." Briefly, he smiled. "The Lion *is* Homana . . . but we are more than that. So, when you put up your pavilion, raise it for yourself. To honor your ancestry. To remind you of what we were."

In silence, Aidan nodded. And then he went out the door.

The family gathered in the Great Hall: Deirdre and Aileen in embroidered Erinnish gowns unearthed from their trunks; Ian and Brennan in soft, dyed leather and clanworked gold. Others were present as well, powerful Homanan nobles and others from the clans, but Aidan felt the absences of far too many people: Niall, Hart and his kin, Keely and Sean, Corin.

But there *was* Shona. And as she joined him at the silver doors to walk the length of the Hall, he knew the absences filled.

She wore green. Rich, Erinnish green, unadorned save for intricate stitching done in delicate gold; and bright Erinnish emeralds spanning a burgeoning waist, laced into unbound hair that brushed the hem of her skirts.

He took her to the dais, where the priest waited for them. Aidan said his vows quietly, damping his *kivarna* so he could last the moment, then listened with great pride as

Shona also said the words. The priest was Homanan, the language was Homanan; in the Old Tongue, and then in Erinnish, Aidan repeated the vows. And then placed around her throat the torque of interlocking repeated figures: a raven in liquid flight, a wolfhound leaping after.

Shona's eyes were bright. And then the moment was past; they were, in the eyes of gods and men, husband and wife, *cheysul* and *cheysula*, Prince and Princess of Homana.

Duly presented by the Mujhar of Homana, Aidan and Shona were free to mingle with the guests. Shona almost immediately declared her longing to be back in trews and boots so she could stride about the Great Hall like herself, instead of a mincing maiden; Aidan informed her he had yet to see her—or *anyone*—mince, and she was obviously no longer— and had not been for some time—a maiden. Shona flashed him a baleful glance, but it was ineffective. The *kivarna* told him the truth: she was as moved as he by the knowledge of their future, bound together forever by something far stronger than vows.

All too quickly the women dragged Shona away from him. Aidan found himself momentarily alone, holding an untouched cup of wine someone had thrust into his hands. Smiling faintly, he looked across the hall and saw Deirdre, elegant in her gown, but hideously apart from the frivolity around her. Grief had aged her in the nearly three months since Niall had died, dulling her hair and etching shadows beneath her eyes. The flesh of her face was stretched taut over bones showing a new fragility.

Aidan was abruptly assailed by the fear she might soon follow Niall. He knew of men and women who, left alone after so many years of companionship, dwindled and died. He had always known her as a strong, spirited woman, conducting herself with becoming decorum in view of her unofficial status, yet knowing far better than most how to run a household as large and diverse as Niall's.

Apprehension increased. He could not sense her, could not *read* her; it was not a gift he could control. Aidan abruptly crossed the hall to intercept her as Deirdre moved from candlelight into shadows.

"Granddame." He presented her with the cup of wine, pressing it into rigid fingers. She thanked him and accepted it, but clutched the cup too tightly. He feared she might spill the wine. "Granddame," he repeated, "I have been remiss. I have not seen you lately."

Deirdre's smile was gentle. "You have had much to contend with of late. A new title, new honor, new wife . . . and soon a new child." Briefly green eyes brightened. "You'll be seeing what your grandsire and father have had to contend with all these years: a proud Erinnish woman with the freedom and facility to speak her own mind."

She had lost much of her Erinnish lilt over the years spent in Homana, but he heard the underlying echoes of Aileen and Shona in her tone. Suddenly he was fiercely proud of the island realm—and the Aerie—for rearing proud, strong women. And for sharing them with Cheysuli.

He took one of her hands and kissed it. "You outshine them all today."

She smiled again; this time it touched her eyes. "How gentle you are, Aidan . . . I forget how little you resemble Niall's children in temperament."

"Gentle!" It was not how he would characterize himself. He was not certain he liked it.

"I think it must be the *kivarna* in you. You understand too well how other people feel, how the slights can hurt. Brennan was always much more reticent to say anything without thinking it over—the diplomat in him!—but Hart and Corin and Keely always said whatever they wished *when*-ever they wished to say it, and suffered the consequences." Deirdre smiled. " 'Tis a trait of Erinn, as well . . . Aileen and I both share it—*and* Shona, no doubt!—though not so much as Niall's children." Her eyes were very kind. "But you have always been different. From the very first. And I have always been grateful for it."

It was not what he had expected. "Why?"

"Because this House is made of warriors." Slender shoulders moved in a shrug. "I do not complain—the world is large enough for all manner of men. Niall raised his sons for a purpose: to be strong and fierce and determined, no matter what they faced, because they would face much." She smoothed back from his brow an errant auburn forelock. "You, too, are a warrior, Aidan . . . but there is more in you than that. You serve your prophecy with less fierceness and more dignity. You do not think of wars with the Ihlini or a treaty with Caledon or a betrothal with this land or that. You think about people, instead. They are *human* to you, instead of sticks in a fortune-game." Her gaze was intent. "That is important, Aidan. You are not so bound, so driven—be who you are, not what the others are."

After a moment, he smiled. "I think I am more bound by the prophecy than anyone here, granddame."

She sighed and removed her hand, cradling the cup once more. "There is more to life than that."

"It *is* life."

Deirdre looked away from him a moment, gazing across the crowded hall toward the Lion. "You are all of you so different."

"Granddame—?"

"You Cheysuli." She looked back. "There are times, I'm thinking, you lack any freedom at all."

"The gods gave us self-rule, granddame."

"Did they?" Her smile was bittersweet. "If that is true, follow your own intuition. Do not let the history of your ancestors warp you from your path."

She sounded uncommonly like the Hunter, or Ashra, or any of the oddities he had met in the past year. "What do you mean?"

"The Cheysuli are so supremely certain that their way is the true way that it is leaving little room for anyone else in the world. 'Tis an insular and arrogant race, because it has had to be." She raised a finger as he began to nod. "But no longer. Now you can loosen the shackles and *breathe*."

"Granddame—"

"D'ye think I judge too harshly because I am Erinnish? That I could not understand?" Deirdre shook her head. "But I do, Aidan. Far better than anyone thinks. I lived with a Cheysuli warrior for more than forty years. I helped raise three more of them—four, if you count Keely with her *lir*-gifts—and yet a fifth when you were born. Oh, I know, Aidan. I know you very well."

The summation hurt. "And do you find us lacking?"

Deirdre's tone was gentle. "Not lacking. Bound. Too bound by customs. There is so little change in the clans . . . change is *healthy*, Aidan!"

His hand dropped to the links at his belt. Change was within him, he knew. Why else would gods speak to him? Why else would they set him a task he had yet to understand? Everyone said he was different. Was he *so* different he would alter the traditions of his race?

The response was instinctive, denial as much as truth. "Too much change can hurt."

Deirdre's hand was cool on his arm. "Nothing is done well if it is done too quickly. But you are less inclined than most to act without thinking. Even Brennan sees himself bound by tradition . . . I think you will be a different kind of Mujhar when you ascend the Lion. And I think it will be good."

Aidan's smile was lopsided. "You give my *jehan* short shrift."

Deirdre laughed. "Brennan will do well enough; probably better than most. He has waited for this all of his life. And he is what Homana requires *now*, but not always." Her green eyes were very warm. "Your turn will come, Aidan. When it does, use it."

Seven

They knelt side by side upon the blue ice-bear pelt from across the Bluetooth River. The *shar tahl* looked back at them, black brows knitted. "Why did you come to *me*? I am only one . . . also the youngest and newest in Clankeep." He studied them both. "You have the right, of course—I am fully acknowledged as a *shar tahl*—but I thought you might go to another."

Aidan smiled. "It is precisely *because* you are not like the others that we came to you."

Shona nodded. "And because of Blais. You were the only one who wrote him of his father."

Burr sighed, smoothing a wrinkle from his leggings. The edge of winter was upon them; he, as they did, wore heavier leathers, thicker woolens, furred cloaks. "Aye. I thought the others unjust, in that. But they viewed Blais' request as unanswerable; Teirnan was *kin-wrecked*, his rune-sign expunged from the birthlines. In their minds, how could they tell him of a warrior who no longer existed?"

"But *you* answered," Aidan said.

Burr shrugged. "I had to. He was a man in need—a Cheysuli warrior requiring information of his heritage." Yellow eyes were very steady. "Had I refused him the information, I would have renounced one of the foremost responsibilities of my position, which is to serve all Cheysuli in matters of heritage, custom, tradition . . ." He smiled. "I am not saying the others *did*. I merely interpreted the custom differently. I no longer believe in the need for *kin-wrecking* at all; Blais' request, therefore, was one I had to answer."

Aidan gazed at him. He wondered anew at the man's commitment. Not its quality or depth, but at its ability to be flexible. Part of it, he believed, had to do with Burr's comparative youth. He was, Aidan had learned, thirty-seven, which made him nearly fifteen years junior to the youngest of the other *shar tahls*. But the rest of it had to do with a different kind of belief system. Burr saw things differently, and interpreted things accordingly. There was room in his world for change, just as Deirdre had suggested.

"So," Shona said, "we've asked it. Will you be giving us our answer?"

Burr grinned. "Of course you may set up a pavilion within Clankeep. Would I say no to you, after permitting Blais to do the same?"

"But he is not here," Aidan said.

"No. But he will return. There are things he must reconcile with himself . . . his *jehan's* withdrawal from the clans is one of them, as well as Teirnan's death." Burr shifted, slipping a hand from his knee to the red dogfox curled by his side. "And have you permission of the clan-leader?"

Shona laughed. "He gave it instantly. Would he dare do otherwise to the son of the Mujhar?"

"Oh, he might." Burr's tone was mild. "Aidan is not well-known here, other than occasional visits. And there is talk of dreams, and nights he walks the corridors of Homana-Mujhar, conversing with the Lion." The *shar tahl's* white teeth flashed as Aidan and Shona exchanged uneasy glances. "But it is thought mostly due to having his spirit chafed by too many walls and Homanan responsibilities. Surely here, in the heart of the land, he will learn what it is to be a warrior of the clans."

"Surely he will," Aidan agreed dryly.

"Just as he will surely learn more about his heritage if he studies with a *shar tahl*."

Aidan nodded. "And may I choose which one?"

"Done," Burr said. "Put up your pavilion, then come to me each day."

"*Leijhana tu'sai*." Aidan rose, reaching down to help an ungainly Shona to her feet. But before he turned away to open the doorflap, he paused. "There was a time you said I had your sympathy. Do I still?"

Burr's lids flickered minutely. "You have many things of me, my lord. Among them my sympathy."

To press him would be futile, Aidan knew. There was a core of quiet stubbornness in Burr he knew better than to test. It was, he believed, much like his own.

Sighing, he pulled aside the doorflap and gestured Shona to precede him into the chilly day.

For three days Aidan and Shona cut, dyed, and stitched the pavilion fabric until it resembled the proper shape. Then they designed and painted the black raven on the slate-gray sides, and with the help of three other warriors set up the frame and ridgepole and dragged the oiled fabric over it, pegging and tying it down as necessary. Finally it stood on its own, rippling in the breeze so that the raven's wings moved, and Shona stepped into Aidan's arms as the warriors faded away, tucking chilled hands into his furs.

" 'Tis *ours*."

Nodding, he gazed at the pavilion as he slung an arm around her waist.

"Ours," she repeated. " 'Twasn't something I moved into when we married, but something we built together."

With the *kivarna*, he knew very well what she meant. He shared it. "Aye. Kilore and Homana-Mujhar have housed many kings, many children . . . but *this* place is ours."

She sighed as a chilly breeze tugged at braided hair. "There is such peace about Clankeep—I'm thinking I could stay here forever."

Aidan smiled. "Forever is a long time, my lass . . . and you not properly knowing what it *is* to be Cheysuli."

"Yet," she clarified. "And I'm knowing *something* of it. D'ye think I'm lying when I tell you how I feel, surrounded by such history? Such security in tradition?" She hooked a thumb into his belt. "I know what you say about change, my lad, but can it wait? I've only just got here. I'd like to see what being Cheysuli is all about before you begin changing everything."

"Only some things," he said distantly. "Things such as the abomination called *kin-wrecking*—" He cut it off. "Enough. I am only a prince, not Mujhar—and even *that* bears no certainty of power. The Cheysuli have always been subject to the power of gods, not of kings . . . it would require more than Aidan the Mujhar to convince the clans to change."

"Then *be* more," she said simply. "Make yourself more, my lad . . . you have it in you, I'm thinking."

"Aye. Perhaps." Aidan turned to her, sliding hands down to splay across the mound of her belly. She had given up trews in favor of loose skirts weeks before, for the child had become intrusive. Aidan felt the tautness of her flesh stretched so tightly under the soft wool skirt and loose tunic. He laughed. "We have put up the pavilion just in time."

Shona cupped his elbows even as he cupped her belly. "He will be Cheysuli," she said fiercely. "Before anything else: *Cheysuli*."

Aidan smiled. "Even before his Homanan rank? Or Erinnish?"

"Even before that." Her eyes were fixed on his in a strange, wild pride. "Gods, d'ye know what it is to come here? To *feel* so much in my heart? All those years in Erinn, cut off from the place I most belong . . ." She drew in a breath and released it slowly, audibly. "I have no *lir*-gifts, but I do have the blood . . . and it burns, Aidan. It burns so *much*."

"I know," he said, "I know. Gods, Shona, how can I not? I feel it the same way."

"But you've *been* here," she protested. "You've had this all your life, since the time you were born; and *Teel*—" She broke off, looking at the ridgepole. "D'ye see? There he is."

He smiled. "I see."

"I'm not knowing how to say it, but you should be able to feel it. All my life I knew the freedom of Kilore, the freedom of the headlands, the freedom of the seas, for my father took me sailing . . . but 'tisn't the same! *Here* I feel free. *Here* I feel whole. *Here* is where I belong."

"But there is also Homana-Mujhar—"

"Oh, aye, I'm knowing we can't *always* live here. There will come a time . . . but for now? They've no need of you in the palace, nor the city . . . can we not stay here as long as possible?"

He smoothed back a lock of hair pulled loose from the braid. "We will stay as long as we can. Gods willing, we will give our child the foundation you lacked." He smiled. "And I, for that matter; I grew up in Homana-Mujhar."

Shona looked at the neat stacks of chests, rolled pelts, cairn stones and kindling, set beside the pavilion. Keely's sword, scabbarded, leaned against the pile of stones. " 'Tis time we made it a home. All the gifts the clan and our kin gave us are worthy of being cherished."

Aidan smiled. Between them flared the powerful pleasure that was more than mere passion, mere physical satisfaction. It was a deep, abiding contentment akin to exultation; a burgeoning comprehension that what they shared could not be extinguished. He wanted to be inside the pavilion, sitting before the cairn. He wanted to share it with his woman. He wanted to be no one but himself: a warrior of the Cheysuli.

This pavilion has nothing to do with that, Teel chided. *You have been a warrior since we bonded.*

Aidan grinned. *Of course.*

The raven cocked his head. *You are uncommonly pleased with yourself.*

I am too happy to argue.

Because of the pavilion?

Partly. There is more.

Because of the woman?

That, too. But more.

Teel's eye was bright. *The child, then. Because there will be a child.*

All of those things, lir.

The raven fluffed wings. *Such simple things, lir: a home, a woman, a child.*

Aidan smiled. *Simple and magnificent. And sufficient unto my needs.*

Teel's tone was amused. *Not so much, I'm thinking.*

Laughing aloud, Aidan hugged Shona. "Let us begin with the cairn, and a fire. 'Tis cold out here, *I'm* thinking!"

Eight

He dreamed. The hammered silver doors of the Great Hall of Homana-Mujhar swung open, crashing against the walls, so that his view was unobstructed. The flames in the firepit died back, sucked away, until only coals glowed. Beyond the pit, crouched upon the dais, was the malevolent Lion

Throne, carved of still-living wood. He knew the wood still
lived, because he saw it breathe.

No. He saw the *Lion* breathe; in his sleep, Aidan twitched.

Wood creaked. Slowly the toes tightened, claws scraping
against veined marble. Wooden flanks tautened, then gave,
rippling with indrawn breath. The tail, carved snug against a
wooden haunch, loosed itself and whipped, beating a staccato pattern against the marble dais.

The Lion rose from its crouch. It shook its head, and the
great mane tumbled over massive shoulders. The Lion of
Homana, no longer a wooden throne, stood upon the dais
and surveyed its royal domain. Within it stood Aidan.

The Lion coughed. It blinked. And then it opened its
mouth—

"*Aidan!* What is it? What is that noise?"

He awoke, sweating, aware of the dream and the not-
dream; the echoes of Shona's voice and the outcry within
the *lir*-link.

"Teel?" he asked numbly.

Lir—lir—Ihlini—

Shona was sitting upright. "Gods—all over, such *noise*—"

Lir—lir—Ihlini—

He scrambled up "Teel?"

Ihlini—Ihlini—

"Aidan?"

"Ihlini," he breathed. "Here? In *Clankeep*?"

Outside, there was screaming.

"Oh, gods," he blurted. "Ihlini—*in Clankeep*—"

Even as Shona hastily pulled on soft boots, Aidan was at
the doorflap. He wanted to tear it open, but did not, instinctively knowing not to give their presence away. A part
of him told him it probably did not matter; if Ihlini were in
Clankeep, they would not search pavilions. They would
simply destroy everything.

Aidan drew aside the flap far enough so he could peer out
one-eyed. And saw the conflagration.

He spun at once. "We have to get out. Now. *Now*,
Shona—they are burning everything."

Lir—lir—Ihlini—

Throughout Clankeep the *lir* cried their warnings, within
the links and without. Aidan heard screaming.

Women and children, screaming.

"Shona—"

She was beside him, cradling belly. "Where do we go?"

"Out of Clankeep. Entirely away—" He had a knife, and somewhere a bow . . . hastily he caught up the warbow and the pitiful handful of arrows. "They are killing the children, *meijhana.*"

He saw it go home. Shona snatched up a cloak and dragged it around her shoulders. She wasted no time looking for anything else, or begging for this or that. She merely waited, grim-faced, as he nocked one of five arrows. Beyond her face, through the slit of the doorflap, he saw the flames lapping at the pavilion across the clearing, and shadows running in darkness.

"We must get beyond the wall," he told her. "We must go out toward the gates, then slip through."

"Or over the wall," she said calmly.

"You cannot climb—"

"I will."

Aidan tore aside the doorflap. A line of flame licked from the burning pavilion and crept across to theirs.

"This way—the back—" He caught her hand and dragged her.

They ducked out, shredding the laces with Aidan's knife. The night was ablaze with flame. The cold, lurid flame that came from the netherworld.

Their pavilion, but newly raised, stood six paces from the wall. Aidan had believed it a safe, cozy spot: shielded by wall at the back, by trees on either side. Only the front was unprotected; there had been no need in Clankeep.

"The children—" Shona whispered, as screams renewed themselves.

"To the wall." Aidan steadied her as best he could, while watching for Ihlini. *Teel?*

Above you . . . lir, they are everywhere—Ihlini everywhere—

Around them, trees caught fire; laces of purple flame danced along close-grown limbs, passing destruction from brother to brother. Burning sap dripped onto the new pavilion even as the lone streamer from the clearing touched their doorpole, and climbed.

Shona clawed at the wall. It was of natural, undressed stone, lacking mortar save for the moss and dirt of years sealing the joints together. In childhood, Aidan had scaled it; it was not difficult to climb because it was not sheer, but Shona was unbalanced by the child, lacking grace and control.

He did not see a way for her to climb it normally, even as she thrust fingers into seams and dug a booted toe at joints.

"I will—" she murmured. "I *can*—"

Behind them, screams and fire, and the shrieking of a hawk.

"Climb, Shona—" He thrust a hand against her spine, trying to steady her.

Lir—lir—Ihlini—

The warning shrilled through the link. Aidan wrenched his head around and saw the horseman come riding.

"Shona—hold *on*—" He spun, raising the warbow, and sighted hastily. Loosed, but the arrow was wide.

He was dazzled by the flames. Throughout Clankeep pavilions burned, falling into charred heaps. Crown fires spread from tree to tree, leaping across the wall into the wood beyond. He saw people running: Cheysuli and Ihlini. He heard people shouting, women screaming, children crying in shock and fear.

The horseman still came on, bared blade gleaming.

Bared blade—a sword—

Aidan did not take the time to think. He ducked beneath the sweeping blade and nocked a second arrow. Behind him the raven-painted pavilion flared into flames, hissing and crackling as fabric was consumed. From all over Clankeep the smell of burning oil and paint hung in the air, as well as the stench of charred flesh. Smoke rolled through the clearings.

Renewed screaming and outcries became an underscore to the macabre dance he entered into with the horseman. The night was moonless and dark, which made the shadows thicker, and the Ihlini rode a black horse. The only thing Aidan saw was the pallor of a face and the glint of the naked blade.

No sorcery here, save godfire—he must use a conventional weapon—

It was something, Aidan thought. At least he had a chance.

Shona still clung to the wall. He saw her pale face turned toward the burning pavilion. The *lir*-torque at her throat glinted in the flames, throwing light into her eyes as she opened her mouth to shout.

The sword scythed by. Aidan, ducking once more, came up and loosed again.

It took the horse full in the throat and brought the animal to its knees, screaming as it died. The rider flung himself free and rolled, tossing off a dark cloak as he came up. Dark leathers polished shiny glistened in the *godfire*. The sword still sang in his hands.

"Shona—*climb*—"

"No purchase," she answered evenly, stepping back to level ground.

Aidan cursed. He could not afford to have his attention diverted by Shona, and yet he could hardly keep it from her. His *kivarna* was shrieking at him: she was frightened, as he was, but also very angry. What he sensed most was rage. A cold, deadly rage engendered by the Ihlini.

They were killing *children*.

He had lost the other arrows. One remained to him. Aidan nocked even as the Ihlini ran toward him with the sword.

The face swam out of the flames. A cool, smooth face, underscored by upswept cheekbones and dark arched eyebrows; the chiseling of nose and mouth. Aidan had seen that face.

"*Tevis,*" he blurted.

The other smiled coolly. "Lochiel," he corrected.

Who had murdered Hart's son.

Aidan loosed. Lochiel sliced the arrow in half.

He cannot be so fast—

But Aidan believed it was possible he could be many things.

He threw down the useless bow and yanked his knife from the sheath, feeling a sickening tightness in his belly. A knife was no match for a sword.

The pavilion burned behind him. Aidan felt the heat, heard the crisping fabric, smelled the acrid stench of burning pelts. Another step, and he would be in the flames.

Shona ran by him, ducking into the burning pavilion. Even as he opened his mouth to shout, she was out from under the collapsing ridgepole. Keely's sword was in her hands.

He caught it as she offered him the hilt, and put his knife into her hands. "Go to the gate," he said swiftly. "Make your way into the wood—"

But it was all he could manage. Even as Shona nodded, turning to follow order, Lochiel came at him.

She ran. Awkward and ungainly, cursing the Ihlini, Shona did as he told her. And Aidan could breathe again.

The sword was a willow branch. It was ground to suit a woman, and then only in practice: the blade was stripped of weight and edge. Its hilt was finer and less heavy than that of his own weapon, and the pommel knot, for him, was unbalanced, hindering his grip. But still it was a sword.

Aidan blessed Keely. Trying not to think of her daughter.

Lochiel was swift and relentless. Aidan parried once, twice, a third time, countering the blows with strength born of rage and desperation. He heard the screaming, the killing, the shrieking. The roaring of the flames. The sound of his own breathing, through a raw and burning throat.

From the corner of his eye, he saw Shona stop running. Saw her swing around. Saw her come back toward him.

No, meijhana—no—

The *kivarna* told him the truth: she could not bear to leave him. She could not bear not to know.

"Run!" he shouted to her.

Irresolute, she slowed. Instinct warred: protect the child, aid the man. Defend what was hers.

A strong, proud woman. An eagle of the Aerie, undeterred by Ihlini. Knowing she could not flee when the man was left behind.

"Run!" Aidan shouted.

The blade broke in his hands.

Gods—

Lochiel laughed. The tip of his sword drifted down; deftly he turned, caught his knife out of his sheath, and threw.

It spun, arcing swiftly, and lodged itself hilt-deep in Shona's breast.

Aidan screamed. The *kivarna* between them shattered, destroyed in a single moment as the knife penetrated. The broken sword fell from his hands as Aidan lunged to grab Lochiel, but the Ihlini stepped neatly out of the way. The blade he had so negligently lowered to aid his knife throw came up with a snap of the wrist. The tip pricked into Aidan's left shoulder as he hurled himself forward, then drove through relentlessly.

Pain. Pain redoubled, and tripled; his *kivarna* reverberated with the outrage done to Shona. His own injury did not matter. What mattered to him was *Shona*—

But his legs would not work, nor his arms. He felt the blade grate on bone as Lochiel twisted the sword, jerking it from his shoulder, and then blood flowed swift and hot.

Shona.

He fell. To his knees. His left arm hung uselessly, twitching from shock and outrage.

Shona.

Lochiel walked by him. Away from him. He turned his back on him. He carried the bloodied sword lightly, easily, deft as a born swordsman. Aidan, twisting frenziedly to watch even as he tried to rise, thought the young Ihlini graceful as a dancer as he stepped across burning ridgepoles and deftly avoided drifting bits of burning fabric. The screams, now, were gone, replaced by a deadly silence.

Save for the crackle of flames.

Lochiel went to Shona. He knelt and pulled the knife from her breast. Her swollen belly pushed toward the sky. Lochiel tore tunic aside. The bloodied knife glistened.

Aidan knew what he meant to do. Instinctively, he *knew*.

In one rushing expulsion of breath and strength, Aidan lurched to his feet. He tried to run. Fell. Lurched up again, staggered, stumbled across the ground. Dripping blood hissed in ash.

Shona.

He had no knife. No sword. Only desperation, and the wild, killing rage.

"Put no hands on her—"

Lochiel, kneeling, slanted him a single glance across his shoulder. And then turned back to his work.

"Put—no—hands—"

Lochiel removed the baby, cut the cord, wrapped the child in Shona's cloak. Carefully he set the bundle on the ground beside the body. With a lithe, twisting turn, he rose to face Aidan.

"I want the seed," he said. "I will make the seed *mine*."

Legs failed him. Aidan fell awkwardly. "Sh–Sh–*Shona*—"

"No more time," Lochiel murmured.

From out of the burning darkness looped the glitter of a blade. The edge bit in, then turned. The skull beneath shattered.

Nine

Muddy ash fouled Brennan's boots. Blankly, he stared at them. How much of the ash was from wood? How much of the ash from bone?

He shuddered. The spasm took him unaware, rippling through from head to toe, stretching his scalp briefly until the flesh at last relaxed. And he knew, with sickening clarity, it was what his son now fought. But on a different level: Aidan had nearly died. Aidan still might die.

Clankeep lay in ruin. Most of the wall still stood, for stone does not die from fire, but nearly all of the pavilions were destroyed. Some lay in skeletal piles, ridgepoles charred black. Others were nothing but coals, or mounds of muddy ash.

Brennan, looking, felt sick.

A man nearby, bending to peel aside a charred husk of bedding pelt, let it fall from ash-smeared fingers. "My *lir*," he murmured rigidly. And then nodded, accepting; he had spent the morning looking, while Brennan inspected Clankeep. Now the man was freed. Now the warrior could go.

Brennan watched him. Deep in his belly the snake of futility writhed. *Lirless*, the warrior would die, though he had survived the attack.

"A waste," he murmured quietly, damning the tradition. Damning the need for it.

The *lirless* warrior stood over the bedding pelt and the remains that lay beneath it. Shoulders slumped briefly; then he made the fluid gesture Brennan knew so well. And walked out of the walls into the charred forest beyond.

So many already dead. And now one more.

Brennan sighed. He was weary, so very weary . . . drained of strength and answers. Here he was superfluous, with nothing to do but watch as the others tended their dead, their living, the remnants of their lives.

"So many dead," he murmured, "and all because Lochiel desired to send us a message. To assure us he *existed*."

"Brennan." It was Ian, walking slowly through ash-grayed mud and charred pavilions. His face was strained, and old. "They found her the day after, over there. She has been attended to. They gave her the Ceremony of Passing six days ago." Ian's gesture was aimless. "There is nothing we can do, save tell Aidan when he wakes."

His mouth was oddly stiff. "*If* Aidan wakes."

Ian hesitated a moment too long. "Given time—"

Brennan's tone was vicious. "Do you think time will make a difference? You have seen him—you have *heard* him! When the Ihlini cracked his skull, all the wits spilled out."

Ian drew in a quiet breath. "You do him an injustice."

"By the gods, *su'fali*—he is mad! You heard his babble! When you *can* understand a phrase, it makes no sense at all." Brennan's face spasmed. "I would be the first to declare him fit and the last to declare him mad . . . but I know what I have heard. I know what I have seen."

Ian's tone was patient. "I have seen men struck in the head do and say strange things—"

"And have they prophesied?" Eloquent irony.

Ian sighed. "No."

"Gods—" Brennan choked. "Why did they let us have him at all if they meant to take him from us?"

Ian offered no answer.

"So many times, as a child, he nearly died. We knew he would, Aileen and I—we tried to prepare ourselves for the night he would wake, coughing, and die before the dawn . . . the fever that would burn him . . . knowing we would lose him, and that there would be no more." Brennan balled impotent fists. "And now, when he is grown, when he is a strong, healthy man—they take him away from us!"

"*Harani*—"

"I should not have let them come. When he told me he meant to bring Shona here, to bear the child here—" Brennan's face spasmed. "I should have refused. I should have said it was better for her to bear it in Homana-Mujhar—"

"You could not have prevented him."

"—where there are physicians, and midwives—and protection from the Ihlini."

"There was nothing you could have done. Aidan is grown, Brennan . . . he makes his own decisions."

"I could have insisted."

"He—*and* Shona—had a perfect right to do as they wished. You had no right to stop them."

"But *look what happened*—"

"*Tahlmorra*," Ian said softly.

Brennan's shoulders trembled. His voice was a travesty. "Why did they give him to us if they meant to take him away?"

Ian put a hand on his nephew's shoulder. "Come, *harani*. It is time we went back. Aileen will need you . . . and, perhaps, your son."

Brennan shut his eyes. "They have destroyed my son," he whispered. "Even if he lives."

He became aware he had been shouting. His throat ached from it, but when he tried to form the words with his mouth, nothing happened. He felt separated from his body, drifting aimlessly, apart from the world and yet still a part of it. And when he opened his eyes, he stared out of the bed into faces he did not know, yet they knew him.

He sensed the violence in his body before it came, and as it came he understood it. His flesh crawled upon his bones, rippling and writhing. And then his limbs began to twitch. Slowly at first, then more quickly, until the convulsions took bones and muscles and made clay of them, molding them this way and that.

Fire was in his head.

He screamed. He heard himself screaming, though he could make no sense of it; he heard voices attempt to soothe him, though he could make no sense of it. He did not know the language.

He convulsed, head slamming back into the pillow on a rigid, arcing neck. Arms and legs contracted. His teeth bit bloody gashes in his tongue until someone forced a piece of padded wood into his clenched jaw. His teeth ground until gums bled, shredding the padding. Splintering the wood.

The seizures passed at last. He lay spent against the mattress, quivering in his weakness. No one spoke to him now. Perhaps they understood he had no means with which to answer.

Memory. It ran around inside his head like a ball set to spinning; spinning and spinning and spinning until at last the momentum ended; then bouncing and rattling and rolling against the inside of his skull.

Memory: Flames. Screams. Stench.

Oil and paint and flesh.

Blood hissing in ash.

His jaws snapped open. His throat disgorged sound. But nothing was emitted, save the rasp of a dying breath.

Memory: Death.

Each day someone held a candle near his eyes. He could see it, but could not blink. Could not tell them it hurt. The words were garbled nonsense. When he tried to put up a hand to block the candle's light, the arm spasmed and jumped. They held it down for him. Some days the spasm passed. Others it spread and worsened. Then they held him *down, pinning arms and legs.*

Someone had cracked his head, like an egg against a rock.

He dreamed. Not of a golden chain. Not of a living Lion. Of a man. A young, magnificent man, strong and full of life. His vibrancy was tangible; his power as yet untapped.

A tall, lithe young man, striding like a mountain cat through the webwork of Aidan's dreams. His eyes were cool and gray, with a gaze so compelling it could stop a hardened assassin from unsheathing sword or knife. The hair was thick and black, framing a youthful face of austere, yet flawless beauty, bearing the stamp of authority far surpassing any monarch's. It was not a womanish face, even in all its beauty; a trace of ruthlessless in the mouth maintained its masculine line. Only rarely did it smile. When it did, power flickered; he could rule or seduce man and woman with equal facility.

Dreaming, Aidan twitched.

The man was not Cheysuli. The man was not Ihlini. The man was of all blood, forged from the heart of war, tempered on the anvil of peace. And his gifts were such that they surpassed all others.

Aidan whispered: Firstborn.

And knew what it meant.

Rebirth.

And death.

The ending of what he knew; the beginning of what he did not.

He cried out in fear, recoiling from the truth; from the man who prowled his dreams.

Deep inside, something roused. Something woke.

He spoke. He heard himself. Saw their frightened faces as they heard him. Saw the horror in their eyes; the comprehen-

sion of madness: surely he was mad? What else would make
him so?

He spoke. He raved. He chanted. The convulsions came
again. And passed.

Lips were bitten. Tongue and gums lacerated. Muscles
shrieked with each dying spasm.

The broken head mended.

He thought perhaps he might, until the child of the prophecy strode through his dreams again.

He woke. He knelt on the floor. Shouting. They all came
running, all of them, and this time he heard himself. This
time he understood. The words of his dream spewed out.

"I am the sword!" he cried. "I am the sword and the bow
and the knife. I am darkness and light. I am good and evil. I
am the child and the elder; the girl and the boy; the wolf and
the lamb."

He wavered on his knees, but none dared to touch him.
Words poured forth. "Born of one prophecy, I am come to
make another. To bind four realms into one; to bind eight
into four. I am the child of the prophecy; child of darkness
and light; of like breeding with like."

He sucked in a quivering breath. "I am Cynric. I am
Cynric. I am the sword—and the bow—and the knife. I am
the child of prophecy: the Firstborn come again."

He stopped. The words were gone. He was empty, and
hollow, and purged.

Aidan tumbled downward, welcoming the darkness. But
hands raised him up again, showing him the light.

The door was ajar, as they always left it now. Deirdre,
who had ordered old hinges oiled so as not to disturb
Aidan, slipped into the chamber. It smelled of herbs and an
odd pungency. Aidan's wounds had been healed; even so,
the smell was not of blood or body.

She frowned, pausing to draw air deep into her lungs.
Exhaling abruptly, she knew. It was a thing she had not
smelled since leaving Erinn.

She looked to the high-backed chair set so closely beside
the bed. "By the gods, Aileen—are you summoning the
cileann?"

Aileen started, crumpling the dried herbs she clutched in
her hands. The pungency increased, then faded as she rose,
scattering broken stems and leaves. As she saw her aunt,

she dropped back into the chair. Color tinged her face. Defiantly, she raised her chin even as she brushed bits of herbs from her skirts. "Neither Homanan nor Cheysuli gods have answered all our petitions. I thought perhaps the *cileann*—"

"This is Homana," Deirdre said quietly. "The *cileann* have no dominion here. 'Tis too far from their halls."

Aileen's face crumpled. "I wanted to try *something!* Nothing else has worked!"

Deirdre crossed the room. A glance at Aidan's bruised, too-pale face told her his condition was unchanged. He had roused but three times since the attack, and only long enough to babble nonsense in three languages: Homanan, Cheysuli, Erinnish.

But now she turned her attention back to her niece. Aileen's red hair was unkempt, twisted into a haphazard plait. She had eaten little since Aidan had been brought to Homana-Mujhar, nor had she slept but an hour here and there.

Deirdre put a soothing hand on Aileen's head, stroking dull hair gently. What she said was inconsequential, much as the words a horseman uses to quiet a fretful colt, but at last it began to work. Aileen wiped away tears and managed to smile at her aunt. "My thanks, for that. But it has been so *hard*—"

"I know, Aileen, I know . . . and may be harder yet. But you cannot be squandering your strength now, when it does no good. He will need you when he wakes. You must eat, and sleep, so he'll be knowing you when he rouses. He will be expecting his *jehana*, not a hag-witch with greasy hair and ditches beneath her eyes."

As Deirdre had intended, Aileen pressed hands against her face. Vanity, in this case, would decoy her thoughts, even if only briefly.

It passed too quickly. Aileen took her hands away and stared steadfastly at her son. "What if he never wakes?"

"He may not," Deirdre said steadily. "I have heard of such things: men and women who, struck in the head, never rouse entirely. They sleep until they die. But Aidan is very strong, and very stubborn. I think if the gods meant him to die, he would not be alive now."

"Brennan says—" She checked.

Deirdre sighed quietly. "Brennan does not know everything. He is upset, as you are. And worried, as you are. And, like you, he has known too little of rest and food. Do you blame him for speaking nonsense?"

Aileen's tone was dull. "Is it nonsense to concern yourself with the succession of Homana? He must, Deirdre . . . he is Mujhar now, and cannot afford to set aside such things. If Aidan dies, or is mad, what is Homana to do? There must be an heir for the Lion."

"There will be an heir for the Lion."

Aileen's tone, abruptly, was filled with self-loathing. "But not from the Queen of Homana."

"There is no need," Deirdre declared. "She has already borne a son. The Lion is satisfied."

The fire died out of green eyes. Aileen looked at her son. "If he lives," she whispered.

He lived. He came awake with a throttled cry and this time remained awake.

The link thrummed within him. *Lir*, Teel said. *Lir, I am well. I sit above you on the bedframe.*

He did. Relief was all-consuming. Aidan, released, trembled. And wondered, as he trembled, if he would lose himself again. If the convusions would steal his body and twist it into knots.

It hurt to breathe. His body, wracked too often, ached from residual pain; from cramps now passed, but remembered with vivid intensity. With exquisite clarity.

His lips were swollen and bitten. His tongue much the same. But his wits were perfectly clear.

I am not mad, he declared. Then, in doubt, *Am I?*

The chambers were deeply shadowed. He lay in his own bed, cushioned by pillows and bolsters. But leather was firmly knotted around wrists and ankles, then fastened to the bedframe.

Aidan spasmed. *Gods—they have* tied *me—*

He stilled. *Am I mad?*

From the corner of an eye, he saw movement. Spasming, he looked, and saw his mother present. Propped in a chair, the Queen of Homana slept. He knew by looking at her she had known too little of it. The truth was in her face.

Memory rolled back: *Screaming. Fire. Dying.*

Aidan went very still.

The reek of burning pavilions, the stench of burning bodies. And blood hissing in ash as Lochiel cut the child free.

At wrists and ankles, leather tautened. "No!" Aidan shouted. "No—no—NO—"

Aileen came awake at once, lunging out of the chair. Her hands came down on his shoulders—had he not been wounded in one?—and pressed him back again, aiding the leather straps that bound him to the bed.

"No!" he shouted. *"NO!"*

Aileen's green eyes were wide. "Aidan, stop!" she cried. "No more of this—no *more*—"

"He killed her!" he shouted. "He killed her and cut her *open*—"

"Aidan! Listen to me!" Aileen shot a frightened glance over her shoulder toward the door standing ajar and shouted for her husband. Then, turning back, she pressed against his writhing flesh. "Stay still. You must remain still. Your poor head can stand no more of this battering."

The pain came in waves. "Shona," he whispered.

Brennan came in, shoving the door open so hard it thudded against the wall and echoed down the corridor. His face was gaunt and strained.

"Awake," Aileen told him, "and remembering everything."

Brennan moved to the bed. The straps bound arms and legs; hissing, Aidan fought them. "No," Brennan said. "No, let them be. We put them there for a reason . . ." His voice trailed off as he looked down on his son. "How much do you remember?"

Aidan wanted to answer. But he felt the ripple in his flesh that presaged another seizure. No matter how hard he tried to retain it, he was losing control of his limbs. His head arched back, thrusting into the pillow.

Brennan forcibly set Aileen aside. He leaned over his son and held him down against the mattress, pinning him tightly. "No, he hissed. "No—you will *not*—"

Aidan's vision flickered. The light in his room changed. Something buzzed in his ears, distorting his father's voice.

"No," Brennan repeated. "Come *back* to us, Aidan—all of you, and whole—not this crazed prophet—"

Jaws locked into place. He tried to say her name. Only the sibilant escaped, like the scrape of broom on stone.

Brennan's hands tightened. "I want you back!" he shouted.

"Do you hear me, Aidan?—*you*. For everyone who needs you. For everyone who loves you."

Aidan forced it between his teeth. "Shh—shh-ona—"

Brennan's fingers tightened. The look in his eyes altered. "No," he said gently. "Aidan—I am sorry."

It was confirmation. Strength spilled out of him. With it went the spasms.

"Shona," Aidan whispered. In silence, Aileen cried.

Brennan unsheathed his knife. With precise care, he cut the leather straps binding his son. Mutely he peeled away the linen cuffs made to protect the flesh, then discarded everything. As Aidan lay slack on the bed, Brennan massaged his wrists.

"Clankeep?" Aidan croaked.

"Mostly destroyed," Brennan answered. "Much of the wall still stands, but little inside. And even outside . . ." He shrugged. "Had it not rained two days after, only the gods can say how much damage might have been done to the surrounding forest."

"How many people?"

Brennan's expression was grim. "The count is one hundred and four. Women and children, mostly."

"Lochiel," Aidan murmured.

"He sent a message. A *written* message, also; Clankeep was the first. That one in blood."

Distracted, Aidan frowned. "What message?"

"That he intends to do as his father—and *his* father—failed to do before him. Destroy the prophecy. Destroy *us*."

"Strahan's son," Aidan murmured. "He was killing women and children. I heard them dying." Attention wandered. He frowned, remembering. "I had a sword wound."

"Healed with the earth magic," Aileen told him. "And the bones of your head—" She broke off, glancing at Brennan.

"But not the wits inside?" Aidan's lips twitched once. "Have I been so very odd?"

"Do you recall none of it?" Brennan asked.

"Nothing but Shona. Nothing but her . . ." Aidan stirred restlessly, ruthlessly pushing away the memory of Locheil's butchery. "He preys on children. First he kills Hart's son, then he turns to my child before it is even born."

"Lie still," Aileen chided. "You have been very ill. It would be best if you slept."

He rolled his head slightly in denial. He was afraid of sleep. He was afraid of what might come, sliding out of darkness into the light where he could see. And where he could be afraid.

His head ached unremittingly. The memory would not go. "He wanted it," he murmured. "He wanted it for a purpose."

Aileen's voice, so gentle. "Sleep, Aidan. Rest."

The pain was increasing. "Lochiel took my *child*."

"Butcher," Brennan murmured. "Even Strahan did not stoop to that."

"He took it," Aidan repeated. "He stole it from her body."

"Aidan, rest." His mother again, smoothing a pain-wracked brow.

He realized they did not understand. He needed them to. He *required* them to. "He took it. Lochiel took the child. He cut Shona open and *took* the child from her."

"Aidan." Brennan leaned down, hands pressing a warning against Aidan's shoulders. "Let it go. Shona is dead—and surely the child, after that. It has been weeks . . . the clan gave her a Ceremony of Passing along with all the others—" Briefly, Brennan broke off. "And I have written Keely."

"*No*—" He twitched away from the pain. "He took the child from Shona. *Alive*. He wanted it for some purpose."

Aileen was horrified, hands covering her mouth. Frowning, Brennan shook his head. "No child could survive that."

Aidan did not listen. "He wanted it. For himself. He said—he said—" Aidan squinted. "He said he would make the seed of the prophecy *his*."

"Aidan, no—"

Consciousness receded. "Lochiel took my child. I will have to get it back."

Ten

His recovery was slow, impeded by weakness and fits. The wounds themselves had been healed, but only outwardly. Inwardly Aidan was still very much aware of the edge he walked. If he lost his balance once, he would be tipped off into the void. It was very like the balance required in *lir*-shape; he chose to think of it as that, since he was accustomed to it, and tried to regain the man he had been before Lochiel.

Winter. Time had passed, too much time; the Cheysuli in Clankeep worked to rebuild what they had lost, but most of the effort would have to wait until spring. And Aidan, walled up in Homana-Mujhar, chafed at the weather and weakness that kept him indoors, prisoner of unpredictablity.

Blinding headaches stole the wits from his head and sense from his tongue. From time to time he came out of a seizure to the echoes of a language he did not know, even though he spoke it. No longer bound to his bed by straps or debilitation, Aidan moved freely within Homana-Mujhar—but often found himself in odd portions of the vast palace without knowing how he got there. He dreamed when he was awake, losing himself even in the midst of conversation. The servants began discreetly eyeing him with pity or wariness, depending on his behavior of the particular moment, and Aidan found himself loathing them as well as himself.

At last he talked Ian into practicing the knife with him in a private chamber. He needed by spring to regain quickness and ability if he was to hunt Lochiel for his child, and only Ian would agree. But Aidan quickly discovered his reflexes had been destroyed. He was slow and awkward with a knife; what would it be like with a sword? And his vision was slightly askew; how would that affect his prowess with the warbow?

Finally, furious, he threw the bitter truth in Ian's austere face. "I will never be the same!"

Ian lowered the knife and regarded him in perfect stillness. "No," he said finally. "It is folly to harbor that hope."

It shocked him. Even knowing, it shocked. Aloud, the truth was so harsh.

His grip on the knife loosened. He shook, as he so often did, no matter how hard he fought it. "Then what am I, *su'fali?*"

Ian sheathed his knife. "A man who has been sorely hurt," he said gently, "in spirit as well as body. Aidan—you cannot expect to be what you once were. Not after that. Do not even hope for it."

Aidan clutched his knife. It shook. "At least you are honest," he rasped. "Everyone else tells me to give myself time; that of course all will be well. All will be as it was before." He clenched his teeth so hard his jaw ached. "It will never be the same."

"No." Ian's eyes were kind. "They lie because they love you, and because they want to lessen the pain. They know no other way, *harani* . . . honesty is difficult for people to deal with when it offers only sorrow. You want *so badly* to go after Lochiel, and yet they wonder how you can. You are not—what you were."

The word was ash. "No."

Ian smiled. "No one knows what to expect of you anymore, and it makes them nervous. There is someone else inside of you, someone else who speaks, someone who *prophesies*—" He sighed. "You always were different. Now it is worse."

Mutely, Aidan nodded.

Something moved in Ian's eyes. "Have you looked at yourself since the attack?"

Aidan shrugged. "My hand is not yet steady enough to shave myself. *Jehana* fears I will cut my throat . . ." Frustration tightened. "Someone shaves me, and I do not require a polished plate to dress."

"Then perhaps you should go and look." Ian smiled as Aidan tensed, eyes widening in horror. "No, no—it is not so bad as that. I promise. Save for one detail, you are much as you were. But it is the sort of thing others will remark on, particularly when they know the contents of your life."

Aidan shrugged again. "I will look." He scowled down at the knife in his hand. There were good days and bad days.

On the good ones he dropped things only occasionally. On the bad, he would do well to touch nothing at all.

"*Harani.*" Ian's tone was gentle. "I know what you want to do. I know how much you need it. But you cannot go alone. You must take someone with you."

"You?"

Ian shook his head. "I am too old now. But there is your *jehan.*"

"He is Mujhar. He has no time."

"A man who has no time for his grandchild is not worthy of kingship." Ian shook his head. "You judge him too harshly. Do you think you were the only one hurt by Shona's death? Do you believe you are the only one who has suffered?"

Anger flared. "You were not there. *None* of you was there. None of you can know—"

"She is dead, Aidan." Ian's tone was level. "Guilt, rage, and recrimination will not bring her back."

Aidan gripped the knife. "You do not know—"

"I *do!*" Ian's eyes were alive with grief. "I watched Niall die, knowing there was nothing I could do. I watched my *jehana* die, able to do nothing as she cut open her own wrists. I watched my *jehan* walk out of Homana-Mujhar, knowing he left his kin to die a *lirless* warrior's death, alone and bereft in the forest." He drew in a shaking breath. "I know, Aidan. Better than you think."

Ian did. Aidan's *kivarna* told him that.

He turned away stiffly, shamed by his selfishness, yet feeling the painful uprush of anguish and helplessness as strongly as before.

And then came the odd little snap in his head that dropped him to his knees. The knife fell from his hands.

"Aidan!" Ian moved swiftly, kneeling to catch both rigid wrists in an attempt to shut off the spasms. "Aidan—fight it—"

"I am the sword," Aidan whispered. "The sword and the bow and the knife—"

"Aidan, *fight* it—"

"I am no one; I am everyone—'

"Aidan!"

"I am Cynric, I am Cynric—"

"Stop this, Aidan. Shut it away. Use the earth magic. Use compulsion. *Shut it away—*"

"Eight into four and four into one. I am the Firstborn come again, and from me will come the others—"

"*Aidan*—"

"I am Cynric. I am Cynric. The sword and the bow and the knife—"

"Stop this madness *now!*"

The spasming passed. Fingers uncurled. Distantly, he asked, "How can I be mad? I am the voice of the gods."

Ian released his wrists. He was ashen-faced, staring. "What have you become?"

Aidan, hanging yet on his knees, knew. He had survived the first sacrifice. He had undertaken the task.

"Their servant," he said softly. "Chosen among all others. Knowing no other master. Not even a *tahlmorra*."

"Aidan!"

"They want me," he told him simply. "They want all of me. There is no room for a wife. Or a child. Or a Lion—"

Ian caught an arm, jerking Aidan to his feet. "Come with me. I will take you to your chambers."

He went with his great-uncle willingly, too numb to do otherwise. As always after a fit, he had a headache, and yet his wits were exquisitely lucid. He knew what he had done, what he had said, and what he was meant to do.

Ian pushed open Aidan's door. "Go to bed. I will send Aileen."

Aidan winced. "No."

"Then go to bed."

Mutely, Aidan nodded. Ian put a hand on his shoulder and urged him through the door.

It thumped closed behind him. Irresolute, Aidan stood in his bedchamber. And at last, recalling what Ian had suggested, he went to the polished silver plate hanging on the wall.

His face was unchanged, save for an unusual pallor. But a wondering hand went to his left temple, fingering the thick new growth of hair that had come back at last after being cut away. At the corner of his eyebrow was a purplish line, a straight slash of a line that stretched across his temple. The end of it was hidden in his hair. Thick new hair. A wing of purest white.

Aiden smiled. It was a cold, deadly smile. "*Leijhana tu'sai*, Ihlini. Now I can never forget."

He shivered. He felt ill, weary, old. He went to bed, as advised.

And dreamed of a chain that shattered beneath his touch.

Eleven

The chamber lay mostly in shadow, save for a single fat candle in a stand near the bed. It cast a sickly light; the wick was half-drowned in wax, sputtering its death. But no one moved to tend it.

Aileen stood in the doorway, staring in consternation at her son. "You can't mean to *keep* them here!"

Aidan did not answer. He linked his hands behind his back and gazed steadfastly at his mother.

"But—you can't," she insisted. "Not so many. Aidan, they are too big—there are too *many* . . ." Aileen's brow creased. "The kennels are kept very clean. They will do well enough there."

Undoubtedly they would. But that was not where he wanted them.

Quietly, he said, "Forgive me, *jehana*. I want to be alone."

She started to gesture, to remonstrate gently, but with authority. "Aidan, those dogs . . ." But she let it trail off. The hand fell lax at her side. He was so *still* . . .

She glanced around the chamber—Shona's chamber, Shona's bed, Shona's belongings—marking the chests as yet unpacked. Aidan and his new *cheysula* had gone too quickly to Clankeep for all of her things to have been arranged. Now they mocked her absence.

Aileen looked back at her son: at the still, white face. "Very well," she murmured, and left him alone once more.

He waited. For a moment longer he stood in the precise center of the chamber, staring fixedly at the now-empty doorway. Then, abruptly, he strode decisively through the throng of gathered wolfhounds and quickly shut the door, dropping the latch with a firm click.

Behind him, dogs whined.

He turned to face them. The big dark male. The bitches. The half-grown adolescents and the gangly, colt-legged puppies. Bright eyes stared back at him, tails poised to wave. But they sensed his tension and turmoil, the cessation of his breathing. Uncertainty dominated.

Ears flattened slowly. Heads sank lower. One puppy soiled himself; another began to whimper.

Breath rushed out of lungs. "*Gods*—" Aidan choked. Grief stole everything else.

Trembling, he walked into the huddle of hounds and began to touch their heads. It hurt to breathe, but he managed; in gasps, and sobs, and spasms. Touching all the heads. Assuaging their confusion. Seeking his own release in contact with her hounds.

Tentative tails waved, then quickened as he spoke. The voice he did not himself recognize, but they comprehended the tone. He was naming all their names: that they understood.

One by one by one: Shona's litany. She believed each dog was born with a specific name, and it was a person's task to discover the proper one, not just tack on anything; they had spent days on the voyage from Erinn trying out names on the two litters, collecting and discarding, until each of the puppies was named. Aidan recalled them all clearly, and Shona's lilting, ritual recital each time she greeted the dogs.

He sat down on the floor and let them gather around him. The puppies climbed over his legs, staging mock battles to claim his lap. The adolescents, too big for such play, snuffled his ears insistently, tending the human hound. The bitches came to his hand and bestowed a lick or two.

Only the male held back, promising Aidan nothing.

It hurt. It was unanticipated, and it *hurt*. Aidan understood the male's reticence well enough—the hound had bonded to Shona in puppyhood, offering no one else anything more than cursory courtesy—but Aidan had believed the dog would be starved for attention, eagerly coming forward to any familiar scent in response to Shona's now-permanent absence.

But he did not. And *would* not, Aidan knew now, on any terms but his own.

The puppies, growing cramped in his lap and weary of dominance struggles, deserted. The others settled quietly, finding places on the floor. Aidan got up slowly and climbed into the bed. It was not night. He was not tired. But it seemed the best place to be.

He lay very still. He stared at the canopy. He remembered what Sean had said: *"There are more ways to geld a man than with a knife."*

Shona.

—striding along the headlands at the edge of chalky cliffs—

—nocking and sighting a warbow with a small, towheaded brother—

—gathering a storm of hounds—

—climbing into his bed—

—gripping locks of his hair—

—winding her own around him—

—tracing the line of hips—

—taking him into her—

The sound escaped his mouth. A throttled desperation.

—other women—too many women—now none of them enough—

"Stop," Aidan gasped.

—none of them enough—none of them *ever* enough—

The sound was repeated: "Stop!"

—the first girl; the woman—

"STOP!" Aidan cried.

"There are more ways to geld a man than with a knife."

Shona. Shona.

Shona.

—everything slipping away—

—the sharpness, the brightness—

—memories of discovery, the exultation of the flesh—

All of it slipping away . . .

Dissolving as he reached, until nothing at all was left save a distant recollection of what he had been.

"Shona," he whispered.

Shona had come to his bed. Now he came to hers, seeking a rapport. A residue of her life in place of the memory of her death.

He floated in nothingness, a cork caught in the millrace, until the millwheel—no, the *Wheel*—trapped him at last and cast him down into the pond.

If I could drown myself . . . But the thought was driven away by the presence of a hound.

The male. He stood at the bedside, pressing his chest into the mattress as he stretched out long neck and head. Nostrils expanded, then closed as he whuffed softly, inspection completed. Folded ears rose, then flattened. Chin resting on bedclothes, he gazed fixedly at Aidan.

Waiting. Deep in his throat, he whined.

Stiffly, Aidan reached out and touched the long muzzle with trembling, tentative fingers. Then traveled the stop between liquid dark eyes onto the dome of the skull itself. Hair was coarse and wiry, the bone beneath crested. A self-possessed, dignified dog of massive, powerful elegance and abiding loyalty.

Deep inside, Aidan ached. For the hound as well as himself. *He* knew what had happened; the wolfhound understood nothing save the woman no longer came.

The ache intensified. Aidan rolled closer and thrust a clutching hand into muscled shoulders, locking fingers into hair. "I know, my braw boyo . . . he has stolen her from us both." Grief narrowed his throat. "But 'tis for me to do *alone*, this buying back of my child. No matter what anyone says."

He took his *lir*, a knife, and a horse, packed with saddle-pouches. He did not yet trust himself to *lir*-shape for any length of time. Eventually, he felt, the strength and control needed for sustained *lir*-shape would return—he had already tested it in several short flights—but for now he could not rely on it. The journey was too important.

If the child still lives. If Lochiel sees fit to let *it*—

He shut off the thought at once.

Much of the harshness of winter had passed, leaving only a residue of frost and wind. He rode wrapped in furs, feeling the cold more; would he ever feel well again? Or was he destined to be different on the outside as well as the inside?

At long last he reached the Bluetooth and took the ferry across, clutching the wooden rails as the barge fought the current. The Bluetooth was the delineation between northern Homana and southern, although the division was not equal. The high north was not as large or as populated because of harsh winters, and was usually called the Wastes; somewhere there was a Keep, but Aidan was not disposed to seek it out. His path went to Solinde, not to northern Homana. Perhaps another time.

The Wastes gave way to mountains. Aidan rode ever

higher, resting at night in frigid passes cut out of wolf-toothed peaks, until at last he crossed over the Molon and exchanged Homana for Solinde.

When finally they reached the narrow defile his father had described as the gateway to Valgaard, Aidan pulled up. Beyond lay the canyon housing Lochiel's fortress, and the wards set by him. He had heard the place described countless times: a field of glassy rock, pocked with smoking vents belching forth the breath of the Seker; huge, monstrous beasts shaped of stone by Ihlini testing their strength. All could be used against him.

He glanced skyward, seeking Teel. *You will have to remain here.*

The raven fluttered down to perch upon a wind-wracked tree. *Is this your choice?*

I have no choice.

Is this what you wish to do?

This is what I must *do.*

Teel's eye was bright. *The Ihlini could kill you.*

Aidan smiled. *He could. He might. He probably will—but not immediately. He will want to gloat, first. And that may buy me the time to do what I need to do.*

Teel made no answer for a very long moment. Then he fluffed black feathers. *Well. I have lived a long time.*

And will longer still, if I succeed.

The raven's echo was odd. *If you succeed.*

Aidan knew better than to ask for explanation.

He made his way through the defile, across the steaming field of beasts, around the rents in the earth that gave way to the netherworld. Never had he felt so vulnerable, so weak, and yet he knew it was required. It did not enter his mind to turn back, or even to think twice about what he intended to do.

Gates. And guards, of course. Aidan walked up the steam-bathed pathway and paused, pushing the hood from his head. In winter light, his earring gleamed. "Take me to Lochiel," he said. "Tell him my name: Aidan. He will be most anxious to see me."

They took him. Having stripped him of all save leathers and gold, they ushered him into a small tower chamber and left him there, alone, as he contemplated the comfort of a fire and other amenities. He sought none of them, neither chair nor warmth nor wine, and waited as they had left him, in the center of the chamber.

Lochiel came. In amber-dyed velvets and soft-worked suede, he was the same man with the same lithe movements and handsome looks Aidan had marked before, gaming with him in Lestra. Pale, ale-brown eyes; short-cropped, thick dark hair; a clarity of feature that reminded Aidan of someone. Someone he should know.

Aidan forced a smile. And then it required no force; a cold self-possession took control of expression and tone. "Surely you knew I survived. You did not intend it, I know; I have come to save you the trouble of seeking me out."

Pale eyes weighed him. Aidan's *kivarna* told him his arrival had taken the Ihlini completely by surprise, who was not pleased by it. But Lochiel gave nothing away in expression, which remained austerely smooth, and nothing away in eyes, which marked in Aidan a certain pallor and gauntness of face in addition to the white wing in auburn hair.

Lids lowered, shielding eyes. His lashes were long, like a woman's; the smoothly defined forehead and arched brows tugged at Aidan's memory.

Lillith? No. Someone else . . .

Lochiel moved. He did not walk: he prowled. Aidan stood very still, waiting mutely, as the Ihlini paced slowly around him. It was unsettling to be so raptly observed, like a mouse beneath an owl, but he made no indication. It was important to show Lochiel a serenity he would not anticipate.

The Ihlini halted before Aidan at last, the heel of his left hand resting idly on his knife hilt. He wore, as always, a sapphire ring on his forefinger: Brennan's. On his right hand, a bloodstone, rimmed in rune-wrought gold.

Aidan watched him closely. Something about the suppleness of the Ihlini's body merged with the line of his brow, the set of his mouth, to tickle Aidan's awareness. He was not an easy man to decipher, even with *kivarna*. He was, Aidan reflected, a wound wire ready to snap.

The chiseled mouth moved. A muscle ticked high in the cheek. Ale-brown eyes, abruptly shielded again behind lowered lids, changed color in Aidan's mind.

Something clicked into place.

"Have you a son?" he asked.

Lids lifted. Lochiel appraised him intently. And then he smiled. "No. I have no son." He paused. "I have *yours*."

Aidan tensed all over. He wanted nothing more at that moment than to rip Lochiel to pieces. But the reaction was what Lochiel waited for, and so Aidan, with great effort, damped down the impulse.

He smiled pleasantly. "Do you know a man called Cynric?"

The smooth brow tightened. "No. And if you hope to confuse me with such babblings, save your effort. I have heard reports you are mad . . . do you think I care?"

Aidan's certainty vanished. The brief likeness he had seen faded. He did not think again of the young man in his dreams, the young man so much like Lochiel, but of himself, of his child, and of the man before him.

Ihlini, he knew, did not fully come into their power until they reached puberty, much as a Cheysuli warrior gained a *lir*. There was a time of learning, of refining, just as there was in Cheysuli custom. And a time of complete assumption, when power was understood and properly wielded.

Lochiel was young, but well past puberty. He was, Aidan judged, of his own age. And in Valgaard, the very font of Ihlini power, Lochiel would have recourse to all the dark arts he needed.

Aidan inhaled a careful breath. "What did you do with my son?"

Lochiel smiled. Aidan, unsettled, was put in mind of the elegant young man who had so charmed Cluna and Jennet—and Blythe. "I intend him no harm. On the contrary: I took him for a purpose. I will raise him as my own. He will come to know his proper place in the prophecy, as all Cheysuli do, so that he can aid its destruction. I will turn him from his *tahlmorra* and make him work against it."

Aidan bit back the retort he longed to make. Quietly, he denied it. "That is not possible."

"Oh?" Dark brows arched. "There *was* a Cheysuli woman, a kinswoman of yours, named Gisella. She was turned, and used."

Aidan shrugged indolently. "I will prevent you."

"You?" Lochiel smiled. "With what? Power? You have none here . . . this is Valgaard, Aidan. The Gate is here, entry to the netherworld. Even if you could summon your *lir*, even if you could summon *lir*-shape, or compulsion— what could you do with either? This is *Valgaard*. I can snuff you out like a spark."

Aidan's sudden smile was brilliant. "Ask Lillith what I can do."

Lochiel recoiled.

There. That touched him. There are *weaknesses in him* . . . Aidan nodded intently, driving home the promise of power. "Because of *me*," he whispered. "At *my* behest. Because the gods *answered* me."

The challenging gaze was unrelenting. Lochiel sought something in Aidan's eyes, in expression, in his tone. And then turned away abruptly, striding to a table, where he poured a cup of wine. None was offered Aidan; he drank it down himself. When he was done, he smiled. "This is *still* Valgaard."

Aidan smiled back. "Would you like to meet them now? *Right* now; *here*?"

Lochiel slammed down the cup. The footed stem bent. "I have sovereignty over this place!"

Aidan tilted his head. "Shall I test it for you?"

The Ihlini's smile was malignant. "*And* I hold your son."

He very nearly laughed. "My gods would never harm him."

"Ah, but *mine* would." Lochiel attempted to right the tipped cup; when he could not do it, he glanced down in distracted annoyance. When he saw the stem was bent, he cast the cup away with a negligent flick of dismissive fingers. He stared at Aidan again. "Do you wish me to summon my gods? They can duel, yours and mine: the gods of light and air against those of death and darkness."

Aidan made no reply.

Pale eyes widened. Lochiel's lips parted minutely. Even his posture was arrested, alert as a hound on a scent. His expression now was intensely compelling. "Is this why you came here? Hoping to set your gods on mine—or on *me!* —and win back your son that way?"

Aidan set his teeth. There was still a chance, he believed, no matter what Lochiel said.

A blurt of disbelief distorted Lochiel's mouth. "I understand, now . . . you thought you could come before me and threaten me—no, *frighten* me—into acquiescence—"

Aidan allowed a delicate tone of contempt to underscore his words. "How could a man do that? How could he dare? Are you not *the* Ihlini, and heir to all the arts?"

Lochiel still stared. "But you *did* . . ." A faint bemused frown tightened brows briefly as he reassessed his conclusion, then faded as he laughed aloud in discovery. "I understand, now—your weapon is *faith!* You believe your gods can win even here in Valgaard!"

Aidan began to wonder if perhaps he had misjudged. If perhaps he had made a mistake. He had been so certain. So determined. His conviction was absolute.

I trust them. I HAVE to. They answered me before. When I faced Lillith.

Lochiel's tone was a whiplash. "Do you think this is a game? Did you come expecting to play Bezat with me?" Pale eyes narrowed. "We are *all* at the mercy of our gods, Aidan. Certainly you and I. I am not so complacent as you. I know better. In the moment of their confrontation, they could well destroy us both. And that is not how I want to die."

Nor Aidan. He had come to threaten Lochiel with a weapon no one else had: divine retribution. He had tapped it once, facing Lillith—but he *had* been complacent. He had believed utterly in his gods, who would face only a single man. A man of great power, but still merely a *man;* now Lochiel threatened a gruesome retribution of his own conjuring, with a god that frightened Aidan much more than anticipated. Asar-Suti, the Seker, had always been an undefined threat, hosted only in vague references.

Now, in the heart of Valgaard, smelling the god's noxious breath, the threat became all too real. He took it more seriously.

As seriously, perhaps, as Lochiel takes MY gods.

Lochiel, face taut, snatched up the silver cup and displayed the ruined stem. "Do you see? This was nothing. I did it unaware. It required no power, no magic. Nothing more than anger." His gaze was unrelenting. "Do you understand? They are *gods,* Aidan! Your gods, my gods—do you think it matters? We are men, and flesh is weak . . . weaker by far than silver . . ." He shut both hands on the rim and crushed together the slender lips. Then displayed the result to Aidan. "I can think of more *comfortable* ways."

Inwardly, Aidan rejoiced. He had found a weakness in Lochiel. He was himself as afraid of a confrontation between the Ihlini's gods and his own, but he had the advantage. He *knew* Lochiel was afraid. And that fear could serve him.

With a serenity he did not entirely feel—Lochiel would call it complacency—Aidan merely shrugged. "I can think of no better way of settling what lies between us. Summon your gods, Ihlini. I will summon mine. We will let *them* decide this issue."

Lochiel threw down the ruined goblet. His smooth face was white and taut. And then, with infinite tenderness, he asked a single question: "Do you recall how easily I killed Hart's son from afar?"

Aidan was very still. Complacency dissolved. Conviction wavered profoundly.

Lochiel's gaze was unrelenting. "I could do the same now, with *your* son."

It burst free before he could stop it. "*No*—" And cursed himself desperately as he surrendered his advantage.

Lochiel smiled thinly, gracious in victory. "But I am remiss. Come with me, my lord. Come and see your precious son."

In an adjoining chamber, Aidan saw the wide, high-standing cradle carved out of satiny wood. For a single insane moment he could not comprehend such a normal and mundane thing being within an Ihlini household.

Lochiel gestured. "There. Alive, as promised. For now."

Aidan stepped closer, then stopped abruptly. The cradle held *two* babies, not one; in infancy, identical.

Lochiel laughed. "You asked if I had a son. No. A daughter. But I invite you to tell me which seed is mine, and which yours."

Aidan stared at the babies. They were swaddled against the cold, hands, head and feet hidden, with only small faces showing. Both slept, oblivious, depriving him of eye color, although even that was no proof. Shona's eyes had been brown; so were Lochiel's. And his *kivarna*, strangely, was silent.

Lochiel moved to the cradle. "Even as I cut the child from the belly of your dead Erinnish princess, my own woman bore me a daughter. Melusine has given suck to your son, so he would know the taste of mother's milk." He saw the spasm of shock in Aidan's face, and smiled. "They share the same breast, the same cradle, the same roof. Tell me again, Aidan, how it is impossible for a Cheysuli to be turned against his *tahlmorra*."

"No," Aidan said hoarsely.

Lochiel put both hands down and touched two heads, caressing each in an obscene parody of affection. "What do you say to knowing your son will think I am his father?" He paused. "Perhaps I should say: *jehan*."

"No." Yet again. Knowing it was futile.

Lochiel bent and whispered tenderly to the sleeping babies, though his gaze remained on Aidan. When he straightened it was with the fluid grace that once more called the dream-being, Cynric, to Aidan's mind.

The Ihlini's voice was hushed, mocking solicitude. "What shall I do with them? Kill one, and let you wonder if it was your son—or my daughter? Or kill them both, so you *know?*"

Aidan nearly laughed. "Do you expect me to believe you would kill your own daughter?"

"I can make more. And if it gives you pain . . ."

The off-handedness hurt most. Desperation boiled up. "You *ku'reshtin!*"

Lochiel cut him off with a silencing slice of his hand. "Choose one, Aidan. Assume the role of a god and determine a child's fate."

It was a cruel twist on a conversation Aidan had had with the Weaver. "And if I say let both live? Would you honor that decision?"

Lochiel spread eloquent hands. "Both are mine regardless."

Aidan twitched. His head throbbed dully. He tried to set aside the discomfort, but failed. Weakness worked its way from head to neck to shoulders, then down to encompass the rest of his body. He knew what would happen if he did not control the weakness. He fought to suppress the trembling before it showed itself.

Lochiel saw it regardless. Dark brows arched slightly, the chiseled mouth pursed. He considered the white wing of hair. "The sword blow," he said softly.

Aidan suppressed the first spasm. "What of our bargain?"

Clearly Lochiel was distracted. "Our bargain?"

"You said I could choose."

But the Ihlini was beyond that. He smiled slowly, replete with comprehension as he watched the tremors in Aidan's hands. "You are pale, my lord. Have you a headache? Have you an illness?"

"Let me choose," Aidan grated. It was something on which he could focus.

Lochiel laughed. "In addition to your manhood, I have deprived you of your health." He saw Aidan's jerk of shock. "Oh, aye—I knew all about the bonding of mutual *kivarna*. I take pains to know such things." He studied Aidan more closely. "Why else do you think I killed her? And *where* I killed her: there, before your eyes. She was hardly a worthy opponent, and of no danger to me that night . . . but her loss would devastate you. Even in the moments before I killed you." His mouth twisted in a mocking moue of pity. "But you survived after all, and now the poor Prince of Homana is unmanned. *Castrate . . . gelding . . .* no more bedsport for *you!*" He paused, lingered a moment. "And no more heirs for Homana. *I* have the only one."

Aidan's head was pounding. Waves of pain poured down, distorting his vision so that Lochiel became a man of two heads and eight limbs. Teeth clenched convulsively. He had no time at all.

"What use *are* you?" Lochiel mused. "With empty head— *and* empty loins—what use are you to the Lion?"

The Ihlini blurred before him. Sweat broke from Aidan's flesh, followed by the first onset of spasms that would suck the strength from his limbs and drop him to the floor, a twisted wreck of a man. Humiliation bathed him.

Not before Lochiel—

Lochiel gazed at him intently. And then a smile began. "No," he said in discovery. "No, I will *not* kill you. What need? You can do more to harm the prophecy by living . . . gods, who would want *this* for a king?"

Please, do not let me fall . . . do not let me lose everything, not here, not now . . . not before this man—

Lochiel nodded. "Better to leave you alive."

Aidan stumbled forward, catching himself against the heavy cradle. Swaddled babies slept on; he wanted to touch them, to wake them, to learn which was his son, but his body failed him. His legs gave way beneath him and he knelt against his will, before Lochiel the Ihlini, whose smile was oddly triumphant.

"Choose," Lochiel commanded.

Trembling, Aidan clung to the cradle.

"Choose," he repeated intently. "This time it is not a game."

"W–why? Why not?"

"Because this time I will abide by it. Choose a child, Aidan. Then walk free of Valgaard."

"Why?"

"Because I want you to go back. I want you on the Lion. I want you where all can see you, so they can see what you are. A man who succumbs to fits . . . or a man who succumbs to demons?" Lochiel made a fluent gesture of multiple possibilities. "I want you *there,* not here. As you are, you will do much more damage to the power of the Lion. To the power of the Cheysuli. Do you think the Homanans will keep you? Do you think they will trust you?" Lochiel shook his head. "I want you *on* the throne, so they can throw you off. Turmoil eases my task . . ." He shrugged. "But you will not go without a child. You would sooner remain here and die of a fit—or my displeasure—than go back without a child." He paused. "So *choose.*"

Aidan still clung to the cradle. "I could choose your daughter—"

Lochiel lost his temper. "Do you think I care? If it *is* my daughter, you will still have to take her with you to Homana-Mujhar . . . an Ihlini witch raised in the bosom of the Lion." Pale eyes glittered. "To destroy the prophecy, I will risk a daughter. I will risk *ten* daughters. But will *you* risk a son in order to save it?"

Aidan pressed his forehead against the cradle, letting the rim bite in. He shut his teeth on his tongue, trying to deflect the pain gnawing at his limbs. With great effort he pulled himself to his feet, standing rigidly. "Is that all?" he rasped. "Or is there something more?"

"The chain," Lochiel declared.

The trembling died on the instant. Aidan clutched a link depending from his belt. "You want—*this*—?"

"Aye. Is it not worth the price of a child who could well be your son?"

"Why? What is this to you?"

"The embodiment of a man, and all the men before him." Lochiel's smile was wintry. "Give me the chain, Aidan. And you are free to go."

The Ihlini knew. He *knew.* "Will you break it?" Aidan asked.

"Only one link," Lochiel answered. "Only one is required. And the pattern will likewise be broken." He shrugged off-handedly. "This alone will not destroy the prophecy, but it *is* a beginning. If I remove that link from the pattern, small changes shall become large."

Aidan knew the answer. If he refused, Lochiel might well kill him anyway, thereby removing him from the pattern in flesh as well as link. If he stayed alive, there was always a chance he could undo things later. And there was the child;

if he walked out of Valgaard with his son, he kept the seed of the prophecy alive. And the human link, he thought, was stronger than the other.

And if I choose the girl—? But Aidan knew that answer, also: choice was a risk everyone took. Choice, and risk, was required.

Aidan unbuckled his belt. Slowly he unthreaded the leather from the links, sliding them free until the chain lay in his hands. He gazed at it, head bowed, realizing in some distant portion of his mind that the weakness in his body had gone. He stood perfectly still before the Ihlini and pondered the ending of his *tahlmorra*.

There will be no afterworld . . . but without Shona, do I want one?

Shona. The Lion. The chain. So many broken links. So many turbulent dreams, harbingers of his fate. So very many *questions*, asked so many times.

But Aidan at last understood.

He pulled the chain taut in his hands. He recalled the binding before Siglyn and Tye and Ashra; how he had drawn the chain from the fire and made it whole again, merely because he believed it. Because it had been required.

Smiling contentedly, Aidan took a final grasp on either end of the chain and looked directly at Lochiel as he jerked the chain apart.

The weak link shattered. Remnants of it rang against stone as they fell, glittering, to scatter apart like dust. He held the dangling end of a sundered chain in either hand, knowing the name of the broken link was Aidan after all.

Lochiel's tone was dry. "Impressive," he remarked. "Now choose a child, and go."

He moved to the cradle. Under his feet crunched bits of broken link. He ignored it.

Two bundled babies. Aidan put down in the cradle the two halves of linked chain. He picked up one of the babies without bothering to rely on *kivarna*; it was as dead as the rest of him. He would take his plight to chance.

"Go," Lochiel said. "You have my leave to go."

Aidan turned and walked from the room, cradling against his chest the son who might rule Homana.

Or the daughter who might destroy it.

Epilogue

Wind whistled through the defile as Aidan walked out of the canyon. Beyond, the wailing stilled. Winter wastes were summer. Trees, once wracked by Ihlini malignancy, now displayed the dignity of smooth young limbs. Buds sprouted leaves.

Smiling, Aidan nodded. With Teel and the horse waited the brown man called the Hunter.

The god matched his smile. "You looked at the child."

"Aye."

"What did you discover?"

"My son."

The brown eyes were wise and calm and very kind. "Do you think the milk he took from an Ihlini woman's breast will curdle his spirit?"

Aidan, turning a shoulder to the sun to protect the child tucked beneath his cloak, sighed. "I think not."

"Good." The Hunter gestured to a boulder near his own. "Sit you down, Aidan, and tell me what you have learned."

Aidan eyed the rock. "It will be too cold. I have a child to care for."

The Hunter said nothing. Lichen and grass crept up the rock, nestling into hollows, until the boulder was covered. A handful of violet clover blossoms bloomed. The throne was offered in silence.

After a moment Aidan sat down. He looked at the Hunter. "I have learned it is sheer folly for a man to try and discern what the gods intend for him," he began quietly. "I have spent my entire life trying to know what you wanted of me, attempting to interpret troubling dreams that denied me a throne and gave me a chain I could not keep whole, no matter how hard I tried." He smiled briefly. "And I have learned how helpless is a man when the gods choose to meddle in his life."

Brown brows arched. "Meddle? Do we meddle?"

"Aye." Aidan grinned at him. "It is your way, I suppose . . . so I will not take you to task for it."

The brown eyes were assessive, the calm face devoid of familiar expression. After a moment the mouth moved into a faint smile. "You have also learned to hold us in some disregard, it seems—to judge from your tone."

Aidan laughed at him, pulling his son more closely against his chest and resettling the shielding cloak. "Not in *disregard*. I have simply surrendered, that is all. You will do with me as you will, regardless of what I want, so I will no longer cause you—*or* myself—any difficulties with my waywardness."

"We cannot *tell* you what to do. We never have."

Aidan's tone was abruptly cold. "No. But you remove impediments from my life. Like Shona."

The Hunter's expression was briefly sorrowful, and then it passed. "There is another way of looking at it."

Grief blazed up momentarily, overpowering in its strength. Then died away to ash, much as desire had. Aidan let it go. He could not, just now, lose control. "What way?" he asked. "Is she not *dead*?"

"She is dead. But do not in any way believe we considered her an 'impediment' to be removed from your life. She was not, nor did we remove her. Shona existed because of her singularly great worth. She was the catalyst. What we did was put her *into* your life . . . and give you such joy in her arms and bed you would not want to share it with another, ever." The eyes were steady. "Was she not worth it, Aidan? The submission of the heart . . . the sacrifice of the body. Even for so short a time?"

He had lost what men most treasured, though they perverted it to common lust too many times in the quest for mere gratification. He himself had done it, regardless of the reasons. But with Shona, he had not. Even knowing, Aidan had not believed the sacrifice of so much would be required of him. Now he understood why.

And did not hesitate. "She was worth everything."

After a moment, the Hunter nodded. "It remains, Aidan: we cannot tell you what to do."

"There is no need for that. I know what to do. *Now*."

"Do you? And what is that?"

Aidan stared beyond the god a long moment, lost in thought, in memory. Then he stirred. Smiling, he stripped the glove from his right hand. The ruby ring glowed bloody in the whiteness of winter wastes only recently touched by summer.

He pulled it from his finger. "First," he murmured, "I rid myself of this, and the title that goes with it."

The Hunter was unmoving upon his rock. His eyes were very dark, and infinitely compelling. "By that, you renounce your rank."

"I do."

"It is a rank many men would kill for, craving the power for themselves, and the promise of more. It is an ancient and honorable title. Your *jehan* held it, and his *jehan*, and his before that . . . many men, Aidan. Very many men. I ask you: do you know what you do?"

"Oh, aye. I know what I'm doing, I'm thinking."

The lilt did not touch the Hunter. "Do you do it willingly, or merely because it seems the easiest thing?"

Aidan laughed. "Are we not done with testing *yet?*" He shook his head, gripping the ring in his palm. "Are you finally asking me the questions I wanted you to ask? Now will you give me my answers?"

"Answer *me,* Aidan."

Quelled for the moment, Aidan nodded. He wet his lips. "I surrender my rank and title willingly, knowing what I do."

"To what benefit?"

"To benefit the prophecy," Aidan answered firmly. "Which I have always served, unknowing; and continue to serve, now *knowing.*"

"You remove yourself from the succession of Homana."

"Aye. Willingly."

"I repeat: to what benefit?"

Aidan smiled, tucking the ring into his belt-pouch and tugging on his glove again. "There was a chain, god of dreams, that once was broken in my hands, and later rejoined. I believed the dreams ended and the task performed, as was intended. But as I stood before Lochiel, I realized that was not true. The joining of the chain, while not precisely *wrong,* was not the desired end."

He recalled Shaine, Carillon, Donal; Ashra, Tye, Siglyn. All who had aided him in his decision, though he had not known it then.

The Hunter's voice was soft. "What was the desired end?"

"To break it." Aidan's attention returned. "The chain

was meant to be broken—and by me—to improve the next link." He gazed down between the folds of his cloak on the bundle that was his son. "To provide *this* link with the strength he requires to complete the prophecy."

The god stirred upon his rock. "What else, Aidan?"

He considered it. The answer came easily. "Chained warrior," he said distantly. "Chained prince; chained raven. Bound, the life goes on. Broken, it is free." He gazed directly at the Hunter. "The chain is broken; the decision made. I wish to go free."

The Hunter's face was expressionless. "Freedom carries its own weight of responsibilities."

"I know that." And suddenly Aidan was laughing with the unhindered joy of realization. The sound rang in the rocks; he let the laughter go out of sheer exuberance and acknowledgment of the truth. He felt so *free* at last. For the first time in his life.

When the laughter died, he grinned at the god. "'Lochiel has lost after all."

The Hunter smiled faintly. "What will you do?"

Aidan's answer was prompt. "Take my son to Homana-Mujhar and give him over to his *tahlmorra*. Mine lies elsewhere."

"Ah. Then you have realized you did *not* break it in Valgaard."

"Oh, no." Aidan shrugged. "I learned what it *was*, instead."

The Hunter nodded. "What of *you*, Aidan, when your son is made the heir?"

He looked down on the bundled child. "The Lion Throne was never meant for me. Gisella was right when she said I would be a throneless Mujhar and a crownless king." He smiled, recalling his fear. "I think I am bound for another realm and another lion . . . for an island floating on the breath of the gods, where lies a fallen altar and a deserted chapel. I think my task is to make it whole again, restoring it to its original purpose so that it may serve Cheysuli in need once more."

"They will call you priest," the Hunter warned. "Half-man. Shadow-man. Warrior without a heart." He paused. "Even coward and castrate."

For a moment only, it pinched. Then fell away into dust,

as all desire had. He was content within himself; with the knowledge of what he was.

"Perhaps the Homanans will," Aidan agreed. "It is their nature to disparage what they cannot understand. As for the others—" he shrugged "—it makes little difference. It is time to bring light to the land again, to chase away the dark." He smiled dreamily, gloriously tired. "Names do not matter. And the Cheysuli will call me something else entirely."

"What is that, Aidan?"

"*Shar tahl.*" He grinned briefly. "Like Burr, only worse— I will teach them things they do not want to hear. I will untwist all the twists. I will show them there are new ways to be honored as deeply as the old." The smile fell away. "And I will prophesy."

"For whom?"

Aidan's breath was a plume. "Cynric."

"Who is Cynric?"

"Child of the prophecy. The sword and the bow and the knife. The Firstborn, come again."

The Hunter gestured. "Is that Cynric?"

Aidan glanced in surprise at the child in his arms. "This one? No. This is Kellin. Prince of Homana. The next link." He looked at the god. "Cynric comes later. Cynric comes after. Cynric is the beginning of a new chain."

"And who are *you?*"

He knew the answer, now. "Aidan," he said. "Just—Aidan."

The Hunter smiled. And then he rose, stepping off the rock.

Aidan stood up hastily, cradling the infant who would one day rule Homana. "Is there nothing else?"

"What else is there?" asked the god. "You have discovered your *tahlmorra*, and accepted. That is all that exists for any warrior." Briefly he put his hand against the lump of Kellin's head beneath the cloak. "Guard him well, *shar tahl*. He has yet to learn what sort of *tahlmorra* lies before *him*."

Aidan, overcome, nodded mutely.

The Hunter smiled. His eyes were very warm as he put his other hand on Aidan's head. "Safe flight, my raven. You are everything we hoped."

And Aidan was alone, save for his son.

Carefully, he peeled back the hooded wrappings shielding the tiny face. The Hunter had left the season warm; he did not fear the cold. In the bright sun of a summer day, Aidan looked upon his son. He touched the delicate forehead, traced the line of the brow, fingered the wispy black hair.

And smiled in a sorrowful wonder. "We made this," he murmured. "The bright, bold lass and I."

In her son, Shona lived on.

Aidan nodded tightly. *Better to have something . . .* Abruptly, he banished it. Kellin was more than something.

He inhaled deeply and blew out a streamer of breath. There was nothing left but to go.

Aidan mounted his horse with great care and arranged Kellin more comfortably in his arms. For now the baby slept; he could not hope for it all the way.

Or *could* he? Did he not converse with gods?

Laughing, Aidan glanced up at the thick-leafed tree on which Teel perched. And then the laughter stilled. "Have you always known?"

The silence between them was loud.

"Have you?" Aidan repeated. "The *lir*, you have always maintained, are privy to many things."

Teel offered no answer for a very long time. Then the raven stirred. *Including all the pain. All the fear.* The tone, unexpectedly, altered from tart gibe to tenderness. *It was necessary.*

"What was necessary?"

Obliqueness, Teel answered. *Obscurity of a purpose: to make you angry. To make you fight something, even a contentious lir.*

"Because otherwise I might have given in." Aidan nodded. "Otherwise I might have broken. The anger was a focus . . ."

Teel fluffed black wings. *A warrior who walks with dead men and converses with the gods does not have an easy road. I was meant to make you take it.*

"*Make* me?"

Teel reconsidered. *To* suggest *you take the road, with whatever means I had.*

Aidan considered that. After a moment he nodded. "Do not change, *lir*. I am used to contentiousness.'

I had not thought to change. Why surrender preeminence?

Aidan laughed. The child in his arms squirmed, then settled once again.

He gathered reins and turned the horse southward. "Ah, well, what does it matter? The Wheel of Life has turned."

He guided the horse one-handed, cradling Kellin with the other. "And the hounds will like the island."

The raven lifted and flew. Southward, toward Mujhara. Southward, toward an island where the standing stones lay fallen, waiting for the *shar tahl* to set them upright again.

APPENDIX

CHEYSUL/OLD TONGUE GLOSSARY
(with pronunciation guide)

Asar-Suti (ah-SAHR soo-TEE) — (*proper name*): god of the netherworld.

a'saii (uh-SIGH) — Cheysuli zealots dedicated to pure line of descent.

bu'lasa (boo-LAH-sa) — grandson

bu'sala (bu-SAH-la) — foster-son

cheysu (chay-SOO) — man/woman; neuter; used within phrases.

cheysul (chay-SOOL) — husband

cheysula (chay-SOO-la) — wife

Cheysuli (Chay-SOO-lee) — (*literal translation*): children of the gods.

Cheysuli i'halla shansu (Chey-SOO-lee ih-HALLA shan-SOO) — (*lit.*): May there be Cheysuli peace upon you.

harana (ha-RAH-na) — niece

harani (h-RAH-nee) — nephew

homana (ho-MAH-na) — (*lit.*): of all blood.

i'halla (ih-HALL-uh) — (*lit.*): upon you; used in phrases.

i'toshaa-ni (ih-tosha-NEE) — Cheysuli purification ceremony; atonement ritual.

ja'hai ([French *j*] zshuh-HIGH) — (*lit.*): accept

ja'hai-na (zshuh-HIGH-na) — (*lit.*): accepted

jehan (zsheh-HAHN) — father

jehana (zsheh-HA-na) — mother

ku'reshtin (koo-RESH-tin) — epithet; name-calling

leijhana tu'sai (lay-HAHN-na too-SIGH) — (*lit.*): thank you very much.

lir (leer) — magical animal(s) linked to individual Cheysuli; title used indiscriminately between *lir* and warriors.

liren (leeren) — feminine version; used by animal *lir* to female Cheysuli.

meijah (MEE-hah) — Cheysuli light woman; (*lit.*): mistress

meijhana (mee-HAH-na) — (*slang*): beloved; pretty one

Mujhar (moo-HAHR) — king

qu'mahlin (koo-MAH-lin) — purge; extermination

Resh'ta-ni (resh-tah-NEE) — (*lit.*): as you would have it.

rujha (ROO-ha) — (*slang*): sister (dim.)

rujho (ROO-ho) — (*slang*); brother (diminutive)

rujholla (roo-HALL-uh) — sister (formal)

rujholli (roo-HALL-ee) — (*formal*): brother

ru'maii (roo-MY-ee) — (*lit.*) in the name of

ru'shalla-tu (roo-SHAWL-uh TOO) — (*lit.*): May it be so.

Seker (Sek-AIR) — (*formal title*): god of the netherworld

shansu (shan-SOO) — peace

shar tahl (shar TAHL) — priest-historian; keeper of the prophecy.

shu'maii (shoo-MY-ee) — sponsor

su'fala (soo-FALL-uh) — aunt

su'fali (soo-FALL-ee) — uncle

sul'harai (sool-ha-RYE) — moment of ultimate pleasure; describes shapechange.

tahlmorra (tall-MOR-uh) — fate; destiny; kismet

Tahlmorra lujhala mei wiccan, cheysu (tall-MOR-uh loo-HALLA may WICK-un, chay-SOO) — (*lit.*): The fate of a man rests always within the hands of the gods.

tetsu (tet-SOO) — poisonous root given to allay great pain; addictive, eventually fatal.

tu'halla-dei (too-HALLA-day-EE) — (*lit.*): Lord to liege man.

usca (OOIS-kuh) — powerful liquor from the Steppes.

y'ja'hai (EE-zshuh-HIGH) — (*lit.*): I accept.